Mrs. C. Jenkin

Who Breaks Pays

Mrs. C. Jenkin

Who Breaks Pays

ISBN/EAN: 9783337234430

Printed in Europe, USA, Canada, Australia, Japan

Cover: Foto ©Andreas Hilbeck / pixelio.de

More available books at **www.hansebooks.com**

"Chi rompe-paga"

"WHO BREAKS—PAYS"

(ITALIAN PROVERB)

BY

MRS. C. JENKIN

AUTHOR OF "SKIRMISHING," "A PSYCHE OF TO-DAY,"
"MADAME DE BEAUPRE," ETC.

NEW YORK
HOLT & WILLIAMS
1873

CONTENTS.

CONTENTS.

WHO BREAKS—PAYS

CHAPTER I.

Alone.

Up five flights of stairs, to the attic of a house in the Rue de Berlin, Paris, that is where I am going to take the reader, on an evening in the beginning of November, 184–. On the square landing-place there are four doors, each with a card, on which is either written or printed the name of the dweller within. Let us examine the card on the door to the left as you go upstairs. Mr. Giuliani, that is the name of the person we are in search of—ring and enter.

The apartment consists of two rooms and a closet, fitted up as a small kitchen. The sitting-room to the front looks down into the street—the bed-room would have a view of the court-yard of the house, but for its dormer window, which allows only of a sight of the sky and of a multitude of chimney-pots.

In the small *salon* a large moderator lamp is burning on the diminutive marble table in the centre of the room. There is no fire in the chimney, though logs of wood artistically laid, and backed by a noble elevation of ashes, show prudent preparation for a cold evening. A black fur rug, bordered by red cloth cut into scollops, lies before the fireless grate; a divan occupies the space between the fire-place and window—a useful piece of furniture, serving as a sofa, a chest of drawers, and, in a moment of necessity, even as a bed. A well filled set of book-shelves, a box for wood, a large Voltaire chair, half-a-dozen small walnut ones, and you have the list of Mr. Giuliani's furniture. A large map of Italy, and four or five pipes and meerschaums, ornament the walls. There is not one object of luxury, not one article for mere show in the whole room.

Mr. Giuliani is seated at the table, and with compressed lips and knotted brow appears to be deciphering Egyptian hieroglyphics, and jotting down learned annotations in red ink with a firm, crabbed, scratching pen. Occasionally he sends forth an angry volume of smoke from the short pipe between his lips. The writer looks thirty, at the least; his head is large, his hair black, with bronze reflections; it is abundant, and curls closely round the nape of the neck, and on the temples; the rest has that waviness which saves much time and patience in hair-dressing; his beard is fine, glossy and curling. his ears small and white, his brow high. the eyebrows full and marked, his nose large, not peculiarly well-shaped, but manly and decided, his eyes black, large, and deep set. His figure is scarcely in proportion to so powerful a head; it is thin, about the medium height, with a stoop forward of the shoulders, which may be the effect of either constant study or of ill-health; but the hands are well-shaped, muscular hands, able to wield something heavier than a steel pen: for the present his feet are in black drugget slippers, but they are narrow, with a high instep. It is not easy to mistake whether a man is a gentleman or not, you discover it in spite of the thread-bare or glossy coat. Mr. Giuliani is a poor gentleman, one of the numerous body of Italian exiles. He is busy with no cuneiform characters, with no hieroglyphics. He is an Italian teacher in Paris. and he is deciphering some of his pupils' carelessly written Italian exercises.

As the little gilt clock on the mantelpiece chimes nine, he pushes away the copybooks with a sigh of relief, leans back in his chair for a few seconds. idly watching the white clouds of smoke from his pipe float away and thicken the already thick atmosphere of the room. Then he rises. opens the window, and sets to work again, but this time reading.

By the way of relaxation Giuliani studies Greek, and is resolved to master that language; a rough task at his age; but it is now his sole ambition. After a youth of enthusiasm, during which he had freely hazarded life and fortune in the cause of liberty, he appeared to have grown philosophically indifferent to every shade of politics, every form of government. the result of weariness at meeting always the same fair professions of goodwill.

and finding ever the same cunning evasions of sacred promises. To rid himself of the remembrance of past hopes, he had taken to burying his wits in Greek roots, as another man might have drowned his in spirits or malt. His calmness was, however, not the fruit of resignation, it was the enforced passiveness of iron necessity.

A true Anglo-Saxon ring at the door bell, a ring which says plainly, "immediate attention, for time is precious," startled the student to his feet. Nervous French ladies, when similar peals for admittance precipitate them from their chairs, never fail to exclaim, "*Voilà pour sûr des Anglais.*"

Mr. Giuliani's visitor was a fair, slim young Englishman.

"Ah! Valentine, how goes the world with you?"

The Italian's voice was strong and musical, and his smile made him agreeable-looking, if not quite handsome.

"What, not dressed!" exclaimed Valentine Ponsonby.

"Not dressed," affirmed Giuliani. "What business have I at a ball? I cannot dance, nor sing, nor perform any tricks to pay for my admittance among fine ladies and gentlemen."

"I could imagine a pedagogue talking in this style, but for a man of real rank—"

"Be kind enough, my good Valentine, to leave my nobility where it is safest—in the dust ; and for Heaven's sake never spread it forth for the curious inspection of my pupils' parents, otherwise you will take the bread out of my mouth. At present the excellent souls look on me as of a course clay conscious of its inferiority, and therefore fitted to teach their porcelain daughters. With what success I do so, these papers could prove," stirring the copybooks with the stem of his pipe. "*Per dio!* one of the prettiest of my scholars, persists in writing *Favoriscara,*" and Giuliani laughed the abrupt laugh of one who lives much alone, without any of that continuity which sympathy imparts to laughter.

Valentine, who was not sufficiently versed in Italian to be much tickled by the blunder, here laid a tiny note before Giuliani, saying,—

"She gave it to me, in case you should stand out for the dignity of a written invitation."

Giuliani examined the writing of the direction and exclaimed—

"That blessed English writing, there is no telling one hand from another!" He next investigated the seal, holding it close to the light. "Now, easy as it may seem," he continued, "I would wager ten to one, no Italian woman could make a seal like this; so round, so small, so neat. How every trifle about this scrap of paper reveals the refinement of your country, Valentine. Its perfume of violets almost overpowers my tobacco."

"You will end by being an Anglo-mane, instead of the Anglo-phobe, you now are," said the young Englishman.

"No, never; you English are a great people, the Romans of the present day, a race of giants, if you will; but disagreeable for strangers to dwell among. I admire, even wonder at your royal Thames—the rendezvous of the world—but I prefer to hang up my harp in the trees bordering the Seine."

Valentine Ponsonby's eyes wandered to the clock on the mantelpiece; the hands already marked the half-hour after nine.

"You then decidedly refuse to accompany me?" he asked.

"Decidedly!"

"Write an apology, then—it is the least you can do; it is not for everybody beautiful Miss Tufton will write an invitation."

"If she be all I infer from your admiration, I should fear to see her, philosopher though I am."

With the unreflecting vehemence of youth, Valentine replied.—

"You may well be afraid. She is creating quite a *furore* in Paris; it is the fashion to be in love with her."

"Indeed! then I need have no more fears. Nothing more odious to me, than a woman whom it is the fashion to adore. In what other terms could you describe one of the celebrities of the *demi-monde?*"

Valentine's honest face showed his displeasure.

"I would not feel as bitterly and severely as you do, even to be you, with your talents and your brave antecedents."

Giuliani smiled grimly.

"I may speak of, and judge my fashionable fellow creatures hardly; but I call God to witness I wish them well, and do them no ill."

"Why not treat them well? Why repulse the kindness they offer you, and that merely because you have taken such a prejudice against the rich, and believe as my sister Alicia does, that the poor and the illiterate have a monopoly of the virtues?"

"The wise of all ages have protested against the rich, friend Valentine; however, I assure you that my wish for obscurity arises principally from self-love. I feel myself to be sadly deficient in those things which are necessary to acquire the good-will of men and women in general. Deficient in fortune, station, and good looks, what wonder if I wish to keep out of the way of offending, or being offended. You have all the requisites for pleasing, my good fellow; so now go and enjoy your evening. Adieu."

The defeated ambassador departed, and Giuliani settled himself anew to his Greek, or tried to do so; but the scent of the violets would not let him forget the discussion; and once more, and as if it were against his will, he took up the note, and examined, with the attention of an expert, the paper, the writing, and the seal. Giuliani, when he had pushed aside the exercises of his pupils, had tasted the pleasure of anticipation. The task had been wearisome, but it had left his mind, as it were, braced for the enjoyment of a favourite pursuit. The discussion with Valentine had, on the contrary, disturbed his composure, put his mind into another frame than that which could sympathize with the woes of Antigone or Iphigenia. A load of ennui oppressed him; the solitude he had just praised, and preferred, overpowered him. More than once lately he had been assailed by a disgust of his position; of being condemned to silence, isolation, and inactivity, at the age most fitted for action and enthusiasm. More than once lately he had been taken unawares by an ardent thirst for freedom from this immobility—freedom, even through a catastrophe. The books were thrust aside, and Giuliani went out, desirous of being jostled by a crowd, that would send him back contented to his attic. Out he went into one of the great thoroughfares leading from the Chaussée d'Antin to one of the Barrières. There Giuliani stopped, and without accounting to himself as to why he did so, examined this poor locality.

Opposite to him, a highly coloured sign, which showed him a beflounced female, holding a new-born babe; at his right hand a tavern, all the faces round the buffet as lurid red as the smoky light from the oil lamp, and shining like the copper vessels hanging round. A yard or two farther on, a flower-shop, exhibiting principally funeral wreaths, woven of yellow immortelles, bordered and studded with black. Heart-rending decorations on them, denoting the rupture of every tie that can exist between man and man. *A ma mère, A mon fils, A mon mari.* The neighbouring dealer was a *revendeuse,* or retailer of cast-off clothes; through the open door, distinguishable by the flickering light, was seen a counter, on which lay the tawdry splendours of much-soiled ball dresses. As Giuliani walked by, the mistress of the tomb flowers (a misshapen mass of female clay) was bidding good-night to the proprietress of the cast-off finery.

He strolled away to the Boulevards—to that division of them which lies between the Rue de la Chaussée d'Antin, and the Rue Richelieu; gaiety and splendour enough there, but under the one and the other he espied the funeral wreaths and the cast-off finery of the Barrière.

He went back to his attic contented with his solitude.

CHAPTER II.

Beginnings.

The next day, as Giuliani was on his road to give a lesson in the Rue de Courcelles, he met Colonel Caledon. Despite a broad difference in their respective ages, the Englishman and the Italian had been fellow-soldiers; and whenever the colonel saw Giuliani, a pressing invitation to dinner was an inevitable consequence. The attraction these two men had the one for the other arose from their acquaintance dating from so many years back; otherwise, with their strong national prejudices, they might have walked in parallel lines for ever without finding or making one point of contact. As it was, Giuliani contemplated with benevolence in Colonel Caledon the peculiarities most disagreeable to him in other English, viz., his faith in England's universal superiority, his unconcealed contempt for every one born out of the pale of the British dominions, his belief that morality was unknown beyond the channel, and that it took two Frenchmen or three Italians to be a match for one free-born Briton.

Colonel Caledon, on his side, freely acknowledged that though Italians were "a set of scamps," his friend Giuliani was a "man," and deserving of a better fate than to have been born one of the Pope's subjects. "When I have seen a fellow, before he had hair on his chin, fight as I saw Giulio Giuliani fight by his poor father's side, in Portugal," would the colonel say, "I am bound to stand up for his character, Italian or no Italian. He is a man—that I'll say for him." In fact, when two men, whose principles of action are the same, are forced into companionship, whatever the differences of nationalities, friendship is sure to follow.

Courage stood as high with the colonel's delicate wife, as with the brave old soldier himself. Mrs Caledon, however, had attracted her rough, burly husband by all that is most feminine in woman carried to excess. Giuliani, and, indeed, most people, liked Mrs. Caledon, she being a person eminently charitable to the self-love of others; listening with an appearance of interest to every pitiless egotist, her large eyes filling easily with tears of sympathy, when most others would have civilly suppressed a yawn of ennui.

"Women," says Mdlle. Necker, "fill up the intervals of conversation and of life, like those down coverlids placed in packing-cases full of china; these *duvets* count for nothing, yet without them everything would be broken."

Mrs. Caledon's mission in life was to be a *duvet*, and to keep sharp angles from meeting.

In compliance with his old comrade's cordial invitation, Giuliani, at seven in the evening, was in the Caledons' drawing-room, in the Rue de Berri.

A peculiarly juvenile old gentleman, accompanied by an elderly lady, were the next arrivals.

"Sir Mark," said the hostess, "allow me to introduce you to one of Colonel Caledon's oldest friends. Sir Mark Tufton—Mr. Giuliani."

Impossible not to remark, and, having remarked, not to meditate on, Sir Mark Tufton's youthful figure, in contrast to a face as lined as those of Michel-Angelo's Fates. He looked as though some draught he had taken of the elixir of youth had only been strong enough to act on his body—the contrary to what happened to the man in the Spanish story, whose head alone lived.

The baronet's face had the thinness of that of a skeleton; his blue eye was glazed, at times almost extinct.

"Cruel and vain," thought Giuliani; a human tiger."

Other guests followed in quick succession—among them some girls, who, seated on a divan as far from their elders as possible, chirped like newly-fledged birds to some young men standing before them. The girls were fair, rosy and puzzlingly similar in dress, manners and complexion.

The young men all had a little turned-up moustache, hair parted down the middle, units sent forth in hundreds by fashionable tailors, hatters and bootmakers: the resemblance went further than dress; their faces were without any individuality of expression, looking as if they had been all set in the same mould, having as much mobility as if they had been made of wood.

They talked fluently, learnedly and sometimes pedantically. Heaven help the one who, in defiance of such wells of learning, ventured on a sharp original observation, which, being original, would necessarily be out of the daily beat of the hearers—out of their narrow, charmed circle. The bold adventurer would be met by a chilling silence, or put down by an authoritative rebuff, either check serving to denounce him as a pert idiot.

As Giuliani listened to the conversation of these examples of the rising generation, of whom the majority were Parisians, as he contemplated their wooden, self-satisfied, half-ennuyed faces, he decided that among them the search would be vain for a dreamy, poetical Werther, with the luxuriant faults and virtues of youth; those faults which, leaning to virtue's side, give promise of generous ardour for a good cause, whenever the hour of action may arrive. He turned away with a sort of longing for the sight of one who belonged to another generation, of one who had loved and fought from heroic sympathy, for the sight of the old colonel's manly countenance, with its keen, impatient, grey eyes, and broad humorous, benevolent mouth. The colonel was oscillating rapidly between window and window of his drawing-room, while into his wife's face, who was fluttering after him, a look of anxiety had stolen, which deepened almost into fear whenever she looked towards Sir Mark Tufton, whose ghastly eyes were fixed on the door, as if it had a spell for him. The conversation at the ottoman died into whisperings, interrupted by girlish titterings.

A solemn butler had twice reconnoitered the party assembled; on his second appearance Mrs. Caledon whispered to her husband, and having received some advice, the hostess, trying to smile, went to the young ladies. To some request there came an eager outburst of assent.

Passing by Giuliani, Mrs. Caledon stopped to explain her trouble.

"We are thirteen," she said; "for that naughty Miss Tufton has failed me at the last, after promising faithfully to be punctual. She knows Sir Mark would not sit down to table thirteen, for an empire. I am not sure he will think himself safe with two of the girls at a side table "

While Mrs, Caledon was still speaking, the folding doors opened, and a young lady glided in, as calm and smiling as if she did not know herself to be a delinquent.

She was dressed in some rich black silk, which, as she moved, showed glossy spots.   A silver grey cloak, trimmed with swansdown, hung over her shoulders. Even at the first glimpse, Giuliani thought her a miracle of loveliness,   For the moment he lost sight of every other person in the room.   Delicate, slight, but erect, and well poised, she looked tall without being so.   Her hair was of that peculiar fairness which has the appearance·of being slightly powdered with gold.   Her eyebrows were narrow, smooth, and darker by several shades than her hair, and so were the long lashes, that caused her blue eyes to look black by candle-light.   Her nose was singularly handsome, and her lips red and curved, closing well over small, white, regular teeth, which must have made any mouth pretty.

The new arrival's beauty was enhanced and set off by an indescribable piquant air of freshness about her whole person and dress.   Every eye was fixed on her, she engrossed the silent attention of the thirteen persons she had thrown into embarrassment, without showing the least symptom of shyness or of self-consciousness ; the smile on her face was puzzling; whoever remembers the Mona Lisa in the Louvre will have seen that sort of mysterious smile.

Giuliani, to say the truth, after the first shock of her uncommon loveliness, gazed at her as he might have done at any charming actress; he almost felt inclined to applaud, when he saw her meet Sir Mark's furious grins with such intrepidity.

Colonel Caledon led the beautiful offender into the dining-room, every ruffle cleared from his brow, and out of his voice almost all the loudness and roughness vanished.   The colonel was not above showing the lively enthusiasm he felt for beauty.

The elderly lady, who had arrived with Sir Mark, and whom Mr. Giuliani had supposed to be Sir Mark's wife, was a Miss Crumpton, a distant connexion of the Tuftons, and considered by the baronet as a dependant, because he did not receive any share of her income of fifty pounds a year, but gave her board and lodging free, for the motherly care she bestowed on his orphan grand-daughter. Miss Crumpton had an old-fashioned, cere-monious politeness, that made her strive earnestly through the long dinner, to induce the gentleman on her right and left to become sociable; but the former was English, and not having been specially introduced to the latter, an Italian, could not be tempted into any informality.

"The count speaks English as well as you or I," said Miss Crumpton, to her stiff right-hand neighbour. She believed every continental gentleman to be a count. "Doubtless," turning to her left hand, "you have spent many years in England, sir?"

"A couple of years, madam," was the reply, and Giuliani ready to laugh at the rank bestowed on him, thought of making a public disclaimer of any right to have his identity so muffled during his uncle's life. But he remembered in time having once tried to undeceive Mrs. Caledon herself, who, after listening, or apparently so, to his explanation, had on the very next occasion, lavished on him more "Monsieur le Comtes," than ever.

So he now said to himself, "*Allons donc, comme ça leur plaît, qu'ils s'en donnent de leur biribi.*"

After dinner, as there were so many French present, the English custom of the gentlemen sitting over their wine after the ladies had left the table, was set aside, and all the guests passed together into the *salon*.

Miss Tufton was immediately surrounded by every man in the room, with two exceptions; Sir Mark, who, seating himself between two of the youngest girls, was very happy to be pelted by the pert answers elicited by his gallant speeches; and Mr. Giuliani, who, as usual, was well cared for by his tender-hearted hostess. She carried on her conversation with him in the lachrymose tone generally used on state visits of condolence, ready to lead or follow him into discussions on "Suffering Italy."

But Giuliani steadily resisting all personal topics, Mrs. Caledon, driven to seek some other subject, asked him if he did not think Miss Tufton "the most lovely creature he had ever beheld."

He said quietly, "Yes."

"Do you put no more enthusiasm than that into your *yes?* I have no patience with the young men of the present day, lifting their lorgnons to examine a charming girl, as if she were merely a muslin doll."

"My admiration is warm and sincere."

"That's right. Come and let me introduce you to her."

"Thank you; but I have a dread of all beginnings."

"You really puzzle me, Mr. Giuliani."

"Have you never heard, Mrs. Caledon, that it is only on first meeting with a person that the judgment is unprejudiced, and that whatever the impression then received, it ought not to be slighted?"

"You think her fantastical; but, poor dear, that is the effect of her education, and the odd life she has led with that queer miser, her grandfather. You must not be prejudiced against my little friend; she is not yet nineteen, remember. Ah, if you heard her sing, you would not be able to think ill of her."

"Though my admiration should reach the highest pitch of intensity, still, believe me, we should never assimilate. Leave me to enjoy the pleasure of the eye, which, in this case, is perfect."

It is not easy to account for the persistence many people show in carrying out a matter which can be of no importance individually to them; unless, indeed, their pertinacity proceeds from having met with opposition, or from an inability to rid themselves of the pressure of an idea until it has become action. Whether from one motive or other, or from being what country-folks pithily call "meddlesome," Mrs. Caledon went direct from Mr. Giuliani to Miss Tufton with a proposal of introducing the Italian to her, beginning at the same time a sort of sketch of his biography.

"I know all about your Lion, dear Mrs. Caledon," said Lill Tufton, rather petulantly; "a silly youth, called Valentine Ponsonby, has given me his history: an ungrateful country, lost illusions, a man with a tragic complexion. Why didn't he come to our dance when I was so good as to ask him?"

"Question him yourself."

"No, indeed; that would be making him imagine

himself of importance. Pray don't introduce him, I should never be able to think of anything wise enough to say; I have no political convictions—"

She stopped suddenly. Giuliani was replying to one of the Englishmen, who, having been introduced to him by Colonel Caledon, was kindly endeavouring to put him, as an Italian, right, as to Italy's safest course, concluding with,—

"You will find I am right, sir; our papers say just what I do."

"Sir," replied Giuliani, "I have the temerity to differ from beginning to end from many English papers."

"I like him!" exclaimed Lill; "I like people who speak out for themselves; besides, I like his voice; it is a gentleman's. I judge of people's rank by their voices Oh, yes, bring him here, by all means."

Beautiful eyes sparkling with welcome, lovely lips speaking welcome, generally are irresistible to men, even to the sourest of misogynists, if such creatures really exist. The hermit of the Rue de Berlin, who feared "beginnings," because he knew they must be followed by inflexible, inevitable consequences, who was so sure of no possible assimilation between him and the beauty, was neither stronger nor weaker than his neighbours when he came under such pleasant influences. In fact, as the lovely face turned itself ingenuously to his gaze, as the tones of a joyous voice caressed his ear, his own heart beats became fuller and faster.

The conversation, if by such a dignified word it may be defined, consisted of short questions and answers; but never had wit, good sense, or learning sounded so captivatingly to Giuliani: yet Lill was not so pleasant as usual. As she had said to Mrs. Caledon, she had heard of Giuliani from Valentine Ponsonby; and, besides his biography, having been told that he was a man of talent, Lill wished to shine before him, and gave way to a sarcasm not natural to her. It is so easy to be satirical, while it is so difficult to be witty. But beautiful eyes and sweet smiles have a way of their own of bribing men's judgment, and Lill's petulant gaiety succeeded far better than Greek roots in banishing furrows and hard lines from Giuliani's forehead and mouth.

Sir Mark's juvenile attentions and lively repartee had, during the last quarter of an hour, gradually run down into gravity and silence. His head had acquired that tremulous motion which the electric current gives to trees before a tempest. The girls on the divan watched these movements and signs of emotion with much the same half-alarm, half-amusement with which they would have looked at the demonstrations of agitation in a fierce inmate of one of the cages in the Zoological Gardens. Presently the baronet asked,—

"Who is that Miss Tufton is talking to?"

"That is Mr. Giuliani, our Italian master," came in a breath from the two girls. "Oh, *such* a delightful man; so clever, so unhappy, so—"

"Italian master!" ejaculated Sir Mark. "What's he here for?"

"He is not a common master, I assure you, Sir Mark," answered Colonel Caledon's niece, Rose; "he is only a master as Louis Philippe was when he was in exile. Mr. Giuliani is one of my uncle's dearest friends."

Sir Mark made no observation in return, but walked up to his granddaughter.

"The horses have been waiting an hour, Miss Tufton."

Lill nodded, without interrupting her conversation. She was saying,—

"I never thought of attending to the story of an opera, I have always supposed the plot of an opera much on a par with that of a ballet; but this of *Ernani* must be interesting. Sir Mark, I should like to go and hear *Ernani*."

Sir Mark lifted one foot, then the other, and made a noise like the ghost of stamping.

"Come, come away:" and Sir Mark seized the young lady's hand, forcing her to rise; he must have been sufficiently violent, for he burst her glove.

She extricated herself from the unkind grasp, and drew off her glove, throwing it on the ground between herself and her grandfather; it was done as defiantly as though she had meant it as a gage of battle. She then turned to the Italian,

"Mr. Giuliani, would you be so very good—I am ashamed to trouble you—would you be so good as to secure a box for us the very first evening *Ernani* is played? Our address is 594, Champs Elysées; and remember we expect you to be of our party. Good-night!" and she held out her ungloved hand, flashing with jewels.

Foreigners are not accustomed to shaking hands with young ladies; Giuliani scarcely touched the beauty's dimpled fingers as he bowed long and low.

She then allowed Sir Mark to trot off with her; and Giuliani, as he followed them down stairs, fancied he heard several menacing snarls.

No one had thought Miss Crumpton of sufficient consequence to be warned that her party were going away. In another minute a servant came hurrying to the placid spinster; she almost upset Giuliani, who was on the stairs. Recovering his equilibrium, he courteously offered her his arm.

"594, Mr. Giuliani," cried Lill, from within the carriage.

CHAPTER III.

Consequences of Beginnings.

IT is a pretty smart walk from the Rue de Berri to the Rue de Berlin, on a wintry night; nevertheless Giuliani found himself at his own door as if he had flown thither. There was elation in his every movement; he had had a sip of the waters of Lethe; pity it had not been a cup-full, strong enough to last through the night. But the sight of the familiar instruments of his daily torture, the copy-books, pens and ink, would have sufficed to set the river of oblivion at defiance, without the aid of his writing-table drawer. It was open, because there was neither gold nor silver in it, to protect from thieves. Giuliani carried all he possessed of current coin in his waistcoat pocket, he had no overplus to make him fret, or keep him from sleep. Nevertheless, he slept that night as badly as any minister of finance, who has the wealth of a nation in his keeping.

The pupils who saw Giuliani well-dressed, calm, dignified, had no idea that the master about whom they gossiped, as girls will gossip, very often went without any other dinner than a piece of chocolate and a crust of bread.

Not more courage had Giuliani shown on the field of battle, than he did in his daily combat with life in the pleasant capital of France. No living soul had ever heard a lament or a request for help issue from those sharply-cut lips. Rent, taxes, clothing, fuel, food; serious items these, to be met by the two or three francs thought sufficient for a lesson of Italian; and what mean haggling too, as to that particular half-crown to be paid for it! It is not only by looking behind the scenes of a theatre, that pleasant illusions are lost. What contemptible tricks are daily played in the behind scenes of every-day life, to permit of a little more external show, a little more dash than our next-door neighbour!

There is yet something else to be added to the list of a refugee's expenses—charity to fellow exiles, who can teach nothing, but how to live on a straw a day.

But why? somebody will ask here, why should a man, so well born, and so rich in intellectual gifts as Mr. Giuliani, stick in the Slough of Despond, which teaching is? Ah! why indeed, have so many illustrious exiles (a long line, from Dionysius of Syracuse, down to the noble-minded Manini), demanded a scanty subsistence from tuition? For this simple reason, that they had no other choice. Be a man's attainments ever so great, they are of small avail towards his turning an honest penny out of the natural sphere of their exercise. But imagine a man, hurled by victorious force into a foreign land, too proud to accept relief from governments or committees, with no friends. no patronage, and no disposition to solicit any. What is left to that man, but to bring into the market his knowledge of mathematics, music, or languages—that which he knows best? Thus it was that Giuliani had advertised for lessons, as a matter of necessity. He did not court it—a hard fate! for his was the belief, right or wrong, that the humblest calling might be made honourable by the manner of discharging it.

New and more brilliant openings had, in course of time, offered themselves to him. Newspapers and periodicals requested political and literary contributions, and he gave them willingly. His articles were highly praised, but they were considered too strict, too unbending, he must modify here, suppress there, soothe, dilute. flatter; in short, substitute other people's tastes and views for his own tastes and views. A man all of one piece as he was, of course flatly refused this advice, and there was an end of his career as a man of letters. This experience had served to reconcile him to his modest avocation as a teacher; he held it to be the only one consistent, under his circumstances, with independence and self-respect. None other, moreover, could half so well satisfy that morbid craving for obscurity, which is the supremest boon to wounded hearts. His life brightened from the day when his lucky star guided a youth named Valentine Ponsonby, at that period meditating a visit to Rome, to his attic.

The new pupil insisted on introducing his master to his mother and sister. Not the most sickly susceptibility ever did or could withstand the cheering presence of the youth's mother. Despondency and fear fled before Lady Ponsonby, as darkness flies at the approach of genial light. Her sunny smile penetrated into the dimmest corners of a benighted heart; the imps of bitterness there ensconsed had to pack up their baggage and depart. When Lady Ponsonby rang at Mr. Giuliani's door bell, and stood before him in the middle of his laboratory of hard work and deprivation, he felt, as he himself expressed it, as if proved by the touch of Ithuriel's spear—with her he was his true self.

The recollection of this benignant friend restored tranquillity enough to the Italian, to permit of his handling his clouded cane with a steady hand, as he sallied forth on his daily rounds the morning after Colonel Caledon's dinner-party. Yes, at the worst he had a harbour of refuge: he had certainly never yet applied to Lady Ponsonby for a pecuniary loan, but he was sure she was a friend, even including her purse. However, he would only ask her when every other attempt had failed. His watch was at this present moment reposing in some of the yawning caverns of the Mont-de-Piété; pledged in order that an old Italian of gentle birth, an exile for conscience' sake, might have a whole suit of clothes on his back when he entered on the situation of a sweeper-out of a house of business. His books indeed! those trusty feres! Giuliani shook his head, they would have been a useless sacrifice; the mass of them would not have brought a sufficient sum to secure for Miss Tufton the use of an opera box for one night. There was nothing for it, but to solicit some payments of lessons long overdue.

Shrinking inwardly as though about to commit a shabby action, Giuliani made his several applications. It is very strange how delicate-minded people, when asking for their money, do so with a timidity that would better suit the debtors, who boldly negative the request as though it were an insult. He was not the man to obtain his money, and returned to his lodging as poor as he left it; nevertheless irrevocably resolved that he would fulfil pretty Miss Tufton's commission. He did specially wish to please her, but more specially wish that she should remain ignorant of his difficulty in doing so: he felt as if he would rather have committed a crime, than meet her wondering smile at any explanation of his poverty.

This was Saturday—Lady Ponsonby always received on Saturday evenings those of her friends who would take the trouble to go to her. He would strive to be the first arrival, so as to have his mind relieved, and be able as usual to enjoy the charm her ladyship diffused around her.

CHAPTER IV.

Incipit Vita Nova.

BEFORE mid-day on Monday morning Miss Tufton received an envelope, containing the *coupon* of a private box at the Italian Opera for the following evening. She was as pleased as a child with a new bauble. Mr. Giuliani was a delightful, kind man, so quiet and unobtrusive: she did really believe that the best people were the most reserved.

Miss Crumpton, to whom these remarks were made, tried to pitch her answers to the height of Lill's tone, but failed; for the young lady exclaimed, petulantly, —

"What's the matter now, Crummie? It's very strange I can never have a pleasure, but some one damps it."

"My dear, I am as delighted as you can be about the box, and I consider this Italian gentleman, I assure you, a most agreeable person; but—"

"Well, as there is a 'but'—must be a 'but' in the case, take courage, Crummie, and out with it."

"Sir Mark, what will he say?"

"Nothing pleasant or polite, that's certain; however, he heard me make the request, and if he had meant to interfere, he would have done so before this. O Crummie, 'sufficient for the day is the evil thereof.' Do, like a good soul, let me enjoy myself this once. I never felt happy about a play before. I am going to write a note to my slave Valentine, to ask him to bring me his copy of *Ernani* this evening. I know he has the whole opera, for he was raving about *Ernani involami* the last time I saw him. I want to know the music beforehand."

Miss Crumpton either was, or seemed to be, deep in the mysteries of a crochet pattern. She nevertheless heard Lill's pen gliding rapidly over the paper, and the anxious look in the old lady's face deepened.

"There; it is done; and admire my diplomatic talent. I have asked Master Valentine to join our party to-morrow, and to tell Mr. Giuliani I expect him to meet us at the great entrance of the Salle Ventadour."

The beauty rang the bell, and desired the footman to

carry the note to its address. A minute or two afterwards Sir Mark entered the room where the ladies were, *The Times* in his hand, and his gold spectacles on his nose. Sir Mark must, indeed, have been excited to make his appearance in glasses, for even with his granddaughter he strove to maintain a show of juvenility.

"Where have you sent Joseph, Miss Tufton?"

"To Mr. Ponsonby, to ask for the music of the opera of *Ernani*."

"Why cannot you buy it for yourself?"

"You know very well that I have no money."

"On the contrary, I am persuaded you have plenty, at least, you give orders as if you had."

Sir Mark was examining, as he said this, the coupon of the opera box.

Lill shrugged her shoulders, and walked to one of the windows. Sir Mark now turned to Miss Crumpton.

"Can you oblige me by lending me forty francs?" he asked, in his most suave voice.

"Certainly, Sir Mark," said Miss Crumpton, with hurried glibness. taking out her purse; "only,—oh dear! I am very sorry, Sir Mark, but I have not more than, let me see——" counting some few pieces of silver.

"Never mind. never mind," said Sir Mark, goodhumouredly; "it's that fool Joseph being out of the way, or I would not have troubled you. I was about to send him to the bank."

Lill had turned to look at the pair: she now burst into an irrepressible, clear, ringing laugh. Miss Crumpton looked aghast; but Sir Mark joined in his granddaughter's merriment as he left the room.

"What a wicked old man that is!" cried Lill. "How slyly he managed to find out that you had no money. He is quite happy at the thought of having made us both thoroughly uncomfortable."

"I guessed he would not pay for that box," said Miss Crumpton, disconsolately: "and now what are we to do? for here is all I have — twenty francs, and my next payment not due for a month."

"He will give me money some day or other, he *must*." said Lill.

"Mr. Giuliani ought to be paid at once, my dear girl; he is quite a stranger, and—and I suspect he is poor; he is only an Italian master, you know."

Lill grew very red.

"Dear good old woman, you are right, as you always are. I know what I will do; I will sell some of my bracelets and rings. I wonder what a box costs. Crummie, let us go at once."

"And if Sir Mark comes to know what you have done?"

"He dare not kill me; and my thoughtlessness shall not be the cause of annoyance to any one who has done me a kindness. Old pet, you shall not come with me; you shall be innocent of my offence. I'll take Ruth. It is of no use arguing, consin Crumpton; I won't let you have a share in my punishment. Could any human being who saw us—saw me—dressed as I am, surrounded by these useless fiddle-faddles" (pointing to tables covered, with a profusion of expensive nicnacs)—could any one believe that I can never command a penny? If alms-giving is to help one to Heaven, Sir Mark and I may make pretty sure that we shall not even get a foot in there."

"My dear girl, the fault is not yours; you have the warmest and most generous heart that ever beat."

"Dear cousin!" and Lill kneeled down by the old lady's side, fixing on her, eyes so radiant with honest affection, that Miss Crumpton may be forgiven if she were always ready to roast the old world to warm Lill. "Dear cousin," went on Lill, "what virtue or grace do you think I am wanting in?"

Lill sighed.

Miss Crumpton had never before heard a sigh from her lovely charge.

"Do not fret yourself, my dear; I'll take the whole business on myself, and borrow the money from Mrs. Caledon."

"You do not, I hope, think I am sighing about my trinkets; no indeed, cousin, I was sighing at a glimpse I caught of my own inner self, and it shows me that I do care about luxury. I revel in what the Catechism calls the pomps and vanity of life; silks, satins, flowers, jewels, perfumes, carriages, idleness, and no contact

with common people : I enjoy even the playing at being
rich ; for after all, but for Sir Mark, I should have to
beg, or work, or starve."

Lill stopped, out of breath and flushed by her confession.

"You exaggerate." said Miss Crumpton, placidly, and
putting a pin to mark her place in her crochet pattern.
"I believe we all prefer being comfortable to uncomfortable."

"Very despicable of us if we do, at the expense of our
self-respect," returned Lill, quickly. "I am a mass of
contradictions ; I had rather be a stock or a stone than
the victim of that old man's tyrannical, capricious treatment. I hate myself for submitting to be decked out
and paraded as I am, just as a sultan's slave might be,
and yet —"

"What alternative have you, my dear ?"

"Keep a little mercery shop, and in the evening sit
in its cozy back parlour, you and I, and have such capital tea and nice buttered toast ; a good novel for me,
while you were counting over our daily gains. I saw
something of the sort one day when we were shopping
in X —, and I thought then that old woman and girl
were happier than either of us, cousin Crumpton. However, I dare say it would not be better than any other
reality, — and poverty !"

Lill had been laughing while she spoke, but she added
gravely enough, —

"Poverty ! I am afraid of being poor."

"Ay ! and no wonder, poor thing."

"Yes, I hate money, hate that continual want of it,
and reverence for it," continued Lill, more to herself
than to her chaperone. "Evil communication will do
its bad work on me ; I don't believe I should feel the
same horror and disquiet now, which I felt two years
ago, when, while I was reading Shakspeare, my grandfather's voice, gloating over his percents, came mingling
with what I read."

Lill's bitter words were the mere expression of the
feeling of the moment, a cry of sudden pain. She wiped
away some stray tears unobserved by the industrious
Miss Crumpton.

"Now, away with all gloom," she exclaimed. ' I shall be off to get money to pay this good-natured Mr Giuliani, and to-morrow night I will enjoy myself if I never do so again."

Before dinner Lill handed to Miss Crumpton five hundred francs.

"Gracious me, my dear!" cried the old lady in alarm, 'that is far more than necessary for an opera box. What have you sold?"

"Oh, a heap of things I was tired of. If it is too much for the box, we will give what remains to some poor person."

"Lill, do promise to be more prudent; you *must* indeed."

"Thank you, cousin, for trying to be authoritative, but I cannot promise, for I should forget just at the critical moment. One good comes of this evil. As long as I have a trinket I can foil Sir Mark's meanness."

"It makes me tremble to think what would be the consequence if Sir Mark found out this business."

"He made his poor wife tremble; and I daresay my poor father and mother also; I do not know whether he could make me tremble; I can only fancy being alarmed at the anger of a person I loved. We shall see."

Lill was in her wildest spirits that evening. Valentine Ponsonby brought her the music of *Ernani*; she undertook to sing all the female parts, forcing Valentine, who had very little voice, and was timid to excess before Sir Mark, to sing Ernani's and Silva's songs. Sir Mark, morose and despotic as was his normal state in his domestic circle, was for a while charmed out of himself by Lill's singing. The voice could not be spoiled by the lively caricature of her manner. She travestied the tragical situations as gracefully as wildly; it was the novice laughing at, and playing with deadly tools.

To Lill's and Miss Crumpton's astonishment, Sir Mark's good humour was unabated the next day. He even advised some change in the flowers in his granddaughter's hair, which, as his taste was universally acknowledged to be exquisite as to woman's dress, the young lady acceded to.

"Little demon!" he ejaculated, as he himself handed

her into the carriage. "How bravely she bears herself! It's not much wonder she fools pleasures out of men."

It was the hour when artisans and workmen were leaving work: many of them were attracted to stand still and watch the ladies get into the smart equipage. Hardworking, toil-stained men they were; but most of them intelligent critics as to ladies and their carriages. There was a harmony between Lill's youth, loveliness and attire which pleased these spectators; but Miss Crumpton, unshapely and grey-haired, in a cap with bright roses, had an undue share of sneers. As Lill leaned back on the soft cushions, wrapped in cashmere, she said,—

"How astonished that bricklayer, who stared at us so insolently, would be if I explained my situation to him; told him, in fact, that I am poorer than he is, for I could not gain my daily bread!"

"You should not look at these sort of people, Lill, it is imprudent—dangerous; these French are a cruel race."

Lill did not continue the subject: she dreaded tears and quotations from the book published by the Valet Cléry, describing the sufferings of Louis XVI. and Marie Antoinette, and which was one of the few books Miss Crumpton had read from beginning to end. Nevertheless, Lill could not banish from her thoughts the ironical expression of those workmen's faces; it had ruffled her composure, and, at the same time, astonished her. She had hitherto felt so secure of being only an object of respect and wonder to the poor. She now received one of the many accidental impressions which get up a battle with one another every now and then in our minds, and which, while their contrary influences render us riddles to ourselves, conduct us to our destiny.

But the Tufton carriage has entered the line of other equipages waiting to set down fair opera-goers, and Lill comes back to her own special world again.

While yet a long way off, Giuliani perceived Lill, and that not a passer-by but turned to gaze again at the beautiful English girl. He could see that she was so busily reconnoitring for some one, as to be quite unconscious of the notice she attracted. A glow of pleasure warmed his heart when the sudden lighting up of her eyes, as her glance fell on him, showed it was himself she had been seeking.

How was Giuliani, any more than the bricklayer, to guess that this brilliant creature, surrounded by all the appurtenances of wealth, was so unaccustomed to any kindly attention to her wishes, as to have magnified a common act of courtesy into one of real kindness? How was he to imagine that this sylph, in celestial blue silk, had been as troubled as himself to find the necessary number of francs to pay for the opera box; that the only difference between their cases was, that she had trinkets to pawn, and no Lady Ponsonby to assist her.

No one comprehends the other's situation in this world.

It was a gala evening at the Italian: every box was full; every stall occupied—the pit crammed. Many who could not find seats were lounging in the corridors and alleys. The curtain was still down, and every man in pit or stall was standing with his back to the stage, his double lorgnon levelled at the *loges découvertes*, wondering from whence had so suddenly congregated such a distracting splendour of eyes, lips, hair, teeth, as he saw there. It seemed as if every young and beautiful woman in Paris had agreed on a rendezvous to dispute the palm of beauty. Not one of the lovely creatures there feared the flood of light falling on her from the great and little lustres; vivid lightning glances flashed round; cheeks flushed, and lips smiled provokingly back to the burning gaze directed to them.

The box into which Giuliani—resisting the longing to offer Miss Tufton his arm—led the chaperone, was one behind the *loges découvertes*, really a private box in its literal sense, few glances, in comparison, penetrating within. Perhaps for an instant the English beauty felt disappointed, as she leaned forward to look at the house, that she was not one of that dazzling circle; but she smiled very pleasantly when Giuliani, who had seen the fair face cloud, hoped he had not mistaken her wishes.

The opera of *Ernani*, as probably every one knows, is founded on Victor Hugo's *Hernani*, so famous as the first piece played at the Théâtre Français, in which the classic unities were set aside—the first play in which the scenery was changed, an innovation that had convulsed all literary Paris.

Verdi's music was in its greatest vogue on the night in question; and at the first tap of the conductor's stick, there was a volte-face in pit and stalls; opera glasses prepared to mark the time, and only one or two ardent devotees kept their eyes on the *loges découvertes*. From the first note to the last of the music of *Ernani*, there is in it the unmistakable accent of deep passion; it keeps every fibre of the heart vibrating, every nerve quivering.

Her arm resting on the dark red velvet of the cushion of the front of the box, her chin in her hand, her eyes fixed, her lips half-open, Lill did more than listen, she drank in each enchanting sound. Giuliani, to whom *Ernani* was a four-fold told tale, now listened with a passionate rapture and vehemence of emotion nearer to pain than pleasure. Those who have not heard such music in the company of one loved, or about to be loved, know not as yet all the irresistible power of music.

Two or three times when the melody was most tender, or the harmony most entrancing—and what other than Italian music ever so entirely sounds the depths of human feeling?—Lill turned to Giuliani in search of sympathy; and to him it seemed as if he read through those clear eyes into her soul. As he sat contemplating her, the first impression she had made on him vanished. Her manners and habits were those of the world she lived in; but beneath all, he felt sure, lay hid a deep sensibility. It was a happiness hitherto unknown, that with which Giuliani felt Lill's arm resting on his, as they left the box. He had quite forgotten his former respectful attention to Miss Crumpton. The crowd pressed her closer to him; he seemed never to have lived till then.

"Ah, what a delightful evening!" said Lill, as he handed her into the carriage; "how much obliged I am to you, Mr. Giuliani!"

She did not speak again for some time after the carriage drove off; she was singing in a whisper, *Ernani involami*. She stopped and said abruptly,

"Cousin, did you remember to pay Mr. Giuliani?"

"Yes, indeed; but, Lill, I could not induce him to let

me pay for the whole box ; he said that the half was his affair, and Mr. Ponsonby's."

"I was sure there would be a blunder ! how vexatious! and that stupid Valentine!" Lill stopped, laughed, and added, "How unjust I am, wreaking my vengeance on the weak! I must never ask Mr. Giuliani to do commissions for me again."

And then she nestled her head into the downy cushions of the carriage, closed her eyes, and plunged into reveries about Elvira, the Doña Sol of the tragedy, and Ernani. The young lady's thoughts, confused and indistinct as thoughts are where one has a perception of thinking at once of two or three subjects as wide apart as the two poles, might be summed up as deciding that for the sake of so heroic and exclusive a lover as Ernani, death itself would be welcome. The very young, for whom life has more pleasures than sorrows, are nevertheless always the most willing to die. They may be said to *enjoy* a sad story. The scene on the terrace, those marvellously tender accents of love, stirred Lill's heart, and sent her to bed enthusiastically devoted to Ernani, to a fantastic unknown Ernani, not at all invested with the features of any one she had ever seen.

Giuliani and Valentine smoked their cigars as they walked homewards.

"Who would have suspected you," said Valentine, "of being chosen a squire of dames?"

"Nothing too strange for your country women to do," answered the Italian. "One may expect from them all that is exquisite, delicate, and charming, and just the contrary."

Valentine's next speech was interrogative.

"She is very beautiful, is she not?"

"Very."

"Like a sylph or fairy," went on Valentine; "she makes me understand the ravings of poets about beauty."

"Precisely so," said Giuliani.

And thus the dialogue continued, diffuse on the one side, concise on the other.

Once safe in the solitude of his attic, Giuliani gave the rein to his sensations. Again the sweet sounds of the music came to his ear, dying away into unearthly melody;

with closed eyes he again saw Lill, now listening, now seeking his sympathy; he saw her bright fair head, framed as it were in the crimson drapery, saw the slender rounded arm, smelt the perfume of the rare flowers she carried in her hand.

Giuliani slept little that night and dreamed a great deal. When he got up the next morning he ought to have said to himself: "This day I begin a new life." On the contrary, he resolved more strenuously than ever not to deviate for the future by a hair's breadth, from his monotonous course of life; solitude, or rather retirement, was his safeguard. His judgment told him he had been right to avoid society—it had not one temptation, but a legion, for men in his position; he had need of all his self-possession to gain his livelihood. Hope or desire of change would not do for him.

CHAPTER V.

Plan of Attack on the Hermit of the Rue de Berlin.

"Now tell me something about Mr. Giuliani, Colonel Caledon. Who is Mr. Giuliani?" questioned Miss Tufton some two or three days after the evening at the opera.

"To answer you categorically, Miss Tufton, he is the only son of my late good friend the Cavaliere Giuliani, of the counts of that name. When his uncle dies this Giulio Giuliani will have a right to both title and estates. But unless matters change considerably in Italy, I doubt much that his situation would be bettered by the count's death."

"Why does his uncle allow him to be an Italian master?"

"Because he is too egotistically timid to risk an iota of his own safety or tranquillity in behalf of any living creature. Since the Cavaliere's death I know that there has been no communication between the uncle and the proscribed nephew; for even Giuliani's request for some account of his father's property was left unanswered. To the demand, however, for an explanation made by a notary, the reply was clear enough — that the cavaliere had spent all he had on his foolish schemes during his lifetime, and that the count did not intend to continue to his nephew the liberality he had shown to his brother. There was no alternative, Miss Tufton, but beggary or work. Poor fellow! I remember him a little lad, with an arm and hand scarcely larger than yours, fighting by his father's-side, always with eyes on the watch, as if he would take all the shots and bayonet thrusts to himself."

"How hard he looks now, as if he had never known what it was to be a child!" observed Lill, the brightness of her face dimmed by the images called up by the Colonel's story.

"Well, I allow he has a stiff character, but it is of good material."

"Miss Tufton," said Mrs. Caledon, "why don't you

take some lessons from him? if you set the fashion, you might make his fortune."

"Oh, dear Mrs. Caledon, I have not the least turn for learning lessons."

"But perhaps you have for doing a kind action; and I am sure you might be of real benefit to Giuliani. He is the sort of person to starve with dignity."

"How can you put such horrible ideas into one's head? A gentleman starving in our very sight!" exclaimed Lill impetuously. She had suddenly remembered that to satisfy her whim she had made Giuliani pay for an opera ticket, and it gave her a spasm of remorse, the cause of which had it been known to her listeners, would have made her vehemence natural.

Lill's manner was accused generally, and not unjustly so, of levity; it was the mask both of the diffidence and the strong feelings she was too proud to show. Masters and governesses had made her accomplished; Nature had gifted her with quick intelligence; but her education had left her character thoroughly undisciplined. She acted first and thought afterwards; sometimes manifesting the simplicity and candour of a child, at other moments displaying a perspicacity that completely effaced the favourable impression made by her artlessness, the which forthwith received condemnation, as assumed. The perpetual contrasts of her moods and manners had earned for her much of the severity with which she was judged. It was the penalty she paid for keeping her judges in suspense as to what she was. Her best friends declared, "She must always be in one scrape or another." Lill herself used to say, "Do what I will, people will always see some evil in it. I wish I had a glass window to my heart, that my motives might be seen; but no, it doesn't matter after all." Such a speech as this would of course be made after she had been wounded to the quick by some misconstruction of her action or her meaning.

Lill had never had a maternal wing to shelter her from the inclemencies of a world she fancied she knew thoroughly at eighteen, while, poor child, she scarcely ever got a glimpse of reality for the tremulous, translucent light of imagination, through which she viewed all things. Miss Crumpton, living so close to Lill, had indeed acquired an idea, though a very misty one, that a romancer was to be dreaded in her, whom others esteemed only to be a pretty worldling. Lill was really alarmingly impressible, both as to moral and physical influences. What she was in the atmosphere of Sir Mark, would be the opposite to what she would be in that of Lady Ponsonby, or any one like her ladyship. It seemed to most of those who knew her that she was either obstinate or yielding, gay or violent, from mere caprice. This supposition it was which brought her the chilling rebuffs she met, when after some terrible outbreak or rebellion she sought to be forgiven by the most passionate repentance. Her nurse was one of the few who believed in Lill's goodness, though even she expressed her opinion by the proverb, "Miss Tufton is one that will either make a spoon or spoil a horn."

This startlish, high-blooded, generous young mortal, quite unable to guide herself along the highways of life, in great want of snaffle and curb, was about to throw herself violently into Mr. Giuliani's existence, and to make a terrible and irreparable confusion there. She set about it in this way — as usual, doing wrong, under the conviction she was doing something vastly right.

On the same day on which she had had the foregoing conversation with Colonel and Mrs. Caledon about Mr. Giuliani, when left *tête-à-tête* after dinner with Miss Crumpton, she began thus, —

"Crummie, I have a plan in my head; now do please put away your crochet, and listen to me."

"Just wait till I am at the end of my row, my dear: if I lose my place, I shall never find it again."

After five minutes Miss Crumpton obediently laid aside her work, and settled herself as an auditor.

"First of all," said Lill, "remember you are to make no objections. I have thought over everything, and I am *quite* determined Crummie."

"Very well, my love."

"I am going to have lessons in Italian of Mr. Giuliani," said Lill, abruptly, to hide, perhaps, her expectation of opposition.

"Have you spoken on the subject to Sir Mark?"

"No, Crummie, and I am not going to speak to him;
— there — there, do not interrupt me; I have all my
plans traced out in my head. How much is there left
of the money I gave you the other day?"

"Every franc, except what I paid for our opera
tickets."

"Then every franc shall go for lessons in Italian. It
is the only way I have of making up to Mr. Giuliani for
my stupid thoughtlessness. He is a gentleman, as well
born as we are, though he is poor enough to be obliged
to teach. Mrs. Caledon says he only gets three francs
a lesson, and I made him spend the price of half-a-dozen
lessons for my amusement — I am so heedless. Crummie, instead of being in danger of starvation here, he
might be living like a nobleman in Italy, if he would renounce his political principles."

"Very sad indeed, Lill!"

"Very glorious, you mean, cousin Crumpton. Are
you not always raving and tearing your hair about the
sublimity of the French emigrants, who lived by dressing hair and salads?"

"For the love of their own legitimate king, my dear:
it was the sacrifice made in behalf of their affection for
the Bourbons, that I so admire. I hate republicans;
and, as far as I can understand, that is what these Italian
refugees are. I do know something about them, my
dear."

"No, you don't, Crummie. The Italians are not all
of them republicans; but they all want to get rid of
those horrid Austrians. Mrs. Caledon explained the
matter to me; and if the French were in England, I
suppose you would not consider it a crime if we tried to
turn them out; however, that has nothing to do with my
present plan. I have never done any good to any one
in my life, and now I am going to try to do some. I
shall have lessons from Mr. Giuliani."

The young beauty spoke authoritatively, but she
looked pleadingly at her chaperone.

"I can't think how you are to manage with Sir Mark,"
said Miss Crumpton, yielding to her imperative, loving
and lovely darling.

"But, Crummie, suppose he never knows of it till too

late. I mean to wait till he goes to England to receive his dear dividends: he will go directly after New Year's day, and then I'll begin my lessons. I dare say we shall have a fight when he comes back; but he won't be able to prevent what's done. I shall pay in advance, you know; so Mr. Giuliani will benefit, even if the lessons are stopped. There now, Crummie, you see it's all nicely arranged, so don't look dismayed. If I have never minded Sir Mark's rage when I was wrong, it's not likely I shall do so when I am sure I am right."

CHAPTER VI.

Different Impressions.

A week before Christmas the English in Paris got up a bazaar for the benefit of their poor countrymen. Lady Ponsonby, Giuliani's friend, had been persuaded to allow her name to be put down among the patronesses, of whom Mrs. Caledon was also one. Miss Tufton had consented to have a stall with Miss Crumpton for chaperone, but no earthly power could have induced Alicia, Lady Ponsonby's only daughter, to undertake any similar office.

At this bazaar took place what Valentine had so long striven to accomplish, that is, the introduction of his goddess to his mother and sister.

Lady Ponsonby was difficult of access to the rich, the fashionable, and the gay; the habits of the children of fortune jarred with hers, and having been once in her life nearly mentally suffocated by the despotism of custom, she had ever afterwards retained a nervous dread of slipping again under such a yoke. What she had hitherto heard of Sir Mark, had made her strenuously avoid complying with Valentine's wish, that she should call on Miss Tufton. But within the last week or two, both she and Alicia had become more and more curious to see Sir Mark's granddaughter.

"That is Miss Tufton, I suppose," said Lady Ponsonby to Valentine, as they were making the tour of the bazaar; "she reminds me of a rosebud sparkling with dew. I never saw anything more fresh and fair."

Lill certainly had not overheard these words of admiration, but as her eyes met those of Lady Ponsonby, she smiled. The old lady and the young one were immediately drawn towards each other; any formal introduction was scarcely needed between them. Valentine was in the seventh heaven of contentment. But the same magnet that forcibly attracts one object fails with another. Alicia examined Lill with curiosity—a curiosity that had something of disquiet in it. She received a deep and lasting impression of Lill's beauty and grace; she even exaggerated both to herself; her sensations were profounder than the occasion seemed to warrant, while Lill's observations as to *her*, were merely that she was not half so agreeable-looking as Lady Ponsonby. By some unaccountable association of ideas, as Alicia looked at Lill, these lines of Coleridge sprang out of her memory,—

> " Her lips were red, her looks were free,
> Her locks were yellow as gold,
> Her flesh made the still air cold."

And yet Lill might have been taken for the very impersonation of glee; it would have been considered an absurdity had Alicia mentioned to any one the lines the sight of the beauty had called to her recollection, and which kept up a ding-dong in her ear. "Spirit of youth and delight," Miss Tufton was deemed by every body else present, one whose mere presence would chase away any thought of the tragedies of life.

After this, visits were exchanged between the Ponsonbys and Tuftons, and a general invitation given to the latter for Lady Ponsonby's Saturday evenings.

"A poor set your new friends, Miss Tufton," said Sir Mark, after a reference to his baronetage; "that old ruin, the Priory, at Bloomfield, you recollect, in the next parish to ours, belongs to the young baronet. It's to be hoped he'll bring back some rupees with him from India. I wonder why the old lady has fixed herself in Paris? The daughter is a dumpy—dresses abominably, without any style; but she has a good line of face, and a pair of uncommon fine dark eyes of her own. Dark eyes, Miss Tufton, I must confess I prefer to blue ones. I think I shall cultivate Miss Ponsonby's acquaintance."

Whenever Sir Mark assumed the airs of a conquering hero, he invariably provoked a retort from Lill.

"I think it would answer capitally," said she, laughing,

"What do you mean by that?" asked Sir Mark, after a second of silence.

"That Miss Ponsonby is more of an age to suit you than your last flirt, Rose Caledon. I am sure your taking a fancy to some one else would be an immense relief to poor Rose, Sir Mark."

Sir Mark, who had been lolling at full length on a sofa, on hearing this, sat bolt upright.

"Pray, Miss Crumpton," he said, "why do you allow Miss Tufton to be so impertinent?"

"Lill, my dear," said the startled chaperone, "you should remember that you are talking to your grandpapa."

The baronet glared at the fault-finder's *mal à propos* invocation of his title to veneration.

"I should remember Sir Mark was my grandfather, ma'am, if he did not himself set me the example of forgetting that he is such."

"Take care what you are about, Miss Tufton; one day or another you may rue this conduct. When you come to ask me some favour, I may show you that I have a good memory."

When Sir Mark had left them alone, Miss Crumpton began to remonstrate with Lill.

"After all, my dear girl, he has brought you up, given you a fine education, and really is generous enough in important things."

"I acknowledge I am wrong to speak to him as I do; I know I ought to hold my tongue; but the temptation is too strong. You never witnessed as I did the way he treated my dear grandmamma. He almost made her an idiot, Crummie. It was his pleasure to torment her, she could not eat or drink or speak in peace; and one day I saw—yes, I saw him beat the poor feeble creature. We were out in one of the lanes near home, and she stayed behind to pick some blackberries; he came back and struck her; he thought there was no one to see him, but a young man on horseback suddenly came up, and laying his whip about Sir Mark's shoulders, shouted out, 'What are you hitting that woman for?' Oh, how glad I was! I ran up and kissed the young gentleman's hand, and told him I would love him all the days of my life, and so I do and will. Besides, I am ashamed of Sir Mark, I am; when Rose and other girls tell me how he speaks to them. The very sight of him makes me feel wicked."

Poor Miss Crumpton was not the one to guide such as Lill into the right road to influence such a man as Sir Mark. She *was all for compromising and temporising.*

"I believe I should behave better to Sir Mark," had Lill often said, "if it were not my interest to do so."

Whether in consequence of his granddaughter's

recommendation of Miss Ponsonby, or from some other caprice, Sir Mark did not accompany Miss Crumpton and Lill to Lady Ponsonby's on the following Saturday. Lill had not the most distant conception of such a person as Lady Ponsonby; had no knowledge of the reality of politeness and respect, between members of the same family, such as existed among the Ponsonby's. She had read of such people in novels, and liked to read of them, but she did not believe that such agreeable pictures could be drawn from real life. She naïvely supposed that every one was uncomfortable at home.

Lady Ponsonby at her receptions always sat in a fauteuil on that side of the fire-place which allowed her to see her guests enter. She wore a cap with a broad ribbon brought into a bow in front, masses of grey hair curled over her forehead; a frilled kerchief of some very transparent material, crossing over the chest *à la* Marie Antoinette, softened the brilliant lights of her ladyship's purple satin dress. In spite of her real simplicity of tastes and character, Lady Ponsonby liked elegance, and was elegant, but she had also the rare knack of dressing in accordance with her age—though with her delicate features and singularly fresh complexion, combined with her spirited voice, retaining many of its youthful tones, and her manner, which had all the vivacity of twenty, Lady Ponsonby rather represented age than proved its possession. Yet she remembered seeing the first Napoleon as consul: "Yes, indeed, I do," she anxiously affirmed to any one who appeared to doubt the fact, for Lady Ponsonby was proud of looking so young, as of an attestation of a well-spent life, and of an easy conscience. "The first consul was walking in the Elysée Bourbon, and I recollect being struck by his shabby coat, with ravelled cuffs: my first lesson not to value people by their fine clothes," added she.

It was apparent that the lesson had not been forgotten, for most of the coats in her *salon* were rather threadbare, and the ladies' dresses of less freshness than their owners might have desired. It was often indeed said that Lady Ponsonby most evidently sent out into the highways and byways for her guests.

When the accusation came to her ears, she had

laughed and said, "What would you have? I cannot interest myself for the fortunate, they do not require anything of me, and I forget them."

It was under the influence of such a character that Alicia had been brought up; her attachment to her mother was a passion. Alicia's affections were less diffuse than those of Lady Ponsonby; she was more exclusive in everything; less of an optimist; nevertheless Alicia had enthusiasms, though they were narrow and one-sided. Her charity and toleration shone almost entirely upon the classes beneath her. She believed sincerely in the poor being nearer to God than the rich; and held to it, that large possessions were a robbery.

CHAPTER VII.

Gioberti.

ALTOGETHER the *coup d'œil* of Lady Ponsonby's drawing-room rather startled our beauty; it was quite different from anything in the way of a party she had ever before seen ; and, to say the truth, she felt herself and her dress out of place. Miss Crumpton, humble and timid elsewhere, had here a scared curiosity, such as she might have experienced if precipitated into a menagerie. A great sound of conversation filled the *salon ;* not at all the hum of agreeable nothings, but the decided intonations of a discussion or debate of interest. Lill slipped into a seat close by Lady Ponsonby, while Miss Crumpton was accommodated with an arm-chair opposite to the lady of the house.

Mr. Giuliani was standing a little to one side of Lady Ponsonby, in conversation with, or rather listening to, a tall large-made man. Hitherto Lill had only seen the Italian with strangers ; she did not know what to make of him as he now appeared. The character of a tragedy hero in which she had clothed him, did not at all harmonize with his present cheerful, eager face, or his frank manner. She turned to observe his interlocutor, to seek in him for the cause of this change.

This extremely tall gentleman's carriage was erect and commanding ; his fair complexion, his hair of a light brown, soft and waving, parted on one side, and hanging round his neck, gave something of freshness to his appearance, like that of a boy just washed and combed ; yet the fair locks flowed round a broad, massive forehead, singularly expressive of a powerful intellect. Lill also remarked, in the close scrutiny she bestowed on him, that his hands were thrust into a pair of new white kid gloves, gaping open, instead of being neatly buttoned at the wrist, betokening haste and carelessness in the minutiæ of the toilet.

His marked accent proved him to be an Italian, but nevertheless his French phrases, delivered in a sonorous, well-cadenced voice, flowed with an abundance, a rich ness, a fertility of thought and expression, which suggested to Lill the image of a river god pouring forth his treasures from his typical cornucopia. Valentine, who had stationed himself by Lill's side, when he perceived where her attention was fixed, whispered to her that "that was the great Gioberti."

"I never heard of him before," said Lill; "why is he great?"

"Do not let my sister hear you confess your ignorance." said Valentine. "Gioberti, you know, is a Piedmontese exile, and a great philosopher. He has written immensely on no end of subjects, among others a book on the Beautiful. One need not be one of the seven sages to understand something about that," added the youth incidentally, with an expressive glance at the young lady.

Lill, who was amused at the strange company, forgot to check Valentine as she usually did when he ventured on being complimentary. "His most interesting writings, however, are about the best course to pursue in order to procure the independence of Italy."

"Ah! indeed," exclaimed Lill.

"But we must listen to Gioberti."

Lill had lost the beginning of the great Italian's speech; he was now saying: "Away with political sects and partial revolts. They retard, instead of hastening, our country's resurrection. I have shown, nay, demonstrated beyond refutation, as clearly as a mathematical proposition, that in the Italian States, the interests of princes and people are identical. Let them unite, and Italy will be at once free, strong and independent. The princes need not fear their subjects, but they must meet, satisfy, and guide the aspirations of the populations; then, governors and governed will form one living wall, impenetrable to all foreign foes, each State ranged round our crowning jewel — Rome."

Alicia, who was standing by Gioberti, turned impatiently towards Giuliani, as if anxious he should speak.

"Gioberti, you have forgotten to take into your consideration, Rome's master, the Emperor of Austria."

"No, no, caro Giulio, the star of Austria already wanes."

"And do you suppose," rejoined Giuliani, "that our relentless foe does not understand as well as you do, that the course you point out. if effected, would be her death-blow? Is it to be imagined that Austria, who has so often clutched at what she would fain tear from the Papal States, and when baulked of actual territory, has taken or made pretexts for her repeated military occupations of the Romagnas, has held the Papal See as her humble useful vassal,— is it to be imagined, I say." continued Giuliani, with increasing energy, "that the power which sees in the brutifying of her own subjects, its sole chance of safety, will not set on foot armies, diplomacy. intrigues of every description, to counteract the working of your noble pacific plan, and checkmate you at last?"

"The power of federated Italy. strong in its internal union, may defy the world," replied Gioberti, rolling over the objection. Giuliani smiled, and remained silent; he knew that the ardent philosopher was so pertinacious and vehement in his convictions, as not only to over rule, but not to hear an opposing argument.

"Now, Monsieur Gioberti," said Alicia, "tell me one thing."

The celebrated author turned upon her a kindly, courteous, and inquiring look.

"You talk of the union of princes with their subjects; do you think that Charles Albert, with his deplorable antecedents, could ever bring his mind to give freedom to his people?"

"I do hope it," replied Gioberti. "In spite of his crooked ways, and of many a dark shade on his past, there runs through his character a noble chord, which does vibrate strongly at times. Has not Goethe written, 'If you would improve men, address them rather as if already such as you wish them to become, than such as you see they actually are.' This thought dictated many passages in my works pointed at Charles Albert. The same idea it was, which induced me formerly, though with less hope of success, to make honourable mention of the Jesuits. Could we have won their assistance it would have greatly helped us."

"The Jesuits!" exclaimed Giuliani; "surely tho

thoughts of enlisting them in our cause must have occurred when you were composing your work on the supernatural."

The author smiled an abstracted smile at this sally; and then, gathering up the reins of his thoughts, set off at an easy pace along the track into which he had been just turned.

"It is a singular thing," he said, "how few of even the most intelligent men are disposed to consider one simple fact, from which, however, flow endless logical and practical deductions, and this is, that we cannot make of the world a *tabula rasa*, upon which to begin our operations. Let us first choose a righteous cause, and then hold steadfastly to it; we can only take for the combat such weapons as are within our reach; if these break in our hands, why then we must look out for others. In this lies the great art of statesmanship.

"Now the Jesuits are a powerful body, and in their day have done some good service in the world. No set of men have more extended ramifications. Their aid would have been profitable; though truly, I did not much flatter myself I should achieve this object; still, it was not a chance to throw away. But if I have given some praise to the Jesuits as they once were, I am at present busy on a work showing them as they now are. Even you, my dear Giulio, will be satisfied with my *Gesuita Moderno*."

Turning to Alicia, whose question he again took up, he added : —

"With respect to Charles Albert, I am much more sanguine. I know the man well — know him personally; and, in spite of his powers of dissimulation, in which none exceed him, and of his simulation, a still rarer talent, in which he also excels, — I repeat, that there are in his soul redeeming aspirations, and in the innermost recesses of his heart burns an undying hatred of Austria. I should not wonder any day to see him draw his sword in chivalrous devotion to Italy's cause."

CHAPTER VIII.

"The Arrow and the Song.'

LADY PONSONBY, who had been amused by the puzzled face of her young guest, now diverted Lill's attention from the political trio, by observing, —

"I am afraid this is very dull work for you, Miss Tufton "

"Harder work, Lady Ponsonby, than I generally find in society: usually it is talk, talk, talk, for talk's sake, is it not? at least to girls. I think I never before re ceived so many new ideas at one time."

"Even that is tiring," said Lady Ponsonby. "I shall stop the discussion by asking Mdlle. Arsenieff for some music. She is a fine performer, and a strangely independent girl. She had the courage to leave her family in Moscow, and to come alone to Paris, to commence the career of a concert player."

"I begin to think," said Lill, "that every one here has an interesting story attached to them."

Lady Ponsonby smiled.

"Do you imagine that to be a peculiarity attached only to some people? But my Russian's story is very simple; I will tell it to you some day."

Lill followed Lady Ponsonby across the room to where the Russian girl was seated, blue-eyed, broad-faced, and broad-shouldered, as if physically prepared to buffet through the world. She had also a gay, unceremonious manner, too much so, to be pleasant to Miss Tufton.

Mdlle Arsenieff would play very willingly: what should it be? She would ask *ce bon cher excellent Giuliani*, and away went the Russian to where the two Italians were standing.

Lill involuntarily watched Giuliani's face and manner when Mdlle Arsenieff addressed him in her free and easy style. There was not the least show of backwardness in his reply, no reserve.

"I thought he had been a man of more refinement than to be pleased, as he looks to be, with so coarse a person."

Giuliani, after handing Mdlle. Arsenieff to the piano, placed himself behind Miss Tufton's chair, saying, in a low voice:

"The performer is a pupil of Chopin's. She is an admirable pianist, though no one can ever give the same effect to Chopin's music that he does himself."

The beauty of the performance was marred, however, by the jerking of a chair, which always seemed to occur in the softest passages.

"We must bear it philosophically," said Giuliani, remarking Lill's annoyance. "The noise proceeds from Mdme. de Rochepont de Rivière's chair; and she is a lady, as her name may inform you, of the French aristocracy, connected besides, with some of the first families of England."

"She looks disagreeable enough for anything," said Lill; "I have been pitying my cousin Crumpton for having to sit near so forbidding a looking person. I cannot fancy her being one of Lady Ponsonby's friends."

"She was a playfellow of Lady Ponsonby's, and Lady Ponsonby forgives her now for being so disagreeable, because, in spite of her pretensions, Mdme. de Rochepont de Rivière is really very poor and neglected."

"I have taken a great liking to Lady Ponsonby," replied Lill. "I think I never saw before such a pleasant, pretty old lady; and when old ladies are nice, they are very delightful."

Giuliani smiled on the speaker.

"Are you a believer in mesmerism?" asked Lill, a moment after.

"In magnetic sleep? yes," he replied.

"Ah! but I mean in the tacit power one person has over another." As he did not answer immediately, she went on: "I assure you, when I am with some people, I feel nonsensical and naughty; with Lady Ponsonby, I think I might grow reasonable and tolerably good."

Giuliani still paused. He knew well enough that in the best kind of women there is much of the ingenuousness of the child. But was not Miss Tufton rather of the stuff of which women of the world are made? It was, however, difficult to be a severe judge of the pretty bright creature addressing him in so cordial a manner

Looking at her, he literally spoke his thoughts, when he said,—

"You give me the impression, notwithstanding your confession, of being a child of light."

"Now, Mr. Giuliani, I don't believe that you are sincere in saying so."

"Indeed! and why not?"

"First, because you had such an emphatic way of explaining *why* Lady Ponsonby asked madame with the double 'd,' which meant, don't imagine it's on account of her birth or her title, as would be the case with Miss Tufton; and secondly, because I read in your face when I avowed how impressible I was—that you were inclined to say, Exactly so—most women have no characters at all."

Giuliani this time laughed out, and Lill joined in merrily.

The unexplained laughter of two persons is very apt to produce a sudden, uneasy quietness in a party. This was the case just now. Every eye in the room fixed itself on Lill and Giuliani; even Lady Ponsonby, who had been talking to the Russian girl, turned round to see what had happened.

"Do you play or sing, Miss Tufton?" asked her ladyship, breaking the silence.

Lill's face put on the little air of wonderment which that of Sontag or Grisi might have worn at a similar question. How strange that she, whose song had been a matter of state, wherever she went, should have such an inquiry put to her! With a little bridling of her slender neck, she answered "yes," that she played and sang.

"Then you will be so good, perhaps, as to favour us," said Lady Ponsonby, laying her hand caressingly on Lill's shoulder.

Accustomed to singing to strangers, the young lady walked without further pressing to the piano. The very first touch of her fingers showed familiarity with the instrument. She played the symphony of a well-known Italian air, paused, and said with graceful bashfulness,

"I don't think I have courage to venture on Italian music before so many Italians. May I sing an English ballad?"

"On the contrary, pray do," said Lady Ponsonby; "it is so long since I have heard an English song—not since my dear boy, Fred, left me. Oh, what a voice his was!" sighed the mother.

"THE ARROW AND THE SONG.

"I shot an arrow into the air,
    It fell to earth, I knew not where;
    For, so swiftly it flew, the sight
    Could not follow it in its flight

"I breathed a song into the air,
    It fell to earth, I knew not where;
    For who has sight so keen and strong,
    That it can follow the flight of a song?

"Long, long afterward, in an oak
    I found the arrow, still unbroke;
    And the song, from beginning to end,
    I found again in the heart of a friend."

LONGFELLOW.

Lill had a true, beautiful voice—one of those voices which unconsciously brings tears of ecstasy to every eye, and swells the poet's heart with a sense of infinite beauty, as he traces in its modulations his own unspeakable feelings.

In this way did the tones of Lill's voice strike on Giuliani's soul, making its every chord vibrate. They bore him up to heaven, then brought him back to earth. He was under the same spell that makes the foot-sore, hungry soldier forget pain and fatigue, and welcome danger.

Lady Ponsonby, who had an organization almost as keenly alive to music as her Italian friend's, hung entranced upon Lill's every note. She gave a deep sigh when the last sound died away, and said, with glittering eyes,—

"You have touched a spring I believed had gone dry. You are a gifted creature, my dear child; excuse me, I can't resist calling you so."

"I am so glad you are pleased: pray call me anything you like, except Miss Tufton. My name is Lilian, but I am called Lill, and sometimes Espiègle."

The little triumph had been complete. Gioberti had been silent, and Mdme. de Rochepont de Rivière had kept her chair and footstool quiet.

Alicia sat down by Miss Crumpton, and spoke with admiration of Miss Tufton's voice, and her style of singing. Alicia's nature had not been stirred as had been that of her mother and Giuliani. Her ear might be duller, or there might be some counteracting charm to Lill's attraction which sealed up the doors of her soul to harmony.

Miss Crumpton thawed under Alicia's praise of Lill, and said,—

"She is so clever, does everything so well, reads constantly; indeed, it is a sad pity she has not a better companion than I am. I wonder she has patience with me."

This humility roused Alicia's generosity. She had hitherto held aloof from the elderly English woman, supposing her to be one of the proud of this earth, who take to themselves the credit of being the salt thereof. But now, penetrating at once Miss Crumpton's nature, she saw in her one born to live in another—to have no great joys or miseries of her own, but to rejoice or lament with those of the object of her worship. Prejudiced, probably, and narrow-minded, not likely to prove a wise friend, but most surely a warm and devoted adherent, whatever backwardness Alicia might feel towards Lill herself, she had none in encouraging Miss Crumpton to converse about her, and she succeeded in making the chaperone better satisfied with her hostesses and the company assembled, than she had been before.

Lill and Miss Crumpton were the first to leave. Gioberti did Lill the honour to hand her downstairs to the carriage. The young lady had no idea how proud she ought to have been at having induced the great Italian to cease his eloquence to become her cavalier.

Once the English strangers gone, there ensued a torrent of questions about them. Lill naturally was the one on whom the conversation principally ran. Even under Lady Ponsonby's roof people would pull one another to pieces, and, as the English girl was indubitably lovely, graceful, and accomplished, the only weak point, her dress, was where the assault was made.

"Ignorance of French habits," pleaded Lady Ponsonby. "In England, my dear friends, it is pretty much

the custom for young ladies to wear low dresses and
short sleeves every day at dinner. Abuse the customs
of a country if you like, but spare individuals."

"Always indulgent, dear lady!" exclaimed Mdlle.
Arsenieff, in her bold clear voice; then sinking it to a
whisper, she said to Alicia, "It appears to me that the
ice of our Hippolytus is melting under the sunny glances
of this daughter of Albion."

"You see even the philosopher *par excellence* was
charmed out of himself by her beauty and her singing,"
returned Alicia.

"Hm! hm!" thought the Russian, "we have a brave
heart of our own, but we are less indifferent than we
would appear."

How strange it is that women so often strive to wound,
in order to track out a secret of the heart, and that, too,
when it in no way concerns themselves.

CHAPTER IX.

Uncommon Domestic Scenes.

LILL, when she went home, wondered why the impression left by the evening was unsatisfactory, why she felt as though she had met with a disappointment. She needed not to have wondered long, had she chosen to take the trouble to look a little closely at the image the most prominent in her mind.

For Lill, mankind was divided into two species—sheep and goats—into the good and bad. She could suppose no faults in those she liked, no virtues in those she disliked. Hitherto she had decided at first sight into which category to place her acquaintances. The Italian master was the first person she had seen who left her undetermined where to put him. His appearance did not prejudice her in his favour, there was too great an absence of symmetry about him. Her imagination, however, had been set at work by the history given of him by Mrs. Caledon and Valentine Ponsonby. Lill could not hear of or see anything like persecution without coming forward as a zealous champion of the persecuted. Once, in London, she had run into the street before Sir Mark's house, bareheaded, to take the part of a little urchin against a big boy. Another time, in Paris, she had stopped to upbraid a carter for ill-using his horse. Feminine to cowardice by character, she was bold as Don Quixote where there was a wrong towards another to redress. It was the indelible recollection made by the ill-usage received by her timid grandmother from Sir Mark, which rendered her so rebellious to him.

Well, the first night Lill met the Italian, her vanity had been tickled by his strong, undisguised admiration, very different from the *fade*, covert gallant glances her beauty had hitherto reaped. Then her generous feelings had been called into play, and she had intended to patronize and protect this unfortunate exile.

Now this evening it seemed to her as if he were not unhappy, and not in the least in want of protection—had seemed as if he wished to give her to understand that his friends, the Ponsonbys, were her superiors, and every other person's superiors. Lill went to bed not at all certain that she should try to make Mr. Giuliani the fashion. How was she to guess that the Italian had acted on a well-digested plan?

Giuliani was not the man to be overtaken unawares by a passion. He discovered that he was on the point of falling desperately in love with Miss Tufton, against his judgment of her character. This, together with a conscientious horror of ever bringing her into contact with his poverty, weighed more with him than any idea of an impassable barrier of rank between them. He knew also that it was only by arresting his course now, he could save himself; one step forwards, and he was over the precipice. His clear-sightedness on the one side, and Lady Ponsonby's perception of the coolness of her daughter's feelings towards Lill, served to check the acquaintance from ripening into any intimacy. Nor did Sir Mark help it on, by cultivating a further knowledge of Alicia's fine dark eyes.

It may be well, in order to explain somewhat Sir Mark's strange and capricious temper, to say a word or two here of his antecedents.

The baronet had begun his career with three lives between him and the family title. He had known the hardships and insults that attend a penniless young man's *début* in the world; he had learned the bitter experiences specially proper to a poor relation, and he had sworn to himself the day he first entered a merchant's counting-house, where he had had to perform something very like a menial service, that one day he would do as much for others as had been done to him. Each tyrant hatches a large brood of his kind; and sends them forth full of spite against the world, to propagate evil from generation to generation. Sir Mark had plenty of strength of will to have been a good man, as witness the self-control which enabled him to conquer his sanguine temperament and to live for ten years the life of an anchorite, saving and starving, in order to secure the possession of that power which would supply him with the means of brow-beating as he had been browbeaten. By a succession of lamentable deaths, he suddenly found himself at the apex of his wishes—rich, titled, one of the class he had so long envied. He was already married, and to a woman many years his senior, whose attraction for him had been her few thousand pounds. She wore the title of Lady Tufton but a few months, then died, leaving Sir Mark with a son of five years old, and more obliged to her even than he had been when she accepted him, or during the many years of her complete self-abnegation.

After this, Sir Mark flourished like a green bay-tree. He was free to begin life again. Loving gold and rank as he did, it would have been consistent for him to marry now some one possessing both these attributes. But men are rarely consistent with themselves; if they were, the arts of diplomacy and of government would be simplified. On the contrary, in speculations as to the conduct of persons, one must make as many allowances for their vagaries as wise mariners do for those of the compass; so many strange, invisible influences attract men and compasses from their right point.

Sir Mark took for his second wife a young, beautiful, penniless girl, the daughter of his jeweller. He separated her entirely from her parents, and every member of her family, and treated her ill all the rest of her life. If one dared to suppose such a possibility, Sir Mark had chosen her to gratify his intense feeling for youth and beauty, and at the same time to have at hand one so unprotected, on whom he could safely carry out the savage vow made in his poverty. This was the poor lady Lill called her dear grandmamma, and who, in fact, did sink under Sir Mark's treatment into gentle imbecility. Few pitied Lady Tufton; her want of resistance against the greatest indignity disgusted, instead of exciting compassion.

Poor thing! to the clergyman of her parish and to the girl Lill she alone explained before her death, that she had thus submitted because she believed it to be her duty to do so; she had sworn obedience, and must keep her oath.

As to his son, who continued to be his only child, Sir Mark despised and disliked him for three reasons: the boy was plain, delicate, and terribly afraid of his father. Sir Mark put him into the army, and obtained a staff appointment for him in India, in order to get him out of his sight.

Captain Tufton married at Madras, and, long a hopeless sufferer from a hot climate, died before the birth of his child, recommending in a touching letter his young widow to his father's care.

Mrs. Tufton came to England, and Lill was born almost immediately after her arrival. Sir Mark was at first furious at the sex of the child, but he allowed the widowed mother to remain at Wavering, the family estate. He was never there himself but during the shooting season, and she might as well have the benefit of a house rent-free, with the attendance of the indispensable servants he was compelled to keep; besides, it looked well in the eyes of the world, her residing under his roof: but she must provide her own living; to do which he allowed her two hundred a year, exacting rigorous payment for the vegetables and fruit she had from his gardens.

In the spring of the year 1832, young Mrs. Tufton died, and Lill was left to the mercy of her grandfather.

The child became dear as the apple of her eye to Lady Tufton, and awoke by her beauty and grace some natural instincts of affection in Sir Mark. The baronet had been remarkably handsome himself when young, and had an unconquerable antipathy to those devoid of good looks. Fancying he traced a likeness in Lill to himself, he began to notice and capriciously to indulge her. Sir Mark, however, was not formed for tenderness; therefore, though he liked and admired the little girl, he could not prevent occasional outbursts of cruelty even towards her. One day that he had been more outrageous than usual in his conduct to Lady Tufton, Lill suddenly struck him with all her baby strength. Sir Mark, as a punishment, ordered her to be let down into a deep, empty water-butt; she was not to be taken out until she promised to ask his pardon. Three, four, five hours went by, and no noise or cry proceeded from the little prisoner. Lady Tufton was ill with grief and terror, and even the baronet began to wish the culprit would give him an opportunity of relenting. At last he desired one of the gardeners to take a ladder, and see what Miss

Tufton was doing. The child looked up at the man, and laughed. There was nothing left for Sir Mark to do but to pretend forgetfulness of the condition on which she was to be released. When she was lifted out of the tub, she was unable to stand, and for weeks after lay a little martyr to rheumatic fever. She would probably have died before yielding to her grandfather, whom she declared she wished to kill for his cruelty to her dear, dear grandmamma.

Under such influences did Lill's childhood pass. In her girlhood she was constantly spurred on to acquire accomplishments, while the atmosphere she breathed was thick with the smoke of the incense burned before wealth and rank.

When the second Lady Tufton died, Sir Mark confided his granddaughter to the charge of Miss Crumpton—a nominal charge, as, from the age of thirteen, the young lady had managed her chaperone. While Lill's distaste to her grandfather was strengthening every year, he in his way had been making her more and more the object of his life.

The estates went with the title; therefore Lill's fortune could only be what Sir Mark had made while in business, or what he might economize out of his present large income. He took to speculating at first, with the view of making her an heiress, but this motive had long since lapsed into a secondary one: the old habit of striving after gain awoke re-invigorated, and to make money for money's sake became once more the main occupation of his life.

CHAPTER X.

The Moth.

A FORTNIGHT after the evening Lill had spent at Lady Ponsonby's, it was Christmas, and the Boulevards of Paris, smothered by temporary booths and a mixed dense multitude, had the air of a country fair. The shop-windows, it may be remarked, were gayer than the generality of faces contemplating them—faces full of careful eagerness to discover trinkets and knick-knacks exactly to suit and do honour to a certain sum to be applied to the purchase of a number of gifts, considered *de rigueur*, whatever inconvenience they might occasion to the giver. The Christmas-box of England assumes mighty proportion when it crosses the Channel and becomes *étrennes*. Frenchmen, however, do not grumble over the change of the *petit cadeau* into a heavy tax; they turn it, as they do every other disaster, into a matter for boast or congratulation.

Amid a gay group wandering from one bewitching window to another, Giuliani saw Lill—not the first time by many since Lady Ponsonby's soirée. Whether chance or involuntary purpose led him almost daily into the Champs Elysées, he did not investigate. The pleasure of a sight of that lovely face, the realization of his most poetic fancies, was at his own cost, and therefore need not trouble him. He knew how gay a life she led; in the mornings driving or walking, in the evenings at balls, concerts, or theatres. Nevertheless the sight of her, who was in search of the most crude realities, always sent him into the land of dreams.

As he now passed her on the Boulevards, their eyes met, and Lill smiled cordially, and gave him a friendly nod of her head, not a dry salute bidding you keep your distance.

"How beautiful everything is, Mr. Giuliani!" she exclaimed.

That evening the Italian consulted Lady Ponsonby as to whether he ought or ought not to pay a visit to Miss Tufton, in obedience to the French custom, which

at Christmas exacts that ceremony from the most distant acquaintance.

"I should be sorry," he explained, "to be wanting in
any attention, and I am sure Miss Tufton would understand my doing so as a politeness; but that terrible old
gentleman is capable of taking it as an insult."

As Lady Ponsonby hesitated a moment, in regret that
the moth *would* singe its wings, Alicia said, —

"Suppose you and Valentine go together."

Giuliani has a disinclination to accept what seemed
like protection in the matter, but he curbed what he
knew to be an undue susceptibility; and it was settled
that the two gentlemen should make their call on the
following day.

When Valentine and his Italian friend entered the
Tufton's drawing-room, they found Lill surrounded by a
crowd of visitors, and Giuliani had time, before she perceived him, to admire her ease of manner, her perfect
knowledge of what to do or say on every occasion. Her
little bright-haired, compact head was held erect with a
dominant air, as if to take cognizance of all that was
going on about her. After a little, she observed Giuliani standing alone in the recess of one of the windows,
Valentine having been accosted by an acquaintance.
Lill at once made her way to him, and remained talking
to him, with a look of interest meant to influence the
other callers; just one of the occasions when Lill's vehement nature led her to over-act a part.

Among the persons present who took most notice of
her behaviour was Mr. Tufton, presumptive heir to Sir
Mark's baronetcy and estates; a very young man, but
lately arrived at his majority. There was that similarity
of feature between him and Lill which attaches itself so
mysteriously to persons of the same original stock. As
a rule it is, the same name, the same appearance.

A very general remark on Edward Tufton was, "What
a pretty girl he would have made!" He had the same
pure lily and rose complexion as Lill, the same curly,
golden hair, the same delicate nose, the same violet blue
eyes; the difference lay in the mouth and chin; in Mr. Tufton both these features were as expressive as possible
of weakness—the chin sloping sillily away into his throat.

This youth was the eldest son of a certain Rev. Edward Tufton, at whose vicarage the rejoicings had been great on the news that Captain Tufton's widow had given birth to a girl instead of the hoped-for boy. The vicar reposed in his own churchyard, and Edward was now mentioned in the last *Baronetage* as Sir Mark's probable heir. Sir Mark, out of respect to public opinion, had sent Mr. Tufton to Oxford, and gave him an allowance of three hundred a-year, hating him with all the hatred due to him for taking money out of his pocket, for not being his *bonâ fide* grandchild, and yet his successor.

Sir Mark had had an idea of marrying a third time, in the hope of having an heir of his own ; but he had grown old, suspicions, and dilatory ; besides, he was inclined to seek for a bride among young and lovely girls, and such hesitated, not so much on account of his age, as of the reports circulating as to his savage temper and miserly stinginess.

Sir Mark, at least once every year, broached the subject of his marriage, and many were the sleepless nights this probability gave Edward's sensible, far-seeing mother. It was in obedience to maternal suggestions that Mr. Tufton had come uninvited to spend the Christmas with Sir Mark in Paris. He had, besides, an admiration in the bud for Lill — strong when in her presence, weak when out of it — and a further tendency to consider her as part of his inheritance, if he should so choose it to be.

Lill and he had been playfellows, and on her side she had that sort of liking for him which early companionship gives. They knew the same people, visited at the same houses, danced together, rode together, but as for ever having had the most remote idea of marrying Sir Mark's heir presumptive, Lill would sooner have thought of a Siamese prince. For all her giddy ways, Lill had her ideal — one she was resolved on finding, or going to her grave a spinster — as wonderful and rare an ideal as ever girlish heart worshipped — a King Arthur, or possibly, as she grew older, a Sir Charles Grandison, but a Sir Charles who had never had a Clementina episode, some one, at all events, grave, stately,

courteous, as superior in talent as in character to the
rest of the world, his only little bit of weakness a passionate love for her, which she would reward by passionate worship. His word should be her law; her motto,
"God is thy law, thou mine." This was Lill's cherished
dream, as she let herself float unresistingly into the
rapids of the gay world.

As soon as the drawing-room was empty of visitors
and Lill was left with only Miss Crumpton and young
Mr. Tufton, she exclaimed, as she might have done to
a brother,—

"How I wish, Edward, you would give up using
that odious eye-glass; it makes you seem so impertinent."

Lill had been made indignant by Edward's having
fixed his glass in his eye, and stared uninterruptedly at
her and Mr. Giuliani, until the latter took his leave.

"Give it up!" retorted the young man; "why your
face where you are now standing appears merely a round
white spot to me; I can't see a feature."

"Sad exaggeration: I know you were not short-sighted
before you went to Oxford."

"Exactly; it was the effect of the midnight lamp
which injured my eyesight."

"Nonsense; it is simply an affectation, and a very
disagreeable one."

Edward was lolling on a sofa during this conversation,
and Lill walking up and down the room.

The young gentleman did not answer for a little, then
shouted out,—

"I know what has made you so cross; it was because
I looked at that Grimgriffinoff with the seedy coat you
were so taken up with. How I hate foreigners!"

"Then why do you come among them?" flashed out
Lill, with sparkling eyes; "and being an university man,
I wonder you have not learned to speak more correctly;
we ourselves are the foreigners in France."

"That's splitting straws," said Mr. Edward, pouting
his pretty lips. "I shall advise Sir Mark to take you
back to England if he doesn't want a horrid Frenchman
in the family."

Lill stopped her walk, and stood with her head turned

over her shoulder to look at the speaker; she laughingly
sang, by way of answer, —

> "There was a little man, who had a little soul,
>   And he said to his soul, let's try, try, try,
>   To make a little speech between you and I, I, I."

"By heavens! you ought to have your picture taken
just as you are!" exclaimed the young man, sitting bolt
upright. "You are a real beauty."

"Good-bye, good-bye." and, waving her hand, she
went away singing, "There was a little man, who had a
little soul," till the passages echoed again.

The words reached Mr. Tufton's ear: their meaning
did not reach his brain.

CHAPTER XI.

If you Doubt—Abstain.

"Gone! Gone!" exclaimed Lill, joyfully, as Sir Mark and Edward Tufton drove from the door on the 7th of January, *en route* for England. "Now, Crummie, let us be as happy as the day is long."

Miss Crumpton looked a little grave as she said,—

"I don't like to hear you speak in that way, Lill. Suppose anything should happen to Sir Mark, and you should never see him again, you would be vexed to think that you had been so glad to get rid of him."

"I cannot tell what I should feel in that case, dear, good cousin, but I know I *am* happy just now, and cannot get up the least little bit of sentiment on the joyful occasion; it is people's own fault when they are not loved. Now Crummie, away with melancholy; you have admonished me as it was your duty to do; and I give you absolution."

Lill went singing to a large cage, opened the door, and let her pet birds fly about the room; they perched on her shoulder, took sugar from between her lips: they chirped and sang to her, and she chirped and sang to them; then she sent them back to their gilded prison, and began to arrange the flowers just brought in, looking as loving and loveable as a girl can be imagined.

"Flowers, and birds, and music, and pleasant people to live with, and clever people to listen to, wouldn't that be a nice world?" she said, half to herself, half to Miss Crumpton. "There, now, look at that rose; I can fancy a man falling in love with such a delicate beauty of a rose, and oh! what a perfume! The perfume of a flower is like—is like—"

Miss Crumpton looked up from her work, Lill answered the mute interrogation:

"Crummie, dear, I am trying to catch hold of my thought to put it into words, and it slips away from me."

Lill was by this time seated before her writing-table, pen in hand, tickling her cheek with the feathered end.

"It is like," she continued, "the sweetness and happiness that good kind people give to one's life. Ah, dear, delicious rose! Words are too poor to say what you put into my head."

Miss Crumpton was deep in her work, and absolute quiet reigned in the room; it even rendered the birds silent.

"Cousin!" exclaimed Lill, at last, "do you recollect my saying I would have lessons from Mr. Giuliani?"

"Yes, my dear; I suppose you have thought better of it. What leisure time have you?"

"That's a secondary consideration," said Lill. "I wish you to know beforehand what I am going to do. I am now going to write to Mr. Giuliani to ask him to give me a dozen lessons—only a dozen; that will make my conscience easy about the expense I put him to. Did you hear Edward Tufton take notice of his shabby coat? It went to my heart! I believe if it had not been for that remark, I should have forgotten the lessons."

"Lill, if you would only listen to me for once—"

"No; I cannot, dear Crummie," interrupting Lill, closing her chaperone's mouth with her own rosy lips.

"It is very imprudent," persisted Miss Crumpton.

"In what way?" asked Lill, in a dry voice, and with a glance that silenced Miss Crumpton.

Lill wrote a few lines, sealed and directed the note, and rang the bell.

"Take that to the address," said she to Joseph.

"Am I to wait for an answer?"

"Ask if there be one."

The messenger brought no reply to Miss Tufton's note, for, as might have been expected, Giuliani was out. It only reached him when he returned at five o'clock. His first sensation on reading it was vexation. "It seems," thought he, "that I am fatally destined to be the teacher of those persons whose acquaintance on a footing of equality is most agreeable to me. This young lady makes no question of my acceding to her proposal, but asks me to name my own days and hours, and to send her a list of the books she must purchase, much in the incisive terms she would use to her dressmaker.

The arrogance of her nation peeps from beneath the embroidery of her polite language."

Satisfied that he had come to an impartial judgment, he even wrote a few lines, expressing his regret that he had no disengaged time, but after a quarter of an hour's fuming, he threw what he had written into the fire, as a subterfuge unworthy of him. He would consult Lady Ponsonby, and to her ladyship he went.

"What causes your hesitation, my good friend?" was Lady Ponsonby's straightforward way of entering on the subject.

"A silly one, you will say," he returned; "it mortifies me, after being on a footing of equality with this young lady, to sink down into her master at so much a lesson."

Lady Ponsonby leaned her head on her hand, and with her third finger gently stroked her nose; a sign with her of inward perplexity.

"If I have judged Miss Tufton rightly," she at last said, "your being her paid master will not alter your present position with her. Should it do so, the loss of her as an acquaintance would give you no regret."

"Then you advise me to agree?"

"There is the old rule, *Dans le doute, abstiens-toi.*"

"And a capital rule it is," observed Giuliani, musingly

"Which you do not feel much inclined to follow," said Lady Ponsonby, with a slight smile.

"Take my advice, Mr. Giuliani, though you have not done me the honor to ask for it;" said Alicia, interfering: "accept of Miss Tufton as a pupil; she will not give you much trouble, I am sure."

"She particularizes, strangely enough," replied Giuliani, drawing the note from his pocket, and giving it to Miss Ponsonby, "that she wishes for a dozen lessons."

"Some whim of her grandfather's; gossip says he is a great miser. What a pretty hand Miss Tufton writes," added Alicia, returning the note.

"And so fond of violets," said Giuliani, without thinking of what he was saying.

The next morning Miss Tufton received a most ceremoniously worded answer from Mr. Giuliani, naming the hours he had at liberty, and begging her to choose those most agreeable to her. He recommended her to procure Robello's Grammar, adding that other books could be decided on when he should have had the honor of examining what was Miss Tufton's knowledge of the Italian language.

"Well, Crummie, here's enough honor and respect crammed into half-a-dozen lines to satisfy you that Mr. Giuliani intends to preserve his distance, or rather, I believe, to make me keep mine. I begin to feel nervous, he takes the matter so in earnest."

Lill fixed on Tuesdays and Fridays for her lessons, because the hour Giuliani had free on those days was from eleven to twelve, too early for any interruption from callers, and, supposing Sir Mark to return before she had had the dozen lessons she had asked for, she was safe from his interference, as he never left his dressing-room before lunch-time.

There was a boudoir beyond the back drawing-room, which Lill had appropriated to herself as a study. There she practised and painted, and it was there that she determined to receive her new master. On the first morning he was to come, she placed pens, ink, paper, and Robello's Grammar on a table drawn towards the window, and then went in search of Miss Crumpton, begging her to instal herself by the fireside, with her crochet-work. "I feel as odd as possible," said Lill, as she heard eleven strike.

Mr. Giuliani was punctual. Lill was going towards him with the intention of shaking hands, but with a slight bow addressed to both ladies, he took a chair at the table, just as the most matter-of-fact master might have done; Lill, not a little surprised, also sat down.

"Will you be so good as to let me hear you read this paragraph?" said Giuliani, opening the grammar at page 9.

Lill began: "Qual havvi terra che il sole illumini con luce più serena, o che riscaldi con più dolce tepore!" she flushed crimson as he corrected each error of pronunciation, provoked at herself for stammering and appearing to know less of the language than she really did. He perceived her embarrassment, and his voice became gentle and encouraging.

"Had Miss Tufton ever read the *Promessi Sposi?*"

"I began it once," said Lill, "but I could not go on with it; it seemed very stupid."

Up rose Giuliani's eyebrows with unspeakable astonishment.

"Stupid!" he repeated, "do you not know what your own distinguished countryman, Rogers said of Manzoni's *chef-d'œuvre:* he declared it was worth all Walter Scott's novels put together."

Lill was not one to yield immediately, even to Mr. Rogers' authority.

"I don't like tame pastoral stories, Mr. Giuliani," she said, with a resumption of her usual vivacity, now that there was no more question of Robello's grammar.

"No more do I," he replied; "but you will find as little insipidity in the *Promessi Sposi* as in Shakspeare; the working of the passions, the tyranny of the aristocrat over the plebeian artisan, the modest but constant, deep love of Lucia, delineated and painted by a master hand, can never be tame; though I allow, you will not find in any of Manzoni's pages the pepper and spice of the French school."

"I will begin it again," said Lill; "I suppose I shall be able to find it at any of the great booksellers."

"Will you permit me to lend you my copy? it is a large one, and I always myself find a foreign language easier to understand in large than in small print."

Lill accepted the offer with gratitude.

"You will be so good as to learn by heart for next lesson, the first exercise, 'Mnémonique,' and a verb, and write out an exercise; you can take the third."

She read over with him the rules for it, and he explained patiently whatever she did not understand, and then it was twelve o'clock. Mr. Giuliani rose immediately, and with another bow was gone almost before Lill could rise from her seat.

"I never was so hot before," was her first exclamation, putting her two hands to her cheeks; and then she stood with a puzzled look contemplating the table and the books. Had she spoken out her thoughts, she would have said that she had not expected Mr. Giuliani to behave so exactly like any other master, treat her so exactly as any ordinary pupil. She had imagined a sort of desultory teaching, a little reading, and a good deal of agreeable conversation on Italian literature, of course; and now she was to learn verbs and vocabulary; and write exercises as if she were a school-girl. Then this jumping up and disappearing as the hour struck was downright preposterous.

On Friday she did not offer to shake hands when Giuliani came in. The grammar was ready open before his seat, and he began at once, "*Le Lundi j'attends le tailleur.*"

Lill repeated her vocabulary perfectly.

"*Bene*," said the master, but the exercise drew down on Lill an avalanche of explanations and references to rules. He then laid before her the first volume of the *Promessi Sposi.*

"I have here and there," said he, "translated into English to the best of my ability some of what I suspected might require a dictionary."

Lill's quick glance discovered a multitude of interlineations in the pages. She was touched by the idea that he had devoted so much time and trouble to help her, and the cloud on her face cleared away, and her voice was cheerful, when she expressed her obligation. But after she had read some twenty lines, she stopped and said,—

"Oh! Mr. Giuliani, I want you so much to explain to me something of these Italian affairs. I have been reading an account of the rejoicings at Genoa, in honour of the hundredth anniversary of the driving out of the Austrians, and also that the present assembly of all the scientific men of Italy patronized by Charles Albert, is a mere cloak to hide a political conspiracy. Why are the Italians always conspiring?"

"You ask me to tell you a long and tragical story," replied Giuliani, in a tone revealing pain.

The English girl, native of the freest country in the world, did not, perhaps could not, comprehend the bitterness to Italians of having to discuss the checks and defeats they had suffered in their pursuit of their legitimate aim of liberty. The majority judge of the attempt by the issue. But Time takes on itself to revise rash condemnations, and to prove over and over again that failures may open an eventual road to success.

"If you are really interested in the affairs of my country," went on Giuliani, " I will bring you a work or two, which will answer your question of ' Why are the Italians always conspiring ?'   At present my conscience will not allow me to take up your lesson by conversation on the subject."

Lill opened her eyes very wide on him, and said tartly,—

"I think I might be allowed to decide the right or wrong of that."

"Pardon me ! you pay me to teach you Italian, not to converse on Italian politics," returned Giuliani, quietly. "May I request you to go on reading ?"

The conversation between master and pupil was in French, of which Miss Crumpton scarcely knew a word. The chaperone heard, however, from the tone of the two voices, that something had gone wrong, and looked inquiringly towards the table.   Lill, aware of this, immediately obeyed Giuliani's invitation and continued her reading.

Though she was nettled at the rebuff she had received, Lill approved of it, and had no intention of confiding it to Miss Crumpton.   That lady was already prejudiced against Mr. Giuliani, and objected to his being where he was ; and Lill knew that Crummie's prejudices were ineffaceable, and that she had the faculty of returning to the charge, and, like her countrymen, never understanding that she was beaten.   Therefore with regard to Mr. Giuliani, Lill, unlike herself, confided no feelings or opinions to her chaperone.   It would have been difficult to say what either were, for they varied with almost every lesson.

Lill now devoted the greater part of her mornings to Italian : she could do nothing by halves.   As she read the *Promessi Sposi*, she compared what she read with her master's description of it.   "A true picture of the working of the human passions, of the tyranny of the great, and of a modest, constant love."

Hitherto she had turned over the leaves of many novels, only stopping to read, when scenes of passion occurred ; and she had preferred those tales most which presented her with pictures of life unknown to her, violent, brilliant, picturesque.

Giuliani's words, "a modest, constant love," had sounded to her like "namby-pamby propriety." How were poor peasants to find time for being in love!

The dark episode of the Signora interested her, and she told Giuliani so.

"It is said," he replied, "that the woes of the great affect us more than the sorrows of the little, and that that is the reason why the tragic poets deal almost exclusively with the misfortunes of kings and princes. The Signora is a princess, therefore you feel more for her than for the poor little country girl."

"And republicans never miss sending a shaft against rank," said Lill, smiling; "you are wrong here, it is not the nun's rank which invests her with such an interest; it is her being made such a victim—oh, the odious, refined cunning of her relations! The way even her father takes advantage of her best feelings; and, when she is driving on the Strada Marina, and, the carriages filled with gay company pass her, you remember how one of her uncles turns to her and says:—'Ah! sly one, you have thrust aside all these frivolities; you are a saint, leaving us poor creatures to stick in worldly vanities; you run away to live a holy life, and go to Paradise in a carriage.' It made me wild to read it," and Lill's eyes flashed and sparkled.

"But Lucia is also a victim," said relentless Giuliani, "and yet her anguish leaves you cold."

"Oh! cold is not the right word to use," remonstrated Lill; "I am sure if crying is to be taken as any sign of feeling, I cried enough when she is in the boat, and appears to sleep, but is weeping silently; I felt every word of the last page of that eighth chapter, as if they came from my own heart. But still I uphold that the Signora is the most interesting. She is so cruelly cut off from all hope; it is so terrifying to see her slipping from weakness into vice, and down into the lowest depths of crime, as if it were unavoidable."

"Do you imagine Lucia would have fallen as the Signora did, however tempted, or that in Lucia's situation the Signora would have walked innocently?"

"Ah! I don't know enough of human nature to decide that: perhaps," added Lill, playfully, "Lucia is too good; one is too sure she will always do right whatever happens."

"A capital reason," replied Giuliani, "which means that virtue is a bore, and that an infusion of wickedness is indispensable to give zest to a heroine."

"Do you know, Mr. Giuliani, you are very much inclined to be unjust to me; you misconstrue into I don't know what absurd theory, a remark made in jest to finish off an argument, in which I was sensible I was getting defeated."

"Forgive my rough speaking, Miss Tufton," said Giuliani, in an earnest voice. "I wished to warn one so young and gifted as you are, against acquiring the habit of finding satisfaction in pictures of what lowers human nature; try, on the contrary, to seek pleasure only in that which elevates our being."

Lill felt as impressible women do, when they receive a serious check for what they had intended as playfulness. She was half inclined to be angry, and half to cry; however she continued her reading with a fair show of composure.

CHAPTER XII.

Hard Lessons.

This conversation took place when two-thirds of Miss Tufton's dozen lessons had been received. It is time, therefore, to examine a little into the state of Mr. Giuliani's heart, after having been so long in a post of extreme danger.

We have tried to describe the sort of man he was; a man in every situation of life more likely to stiffen himself than to be pliant. One who had voluntarily renounced a high personal position because it entailed the denial of his political principles; who had failed as a writer, because denied the liberty to write according to his conscience. One who was indifferent to the glitter of riches or pleasures: who was contented with an obscure sphere, whilst waiting for a fitting occasion to devote himself to his country usefully — an occasion that he was convinced would soon occur — and in the meantime employing his circumscribed leisure for the acquisition of knowledge. This was the Giuliani Lill had met at Mrs. Caledon's. What neither kings nor governments, nor " times out of joint," nor literary time-servers, had been able to do, a slight girl had effected. She had destroyed his healthy resignation, thrown every faculty of his soul into deadly struggle, keeping his spirit floating between two opposed influences, love and reason.

Under his grave exterior, the continual warfare raging between these inimical adversaries was difficult to discern. He had been at the first a little afraid of his own lively admiration for Lill, and had narrowly watched himself; but when he found that he had no feverish impatience to see her, that even the interval of a week (when, for some reason or other, she had put off a lesson), did not seem long to him, — he breathed freely, convinced that danger did not lurk for him even in her sweet presence.

This happy conviction faded almost as rapidly as it had sprung up. Giuliani was no self-indulgent dreamer With the certitude that he loved Lill with all the concentrated energy of his nature, came also the knowledge that he had an enemy to conquer. Spare it to-day, and to-morrow it would be too late. Love held an inebriating cup to his lips, Reason snatched it away, took from it Hope, and gave it back to him, a bitter yet divine draught of struggle and suffering. His probing spirit had detected that though Lill's ingenuous trust in his judgment and unconscious adoption of his opinions, might be fostered into attachment, her heart did not spontaneously incline towards his. That versatility of her impressions, which exercised so great a fascination over him, was but a reason the more for his protecting her against himself. He was neither a blind adorer nor a blind detractor of the sex—the two camps into which the men of his time seemed divided. He knew that good, strong-hearted women, were capable of the most sublime and unselfish missions; women from out of whose infinite benevolence and gentleness, men wearied of battling with the egotism of the world, could gather hope for the future and forgetfulness of present evil. But Lill, lovely, sprightly Lill, with noble impulses, was a spoilt child of fortune; acting from sentiment, with only confused notions of justice, without any firm convictions of what was right or what wrong. Love her he did; avoid her he must. His first impulse was to leave Paris immediately, but he was not master of the situation. He had no money to live upon, except the produce of his teaching.

A moment of escape offered itself to Giuliani; the dozen lessons which Lill had asked for were at an end. He did meditate excusing himself from further attendance on her; but the weakness of human nature and the repugnance to seem to press the pecuniary part of the affair on her notice, withheld him, and the happy occasion was lost.

Lill, in the meanwhile, was greatly distressing herself as to how she was to manage to pay him. She had held the money in the hollow of her hand during the thirteenth and fourteenth lessons.

"If it were fifty or a hundred pounds," said she to herself, "it would not be so dreadful to do; but a paltry sixty francs!"

She thought of confiding the task to Miss Crumpton, but she was afraid of the way her chaperone might acquit herself of the commission. Miss Crumpton was extremely particular about having receipts for every payment she made. Lill would never recover it, should Miss Crumpton ask one from Mr. Giuliani. No: she must give the money herself, and she would spare him as much as possible by having no witnesses to the fact.

In pursuance of this determination, she said to Miss Crumpton on the ensuing lesson day, —

"I am going to pay Mr. Giuliani to-day. Give me the money, please; and, Crummie, just go out of the room at five minutes to twelve, I am sure he would rather I paid him without anybody looking on"

"Ah! just as you please, my dear; it's very lucky your lessons are over before Sir Mark's return.

"They are not over," replied Lill. "I have begun another dozen. I did not exactly mean to do so, Crummie; but somehow I had not the courage to say I did not wish for any more."

Miss Crumpton was really vexed, and moreover frightened. A thought that had more than once troubled her lately, suddenly made her use now these warning words:

"Take care what you are about, Lill!"

Lill turned at bay like a young lioness on the poor lady,

"Pray what am I to take care of, Miss Crumpton?"

"I did not mean to offend you, my dear."

"But you do offend me. What irretrievable scrape is there in having two dozen, instead of one dozen Italian lessons?"

The door bell rang, or probably Miss Crumpton would have very sufficiently succeeded in opening Lill's eyes to the feelings Giuliani entertained towards her; in short, played the part of destiny, as it was not unlikely that the knowledge that she was adored by a man for whom she felt such respect and esteem, might have so wrought on Lill, as to make her give him her maiden heart in return. However, fate willed the door-bell should ring, and prevent Miss Crumpton's answer. It was not Mr. Giuliani, as the ladies had anticipated, but a letter from England, and from Sir Mark. In spite of all her show of bravery. Lill opened it with trembl...g fingers, that betrayed an inner trepidation, her eyes glancing eagerly over Sir Mark's extremely well-written epistle.

Sir Mark, who always wrote agreeably, as if to make sure that no line of his should ever hang him, surpassed himself in his present composition. He was affectionate, and actually liberal in deeds as well as words. He began by apologizing to his granddaughter for being a remiss correspondent—wished to know if Miss Tufton were still pleased with Paris, and if she could make up her mind to remain there a little longer—till Easter perhaps? He had unexpected business which would probably detain him until then. London was empty: no gaiety—never was till after April. He enclosed a letter of credit on Hottenguer and Co. for household expenses; he believed it was ample enough to allow her also to amuse herself as much as she liked.

Lill drew a long breath, like one relieved of a load, and gave the letter of credit to Miss Crumpton, saying,—

"To be so generous and so very kind Sir Mark must be ill: however, Cousin Crumpton, set your mind at rest, the evil hour you anticipated for me is adjourned."

It was with great elation of spirits at what was unavowedly a happy reprieve, and forgetful of either warning or offence, that Lill received her Italian master. She was at a flower-stand when he came in, trying to twine some ivy branches round the bars. The face she turned towards him was as bright as ever that of Aurora appeared in dreams to poet or painter.

" Please come here and help me," she said.

He went to her side.

"No, no, not that way, Mr. Giuliani," as he attempted to weave in the branch she gave him. " You are forcing it against its will: don't you know that even creepers have a will of their own ?"

" Indeed I did not ; I am a thorough ignoramus about flowers."

" But you love them, I hope."

" I enjoy them when I see them ; but they are not a necessity of my life."

"Oh, I am sorry to hear you say that ! I am so fond of them, and they are so grateful for fondness. At home, the first thing I do in the morning is to run out and look at my flowers, and I have a positive remorse if I see one drooping; I know it is through my neglect; I water it, and presently up rises its sweet head, as if to thank me," and while Lill spoke she was busy tying up her plants, or relieving them from old blossoms or withered leaves, all of which she put quite naturally into Giuliani's hands, her own small white fingers touching his at every moment.

Miss Crumpton had been over-anxious to obey Lill's injunction, and had left the room before Giuliani's arrival.

His pupil was so confiding, so gentle, so almost affectionate in her manner towards him, that the master had a wild desire to catch her in his arms, and tell her that he worshipped her. While he remained silent from his extreme emotion, she talked on to him ; but he did not seize the sense of her words for the dull, heavy sound in his ears ; his head felt as if bursting. Could he have thought at all, he would have been afraid he was in danger of a fit.

"There, thank you," said Lill, moving away from the *jardinière.* "If you lived in the country, and had a garden of your own, you would soon adore flowers."

She was at the table busy with her desk, he standing always motionless where she had been. She came back to him.

"Mr. Giuliani," speaking now in a low voice, "you know I owe you something," and with the deepest of blushes she held out a little packet, in which were three napoleons.

He was sobered at once, and the "thank you" with which he received the money had reference rather to the service so unconsciously rendered him, of bringing him back to his senses, than to the money she gave him.

That day's trials were not at an end for him. Lill was reading Dante, and this day she had to read the end of the fifth canto—the story, in fact, of Paolo and Francesca. When she reached the line—

"*Amor, ch' a null' amato, amar perdona.*"

he started up, saying abruptly,—

"I must interrupt you; we lost some of our time to-day. I have a pressing engagement; you can read the remaining page to yourself, and prepare the sixth canto for next time."

Many years after Giuliani read in his diary at the note made of that lesson these words,—

"If I were twenty-one, instead of thirty-one, I should be a happy blockhead this day—being thirty-one instead of twenty-one, I am a blockhead without the happiness. How enchanting she was to me—familiar as with a dear brother—yet with a touch of shyness that would not have existed between brother and sister.

"What the deuce! was I ignorant when I adopted the career of a teacher—was I ignorant that I was no longer to be a man, but a species of monk or father-confessor—that I was to be dead to all the temptations of youth, beauty, and grace, to the sweetness of an angel? It went very well with me for years. I have seen rosy cheeks, sparkling eyes, pretty creatures enough to turn any masculine head, and I declare to heaven, they might have been so many dolls for aught I cared. Last year those two sisters from England, so noble, gentle, lovely, even kindly, never hurried my pulse. I had come to believe myself bomb-proof. Query.—What's to be done now?

"Answer.—Cut off your right hand, pluck out your right eye if it offend you." The next words showed by a change in the color of the ink, that they had been added at another time.

"I have never been able to absolve Othello for his theft of Desdemona. No matter that she was willing, or her father unreasonable—if indeed he were so—of which fact I know nothing. Capital Shakspeare! how he prepares that through that rent in the armour of her discretion, a doubt may be shot into Othello's mind as to his bride's truth.

"There is a spice of Othello in every man, the less or the more makes a tragedy or a comedy. Probably I have a larger dose. Miss Ponsonby compared this English Pearl to Desdemona, when noticing her neatness in all the delicate works of women. As far as I am concerned this Pearl shall receive no injury, not have a flaw in her perfection, to be discovered by a microscope She might pity me, might lend her ear to my sad story. I shall not tell it to her. A man does not cry out when he is hurt. Heroics! I declare: well, I am ready to laugh at them, and write myself down no hero—but an ass."

CHAPTER XIII.

Under Strange Circumstances.

Possibly the hiatus between these two paragraphs, marks the moment when Giuliani might have retreated, and did not. from the temptation Lill's presence was for him. The period when he invoked the sacred injunction as a guide, and did not obey its behests. The spirit of the last observation is unlike that of the first : there is in it a perceptible subtle protest against himself and a recorded promise in favor of his pupil.

One morning that Lill was on her way to call on Lady Ponsonby, she saw her ladyship and Alicia in the street. She pulled the check-string, and jumping out of the carriage. joined them, saying,—

"I was on my way to you."

"If you will wait a few minutes for me," said Lady Ponsonby, "I shall be home again. We are going to Giuliani's apartments with one or two little presents; it is his fête day, and we don't wish him to feel himself alone in a foreign land."

"Oh! let me go with you, will you?" asked Lill. "I am sorry I did not know sooner, but I can leave my pencil case with your presents. I don't think he will care for its not being new."

Lady Ponsonby had nothing to say against this arrangement. There was no impropriety in Lill's giving her master a pencil-case, nor in her gift being left with those of her ladyship. Still Lady Ponsonby would rather not have met Lill at that instant. Giuliani's porter when asked for the key of the apartment by Lady Ponsonby, who was well known to him, answered,—

"*Monsieur est chez lui, madame,*"

"Well, what will you do now?" asked Lady Ponsonby, turning to Lill.

"Let us go up by all means," replied Lill, laughing. "How surprised he will be to see me!"

Surprised was scarcely the word to describe Giuliani's sensations, when on opening his door he descried Lill's bright face peeping from behind Alicia.

"The devil plays against me," thought he.

The ladies entered the little salon, Lady Ponsonby explaining how she had met Miss Tufton, and brought her with her, carefully taking all the responsibility of the act on herself.

Lill's beautiful eyes grew actually round with astonishment, when she saw on the table the bread and the square of chocolate, which Giuliani had been in the act of eating when they went in; a clasp-knife like that used by English labourers to cut their bread and cheese, lay by the bread.

After the first shock was over, Giuliani was glad that Lill should see his poverty in all its reality; he knew that things imagined have often a charm which vanishes when witnessed. He fancied that henceforth any idea of equality between herself and him, would cease, and that thus his task of self-control would be very easy.

The contrary of this occurred. The sight touched the warmest springs of Lill's heart. A gentleman so excellent, so accomplished, living in this way, without any one to wait on him—she felt wild to say something kind, to do something to show how much she respected him; and yet oppressed by a new-born timidity, she remained for a little like one ill at ease.

Giuliani had, however, one of those sincere, immutable natures which, though not of the kind to conduce to self-advancement, always leaves a man master of himself.

He was now so perfectly unembarrassed, explaining how he came to be so late in breakfasting; so little in need of encouragement, that Lill forgot to feel awkward for him, and began flitting about the room, reading the titles of books, examining the map of Italy, the pipes ranged against the wall, and trying to get a peep down into the street.

In the meanwhile, Lady Ponsonby was busy spreading a thick cover on the table, as she said to prevent his fingers from being numbed with writing on the cold marble, while Alicia was adorning his lamp with a shade composed of the tricolour of Italy.

"*Tante e tante grazie, Madonne mie,*" said Giuliani, "if I had had a presentiment of my good fortune, I should have tried to be prepared with a sonnet." Lill was standing apart, wishing to present her pencil case but seized with a fit of shyness not to be overcome.

"I think I have something better worth your attention than these meerschaums, Miss Tufton," said Giuliani, as he drew out one of the drawers below his sofa; and taking from it a wooden box, he arranged before the young lady a collection of plaster casts of the monuments of Rome.

"My kindest of pupils, Valentine, brought me these remembrances from home."

"Are you a Roman, Mr. Giuliani?"

"An Italian born in the Romagna," was the answer.

Lill said, going to the map, "Show me where that is."

"You see, Lady Ponsonby," exclaimed Giuliani, "that in England there is about as much known of Italy as of China."

"That is not a just accusation, Mr. Giuliani," returned Lill, with spirit. "If you were to be told I came from Staffordshire, or Shropshire, would you know exactly where to put your finger on those counties in an English map?"

"But the Roman Legation is a state, not a shire, Miss Tufton; as much a state as either Scotland or Ireland. By the way," turning to Lady Ponsonby, "do you see that the Tuscans are beginning to join in the hymns of praise to the Pope, and manifesting a considerable degree of aversion to their own government."

"Everything that seemed most unlikely to come to pass appears now about to happen," said Lady Ponsonby. "Indeed, after the miracle of a Pope being chief of the party of progress I have begun to expect to live to see an Italy independent and free."

"It is difficult to expect regeneration from such a source as a Pope," replied Giuliani. "The man as a man, I believe to be honest and benevolent; I allow it, but he is the head of a body which holds to influence, riches, dignities; and to preserve these Pius IX. or any other Pope will be constrained by the princes of the Church to retain temporal power; and the Pope as temporal sovereign, must prevent the union and independence of Italy. Nevertheless I hail the daily increasing agitation, and the forthcoming disorder. Fire and sword are before us; let them come, they bring a resurrection—life not death."

Alicia, who had not been speaking, remarked that notwithstanding Giuliani's interest in the subject on which he was conversing, his eye was always seeking the pretty head bending over the casts of Roman monuments. Lill had untied her bonnet, and taken off her gloves, and altogether she looked as if she were at home; and not the least like a fine lady under strange circumstances.

The striking of the clock made Giuliani start, and reminded him that time was not his own. "I must go," he said; "Miss Tufton knows that pupils do not like to be made to wait. I see her sometimes look significantly at the clock, when I am five minutes late; and to-day I give my first lesson to a very great and very busy lady, who entreated me to be punctual, as every hour of her day was allotted to some particular pursuit."

He accompanied the ladies down stairs, handed Lady Ponsonby and Lill into the carriage,—Alicia had declined going with them,—bowed, and Lill saw him walk away by the side of Miss Ponsonby. The sight of the elegant equipage, the spirited horses, the powdered men servants, obliterated the pleasant homely picture of Lill seated in his room. "A precious fool I am," was the agreeable conclusion he came to.

The first words Lill said to Lady Ponsonby were,—

"I had not courage to give the pencil-case to Mr. Giuliani."

"Perhaps it was better not," said Lady Ponsonby; "it is always awkward for a man to receive presents from a young Lady."

"Miss Ponsonby gave him one."

"Alicia? Oh! that's a different affair. Alicia can scarcely be called a young lady; and do you not see they are on the terms of brother and sister, or rather, to give up a hackneyed and not a true comparison, like honest friends." And here the conversation dropped.

Although no list has been furnished of the gaieties which occupied Lill's evenings during the period of her Italian lessons, it must be understood that her routine of engagements was in no way interfered with by her new studies. Many were the glimpses Giuliani had of

her on her way to balls; and each time he received a
new warning of the impracticability of sympathy between
their lives. But this was not quite so impossible as he
imagined. After having danced a whole evening with
men, young, fashionable, and, for the most part, rich
and titled, Lill, on her return home, would subject them
to a criticism, which testified to her shrewdness, and
showed that these partners of a quadrille and a waltz
had no chance of interesting her heart. Hitherto Lill
had reflected little on any subject; the habit of thinking
out a thought is not a general one; and the curiously
far-seeing perspicacity which she had at moments lasted
but the length of a moment.

CHAPTER XIV.

Clouds.

THERE came an epoch in which not only Robello's grammar and Dante were discussed between master and pupil, but music, painting, poetry were talked over with spirit; when sometimes the melody of Lill's voice had rendered Mr. Giuliani deaf to the strking of the noonday hour. The progress of many things in this world is never verified until a great change has been effected. For instance, the course of a river eating away the soil, and creating picturesque windings, where formerly none existed; or the growth of a great national idea, and still more the influence of mind on mind. Many sow the seed who are not destined to reap the harvest. Thus the intercourse primarily with Mr. Giuliani, and secondarily with the Ponsonbys, was giving to Lill a wider mental view, a clearer perception of good and evil. She began to live under more delicate laws than those which had ruled her when she first came to Paris. One proof of this was, that her belief that she had a right to meet tyranny by cunning was uprooted. She would not for the world that Mr. Giuliani should know of her management with regard to her lessons. She acknowledged to herself that she needed a firm hand to guide and protect her from the sallies of her own imagination.

But the pleasant intercourse alluded to above, had come to an end. Mr. Giuliani's renewed reserve held out against the winning kindness of Lill's manner. The same incident had affected them differently; his pride had enlisted itself on the side of his judgment. He fancied that the greater gentleness he observed in his pupil, immediately after her visit to his apartments, was the effect of compassion; that the vanishing of that little asperity with which she had seasoned their arguments, denoted that she no longer spoke to him as an equal; he must show her that he would neither permit her to be his benefactress, nor to patronize him; and accordingly he stiffened himself once more into the character of a pedagogue.

Lill, distanced by this invulnerable reserve, began to care less for her lessons; she resolved to take no more after the end of the second dozen. She began even to reckon on their close, though it made her a little melancholy to think that Mr. Giuliani had lost his first goodwill towards her. After having thought over her behaviour to him, she found only one cause for self-accusation; the tacit deception practised against Sir Mark; but that was no wrong surely to Mr. Giuliani. She had, however, an intuition that Giuliani would view it as an offence.

Just as Lill was making sure that her lessons would be finished before her grandfather's arrival, she received a second letter, notifying his immediate return, and desiring Miss Tufton to provide a small but elegant and comfortable suite of rooms for a lady, a particular friend of his. The apartment was not to be in the same house they occupied, but in the vicinity. Sir Mark mentioned that Edward Tufton would accompany him to Paris.

Something in the tone of this letter startled Lill. It was less carefully worded, and she fancied she traced in it signs of disquietude, as though he were vexed or uneasy.

"I wonder who the lady can be?" crooned Miss Crumpton. "It can't be Mrs. Tufton, or he would ask her here, as Edward is coming over; nor his cousin, Mrs. Blake. She's too old to travel; besides, he hates her. Nor that pretty Miss Stavely he used to talk so much about. Dr. Stavely wouldn't let his daughter be in apartments by herself; nor—"

"Oh! Crummie," interrupted Lill, "how can you go on stringing together the most unlikely people for Sir Mark to have anything to do with! Depend upon it, it's some middle-aged widow he fancies himself in love with."

"Lill, my dear, I wish you would not talk in that flighty manner about Sir Mark."

"It does seem strange to myself that I talk so," said Lill, a little sadly. "I had almost forgotten my old ways. You see how easily I am influenced; one person makes me good and another bad."

"My dear, what can be the matter with you?" asked Miss Crumpton

"It's the horrible change I foresee in our lives. Crummie, that's worrying me. However, we can't talk about it just now. I must go and get my books ready; it is close on Mr. Giuliani's hour."

"Lill, I do beg of you to give up these Italian lessons before Sir Mark comes; do, my dear girl, they will get you and me into a scrape for no use; and Lord knows what may be the consequence. You will do me the justice, my dear, to allow that I always did object to them."

"I will bear witness to that, Crummie," said Lill."

"It's not to save myself from a little more or less rudeness from Sir Mark, I say so," replied Miss Crumpton; "it's to pacify my conscience. Now, Lill, don't fly off! listen to me. I don't approve of Mr. Giuliani, he takes too much on himself. I sit by and see more than you think for. What business has he always to be lecturing and advising you?"

"You are all wrong, Crummie," said Lill, in a sort of exhausted voice; "but it does not matter now. I intend this to be the last lesson. Are you satisfied?"

When Mr. Giuliani came in he observed at once the disturbed faces of the two ladies; but had he overheard Miss Crumpton's opinion of him he could not have devoted himself more carefully to the ostensible reason for his being in Miss Tufton's boudoir. He was patience itself with the endless mistakes Lill made; he waited quietly to discover the cause of her absence of mind, which, as the lesson proceeded, he did not doubt regarded himself.

"I have been annoyed this morning," said Lill, after a more glaring blunder than the preceding ones.

"Only an annoyance, I trust, and not any matter of importance," he replied, calmly.

She closed her eyes violently, to press back the tears of vexation that were ready to fall. Why did he speak in that unfeeling tone, when most of her discomfort was about him? When she looked at Giuliani again, he saw the repressed tears hanging like drops of dew on her long eye-lashes.

"Mr. Giuliani," she said, impetuously, "may I reckon on you as a friend?"

He looked surprised, and a shade of distrust, innate and common to all Italians, darkened his face as he answered.—

"In as far as your Italian master can presume to be your friend, Miss Tufton."

Lill more and more dissatisfied, said petulantly—

"Had Miss Ponsonby asked you the same question, that is not the answer you would have made."

"It is so different," he said, gently.

Lill sat silent, patting the book before her with her pencil-case, greatly minded to tell him frankly how she had acted with regard to her lessons; but she dreaded his keen way of going to the bottom of every subject, and feared to give him an opportunity of making her own that she had taken lessons, because she wanted to pay back the opera ticket, knowing him to be so poor.

He, on his side, studied her face, which was an honest witness to some struggle going on in her mind. Observing, however, that Miss Crumpton's attention was excited by the protracted silence, he said,—

"Forgive what may have seemed a churlish reply to a question which only does me too much honour. I am ready to serve you to the utmost of my power."

"Thank you; I asked you if I might reckon on you as a friend because I am going—" She began again. "What I wish is, that you should not quarrel with me or consider me capricious," another pause. At last she added, "I don't think I must take any more lessons."

He was really astonished, and recollecting the appearance of disturbance in the two ladies when he arrived, he felt sure that behind this sudden determination there lurked something painful or offensive to himself. Maintaining, however, a composed exterior, he drew out his memorandum-book, glanced over it, and remarked,—

"In fact, you have only two more lessons of the second dozen to receive."

"Can I have a double lesson to-day and to-morrow?" inquired Lill, with growing embarrassment.

Giuliani could not resist saying,—

"Are you going to leave Paris?" and as he spoke, his heart contracted with a spasm.

"No, not yet;" then hurriedly, as if compelled by the

interrogative, searching gaze of his eye, she stammered out, "Sir Mark is coming back directly."

Giuliani understood it all in a minute.

"And you are afraid of his finding me here?" She did not answer, "I should be sorry to be the cause of any dilemma to you; to myself, the game of *cache-cache* is peculiarly distasteful!"

He was standing up hat in hand, silent and abashed, Lill placed a tiny packet on the table, similar to the one she had given him at the end of her first dozen lessons. He opened the paper, saw within three napoleons.

"Ten lessons only, Miss Tufton," and he laid down two five franc pieces before her, blessing Providence that he happened to have them to return.

With a bow to Lill, and one to Miss Crumpton, he was gone.

"There, we have banished a real gentleman, Crummie dear!" said Lill, protecting her face from her chaperone's scrutiny by looking out of the window. "We see so many in Sir Mark's house, that we can easily spare one from the number." Suddenly raising her voice from quiet irony to passionate excitement, she went on; "Do you know, cousin Crumpton, you are my Mephistopheles. I should never have had the audacity to do what I have done to-day to shelter myself, but for you and your terrified face."

Miss Crumpton shook her head, and sat patiently enduring the storm — truth to say, so relieved by the renunciation of the Italian lessons as to be case-proof against anything, Lill might say; but Lill gathered her books together in silence, a great knot tightening her throat as she closed Dante.

"There's an end of one piece of happiness," was her inward ejaculation. Then unable any longer to bear the sight of Miss Crumpton trying to look sympathizing, and yet with her attention engrossed by her work, she retreated to her own bedroom. She stared long out of the window, wondering at those numerous strangers who pass — pass perpetually through the streets of a great town, wondering what their aim, for what their eager movements on foot, on horseback, in carriages, thinking that perhaps they were all straining after some luxury some pleasure. She felt a sort of consternation, knowing those so busied mortals to be also immortals. How strangely insignificant were those houses called mansions and hotels, merely larger nests than the birds make! How high the skies above the loftiest! how puzzling that for this crowd, and other similar crowds, running aces after such puerile prizes, a Supreme Being should nave suffered in order that they should inhabit the same Heaven as Himself.

Be grateful Lill to Ginliani. Let the tears drop swiftly from your eyes for the loss of his society: he has a right to your eternal gratitude; he has taught you to raise your eyes above the sky line that has hitherto been their boundary.

Ruth, her maid, came to inquire at what hour Miss Tufton would require the carriage.

"I shall not want it to-day," she said, without turning from the window.

No sooner was Ruth gone than she repented her decision. What was she to do with the afternoon? She was disinclined for everything that had occupied her yesterday or the day before. She went to lunch with the wish, unfelt for weeks, that some one would call.

Miss Crumpton took the opportunity of reminding her of Sir Mark's commission. No, Lill could not be worried with that to-day. The letter had only arrived in the morning, next day would be time enough; well! perhaps she might go and ask Mrs. Caledon, if she could recommend her any apartments.

Mrs. Caledon was at home, and held Miss Tufton's two hands in hers to express her joy at seeing the dear girl again; such a stranger as she had lately been! Lill could not return this warmth, and ill at ease with herself, she was ill at ease with others. She set aside Mrs. Caledon's coaxing ways, and abruptly entered on the subject that had brought her there. The good-natured woman was full of *empressement* to help in obtaining the required apartments for the "Anonyma," as she nicknamed Sir Mark's mysterious friend. She recollected having seen a delightful entresol in the Rue de la Madeleine, the very thing for a single lady. "It had *this* advantage, it had *that* convenience; and really the person who wished to let it, was so charming and delightful, quite a lady. She had a son in Algiers, and the way she spoke of her dear soldier, and the way she described her feelings, the feelings of a mother separated from her son, actually made her cry," wound up Mrs. Caledon, her eyes ready to do homage again to the interesting lodging-keeper's eloquence.

Mrs. Caledon's *couleur de rose* representations set Lill's teeth on edge, who was just now looking at everything through a very black medium: with irrepressible impatience she replied, —

"If it were paradise itself, my dear Mrs. Caledon, and the landlady an angel, it can't do; I explained to you that Sir Mark particularized that the apartment was to be near us:" she jumped up with the intention of going away.

"And you really have no idea who the lady is ?" inquired Mrs. Caledon for the third time.

"We have been puzzling over it all the morning," here put in Miss Crumpton. "Miss Tufton says it can't be Mrs. Blake nor Mrs. Tufton."

"Nor any one we ever heard of," interrupted Lill.

Mrs. Caledon now began to discern the cloud on her young visitor's brow, and being a wonderfully penetrating woman, she guessed that it was caused by the young lady's jealousy of any strange influence over Sir Mark. Her next remark showed where her ideas were; she said,—

"Sir Mark is certainly very young-looking of his age."

"Seventy next birthday," pronounced Miss Crumpton.

"Ah! then I think you may make yourself easy about the occupant of the apartment, my dear Miss Tufton. It's not likely at that age, and it's just as well—men are so very contradictory—not to seem apprehensive of anything of that sort; you understand me, dear !"

No, Lill did not understand, and did not care to understand; she thought Mrs. Caledon more incoherent and more stupid than usual.

Other visitors came in, and Mrs. Caledon went through a similar ceremony to that she had used with Miss Tufton, holding their two hands, and reproaching them with their long absence, and exclaiming at her joy in seeing them, and at their goodness in coming to see her.

In Lill's state of mind it was like a scene in a comedy, meant to caricature the empty inflation of worldly intercourse, yet she had witnessed many similar displays without any such disgust. She must play her part though, for Mrs. Caledon was relating how her dear young friend was seeking for a pleasant, small apartment, for a lady coming to Paris. But it must be in the Champs Elysées. Ah! but for that condition each of the new-comers had one to recommend.

Lill hereupon deliberately rose; Mrs. Caledon in a half pathetic voice found fault with her for being in a hurry; the last words almost doubling the length of the visit.

The instant Lill returned home, she made out a list of books, and despatched one of the footmen to Galignani's; no use to bring her the first and second volumes of anything, she must have a whole set at once. She felt as if she should read all night. The book sent to her was *Alton Locke;* it was one that six months previous she would never have read fifty pages of, as at that time, as we know already, she never read anything except what she called "interesting scenes." The page at which the book opened, at once fixed her attention. Surely these were the very same opinions she had heard at the Ponsonbys'; then there were other people, and downright English people also, who had such sentiments about the poor and the rich. Hitherto, though half inclined to believe that the Ponsonbys and her Italian master might be sometimes right, still in her heart of hearts there had lurked a suspicion that their ideas were very extravagant, and terribly republican. Lill's notions, by the by, of republicanism were drawn from descriptions she had read of scenes in the American senate-house, and from satirical works on the habits of those on the other side of the Atlantic.

In *Alton Locke* were the same prophecies of evils to come from the terrible inequalities of class and wealth, the same deprecations of the consequences, she had listened to at the Ponsonbys'. The more she read, the more the conviction grew that Giuliani and the Ponsonbys were better and wiser than those of her own society, for Lill was thoroughly patriotic, and this endorsement of their opinions by an Englishman gave a validity to the sentiments of her new acquaintances. She read on till the small hours of the night, and mixing with the interest of her book, ran an under-current of vexation, sorrow, and scorn, at the pettiness of her own conduct that morning. After her bravado, too, that she should defy Sir Mark on the subject of her Italian lessons, to have lowered her flag before a shot was fired. She really could not explain to herself her sudden fit of cowardice —it had been a panic.

Lill went to bed in a sort of despair, but the morning light inspired a more hopeful view of the case. She would go to Lady Ponsonby and tell her the exact truth from beginning to end, and beg her ladyship to ask Mr. Giuliani to forgive and make friends with her. After having on the preceding evening viewed her fault as irreparable, she now each moment believed it easy of remedy. No sooner did she begin to be reconciled with herself, than she considered that Giuliani would be reconciled to her also. What did she know yet of those stings to a man's self-respect or self-love, which are more difficult to forgive than the theft of half one's fortune?

At breakfast Lill told Miss Crumpton of her intention to call early on Lady Ponsonby: that she should go thither in a hackney coach, and be back in time to hunt for lodgings in the afternoon.

Miss Crumpton said nothing, as usual, but she ate her toast with an air of meditation which made her silence indicative of the contrary of consent. Lill unfortunately for herself, was one of those who always, even when taking her own way, desired that those about her should approve of what she did. Many rash, even bold acts was she guilty of: but she was timid at heart, and extremely alive to disapprobation. The weakest person, one for whose judgment she had no respect, and for Miss Crumpton's she certainly had none, even one against whom she rebelled as she did against Sir Mark, had nevertheless always the power to make her waver in her purposes.

" Why don't you like the Ponsonbys, Crummie?" she now asked, in consequence of the old lady's taciturn op-position.

"If I am to speak frankly, my love, because they are not like other people: really one does not know what to talk to them about. Miss Ponsonby puts on a look, if one but happens to speak of dress, as if it were an improper subject for a woman. There's always something queer about clever ladies; and when I was a girl I remember being advised to keep clear of them. In a book I was reading the other day it was remarked, that it was a positive blessing now-a-days to find a woman who could do nothing. Sir Mark for one cannot endure learned ladies; and my poor father used to say, that when a woman had so much head she had precious little heart."

The spell that had been cast by the old lady's silence, was broken by her loquacity, and Lill sent for a coach and proceeded alone to call on Lady Ponsonby. Till she heard that her ladyship was at home, she had never had any doubts as to her reception; when it flashed on her, that perhaps Mr. Giuliani had complained of her, and they would perhaps be very angry with her, she felt inclined to run away again.

"I have come to complain of your friend, Mr. Giuliani, Lady Ponsonby," said Lill, with not a bad assumption of fine lady indifference as she entered the room.

"Indeed! how can he have deserved your blame?" asked her ladyship in a soft access of reproach.

Alicia, who had but one yea and one nay, looked the serious displeasure she felt.

"Now, Lady Ponsonby, tell me," went on Lill, "has Mr. Giuliani told you of our quarrel?"

"Of no quarrel, my dear child, but of a little misunderstanding caused by a kind heart and a giddy head," returned her ladyship.

"Yes, that is it exactly," said Lill, won into candor and gentleness by the tone of Lady Ponsonby's voice. "You take all naughtiness out of me, dear Lady Ponsonby. But I meant no harm, no disrespect to Mr. Giuliani, I assure you."

"I am certain you did not: but why make any mystery of so simple an act as having a few Italian lessons?

"You don't know Sir Mark, Lady Ponsonby:" here

there was a little pause. "May I tell you quite the truth, you won't be angry, nor Miss Ponsonby neither?"

Encouraged by kindly assurances Lill said, "I wanted to help Mr. Giuliani; I have never done any good in my life, and I wished to make up to him for having forced him to buy that foolish opera ticket; and Sir Mark would have insulted him, had he met him giving me lessons, perhaps, not even let me pay him:" Lill's delicate complexion crimsoned more and more with every word she spoke. "I don't know how it is," she added, "but everything I try to do right, turns out wrong: I am so sorry."

"Poor child! I am sure you are; I will undertake to set everything right between you and Mr. Giuliani."

"You must not tell him that I took the lessons to give him, money—oh! pray don't; I would rather he thought ill of me all my life."

"You are a dear, generous-hearted creature," said Lady Ponsonby. "Trust me, my child, I will not hurt our friend's feelings; I believe he will be so comforted to have you vindicated, that he will not be at all sensitive as to your wish to assist him. Have you no idea how painful it is to suspect a friend of being unworthy of our esteem?"

"You don't think he will mind my trying to help him?"

"Not at all," interrupted Alicia. "Mr. Giuliani gave you instruction against its current price in francs. He is therefore under no obligation: you did not give him money without having more than an equivalent. His is a commerce as respectable as any in the world, though perhaps the least lucrative. And as to his feeling any inferiority, because he is a teacher—I confess *I* feel the superiority to be all on his side, inasmuch as knowledge and the experiences of a hard-spent but honorable life are superior to the white paper of a girlish mind. I don't ask you to adopt my theories, however; indeed one is always wrong to borrow other people's ideas."

"I never dreamed of Mr. Giuliani's being inferior to me, Miss Ponsonby; I know he is a gentleman born. I am very sorry for the instant's pain I gave; and I would ask his pardon, but he will not give me an opportunity."

"There is no necessity for making windmills into giants," said Lady Ponsonby; "and that is what I think we are doing now."

"Tell Mr. Giuliani, I do beg he will come and see me," was Lill Tufton's whispered request as she took leave of Lady Ponsonby.

CHAPTER XV.

Man proposes.

IN answer to Lady Ponsonby's explanation, Giuliani replied: "I see that in being so angry I have been more childish than my poor pupil. It is better to be born lucky than wise; and Miss Tufton and I have had a fortunate escape out of a false position. Be so good, my dear friend, as to make my apologies to the young lady for my rough behaviour, and assure her of my entire respect."

When he was gone Alicia observed:

"He feels it more than he would have it imagined."

"Better the acquaintance should end now than later," said her mother.

"It is not this rupture that will end it," was what Alicia thought, but did not say.

This explanation, coupled with several messages from Lill, caused the Italian a great contention of mind. His excessive annoyance at her conduct supplied a gauge by which he could measure the attraction she had for him. He was no boy, unaccustomed to reflect on his actions and to weigh their probable consequences. He turned the subject, therefore, of any further intercourse with Miss Tufton round and round, viewing it in many lights. Though a man not to abuse the opportunities afforded him as a teacher, yet once freed from the responsibility of what he considered a post of confidence, nothing but his own will need prevent him from openly wooing her, as any other man of her acquaintance might do. In seeking her love, he should break none of God's commandments; he made light of the world's law, that none but the rich should mate with the rich. Except in fortune there was no other inequality of circumstances between them. He was as well born, as well educated.

Giuliani had no want of manly self-reliance. He would have no fear to take a woman's hand in his, and bid her trust to him for everything; he was capable of gaining the daily bread of two as well of one. But not that of a woman like Sir Mark's granddaughter; the whole of the emoluments of that professorship he expected shortly to be offered to him, would not suffice to procure her the half of the daily comforts she was accustomed to, setting aside the luxuries.

There was nothing of morbid punctiliousness, nor of overstrained, sickly sensibility, when, after summing up the pleadings of his judgment against those of his heart, he decided on avoiding beautiful Miss Tufton for the future. The recollection of her sweet face, her winning voice, her pretty playful ways, went with him wherever he went. Charming, most charming as she was, dear, most dear, as she was; gentle, nay, he might without lack of reverence for her, add, encouraging as her manner to him had been, he nevertheless would renounce all effort to win her. The barrier built up by their different ways of thinking, by their different appreciation of things, by their different habits and requirements, by their mutual national prejudices, strong in both, was one that love would never overthrow. He allowed to himself that there was small hope of such discord being resolvable into harmony. He should fail to make her happy. Love combated love. The idea of her having to suffer in the future, opposed his desires in the present. If not wholly responsible for the birth of his passion, he was entirely responsible for its consequences. This was the moment to decide whether to allow of its growth, to assist, as it were, his own defeat, or to resist with the utmost vigor of his soul.

Most young women have a notion that the man who does not allow his feelings to master his judgment, who respects propriety or justice, or any social claims, including their own, must be a sorry lover. However, disciplined habits of thought, and a cultivated love of justice, are not bad foundations to build happiness on. But this is a mere story, and not a book of good advice.

CHAPTER XVI.

Woman Disposes.

Lill was not satisfied by the polite messages she received in return for the explanation Lady Ponsonby had given Mr. Giuliani. Lill liked her master; he was the first clever man with whom she had ever been on intimate terms. At eighteen a beautiful girl seldom hears much else from the men she meets than compliments, even though they may have the largest and longest of heads. Lill had never been argued with as Mr. Giuliani had argued with her. He had treated her in all their discussions as an equal. When she opposed his opinions, he supported his arguments warmly, hitting hard, as though he had been discussing a point with another man. She had been first startled, then flattered, by this treatment. The more independent he was with her, the more pleasant and gentle her manner had been to him. He had often been on the verge of losing his head in her society, but in the moment of peril, some little word spoken with the unconsciousness of habit, had reminded him his pupil was the fashionable Miss Tufton.

As he had written in his diary, had he been twenty-one instead of thirty-one, he might have been a happy blockhead. Experience of life is a great rival to love, and Giuliani, with his terribly acute sight, had seen and did see so many weaknesses clothed in the garb of amiabilities, and accepted as such, that he was grown apt to judge severely.

To all Lady Ponsonby's assurances, that Miss Tufton was sincerely distressed at his avoidance of her, he replied.—

"Mere matter of self-love; she is not accustomed to opposition from her male acquaintances, and my resistance causes her attack. Let me guide this matter to a safe haven."

But Lill was obstinate, and like a child as she was, determined to see him again, and make friends. So many were her visits to Lady Ponsonby, that at length one day she did meet the Italian. He on his side, had heard the carriage stop at the door. Philosophic Mr Giuliani recognized the peculiar sound of those wheels, the trot of that special pair of horses, and he hastily took leave of Alicia who was alone at home. He was issuing on to the landing-place just as Lill reached it. He could not close the door of the apartment in her face he must hold it open to allow her to pass.

She had run up the stairs so fast, she was so surprised, so overjoyed to see him, that she had scarcely any breath to speak with — only enough to say, with outstretched hands,—

"Oh! stay a minute, Mr. Giuliani, I want to say two words to you."

A party of young people were coming down from an upper story. Giuliani saw by Lill's eager look that she would speak then and there, let who would be present. There was nothing for it but to reply: "I am at your service, Miss Tufton," and to motion to her to enter.

Alicia, meanwhile, had come forward to receive the visitors; they were scarcely in the salon before the impetuous girl exclaimed, —

"Mr. Giuliani, pray forgive me!"

"Ah! mademoiselle, you punish me, indeed, by using such an expression;" adding, with a hearty wish to turn the matter into a jest: "The enraged master ought to ask pardon of his pupil; he is quite placable now, I assure you."

"Why does he not shake hands with his pupil?"

"You honour me," he said, slightly touching the little gloved fingers.

"Now, then," continued Lill, "you must promise to come and see me again."

Mr. Giuliani found out that it was one thing to come to a decision in his own chamber, and quite another to do so with a pair of eyes very dear to him, pleading for a favourable answer. Perplexed, he replied, —

"The hours you had are already filled up, Miss Tufton."

"I did not mean that sort of visiting," said Lill, crimsoning; "I meant you to come as — Sir Mark has not returned yet, when he arrives he will call on you."

"Thank you," said Giuliani, with an embarrassmen

that took the appearance of pride. "Thank you; but I must decline the honour of a visit from Sir Mark."

"Then you have not really forgiven me. I will tell him about the lessons, quite candidly."

This promise, made with the intention of pleasing him, for he was pretty sure it would be a real self-sacrifice to confess what she had done to Sir Mark, threw Giuliani off his guard. Did she, then, care so much for his society?

It was Giuliani's turn to change colour; his dark complexion grew darker, and a brown ring encircled his eyes. Joy rushed into his soul; softened it; laid it open to temptation; he made one more struggle.

Lill's eyes looked at him with some surprise.

"Miss Tufton," he said, "I am not ungrateful for your kindness, even though I cannot accept it. It would be a legal fiction, Sir Mark Tufton's calling on me. You know, and I know, the estimate he has of me, and of my present position. Perhaps I have a morbid susceptibility; will you be without compassion for my weakness? Come, you owe me some indulgence. I was not a severe master."

He spoke gaily, but his real dejection pierced through the thin disguise.

"But if you mean never to come and see me, then there is an end to our acquaintance," said pertinacious Lill, glancing round the room to avoid looking at him; she missed Alicia and spoke more at her ease.

"Mr. Giuliani, why do you choose to be an Italian master?"

"Necessity, not choice, makes me one."

Lill moved her shoulders with the contradicting jerk of an impatient child.

"And do you mean to continue to be one all your life? Have you, who profess to think so much of friendship, no feeling for the mortification you may give your friends and relations?"

He laughed.

"As for relations, it is droll you should invoke my forbearance towards mine; they who have never troubled their heads as to whether I starved or not; and as to friends, dear young lady, I am afraid you confuse them with the mere companions of an hour. Friendship depends on esteem and respect, and should I not inevitably lose yours and my own if I became, under the circumstances, one of Sir Mark Tufton's visitors?"

"I don't see the force of your objection; but you are determined to quarrel with me," was Lill's answer.

She was pained and mortified. To persist any longer would be demeaning herself; she turned away.

Giuliani's firmness was not proof against the idea of her leaving him in anger. An evil fate lured him to say,—

"Be sure, Miss Tufton, that if you should ever stand in need of the services of a devoted friend you will find one in me."

"Nonsense," she exclaimed, sharply; "I am not likely to fall into the water to be pulled out by you, or my horse to run away with me, just so that you should be on the road to stop it, nor to be in a house on fire, where you will come in the angelic shape of a fireman to rescue me. I don't want that sort of friendship which is to come out once in a life, like coronation trappings. I want society, and sympathy, and confidence, such as I see you give the Ponsonbys."

"I have been intimate in this house for years; and besides your orbit and mine, Miss Tufton, are cast too far apart to allow of the intercourse you describe."

"You put me out of all patience, Mr. Giuliani, with your prudent diplomatic words."

He was silent.

Here a sudden thought flashed upon Lill, and with her usual impulsiveness she added,—

"May I ask you one question?" he bowed. "Are you and Miss Ponsonby engaged to be married?"

"God bless me, no," replied Giuliani, with frank alacrity.

Alicia, in the next room, with the door open between, heard this prompt, decided answer.

"You seem to like her very much."

"Certainly; there is a great conformity of tastes and opinions between us."

"Can you not have the courage to speak out plainly for once, Mr. Giuliani?" said Lill, with growing asperity "How I do hate and despise caution!"

"Why, what in the name of heaven would you have me say?" asked he, with a half smile. "I do not know myself what my feelings might have been with regard to Miss Ponsonby had I ever allowed myself to dwell on the possibility of my having the blessing of a companion. I am too poor to marry; I would never marry a woman richer than myself; and I am too clear-sighted not to be aware that the whole of my yearly gains would not suffice to furnish the mere ornaments ladies think so necessary," and his eye glanced casually at the bracelets Lill was wearing.

Lill impetuously unclasped the two rich bracelets, and flung them into the fire, saying,—

"Ladies may wear them and not value them."

"Childish!" exclaimed Giuliani; but his face flushed, and his heart beat violently: he had a fierce struggle with himself not to fall at the feet of the passionate, generous girl, so unconscious of the interpretation that might be given to this action.

"If I am childish, you are vindictive, like all Italians; you can't forgive me for what in truth was meant kindly."

Her voice had that peculiar break in it which tells of repressed emotion; it forced itself into the very citadel of his will.

"You are mistaken in every one of your conclusions," he began, with some heat; "there is nothing but good will towards you in my heart, Miss Tufton; but no woman of sense and spirit would require a man she esteemed to put aside his own judgment, and be a puppet in her hands."

Lill's impetuosity was overmastered by Giuliani's earnestness; she shrank from him with intuitive alarm. Her softly sighed, "Oh, no!" to his question, and her alteration of colour changed his mood.

He asked himself hastily, "Was this use of feints to escape danger manly?" Passion is the greatest of all sophists, making men and women do the thing they would not, and leave undone the thing they would.

"Speak out like a man," urged Passion, on Giuliani; "it's the only way of extricating yourself honourably from your difficulty." Passion, to seduce her victim, took the form of Reason.

However others may make us suffer we ought always to remember that the fault is never confined entirely to one side; we may be sure some laxity of our own mixes in the matter. Mr. Giuliani had always respected his own strength of purpose, and struck hard on any feebleness he saw in others. He lived to be more indulgent.

He now fixed his eyes firmly on those of Lill, keeping them by the force of his will all the time he spoke riveted to his own. His voice was firm, but the lurid red of his complexion showed the storm within.

"I will be your daily, constant visitor, Miss Tufton, if you desire it, after you have listened to me for five minutes. I will not skirmish any longer with you. In plain words, Miss Tufton, I love you—you start—I have no eloquence to wrap my meaning in. What I feel, if I speak at all, I speak candidly, and without palliatives. You wonder at my audacity; but," and he went on with increasing force, "a whole, an undivided heart is a precious gift, that does not fall in a woman's way often. Riches, beauty, station may all vanish; a true heart knows no change. If you think mine worth having, take it. Have no fears for the future; I will bear you through life more tenderly and softly than you have yet any idea of; if not, bid me go."

Words read cold that spoken can cleave their way irresistible through the thickest coat of mail to the heart addressed. Lill trembled not so much at what Giuliani said, as at the travail of soul that looked out of the depths of his eyes into hers, as he laid his fate in her hands. Her whole consciousness merged into the one idea of his pain. She could not bear it, and with no other thought than of that, she remained standing by his side; remained willingly standing by his side; her colour going and coming, lovelier than he had ever seen her; his soul was entranced by her beauty. He did not know her Christian name, or it would have sprung from his lips; some inarticulate sound did come from them, more expressive than any clearly uttered syllable.

"Am I to go?" he said, after a pause that seemed interminable to both.

"I—I—don't know," she stammered. He studied her

face with all the little presence of mind left him; her eyelashes were heavy with unfallen tears. "Your peace before all other things," he said: "God bless you, Miss Tufton."

"No, don't go in that way, Mr. Giuliani. I cannot bear you should go away so."

"I have no wish to hurry you," he said coldly.

"Pray, pray, don't speak to me in that tone," said Lill. "I don't deserve it—indeed I don't."

"I take God to witness, I would not even for the possession of your hand, hurry you; but I am sure of this, if you hesitate, you should say no. Resist the pity I see your gentle heart is moved by. Pity is not akin to love—at least I refuse all love so born. Go home, Miss Tufton, and of all I have said, remember only, that you have one more firm friend in the world."

Lill was thoroughly overcome by this resignation; she did what an inexperienced, warm-hearted girl would do, when the man so speaking was one whom she held as a sort of hero. She put out her hand to him with a deep blush, and the long repressed tear-drops rolled freely over her cheeks.

Giuliani took the pledge thus proffered with a feeling more allied to pain than joy. He felt more as if he had caught or snared some lovely timid thing, than that the timid, lovely thing had come with its large loving eyes, willingly to his arms for love and safety. That moment, single in man or woman's life, when heart goes spontaneously to heart, that moment which ought to have weighed them to the earth with its freight of bliss, kept them standing hand in hand like traffickers, sealing a bargain. At last he raised her hand to his lips:—

"It is an awful responsibiliy," he said, "to take upon one-self to influence the fate of a fellow-being. God do so unto me as I am true to you. Be you so to me. If you repent of your goodness to me this day, tell me so—even at the foot of the altar;" with a sudden, unusual violence, he added,—"I am an excellent friend, but a demon of a lover."

The sound of a key turning in the lock of the outer door of the apartment, made Lill snatch her hand from Giuliani's, and seat herself on the nearest sofa. Lady

Ponsonby came in serene and smiling as usual—but stopped and asked in some surprise,—

"Where is Alicia?"

Giuliani and Lill had forgotten Miss Ponsonby; she had slipped into an adjoining room, when the tone of their conversation became one to which no third person is ever willingly a party.

Giuliani, like men in general, had a special horror of explanations, which might involve any display of emotion on his part; he had no idea that he could do anything but give a straightforward account of what had just passed, had no conception that Lady Ponsonby was acute enough to comprehend the situation without words. So with a hasty muttering of want of time, and one anxious look at Lill, in the hope of one in return, he fled.

"Well, my dear," began Lady Ponsonby to the silent young lady, the transparent evenness of whose cheeks was troubled by agitation, "Well, you have made peace with Mr. Giuliani, I see."

Without asking how Lady Ponsonby perceived this, Lill burst out crying; Lady Ponsonby sat down by her, and taking one of the little hands, began stroking it in a soothing, caressing way.

Not understanding that her new secret was no secret for her friend, Lill exclaimed,—

" I am stupidly nervous to-day, I'll go home now, and come back some other day."

She threw her arm round Lady Ponsonby's neck, kissing her with that energy which betrays an inward craving for help. Lady Ponsonby gave a caress in return, full of promise of the help demanded, and without a further question let Lill go.

As soon as the visitor was gone, Alicia came from the next room. Lady Ponsonby was about to speak, but the words died on her lips at the sight of her daughter's face, quite bloodless, with a certain stony look about her mouth. Alicia said,—

"My dear mother, you look at me as if I were a ghost."

The voice was composed, but hard, as if it came from a dry throat, or from that of a person who has been for hours silent. It cleared quickly as she went on. "I had to leave the door open between the rooms, that I might be close at hand, in case of some one coming in who might gossip about the *tête-à-tête*. I had no choice left but to overhear their conversation."

Lady Ponsonby could not give her attention to what Alicia was saying. For the first time a most painful suspicion had entered her mind. Was it possible that under that usually calm exterior lurked concentrated passion? Her suspicion became certainty, as Alicia went on with tight-drawn lips:

"He told her he loved her; it was quite natural she should do as she has done. She is a more generous-hearted girl than I fancied; he bid her beware of her pity misleading her—it has misled them both. Oh, mother! how I wish she could have really loved him, but —" here the speaker's fortitude, strong against her own sorrow, gave way when fearing sorrow for him.

Lady Ponsonby took her daughter into her arms, and Alicia lay there, as one thankful for so sure a haven; she whispered,—

"Always his friend, mother, whatever happens."

"Always, my daughter," said the mother, fervently.

How well a mother knows how best to comfort her child!

CHAPTER XVII.

Yes or No?

AND Lill, what were her feelings during her drive home? They were mute, quite mute, except insomuch as she was longing to be in her own room locked in, sure of no interruption, so that she might think,—she wanted to think, to get rid of the confusion in her mind; no possibility of thinking in such a distracting noise.

The carriage was driving along the Champs Elysées, bright with that air of universal rejoicing which a fine day in early spring is sure to impart. Leaves open and flicker like gold in the sunlight, birds twitter and bury themselves in the dust and quarrel, children laugh and shout and scamper, horses caper, shrill trumpets, tinkling bells, mingle with street cries in unmusical but cheerful chorus. The sound of "plaisirs, plaisirs, mesdames," came back in all her after days of sorrow.

Miss Crumpton's broad face within its wide aureole of lace and ribbon was looking forth as Lill alighted. It appeared to greet her at the outer door of the apartment, "I am so glad to see you, my dear; I was growing uneasy."

"Can't I be away two hours without your fretting? one would almost be glad not to be cared about," said Lill peevishly: she was thoroughly unhinged, poor thing. Miss Crumpton made no reply, and went quietly back to the salon.

Lill, sorry that she had been cross, but too cross to say so, opened her room door; Ruth was sitting there at work. "Oh! dear, it seems one can never be alone," cried Lill. "No, I don't want you to take off my cloak," continued she to her maid.

"I have put out your grey silk for dinner, Miss Tufton."

"I shan't change my dress; do go away, Ruth; I really should be glad if I might have a quarter of an hour to myself."

Ruth gathered up her work with the method and care of a well-trained lady's-maid whose business is with her mistress's wardrobe, and not with her mistress's moods. Lill was ready to take the girl by the shoulders and turn her out of the room; her slowness was exasperating.

"At last!" and the door is double-locked, the bonnet tossed off, and Lill lies back in a large chair. She has quiet enough to think in; she tries, but it is as difficult to think to any purpose now as it was in the bustle of the Champs Elysées. It was by an exertion of will, however, that one distinct impression was kept under; she dared not acknowledge it,—it would be wicked, cruel : the mischief was done, and she must abide by it. What could have made her ask that question about Miss Ponsonby? It was that which brought it all on. It must have made him think she cared for him : O heavens ! and did she not ?

Then came a crowd of images, whirling and toppling over one another; everything that had been in her world was turned topsy-turvy.

"Is it possible that it is dinner-time ?" asks Lill, as Ruth knocks at the door to tell her that dinner is on the table.

All through dinner Lill sat absorbed in the effort to think; she said, "Yes," and "no," to Miss Crumpton's observations, nevertheless, with a tolerable correctness. After dinner, with the excuse of a headache, she coiled herself on the most distant sofa from her chaperone, and once more gave herself up to the hard task of thinking. Some distracting questions presented themselves. What would Mr. Giuliani expect her to do now ? What would he do ? Tell Sir Mark ? That was one thing she might be certain of. And the consequences ? Well, she had brought them on herself, and she must take them, whatever they were. No doubt she would be called a fool,— perhaps she had been one. He was a very good man, far better than she was, — very clever and very much respected; he couldn't be mistaken, thank heavens, for aught but a gentleman. It was very odd that such a marriage should be her fate; it was about as unlikely a thing as could have been conceived. She recollected how she used to long for her lessons; she had really been unhappy when he had quarreled with her, and yet she certainly was not happy now; perhaps it was because

she was frightened at the idea of what Sir Mark might
say or do.

Lady Ponsonby would know, and Alicia, and they
would come and congratulate her; at all events, they
would approve of her. Whenever Lill thought of Mr.
Giuliani in connection with the Ponsonbys, her spirit
rose, she steadied herself by leaning on their liking and
estimation of Giuliani — she even felt elated at having
won the hero of their circle.

CHAPTER XVIII.

A True Lover.

This earth had suffered no change for Mr. Giuliani, when he went forth from Lady Ponsonby's house; the air was not full of music, nor did he perceive in it ambrosial odours, his step was not elate, nor his head erect with the triumphant air of one who has been admitted into the beloved one's heart. There was nothing about him which said to the passers-by, " Look at me; she, that lovely one, at whose feet the greatest might be proud to kneel, is my affianced bride; she has laid her small dimpled hand in my broad palm, has accepted my arm for the support of her life."

No, certainly the world had no peculiar air of gladness for Giuliani, nor he for the world. He found no difficulty in thinking with pitiless logic over what had occurred during the last hour; every gesture and word of Lill's in that portentous conversation were present to him, and perseveringly accompanied by the presentiment of a coming new misery in his life. He was pursued by that look of timid pity he had caught, as it entered her eyes, when he told her that he loved her; it was harder to bear than her letting him go without even a parting glance.

His pupils of that day thought him sterner and more difficult to please than usual. One little girl, full of tricks as a pet monkey, had the glory of making him really angry; the possibility of accomplishing which had been hitherto doubted by his classes.

As he left the school he laughed inwardly. Preposterous! the idea of his being the accepted husband of that fine lady Miss Tufton. Had he been mad or drunk, when he proposed anything so monstrously out of nature? He was ashamed of himself and ashamed for her also; could not a woman then resist a man's importunity? Was audacity the one thing needful to obtain her? Giuliani was very bitter that evening; he was mortified at having let himself be carried away by the impetuous current of his own passions; he would have been grate ful to her; would have placed her on a pedestal beyond all other human beings, had she had the courage to withstand the weakness of her own pity.

He sunk in his own estimation when he probed his heart and brought himself to confess, that it had been conquered by her beauty, that he could not see that softly rounded cheek with a colour like that of the outer petals of a rose, those liquid eyes of the dark blue of Italy's heaven, the slender, exquisitely rounded throat, the graceful little form, without his soul's firmness melting as wax in the sun. He worshipped the perfect temple without having learned what gods dwelt within. For a time he took a revengeful pleasure in bespattering himself with the mud of mean motives. But the nearer the hour to midnight the more fervently his imagination worked, nor was his will at last strong enough to thrust away Lill's image. She was so young, so inexperienced; what wonder if she should be afraid to step beyond the limits of those conventionalities she had been bred up to respect ! He had done her great injustice and consequently himself. Why had he said he was ignorant of all but her most perfect exterior? Had he not had instances of her being gentle, pitiful, teachable? He quarrelled with her pitying eyes, had wished them haughty and forbidding, had wished her to show herself unwomanly, because he had made a fool of himself. Once on this track, his fancy, leaving fears far behind, devoured space at a gallop towards hope.

After all these turns and twists of feeling and thought, wearied in mind and body, Giuliani slept more soundly than usual. A good night's rest and a bright morning are very efficient aids in helping mortals to a healthy view of their position, and to making a healthy resolution. Giuliani got up with a clear perception of what he owed Lill. Respect had always been her due from him, now he owed her the homage of a loyal lover. What though the world would stamp his offer as absurd and audacious? what though his attic was the antipodes of her lordly dwelling? she had seemed to think his love might span the gulf between them, therefore no promptings of self-love should deter him from upholding the claim she had allowed

It would be unmanly to leave her in a dilemma, or without a clear understanding of her position. In the circumstances, the best course was to write to Miss Tufton; easy to decide, difficult to execute.

He sat a long time, pen in hand, before he wrote a a syllable; then the three lines accomplished were destroyed. He took a turn up and down his little *salon*. He had a rather heroic air in his red-lined *robe de chambre*: its colour threw out, in good relief, his black hair and beard, and by its flowing outlines gave breadth to his thin figure. He takes down his pipe, not for inspiration, but for soothing—tobacco is a calmer. He lays it aside lest the odour should attach itself to his writing-paper; he is again at the table, on which is spread the thick cloth, good, kind Lady Ponsonby's present. As he leans his elbow on it, he cannot but think of that excellent friend of the cheerful aspect. His heart softens unusually towards the whole Ponsonby family. The thought intrudes unwillingly and involuntarily, that had he been about to address his letter to Alicia, he should not have felt that there was the same discrepancy of situation between her and him.

The fingers of his left hand twisting his beard, he sat on, musing on the contrariness of human beings, who will not pluck the good fruit within reach, but must climb the tree for that which, when attained, is found to be inferior in flavour.

The letter advanced not a line for this new chain of thought; nine o'clock, and he ought to be out by ten. It must be written, however, and in English, in case she might wish to consult Miss Crumpton; a smile relaxed his face at the thought of the chaperone's astonished horror, if his letter were presented to her for perusal. He could not even help himself by writing, "My dear Miss Tufton;" that was too little between them now, and he did not choose to hazard any more endearing term, until he had more solid ground for believing such would be acceptable. Again, it was difficult to press upon her anew what he had urged yesterday, that if she repented of her goodness to him, to consider herself free; such persistence might assume the semblance of backward-ness on his part. Undoubtedly an interview would have less chance of giving her this faulty impression ; but as he was not playing a double game with his conscience, he shrank from the witchery of her presence ; certain it would again mislead him, and make him utter words foreign to his intention, and that he should leave her as full of doubts and misgivings (on her account, mark) as he was now. It is not in the moments of our sharpest anguish, or most ardent desires, that we are ever most eloquent. There must be self-possession to write or speak with grace and effect ; and in this moment not an atom of Giuliani's moral or physical being but was engaged in combat with another force.

Thus it came to pass, that after plunging for the twentieth time his pen into his inkstand, he resolutely set to his difficult task. The passionate thoroughness of his love hid itself at first under a little pedantry, and never rose above the earnestness of a friend. Before eleven, the letter was in Lill's hand.

CHAPTER XIX.

All or Nothing.

ONLY yesterday! thought Lill, as she awoke next morning. An indefinite period seemed to her to separate herself of to-day from herself of the day before. Her first sensations were the continuation of the last of the evening before. She had done with her world of hitherto; that morning she entered a new one. A desire, till this moment unknown—a desire for guidance—was one of the effects of this change of atmosphere. Lill had never before experienced any doubt that she was able to pilot herself and others, through the most difficult straits; she had always carried her point with a high hand, even with Sir Mark. She would have been mightily indignant had she been told that she now had an inclination to ask aid from the persons she most despised, or that she sorrowed over the want of those family ties she had hitherto only considered in the light of tormenting limits to independence; they might be occasionally obstacles in the way of a free course; but with a growing experience, she discerned that they also might be a welcome shelter. Never till now had she discovered her real loneliness. She had talked of friends and friendships, had written long letters, and received longer ones, with the inevitable garnishings of "dearest" and "darlings," profusely strewed from beginning to end. Yet in this crisis, she had, and she well knew it, of honest and sincere souls to depend on, none but her old cousin, to whom she had the sort of affection we give a favourite spaniel, because we are flattered by his slavish fidelity.

Just at the moment Lill was feeling that she was a very friendless creature, and moreover sore to think she was so, Giuliani's letter was handed to her. The sight of his handwriting stirred her as though it had been a supernatural reproof to her thoughts. She had a friend —a very different one from poor Crummie—a friend, and not the mere shadow of one. Lill was not much versed in definitions, but she had an intuition of the reality and unchangeableness of Giuliani's sentiments. With more complaisant feelings than the writer had dared to expect, she broke the seal and read the contents.

How unlike the man and his emotions were the first lines !

"May your dreams last night have proceeded from the ivory door, and pleasant visions have soothed any unrest an importunate friend may have caused you !

"I told you yesterday in my hard pride, that I would have no love born of pity. Sweet one, to-day I will take your pity without your love ! and yet my love in the night past has grown as immeasurably as did Jonah's gourd. It burst from the silent calyx of my heart; it bloomed at once into a hundred-leaved flower. I am troubled with anxiety for you. Your eyes with their pitying look haunt me; it is not clear to me, that your heart is drawn towards mine. A great fear has come upon me: for I love you for yourself, not for my own pleasure. You are so young, so inexperienced, so friendless. To others you may be one of the fortunate ones of this world; to me you have seemed, ever since you were my pupil, as a pretty, uncared-for blossom. My soul yearned over you with a father's, a brother's tenderness. It is in one or other of these characters I now address you, pleading, not against myself, but as counsel for you, in this great crisis of your life.

"Having listened to a proposition of marriage—listened for the first time, as I gathered from the alarm in your face—it becomes the duty of the friendly counsel, who stands in lieu of parents and brethren, to make you understand what marriage means. It is not an abstruse subject requiring a long commentary; it simply means, *consent*, the entire consent of two beings to belong entirely (for better for worse) to each other. You understand this coupling together may be like that of galley-slaves the dead to the living— the executioner to the condemned; or it may be like the heavenly kingdom, where weariness and sorrow are to find their rest and consolation. So far your counsel. I now speak to you in my own name. Wifehood is synonymous with heroism; she who enters that order engages herself to help, to redress all her husband's injuries by her sweet ministrations.

"Sorrow and death have many varieties; joy and birth, none. Joy comes from within, not without. Had I all the kingdom of the world to bestow on you, I might yet not render you a happy woman, I might be the poor soul I am. and still have the power to make you, thank God! joyful for your life. Pause, then, and say to yourself, 'Would it pain me more to lose this man—never to see him more—than it would to lose my pet canary, who refuses liberty to sit and peck his sugar from my lips?' If the man be no more to you than this—a tame creature cherished because it worships you—do not let him see you to-morrow evening at Lady Ponsonby's. There is no fear for the result of the wound he may receive. A man does not die because he may wish it. 'All or nothing, is my motto.'" G. G.

The smart of the wound that her pitying eyes had inflicted was betrayed by these last lines; indeed, any one experienced in passion could have traced in this letter every fluctuation of Giuliani's feelings—tenderness, passion, effort after self-mastery, irony, doubt, and despair. Giuliani, in truth, worshiped Lill. All very well to try and persuade her and himself that there had been a gradation in his sentiments, when his soul had been taken captive at once by the charm of her person, her manners, her talents. He loved her, as many a man does a woman, because she charmed him. It was now only that he was about to have a chance of seeing into the depths of her soul, though, supposing she allowed him to love her, the chance, after all, would be very small, that he got beyond seeing himself in the blue depths of her eyes, a sight that makes a Narcissus of many a man.

Lill, startled and silent, sat looking at the outside of the letter long after she had mastered its contents; at first they weighed so heavily on her, that she turned uneasily from side to side in her chair, as one who, in composition, struggles to bring a thought clearly forth from a misty conception. But instead of clear thinking, came remembrances in a serried troop—remembrances assailing her with persuasions and warnings to take flight from Paris. In most coming difficulties, there is an instinctive foresight of them; we resist the impression which might, oftener than not, save us. Lill heard the hill streamlet that rippled so noisily athwart the west wood at Wavering, and strangely present to her were the little lights trembling now in, now out, as the breeze waved aside the leaves to let the sun peep into the shade; she seemed to smell the stringent perfume of the fir plantation, to see beyond it the expanse of cornfields, made by the wind to look like a green sea, with tender gray waves, and then the home park with its knolls and dells, roamed over by speckled cattle, those objects of alarm in a hot, breathless summer day. And suddenly there came upon her a great desire for home, the home of her childhood and girlhood; had she wings, she would fly away thither; she wanted to be among familiar faces—wanted to see the bluff farmers and their wives again, to hear the village bells, to be scolded again by old Bates the gardener. Her bosom heaved, and she sighed short quick sighs.

"My dear!" exclaimed Miss Crumpton, who, in spite of her crochet, had had her eye on the letter and on Lill.

Lill raised her head, shook aside the thick clustering hair that had hung so close to her cheek, and thrusting Giuliani's letter into her apron-pocket, said,—

"Crummie, I'll give you an empire if you'll tell me whom I have thought of, and nearly cried about."

" I was never a good guesser of riddles, my dear; but though I am rather dull at finding out enigmas, I am not as blind as a mole; I can see what is before me."

"I can't remember just now what creature it is sees behind it; but something does,—a fish or a bird. And you are neither, dear Crummie," said Lill, rising. Placing her two hands on Crummie's shoulders, and looking into her eyes, she added: " I was nearly putting my finger in my eye a little while ago, for thought of cross old Bates."

Miss Crumpton shook her head.

"True, indeed!" went on Lill; "and fancy, I am homesick, longing for Wavering Park, wearying for the sight of the ugly church, and John Larke's timber-yard, and the Pillory Pond, with the white may dipping into its brown waters. I want to hear my native tongue in all its ugliness; every 'o,' and 'i,' and 'a,' changed into something not 'o,' nor 'i,' nor 'a.'"

"To tell the truth, Lill," replied Miss Crumpton, folding away her work, as if willing to act on the thought, "if I am to say what I think, my belief is, we should be better there than here."

Lill went away to her birds, and let Dick out of his cage; who after fluttering round the room, came and perched on her hand, with tiny flights up to her lips, where he was used to find sugar.

"Ah! self-seeking Dicky," said Lill, stroking the little yellow head with one finger. "You ask sugar for your love. Now *I* love you because I love you, and would give you freedom if it were good for you; that's what people call love, is it not Crummie?"

"My dear, I can't make you out."

"But you are my chaperone, and it's your duty to make me out, and to explain to me what I don't under stand of life and society. Now, what is real love? I want to know it from sham."

Miss Crumpton shook her head.

"I can't tell you, my dear."

"When you want to find out whether the stone you have is a true or false diamond, you go to a lapidary," said Lill; "now, Crummie, girls ought to have some one who can tell them the right from the wrong love."

"Men are so deceitful when they are in love," began Miss Crumpton.

Lill stamped her foot impatiently.

"Don't go off into platitudes, cousin."

"I'll give you one good piece of advice, my dear, platitude or whatever you choose to call it," said Miss Crumpton, now on her defence. "Love flies out of the window when poverty comes in at the door. And it's best for such as you, my dear, to repent in a coach and four."

CHAPTER XX.

Femme qui Écoute.

LILL TUFTON had given ear to the words in Mr. Giuliani's letter, and she went to Lady Ponsonby's the next evening.

Giuliani was standing behind a sofa in the farthest part of the room, opposite to the door, when she entered. Their eyes met for an instant, then glanced away from each other. Lill seated herself between two ladies she did not know, all her wishes limited at that moment to a desire of keeping clear of Mr. Giuliani. No sooner had she warranted him by appearing where she did to claim her before all the world, than she wanted to avoid him. Absent he had much more power over her than present. Absent she pictured him as lonely, poor, sorrowful. Present his firm countenance, a something of authority in his look and manner, occasionally a dash of humour in what he said, made her, she could not tell why, half resentful, and inclined to be haughty to him. His voice, always peculiarly pleasant, and perhaps so because it had in it so much of his prevailing moral qualities, sincerity and decision (he never mouthed, nor gabbled, nor hesitated, nor minced his words)—even his voice, which had at first attracted her attention at Mrs. Caledon's this evening displeased her.

He ought not to be speaking so calmly and fluently, even sportively—she had not expected *that*, after such a letter. She might have stayed away, and no fear but that he had been quite as much at his ease. Had he covered his head with ashes, and his shoulders with sackcloth, been silent or spoken in a dolent voice, Lill would have found him equally in the wrong.

He had, poor fellow, one irreparable fault, really an unpardonable one for her— he had not been able to make her love him. He was, however, most excusable in not himself suspecting it, when of her own free will she had come to Lady Ponsonby's that evening. She had yielded, indeed, half to the influence he did possess over her, half to her own vivid imagination, and her present disturbance proceeded from the alternate attraction and repulsion he had for her.

She scarcely krew what she was saying when he at last crossed over to where she was; she supposed she must shake hands with him. The indifference she had heard in his voice, she certainly could not attribute to his eyes; nor did his tremulous pressure of her hand express exactly superabundance of calmness.

He sat down and talked to her with serious pleasantness and as he talked an air of repose spread itself over him. He relaxed from head to foot, like one who, having had his heart's full desire granted, is at rest in soul and body—an impression seldom given by men, who when conversing in society, have the look rather of prisoners on the watch to escape. Not a word but that the whole party might hear, and yet Lill felt that he would not have spoken so to any other than herself. Gradually the subtle influence of a strong love subjected her, and the feverish irritation of her humour was lulled. Her head no longer pendent like a drooping flower, rose on the flexible, arched throat, the lovely face turned full to him; the blue eyes thanked him for setting her at peace with herself.

Mdlle. Arsenieff and Miss Crumpton were the only two of Lady Ponsonby's guests whose curiosity was awakened by Mr. Giuliani's so completely engrossing Miss Tufton's attention.

It was one of the Italian's peculiarities, whatever he might be doing, to see all that went on round him. Alicia had often remarked, "Mr. Giuliani sees with the back of his head; I believe nothing escapes him. Without appearing to look, he knows how every woman is dressed in any room he goes into." Miss Ponsonby spoke feelingly, being conscious of her own failings in that respect—carelessness as to dress. Lill's elegant nicety was one of her special attractions for Giuliani. What he did remark this evening was, that Mdlle. Arsenieff and Miss Crumpton were watching him and Miss Tufton; Miss Crumpton in fidgety silence, and Mdlle. Arsenieff more demonstratively by hovering incessantly in their neighborhood. The Russian discovered once that they were talking of horses, and she came near enough to hear; Giuliani was saying he did not like to see a woman on horseback, the sight alarmed without pleasing him. The next topic of their *tête-à-tête* she discovered to be birds and flowers.

Nevertheless, in spite of Mdlle. Arsenieff's active surveillance, Giuliani did find a moment to say unheard to Lill, "Miss Crumpton ought to be in our confidence." These words made Lill as hot as fire for a momentary interval; she had another of those prompt, vehement inward agitations which might pass for divine inspiration. She had only courage to say to herself, "Too late." To Giuliani the deep crimson flush that covered her face and throat was a most ecstatic vision. His sharp sight was of no use to him here. "He hurries me too much," was the meaning of that blush. Women's emotions are always complex, not seldom inexplicable to themselves. He gazed with grateful confidingness at her; suspense, conjecture, doubt, had ended from the moment she had entered Lady Ponsonby's *salon*.

As Lill's blush faded, and her silence continued, Giuliani took another favourable opportunity to ask,—

"May I pay you a visit to-morrow evening? Sunday is my only free day."

"Why not call after church?" inquired Lill.

"First, because I ought to go a little way from Paris to visit the friend who is canvassing for a professorship for me, and then in the forenoon you may have visitors; and am I very exacting, in wishing to see you for a half hour alone?"

"But what will Miss Crumpton think?"

"Why should she be left to conjecture? Tell her the truth."

"That is not perhaps so easy," was the rather pettish rejoinder.

Giuliani was that evening overflowing with the milk of human kindness, happy to have to exercise patience with her.

"Suppose you allow me to tell her—it is my right now to save you any trouble."

Lill shook her head.

"No, she will bear it better from me."

That was the end of their conversation for that evening. Lady Ponsonby called away Giuliani purposely, to prevent officious remarks, and Alicia came to Lill's side. Probably Alicia had never before tried so hard to make herself agreeable to any one as she now did to Lill. As Giuliani's betrothed, Lill was to her the interesting person, which as Miss Tufton, a mere young lady of fashion, she could not be. Alicia's stern heart softened with something of maternal tenderness to the delicate nurtured girl, who had agreed to cast in her lot with that of the rugged patriot. Alicia herself, with her high ideas of Giuliani's worth, of his talents, and of the grandeur of the cause he supported, yet could not resist a little surprise that the brilliant fairy had consented to turn simple mortal for him. Alicia could not fancy Lill in the homely dress suited to the fortunes of Giuliani's wife— could not imagine her in the tiny attic *salon*. Little fanciful as she was by nature, legends of the fatal destiny of all mortals who had sylphs or demigoddesses for wives came into her head.

But Lill's sentiments for Miss Ponsonby had undergone no sympathetic change. She had discerned at the first the backwardness and the shade of mistrust scarcely recognized by Alicia's self; besides, Miss Ponsonby's and Giuliani's respect and friendship for each other, far from creating any corresponding friendliness in Lill, was likely, in her present state of fluctuation, to produce more decided hostility.

Alicia, all unused as she was to talk of theatres or other diversions, reproduced as she thought, with tolerable fluency, what she had gathered from Valentine and others; Lill listened and answered with a smile—an indefinable smile, Giuliani considered it so, for, though some way off, his eye seldom wandered from the lovely young creature. In an obligatory pause, for Alicia had come to an end of her fashionable news, Lill said,—

"Now I'll try and talk politics, or of Italy, and the patriots, and independence—try to raise my intellect to your level, in return for your kindness in coming down to mine."

Alicia was petrified.

"I do care for some other subjects than dress and

amusement," went on Lill; "I hope some day you will do me more justice."

Alicia could not, of course, guess what a relief it was to Lill to let her petulance have its way. It was the sting of an insect struggling for liberty.

On taking leave of Lady Ponsonby's, Lill found Giuliani again by her side. Valentine was there also, but he had to retreat, so pointedly did Giuliani offer his arm to the young lady. As they went down the stairs, Giuliani took her hand in his.

"I almost wish I could die to-night," he said. She turned with a gesture of surprise towards him. "It is my happiest moment," he added and raising her hand, he pressed his lips on the delicate wrist.

Her pulse was as calm as that of a sleeping child. Valentine and Miss Crumpton had both a glimpse of Giuliani's actions; Valentine believed his eyes, Miss Crumpton doubted hers.

When Valentine returned to his mother's *salon,* Mdlle. Arsenieff was saying, in her clear voice, to Alicia, with little care who overheard her.—

"Pray, is there not something between Mr. Giuliani and *la belle Anglaise?*"

Alicia answered: "I am not in their confidence."

"They two are fire and water," said Mdme. de Rochepont de Rivière, "and the something that will be between them will be thunder and lightning. However, thank goodness, they have not chosen me as confidant, so I shan't be the worse for it. Good-night."

Miss Crumpton sat silent during the drive home. What her mightiest efforts of speech would not have accomplished, her silence won. Before she went to bed Lill confessed to Miss Crumpton that she was engaged to Mr. Giuliani.

The old lady, though she had more than suspected the fact, when her dread was confirmed refused to credit her ears any more than she had done her eyes a few minutes before.

"He's a downright villain!" burst forth the alarmed chaperone; "and so I'll tell him: stealing into people's houses, and making his own of them. Oh! I always did hate foreigners."

"You are talking infinite nonsense, Crummie," Lill replied; "if you wish to call any one bad names, or to accuse any one, pray let it be me. Truth, dear old lady, helps a cause mightily. I begged Mr. Giuliani to come to this house, and he did not try to make me like him."

"I don't believe you do like him—you can't—it's against nature!" exclaimed Miss Crumpton, with a gesture of despair, which set her cap all awry.

"Don't storm about it, it won't do any good," said Lill, with a quietness unusual in her; "I don't wish to put Ruth in our confidence. There, read that, and you'll see that I have not wanted for good advice."

Lill while speaking had taken Giuliani's letter out of her desk, and given it to Miss Crumpton.

During the time Miss Crumpton was reading it, Lill sat very still, her eyes on the old lady.

"He knew the way to take to make you say 'yes,'" was the indignant spinster's commentary; "tell you not to do a thing, and you will be sure to do it."

"Thank you," said Lill.

"Didn't you always take the part of the servants when they came to you with a pitiful tale?"

"Oh, Crummie, what a confusion you make! Do listen to me patiently. Mr. Giuliani really loves me—loves me for myself. No matter what might happen to me, if I were to have the small-pox, or become a cripple, unsightly to every one else in the world, he would still cherish me as his love. It's so very rare, you know, to find that sort of attachment; I have seen enough of life to know so much. Mr. Giuliani's feeling for me is not a question of money and settlements—"

This word was a new cue, and set Miss Crumpton off.

"How are you to live? I am sure Sir Mark will turn you away without a penny; and I have so little in my power." The old woman was already drifting over to her adversary's side. "But, Lill, my dear, he loves you, and no thanks to him; but you—*do* you love him?"

Miss Crumpton's voice and look were full of the disgust that the idea of such a possibility gave her.

"I never saw any one else I ever thought of as a husband," said Lill.

"But you might, if you took time to look about you."

"Hush, Crummie, you must never say such words to me again; it would be too dishonourable. For my sake —for your poor Espiègle's sake, do try and like Mr. Giuhani. If he were English, I am sure you wouldn't be able to spy out a fault in him; and he will be as a son to you, Crummie. I shall not have to beg him to care for you. Whoever loves me, and is kind to me, he will love; that is more than you are inclined to do."

"You persuade me out of my senses, Lill, my dear; but you'll never get me to say it's anything but a most unnatural business; and then Sir Mark—"

"We have settled about him already," said Lill, with a smile, half sad, and a weary look: "he is to hurry my marriage by turning me out of doors."

CHAPTER XXI.

Passionate Heart.

One of the Caliphs of Granada, designated "The Happy," was able to reckon up, nevertheless. how many had been the happy days of his life; twenty-three was it? not more, certainly.

Giuliani was not so far behind the Moorish monarch; he marked down at this period sixteen days of happiness, beginning with his Sunday evening's visit to Miss Tufton.

Lill accepted from him a ring. allowed him to place it himself on her finger, allowed him to wonder at and go into ecstasies as to the slenderness of the finger, to study the hand and doat on its every blue vein and on the tiny dimples that marked the whereabouts of the knuckles.

The unbending of the grave man, his childlike frankness, were really touching. For a time Lill sat and watched him with the satisfaction of one who sees the admirable working of a new mechanism. This new Mr. Giuliani was of her creating. Miss Crumpton's frigidity lasted throughout tea; after that she lost her chilling power by nodding most charitably in her easy chair. Giuliani lowered his voice in reverence to so convenient a slumber. Miss Crumpton only slept on Sunday evenings when crochet and knitting were forbidden pleasures. It was then he had the opportunity of offering his ring. Lill rather liked to hear him talk fondly and foolishly. He spoke to her for the first time of his own family, told her stories of his schooldays and made her laugh, that laugh which seemed to him like silver bells; he spoke to her of his father, of his bravery, his high hopes, and their fading; and won from her something dearer than her laugh, precious tears of sympathy. At last he fell into sudden silence. Good heavens! what a rush of growing tenderness it was. that filling his heart, stopped his speech : words came dropping slowly from his lips, like drops out of an overfilled narrow-necked vase, passionate words that scorched Lill's cheeks, but froze her heart. her satisfaction was gone, but not her courage. She had made many a pious prayer that

Sunday morning in his behalf. Having promised to be his wife, she had prayed God to make her loving as well as dutiful to him; but she listened so gently, her long eyelashes bashfully sweeping her hot cheek, that he thought it better so, than if her blue eyes had darkened in answer to his.

The next morning Lill received a bouquet of exotics, left with Giuliani's card. Lill was not pleased. "I wish he would not act so openly the lover," was the thought with which she took the flowers. Growing in her heart was a seed of resentment at the equality on which he placed himself with her; she did her best to keep the feeling under, always asserting loudly that his social rights were not altered by the accident of his being an Italian master. Nevertheless ever since she had entangled herself in an engagement with him, whenever he assumed the air of a lover, she was inwardly revolted, as if he were taking an undue liberty with her.

Unluckily for all parties Giuliani maintained towards Lady Ponsonby and Alicia an unexpected reserve; the more unexpected as he must have known that Alicia had been almost a witness of his declaration of Lill.

Perhaps Giuliani felt his position to be one of those which a sincere friend would be bound to handle boldly, and he might have a latent dread that his happiness was built on sand, not rock, and would fall with a great fall at the first shock. The strongest of us are but cowardly compromisers when passion has the upper hand.

Had there been anything to do, any overt struggle to make, Lill would have shown both strength and constancy. But she was not proof against mere endurance. She could not rise superior even to Miss Crumpton's repugnance to the Italian; she was for ever trying to get the old lady to confess herself wrong, it was like hitting a down cushion, which yields to the blow, and straightway recovers its form; Miss Crumpton's *non possumus* was taking effect on Lill. Giuliani was soon made to feel the consequences of this enemy at court.

The first cloud that darkened the heaven of his love was the evident fear with which Lill looked forward to Sir Mark's arrival. Do what he would to be indulgent on this score, to see in it nothing but girlish timidity,

his self-love, rendered extremely ticklish by his circum
stances, was wounded. He had expected something
very different, recollecting as he did very distinctly
Lill's defiance of her grandfather in the beginning of
their acquaintance. The first expressions of alarm he
had met with soothing encouragement, with those
assurances which when a woman loves a man, make her
feel ready to dare the whole world for him. But at last
Lill's terrors lest Sir Mark should arrive and find him
there, more openly expressed at each succeeding visit,
provoked from him the utterance of some of the displeasure that had accumulated in his mind.

"This alarm is overmuch," he said. "There is something grating to my feelings in it. It is painful when
duties clash, and you have a duty to perform to Sir
Mark as well as to me; but I supposed you had already
considered where the one ended, and the other began;
above all, let there be no concealments."

"You don't know Sir Mark's violence," said Lill, pale
with a quiver on her lips. Giuliani's new tone was in-
expressibly painful; it revealed something like contempt,
she thought. A tear in those beloved eyes, brought
thither by his severity, filled him with remorse.

"I am wrong," he said; "forgive me; you shall
choose your own time and opportunity for speaking to
Sir Mark. I will leave you now, and not return again
until you recall me."

"I don't wish that," said Lill; "all I wish is, that if
Sir Mark should arrive and find you here, that you
would not explain anything to him."

Giuliani hesitated, and his brow lowered.

"I do think," said Lill, "you might be a little more
indulgent to me. I can't help dreading the first outbreak of Sir Mark's rage; I must bear that; you promised you would never willingly make me shed a tear. I
thought when a man really loved a woman, he was not
ready to suspect her of faults."

"You thought," returned Giuliani, "that love was
necessarily blind. A great fallacy: any one who avers
that any human being is faultless, uses flattery to gain
some selfish end. Is that love not greatest which loves
in spite of blemishes?"

Lill shook her head.

"I begin to believe you don't know what love is."

Giuliani here turned frightfully pale : the effect of her words was so beyond her intention, that Lill was like one thunderstruck.

"Child, child !" he ejaculated, "you cannot then understand me :" he went towards the door.

"No ; you must not go away angry with me."

"But I am not angry."

"Yes, you are ; come, forgive me for whatever crime I may have committed," said Lill, playfully, yet but half pleased. "You won't ? well, then, I won't have your ring." He turned from her. "Take it or I'll crush it under my heel," she threw the ring on the floor.

"Even as you please," he replied, without stooping to lift up the ring. They stood eyeing one another like two combatants about to test each other's strength.

It was Lill who picked up the ring.

"Put it on my finger," she said, imperiously.

"Not so," he answered; "you must resume it of your own will and deed."

She continued to hold the small circlet on the tip of her finger. What a strange battle was fighting in her heart ; not one between love and pride, nor between pride and pity. She valued him for his very resistance, and she could not resign her power over him.

She held up her finger and the ring slipped back to its place. She held out her hand to Giuliani, he took it, kissed it fervently, saying,—

"Lill ! have you then had no idea that I give up something for you ?" she opened her eyes very wide. "If I have never before told you," he went on, "it was because I feared to appear a boaster. I must tell you now that you may understand how much you are to me. My pride I have laid, not only beneath your feet, but I lower it in the dust before your grandfather, and submit to the contempt of the rich for the poor. My independence, for I stoop to seek a place under a government not my own, the same which has played false with my country. For you, I renounce my obscurity, and lay myself open to all the rancour and calumny, which, like sleuth hounds, pursue the Italian, who, having been once marked as a republican, accepts anything from the ministers of a monarch. A man makes no little sacrifice, my beloved one. when he gives the slightest hold for the accusation of deserting his principles."

Lill stood by his side silent and subdued, her own sensations and conduct at that moment seemed to her so mean and trifling.

The tone of Giuliani's feeling was too high strung to be brought down easily to the diapason usual to a drawing-room. This conversation had taken place in the little room where he used to give Lill her lessons, and where indeed Lill generally received his present visits. When Miss Crampton, from the door of the adjoining room, called them into tea, he bade Lill goodbye; he stood with her hand still in his, surveying every object in the well-known room. Birds, books, flowers, Lill's work-basket, all the hundred trifles that remain in the memory, as making up the individuality of a friend. At last his look returned to Lill, there it lingered, noting hair. eyes, lovely hues, and the slight bending figure.

" My beautiful one !"

" Don't go." whispered Lill.

" I must be alone, God be with you :" he left her. Lill stopped a moment, then ran after him.

" Come back," she cried, but he was out of hearing.

The next morning, before Lill had left her room, a small packet was brought to her, instead of the usual bouquet from Giuliani. Several scraps of written paper, evidently just cut out of a note book, were inside an inner envelope, on which was written in Italian, " I send you some of my diary : judge for yourself of what I have felt for you and for how long. My heart reproves me for enjoying your dear society, at a cost to you of anxiety. Till you bid me, I shall not come to see you ; Sir Mark must soon be here; and then —" Lill took up the bits of paper one after the other. Some were of two or three lines, some of half a page. He wrote of her under the name of Perla. Ah ! he had longed to kiss the ground on which she trod : all the time he had played the austere master, repressing her friendliness, she had been dearer to him than his eyes ; her image had filled his soul ; and yet he had struggled, and but for ac accident she would have known nothing of the matter. He had even doated on her petulance : it was, indeed, not commonplace prose, it was more like a beautiful hymn, thought Lill, with exultation ; the passionate words went to her head, there was a beating in her ears. " I suppose I do love him," she said ; " I must, he loves me so much," and she put the envelope containing the scraps into her desk.

After breakfast, Lill, still under the influence of the spell, wrote him a few frank, affectionate lines, in perfect good faith at the moment, begged him to forgive her cowardice ; it was not alone for herself she trembled ; he was to trust to her to make his banishment as short as she safely could ; she took out of his last nosegay a sprig of " Forget-me-not," and enclosed it ; the signa-ture spoke volumes to Giuliani — Lill signed " Perla." It was almost as if she had assumed his own name.

CHAPTER XXII.

Grandmamma.

SIR MARK had arrived. He had seen his friend Mrs Townsend installed in the apartments secured for her by Lill, and expressed himself satisfied with the choice

This approbation sounded strange enough to Lill accustomed in former days to accept Sir Mark's silence as the surest proof of his satisfaction, and she looked at him to see if he meant what he said; then she observed he had a sort of paleness as if ashes had been rubbed over his usually florid complexion.

"Have you had the gout, Sir Mark?" she asked.

"Gout! what makes you say that? It's not the gout; you and Miss Crumpton were always dinning the word gout into my ears, until you made me believe I had it. I have had Dr. Whyteson's opinion; it is neuralgia; you women are always so knowing with your gout and rheumatism."

"The name is not of much consequence," Lill began.

"That's all you know about it," interrupted Sir Mark. "Call things by their right names; gout is gout, and neuralgia is neuralgia, and not gout."

"Very well; have you had neuralgia?" asked Lill.

"I have not had anything, Miss Tufton; my health has been excellent, is excellent, and will be excellent, if you do not worry me."

Lill here walked towards the door, with the intention of leaving the cross old man to himself.

"Where are you going now?" he said, pettishly.

"To my own room."

"Wait a minute; I have something to say to you."

Lill reseated herself, with a treacherous change of colour; her conscience made her a coward. In the moment that elapsed before Sir Mark spoke again, the wildest, most extravagant conjectures whirled through her brain; no doubt Sir Mark had heard in some way or other of her Italian lessons; he suspected her, and was about to attack her on the subject of Giuliani; she turned hot and cold, then braced herself up to meet the attack

"You must call on Mrs. Townsend this afternoon," said the baronet. "I told her you would be with her about six o'clock; she said she wouldn't be ready to receive you before. Take the carriage, and see if she wants to drive out."

All Lill's muscles relaxed; she burst into a hysterical fit of laughter.

"What are you laughing at?" asked her grandfather. Miss Crumpton also looked inquiringly at her.

"Nothing; only that in general owls, and not fine ladies, begin to fly about at twilight."

Sir Mark's eyes darted fire at the speaker.

"Just pay attention to what I say to you, Miss Tufton. You had better not show any of your impertinence to Mrs. Townsend, or by G— you'll live to repent it."

"In what way?" she said, with a peculiar intonation Sir Mark could not understand; it sounded most like a mere interrogation from curiosity.

"I'll turn you out of the house."

"I don't know that that would be the worst thing that could happen to me."

"By G— you women are enough to drive a man mad!" exclaimed Sir Mark, and flung out of the salon.

Lill turned to Miss Crumpton, the silent spectator for years of the turbulence of the house of Tufton, not only silent, but looking on with a face as round and placid as a full moon in July; still and unmoved—but for her crochet-work—as one of the large-lipped, serene-faced Ethiopian statues in the British Museum. Turning to her, Lill said,—

"Shall I tell him now about Mr. Giuliani, or wait to see if he is really going to be married? a touch of kindred feeling, you know may make him kind."

"I knew a gentleman who married at seventy-five," said Crummie "and he lived to be eighty-six, and was very happy; you had better wait and see the lady first."

This advice was like a respite to the condemned, and was acted upon.

At six o'clock Lill drove to the Rue de Cirque, expecting to see a dashing, dark-eyed woman, who would overwhelm her with cajolery and coaxing—exactly as the present Baronne de Tircourt had done before she married the young French baron instead of the old English baronet. Miss Tufton was admitted by a French *femme de chambre*, who said that Madame would be with Madlle. immediately.

Lill was astonished to see the metamorphosis already effected in the salon; every table, sofa and chair seemed to have been moved; the curtains were differently draped, and flowers were everywhere that a vase or glass could stand, while every seat was encumbered by cushions. The inner doors being open, Lill could not help having a glimpse of what was going on behind them, and a pretty scene of disorder it was. Great trunks, with their lids thrown back, and the floor strewed with their heterogeneous contents.

Lill was left half an hour by herself; at the end of the first quarter of an hour the same French maid, Madlle. Athenais, brought in a splendid camphene lamp, lighted, and a book "pour Madlle. Tufton, Madame était deso-lée, etc."

The book was one of Balzac's, and the very first page fascinated Lill's attention. It began, "Qui est Madame Firmiani?" Was this meant as epigrammic on the part of Mrs. Townsend? Lill had reached the last of the conjectures about Madame Firmiani, when a rustling made her look up. A little fragile-looking being — her fair hair simply wound about her head, in a black silk dress, made like a peignoir, was coming towards her. Mrs. Townsend took Lill's hand, and raising herself on tip-toe, kissed the young lady.

"You are very good to keep the promise Sir Mark made for you, Miss Tufton," said she, staring at her visitor unceremoniously, and not with an exactly satisfied look.

"I hope you approve of your apartments?" said Lill.

"I like the position, and the rooms are well-sized. When I have changed some of the furniture I shall like them well enough. I hate Utrecht velvet for chairs, they catch hold of your dress so; and yellow is my abomination—my hair doesn't allow of it, nor yours either,' she added, "though it's some shades darker than mine."

Again she stared at Lill.

"Sir Mark thought you might like to drive out," said

Miss Tufton, remembering the injunctions he had re
ceived.

"Dear old man! did he? very kind of him; but pray
tell him I am not crazy; the gas is lit in the streets, I
believe. Do you like French plays? do you go often?"

"Very seldom," was Lill's reply.

"Are you one of the serious?" asked Mrs. Townsend.

"Not at all," and Lill laughed; "but since Sir Mark
has been away we have had no gentleman to go with us."

"We!" repeated Mrs. Townsend, inquiringly.

"Miss Crumpton lives with us."

"Oh, the companion."

"No, my mother's cousin; she stays entirely out of
kindness to me. Can I be of any service to you, Mrs.
Townsend?" added Lill, rather nettled at being so cross-
examined.

"No, I don't think so—for this evening at least. I
mean to have a cup of tea and go to bed. Tell Sir Mark
I am invisible till to-morrow afternoon,"

"Then I will leave you," said Lill. "We dine at
seven."

"Always?" asked the other lady.

"Yes."

"When you have no evening engagements?"

"It is our regular hour."

"You must change it. I can't bear dining before nine,
it makes such a horrible long evening. Tell Sir Mark
you are very different from what I expected; much better
looking."

"More than I can say for you," thought Lill; "poor
little half-dead looking creature, with not even pleasant
manners."

"Well!" said Sir Mark, when he met his granddaughter in the drawing-room before dinner, "how did you
and Mrs. Townsend get on.

"We examined one another very minutely, and Mrs
Townsend desired me to tell you she was not crazy,
therefore did not take a morning drive by gaslight."

Sir Mark laughed as if delighted.

"Well? anything more?"

"And that I was quite different from what she ex
pected, and much better looking."

"Not a bit of feminine jealousy about *her;* you won't hear *her* pulling other women to pieces; and Miss Lill, clever as you think yourself, you'll find your match there for mother wit. Lord, what a wonderful creature she would have been had she had an education like yours!"

Lill was not only in most perfect astonishment at Sir Mark's way of speaking, showing as it did some of the usual marks of a real preference, but she was moved by it. She had half a mind to throw herself on his mercy; he was become more human; who could tell but that he might be glad to get rid of her?

They were yet at dinner when a ring at the bell of the great entrance door announced some visitor.

"Probably Mr. Edward," observed Miss Crumpton.

"Why the deuce couldn't he have come sooner?" said Sir Mark gruffly.

"It is not a *he* at all, come to disturb your digestion," said a winning voice.

Mrs. Townsend was standing laughing by his side, in the most coquettish and becoming of bonnets, a *sortie de bal* over her shoulders.

Lill was amazed at the transformation wrought in the lady's appearance since six o'clock. Pretty she was not, rather something more, very piquant, her large sunken eyes launching forth flashes of light.

With a careless glance at Lill and Miss Crumpton, she said,

"Don't let me disturb any one; I am so glad you are at dessert. I shall sit by you, Sir Mark; and you must give me quantities of dragées."

"You know Whyteson said your way of living on sweet things was what hurt your health."

"That," snapping the smallest fingers woman ever had, "for Whyteson. I do not care to live a year or two longer if I am never to do as I like; so give me my sugar plums."

"Why have you not a '*nougat*,' Lill?" began Sir Mark

"Oh, don't scold me, Sir Mark, scold the *chef.*"

"I won't have any scolding here," said Mrs. Townsend. "I have come to carry you off to the Palais Royal Theatre; I have got a box, and a carriage is at the door."

"Why, how have you managed?" Sir Mark asked.

"*Force de volonté*, sir. I felt dreadfully stupid after Miss Tufton went away, and I sent Athenais to find out if there was a *valet de place* to be had about the house, and that brought down *Madame la propriétaire* from the *troisième*. Sir Mark, be on your guard, she is an uncommon pretty Parisian; she and I fraternized or sorrowized at once; she managed the whole business. I don't know the least what the play is, but madame told me she knew that some of the Princes were to be there."

Lill, who had been growing more impatient at each of Mrs. Townsend's words, felt for an instant as if the last speech had been personally aimed at her. It was almost a reproduction of what she had once said to Giuliani, and the odiousness of such trifling was now made apparent to her. While Mrs. Townsend was eating her sugar plums, dipping sweet biscuits into her wine and chattering to Sir Mark, her eyes were busily scanning Lill.

"I see you don't wish to go, Miss Tufton," she said at last.

"Lill! not like to go to the theatre!" exclaimed Sir Mark; "why she is forever teasing me about boxes; by the by, Miss Tufton, have you screwed any more out of that hero of Mrs. Caledon's;" and chuckling the while, he went on to tell the story as he understood it, of Lill's having made a stranger she met at Colonel Caledon's, give her a box at the Italians'.

"You are mistaken in one point," said Lill; "I paid for Miss Crumpton's ticket and mine."

Sir Mark looked furiously at her.

"You did, did you? Where did you get the money?"

"You had better not ask me before strangers," she said.

"Never mind me," said Mrs. Townsend, laughing.

"Well, then," continued Lill, "I have no idea of cheating any one, and as I had no money I sold some of my ornaments."

"Quite right," said Mrs. Townsend, staring Sir Mark in the face. "There is no reason for your being unlady-like because Sir Mark is such a screw;" then she added in a low voice to the astounded baronet, "What a tempting prospect this story opens to me!"

Sir Mark made no reply, but the look he threw at his granddaughter was awful. Once more Mrs. Townsend whispered to him, "If you fly into a rage with Lill, it's all over between you and me;" then aloud, she said, "I see you would really rather stay at home, Miss Tufton; don't be afraid, Sir Mark shall not make you do anything for me against your inclinations. I shall beg Miss Crumpton to be our chaperone, for I am not going alone with your grandfather."

It was so arranged. When they were gone, Lill burst into a fit of tears. She remembered Giuliani, his tenderness came back on her as the thought of green pastures and clear streams does on the parched traveller in the desert; she must be happy with any one like him; she would get out of this wretched thraldom to Sir Mark and his set. Let him do his worst, she would be safe with Giuliani. Time was, that Lill would have laughed at the late scene instead of crying; the evil spirit had come out of her. but what if seven worse should take up their abode in her? She was yet weeping, when Edward Tufton, fresh from England, came rushing in. She had never been so happy to see his well-known face; even his loud unmusical voice was welcome; she felt, as he almost shook her hand off, as if she had found a support, one who would help and like her without analyzing whether she were right or wrong.

"So they are all out but you, Lill; what a lark! Well what do you think of grandmamma to be?"

"I pity her," said Lill.

"Pity me rather and yourself; but while you *are* mistress here, order me something to eat, I am starving."

Lill rang the bell.

"What will you have?"

"Oysters to begin with, then any cold meat that the cook can spare me."

Presently the two cousins were seated at the dining-table, an immense dish of oysters before Edward.

"There, you eat those," he began, giving her a plateful.

"No, I can't."

"Yes, you must, you look horridly down in the mouth,

I can tell you. You have got a suspicion of a hollow in your left cheek ; what's the matter ?"

" Nothing's the matter, only I want to know something about Mrs. Townsend."

" A queer fish, ain't she ? Such a spirit in that little body of hers ; she cows Sir Mark famously, don't she ? I'll stake a hundred to one that in a year she'll bring him to be only the husband of Lady Tufton."

" But is it all settled then ? and who is she ?"

" All right as to respectability and that sort of thing, for that's what you are driving at, I know ; as to your first question, you must ask her. I say, Lill, don't you go for to be taking a dislike to her because of her odd ways. She's not an ill-natured woman, and she is open-handed as the day ; and she can be, when she likes, the best fun in the world."

" The idea of a grandmamma the best fun in the world !" repeated Lill.

" You should see the state my mother is in, she wants me to go into the Church and secure the family living at all events ; she looks on my chance of the baronetcy as gone, and declares this marriage will be her deathblow. Every day she writes me some new plan ; her last is that you and I should unite to prevent its ever taking place. If wishes could kill, alas ! for Sir Mark."

" *A la grâce de Dieu*," said Lill ; "as for me I don't grudge Sir Mark his happiness nor his money, but now good night : he was in a rage with me as usual before he went out, and I don't want to meet him till he has slept it off."

" Then, perhaps I had better toddle to bed also," said Mr. Tufton.

CHAPTER XXIII.

Drifting Away.

On the breakfast table next morning lay a tiny note for Lill, written in pencil; it ran thus:—

"What is the first duty of woman on arriving in Paris? Guess, and come in the carriage at half-past one, and tell me."   "Honora T."

Lill had lately had such an uncomfortable time of it with herself, that, truth to say, she was rather glad to have some other subject forced upon her. So, on the whole, she welcomed Mrs. Townsend's note, and was punctual to the hour mentioned. As a matter of course she had to wait half an hour, and therefore had the opportunity of finishing Madame Fimiani. The hero, as every one knows, lives up in a garret, and gives lessons in mathematics, which does not make him the less of a fine gentleman, or the less beloved by a very fine lady. The story interested Lill, as stories do which trench on the domains of our own private history.

The two ladies drove first to De Lisle's. Lill sat there for three quarters of an hour, patiently enough, amused with the variety of materials exhibited; but at last Mrs. Townsend's caprice bewildered and fatigued her. That was nothing, however, to the impatience that ensued when, the dresses being chosen, the quantities required were to be discussed. Mrs. Townsend disputed every point, accused the shopman of wishing to make her take too much, and ended by ordering more than he had said was necessary.

"I declare it's nearly dark," she said, as she was walking to the carriage.

"We have been four hours here," answered Lill.

"Ah! well, if it had not been for your solemn face, I should have been longer; it will be your fault if I have taken what I don't like."

Sir Mark's fine horses had been dawdling and standing in an east wind all this time; the coachman looked down upon the ladies, with a face as rough as the wind itself; Lill observed this to Mrs. Townsend.

"What else is he a coachman for?" she said, which, however, did not prevent her sending him a large *pourboire* when she got home.

In the meantime they drove to Jeoffroy in the Rue Richelieu, where another hour was spent in choosing coiffures and bonnets; then elsewhere for artificial flowers, elsewhere again for gloves, for shoes. At half-past eight Lill put down Mrs. Townsend at her own door, who, as she alighted, exclaimed,—

"I shall not dine with you to-day, but come and see me early to-morrow."

Mrs. Townsend had engaged herself to dine with the Tuftons, and had made them alter their dinner-hour.

The next day Lill walked with Edward Tufton to the Rue de Cirque. They were arm in arm, and really made an interesting couple. Many of the passers-by turned to look at them, and all had more or less of a smile on their faces, the pleasant sensation with which one greets spring-time.

"Well matched indeed!" was the thought of one who had been some time (himself unseen) contemplating them. As the cousins were about to turn into the Rue de Cirque, this moralizer passed them hastily, and without giving any sign of recognition: Lill flushed crimson: "he must have been behind them, he might think all sorts of things;" she made a dash forward to stop him, she half called out his name, and then stopped.

"What's the matter?" asked Edward, putting his head forward to see her face.

Of course the answer was. "Nothing."

"Yes, it is something; that fellow who passed us is that Grimgriffinoff you were in such a passion with me about."

"Perhaps it was," said Lill; "I suppose he did not recognize us."

Mr. Edward looked rather sulky.

That Saturday evening Lill could not go to the Ponsonby's, but she wrote an apology and explanation.

Within a week of Mrs. Townsend's advent in Paris, she had a dashing, low, open carriage, with a pair of spirited ponies, in which she drove herself and the beautiful Miss Tufton to the Bois de Boulogne, and in doing which both ladies met with their due share of admiration; the one for her beauty, the other for her graceful, daring coachmanship. At the end of that week the two were mounted on equally first-rate horses, with plenty of cavaliers besides Sir Mark and Edward Tufton; cavaliers agreeable, gallant, and talkative, to whom Sir Mark and his heir presumptive only were an exception, their rule being to be sulky and silent. The ladies were also *en évidence* in the evenings. After the ride, or the drive, came the dinner. There was always either company to dinner or in the evening; or they went to a theatre, or a concert, or a ball, or a soirée.

Mrs. Townsend could not endure a family party, and wherever she went, Lill must go, or else Sir Mark should not accompany her. Lill yielded to this exigency with evident reluctance at first, then more and more readily.

But wherever she might be, or whatever she might be doing, abroad or at home, alone or in a crowd, the recollection of her promise to Giuliani, of his right to claim its performance, lay heavy and cold on her conscience. Why did she linger so? was a question never candidly answered.

She was already once more living in the zone of fashion, breathing easily in that malignant air which leaves no one the master of either his thoughts or actions.

All that can be said in Lill's defence is that, throughout this period, she never laid herself out to attract; her manners, indeed, were so retiring, that more than one of those who dangled in her train supposed her to be the betrothed of the ill-tempered looking youth who was always at her side.

After that morning when Giuliani had passed her in the Champs Elysées without any sign of recognition, Lill had had many glimpses of him when she was on horseback, or in the dashing pony phaeton; and each glimpse had sent the blood violently to her heart, leaving her face colourless for an instant, only to steep it in crimson the following moment. Giuliani never seemed to see her, but she was certain, as of her life, that he always did.

One day in particular she had had a good inspiration.

She had been riding with Mrs. Townsend and a gay party in the Champs Élysées, and she had caught sight of him about to enter the courtyard of a building on which was a huge board with staring gold letters, announcing it as a "*Pensionnat pour jeunes demoiselles.*" She saw perfectly well that he looked pale and thin. She had fine gentlemen on either side of her, well mounted, and as sleek and shiny as their steeds: they were all trotting, and the cloud of dust they raised reached Giuliani. He stopped and shook it from his coat. This accidental circumstance smote her heart. In the smart of the moment, she curbed her horse so tightly, that he reared: the gentlemen on either side made a snatch at her bridle, but she struck the spirited animal with her whip between the ears, so that he set off at a wild gallop. No, *he* should not see any man paying her attention. And Giuliani thought the gallop a bravado! Did not Lill well know his aversion to a woman's riding?

On her return home, still under the impression she had received, Lill wrote to Giuliani a very few lines, but strong with real feeling: she concluded by saying that nothing should prevent her going to Lady Ponsonby's next Saturday evening. She gave her note to Ruth, bidding her take it to the post herself. Ruth had often seen notes addressed by her young lady to Mr. Giuliani, and had not given a thought to the matter. She was accustomed also to Lill's forcible manner about trifles, yet this day the lady's-maid imagined, for the first time, that there was something between Miss Tufton and Mr. Giuliani, and hers was the memory of a servant for those sorts of things.

Giuliani received the note with more of surprise than pleasure; he read it, and laid it down with a quietly muttered "*Pauvre enfant.*" His heart was as heavy as a stone.

That morning he had heard that he was sure of being named to the professorship of history at the college of the provincial town of B—. "An evil fate follows me," he had thought; "the nomination is of no use for the end I solicited it, and will only serve to separate me from the best of friends, and a life that suits me. I have deserved this."

CHAPTER XXIV

Fetters of Intimacy

"No, no, no,—I can't spare you this evening," said Mrs. Townsend to Lill, who was pleading a pre-engagement. "I don't know another English woman I can ask to meet these French people. *You* will do me credit; besides, I can't bear to see any one pursing up their mouths in fear of what may be coming next, or else dropping out from the end of their lips, in answer to a joke upon some of our national absurdities, 'That's exactly what we pride ourselves upon in England.'"

The mimicry of some of their *collet monté* acquaintances was so capital that Lill burst out laughing.

"You are a charming creature," said Mrs. Townsend; "I knew you could not resist me."

"I must this once—only this once, dear Honora."

"Where do you want to go?" asked the dear Honora, her sunken eyes fixed on Lill with curiosity. "I am your chaperone now; Sir Mark gave you into my charge, and I have a right to know, and I will know."

Intimacies generally end in being tyrannies. Lill was by this time aware that what Mrs. Townsend said in play she often meant in earnest.

"There's no mystery in the case," she said? "I wish to go to Lady Ponsonby's Saturday reception."

"You never mentioned Lady Ponsonby to me before. Where does she live? who is she? why have you not introduced me to her?"

"I should be very glad to do so; she is a charming person; oh, so good, so unlike any one I ever saw," said Lill, warming with her subject. "I used to go there almost every Saturday evening before you came, and she has a right to be offended at my neglect of her lately."

"Is she old? has she sons?" pursued Mrs. Townsend.

"One son at home, the other is in India; but you needn't imagine any love affair between Valentine and me; he is just such another as Edward Tufton."

"Ah! by the by, Lill, why don't you and that Neddy

make up a match, and keep the title and wealth in the
family ?"

"Heavens, no !" exclaimed Lill, again laughing;
"that would be preposterous ; his wife to be should still
be in the nursery.   Besides, we expect you to be Lady
Tufton."

"Hm ! hm ! hm ! come, confess, and I'll let you off
this evening.   *Notre cœur a déjà parlé*, eh ! some mer-
curial Parisian whom we think to meet at this Lady
Ponsonby's ?"

"No, indeed," said Lill, firmly.

"You swear it is not so — very well; then you must
give up Lady P. and all her amiable *bataclan*."

Lill was afraid to insist, so she sent off at once a note
to Lady Ponsonby.

"Please not to think ill of me — but, indeed, I do not
believe *you* ever judge one unkindly — I would give
much to be with you this evening, but I am prevented.

"Your most affectionate,

"LILL."

"Show it to Giuliani," said Alicia, who was suspicious
that all was not right between the Italian and Miss Tufton.

Lady Ponsonby accordingly placed it in Giuliani's
hand as soon as he came in.   It was the first time she
had ventured on the slightest act that could give a hint
of her being aware of his feelings for Lill.

He read the few lines in silence, the moment was not
come for any outpourings of the pain he felt.   Alicia
picked up the note afterwards, so crushed, that the
writing was nearly illegible.

CHAPTER XXV.

Soiree Townsend.

THERE was a pleasant subdued light in Mrs. Townsend's drawing-room, when Lill entered it with Sir Mark and Edward.

A lady and two gentlemen had preceded them. The lady was presented as Madame de Verneuil, one gentleman as Mons. Ix, the other as Mons. Vertengris. The *partie carrée* opened their circle to admit the new arrivals. Madame de Verneuil retreated to a sofa, in one corner of which she shrank herself up, looking — no other description will answer for her — like a portrait by Watteau. Her hair, of that peculiar shade called black in England, and *châtain* in France, was drawn back from her face, falling in the studied disorder produced by a clever hair-dresser, behind her ears down on her white throat. The blue knitted capuchon on the back of her head remained as she had put it on, to walk down from the *troisième* to Mrs. Townsend's second.

Mrs. Townsend looked that evening in her flowing white dress with green ribbons, like Lorelei, so said Mons. Vertengris. The something strange that characterized her appearance, was one of her attractions; she made people look and look again; it was easy to imagine her Lorelei or any spirit in pain, even a victim to some supernatural influence. The extraordinary brilliancy of her dark gray eyes was really suggestive of an inward fire gradually consuming her; and the inevitable impression of every one on seeing her for the first time was wonder, how so frail a bark could carry such a cargo of life.

The conversation broken by the entrance of the Tuftons was not easily reknotted. Mrs. Townsend called Lill to sit by her, and introduced Mons. Vertengris to her. Mons. Vertengris was much younger than Mons. Ix, and was exactly the sort of a person whom gentlemen like Sir Mark and Edward Tufton consider as the worst species of Frenchmen. He was tall, well-made, hair and eyes black as jet   both lustrous; in short, very handsome. Mons. Vertengris made a little sign expressive of his approbation of Miss Tufton's appearance to the lady of the house, with whom he continued his conversation, which, however ingeniously he paraphrased her observations, did not prevent Lill's attention wandering to what was passing between Mons. Ix and Madame de Verneuil. Mons. Ix might be a man of forty, but he wore a wig, at least so it seemed—a scratch auburn wig, which came down in a point on the forehead, and retired very much from off the temples. He had a scrutinizing eye, and not a pleasant mouth, with dazzling white teeth, as had also Mons. Vertengris. His thin lips twisted scornfully as he spoke. To Madame de Verneuil's observations as to Lill's beauty, he answered,—

"Yes; she rather justifies those charmingly impossible English engravings, but she makes me think of *ce rosier blanc qui doit me donner des roses noires;* in short, fit to obtain a prize at some flower-show."

"Very unjust," responded Madame de Verneuil. "*Que voulez-vous? moi j'ai le malheur de ne pas avoir de goût pour les blondes filles d'Albion.* If it were only their unnatural habit of shaking hands with every man they meet, I could never adore them. I should prefer to be the first man to press the hand of my future wife."

Madame de Verneuil, by a glance, guided Mons. Ix's eyes towards Lill, who, by her deep blush, showed she had overheard the criticism.

"Have you seen the dear political, theological, sentimental princess? how goes on her amiable recruiting for the cause of Italy?"

"Badly, since she broke with the *Giovane Italia;* her fine eyes have quite failed in melting the hard-hearted Giulio; he holds out against all her stratagems!"

"Giulio? don't know him," said Ix, nonchalantly.

"The man of wood, son of the Cavaliere Giuliani;" here were some words unintelligible to Lill, whose whole attention was engrossed by this conversation.

"Ah! ah! The *protégé* of Gioberti—he that is to marry the daughter of an English Miledi."

"But the princess will have him if she cares to do so; her motto is: '*Labor vincit improbus.*'"

A bustle at the door announced a new arrival. A tall, dark woman, between the two ages, to translate the graphic French phrase, entered, leaning on the arm of a gentleman. Lill heard this same lady accosted as *Notre chère princesse*, and coaxed and cajoled by Madame de Verneuil and Mons. Ix.

"I come with such a history," exclaimed the princess. "What a world! what a base, hypocritical world, Mons. Ix! You don't hit it hard enough in your writings. I shall become a greater pessimist than you. I shall retire to the summit of Mount Lebanon."

"I ask nothing better than to be allowed to accompany you," said Mons. Ix. "There under the broad spreading cedars, through the fine leaves of which comes filtering the silver light of the full moon —"

"And when there is no full moon?" interrupted Madame de Verneuil.

"Or no trees?" suggested Mons. Vertengris, believing he was very original.

"My faith, the case is not foreseen by poets," answered Mons. Ix.

"But my story, my story; has no one any interest in my story? listen!" Everybody was silent and the princess began:"Count C—, — ah! I see you guess the name—wants to marry his son. Well, he hears of the daughter of a wealthy merchant in L—, and sends a confidential agent to enter on the preliminaries. The father, Mr. R—, presses for the name of the future —, the agent is not authorized to reveal it, but allows that the father of the young man is a count and hereditary peer. The well-pleased confident returns to Paris and finds his principal at dinner with his intimate friend, Count D—. Count C— tells him to speak out, for that D— is his bosom friend, whereupon the agent announces the success of his negotiations, gives the cipher of the young lady's dowry—a sum that makes the mouths of both counts water —and winds up the narration by saying, that the father had greatly urged him for the name of the person who was in treaty for the young lady's hand. 'To pacify the good papa,' continued the agent, 'I told him that I was acting for a count and peer.' 'Bien,' said Count C—;'you may communicate the name and title.' Count D— took his leave immediately after dinner, went by rail to L—, introduced himself to the merchant; he was a count and hereditary peer; *bref*, the young lady's hand was promised to *his* son when Count's C—'s agent reappeared at L—."

There was one burst of laughter, as the princess concluded her story, from all in the room with the exception of the Tuftons: Sir Mark and Edward could not follow the lady's rapid French, and Lill was indignant. "It was down right cheating," she exclaimed.

"You are right, mademoiselle," said Mons. Ix, addressing her with a sort of benevolent look. "See what it is to be young! there is still a fibre of honesty in your heart; I perceive it is a bad thing to be no longer young. Mademoiselle, I congratulate you on the power of being indignant; in ten years you will laugh like the rest of us when an infamy is related.

"I hope not," said Lill, with a little too much emphasis for society.

Both *cette chère princesse* and Madame de Verneuil stared at Lill coldly. But Mons. Ix had made his reputation, he wielded a waspish pen, his books were popular; therefore when he spoke every one listened, and took it on trust that what he said was witty or sagacious.

Mons. Ix sat for a time with his head hanging down on his breast: then, as if awakening he said.—"Yes, my mind is made up. Youth is our consolation and supreme resource: the best thing in the world,—you shrug your shoulders, ladies,—not for its smooth skin and bright eyes, though such gifts are not worthless,— far from that; but I adore it for its folly and exaggerations, generally the exaggeration of some generous sentiment."

Mons. Vertengris kindly wished to interpose some praise in behalf of those whose youth had fled; he resorted as usual to a paraphrase of something he had heard or read. "True, a smiling plain is charming, but a fine ruin excites our curiosity."

"Bravo," exclaimed Ix, with a twist of his mouth. "Well, for my part, I accept your simile with gratitude."

After this Ix ensconced himself between the princess and Madame de Verneuil, and of their conversation only unconnected sentences reached Lill; but they interested her, for the subject was Italy.

"'Waiting for his star;' it will be long enough before it comes to him," said the princess.

"*J'attends mon astre.*" Lill knew that was Charles Albert's device.

Here more guests entered, and what followed was lost to her. Sir Mark at every new entrance turned a reproachful glance on Mrs. Townsend, who did the honours with a perfect grace, that even Mons. Ix allowed to be worthy of a Parisian. Suddenly Lill saw Mdlle. Arsenieff. The Russian came up to her, and in her careless, loud way, said,—

"I drop from the clouds; I believed you were already on the other side of the Channel. You have, then, turned a cold shoulder to Italy?"

Lill asked for Lady Ponsonby.

"Ah! poor lady, she has had bad news of her son in India; but there is compensation,—he is about to return to Europe."

Mdlle. Arsenieff's business there was to play, and not to gossip; so she left Lill with her curiosity quite unsated.

"Always that German music," exclaimed the princess. "Italian music is as much avoided as if it were a political prisoner. *Mon dieu!* how I detest those ti, ti, ti, echoed by tom, tom, tom! *Ah! cher ami,*" to Mons. Ix, "*la guerre sortira de ces faux accords,*" said she returning to her former subject.

"That may well be; they are very irritating to the ear," said Ix, laughing.

"The idea," continued the princess, perfectly unconscious of the *quid pro quo* of what she had just said, "of a pope at the head of a liberal movement, and Francis of Modena granting concesssion! God give me patience! we are not yet in the millennium, when the tiger will lie down with the lamb."

Lill only once caught a word which she believed referred to Giuliani.

"As to him, he has retrograded into a constitutionalist, sees no hope for Italy but in Piedmont; that party increases. It is not he individually, but his name counts, and he is honest."

To an observation of Mons. Ix the princess replied,—

"*Affaire de cœur.* Bah! one of those men who has no blood in his veins"

Mons. Vertengris was singing, and just at this interesting crisis sent forth a volume of voice that overpowered every other sound.

Mrs. Townsend afterwards tried to persuade Lill to sing, but in vain, spite of Sir Mark's frowns; the English girl was really afraid of the two Parisian ladies.

The guests at last slipped away one by one; Mons. Vertengris standing before Mrs. Townsend for at least three minutes and a half, and then for as long before Lill, with his feet drawn close together, his hat in both hands in a line with his knees, and his head bent down on his chest. It was Mons. Vertengris' way of taking leave, and expressive of his most distinguished sentiments. The ladies bowed and curtsied themselves away under Mons. Ix's guard, and the Tuftons alone remained.

"Who is that woman with the moustache?" asked Sir Mark, gruffly.

"Woman? what woman?" repeated Mrs. Townsend with an artless air. She had drawn Lill down on the sofa by her side, and was playing with a curl of her hair.

"Well, that lady, if you choose to call her so."

'Oh! Madame la Princesse de —, born Countess —"

The names were too historical for even Sir Mark to sneer at.

"And the other, with her saucy face?"

"Madame de Verneuil. I believe she has no title to offend you."

"And where are the husbands of these great dames?"

"The prince is in his own country, and as for Madame de Verneuil, she has too much *esprit* to be anything *but* a widow;" and, with one of her sweetest smiles, Mrs Townsend pointed to the clock, which marked an hour after midnight.

Home the three Tuftons drove in inimical silence; for silences have as many meanings as words. Each received their candle with a muttered good-night. Certainly, never in any family was there less of ceremony, less of politeness, than in that of the Tuftons: it may be added less of cordiality also, which, in many cases redeems the rudeness of home manners.

Sir Mark had always been and was the last person in the world to whom Lill ever applied for any indulgence, or advice, or assistance. She had never heard the door close against him but with a sensation of pleasurable relief.

As for Edward Tufton, he was a specimen of the sort of youth Mr. Carlyle would keep for some years under a tub; full of lively sympathy for the powers that be, very good-natured when he had his own way.

Lill did not intend to be cruel to Ruth, but she allowed her to go on brushing her hair indefinitely. Twenty-one days since she had spoken to Giuliani. She was glad now she had been to Mrs. Townsend's. Poor Lill! to think of her finding consolation in the windy words of two women of the world! Nevertheless, it was a balm to her pride that Giuliani was canvassed for by a princess of great lineage; that his name was held as a power by one of the most noble of his own nation.

Madame de Verneuil and Mons. Ix spoke of him as on a par with this lady, whose escutcheon had figured in the Crusades. His giving lessons had not been alluded to. How she wished Sir Mark and Edward Tufton had heard how respectfully he was mentioned! they would not dare then to treat him with contempt. Mons. Ix did not seem to think there was anything out of the way in Giuliani's marrying Miss Ponsonby; and she was the daughter of one baronet and the sister of another, quite of the same rank as Lill herself.

" If English people," mused Lill, " were only as liberal as the French; but they are so ferociously exclusive. You must be English to the very marrow of your bones to please the English. A grain of continentalism, and one is lost."

She remembered feeling in this way once herself. Poor Lill! what a vexed sigh she gave!

It was a curious illustration of the impression of truthfulness Giuliani had made on her, that she entirely set aside as nonsense all the gossip that associated his name with that of Miss Ponsonby.

At last Ruth, who had fallen asleep in her operations, gave her mistress's head such a knock with the brush, that Lill uttered a little scream, and repentantly sent Ruth away to her bed.

CHAPTER XXVI.

Schahabaham

MADEMOISELLE ARSENIEFF was a Cossack from the borders of the Don. Scarcely yet tamed by her two years' residence in Paris, Lady Ponsonby and Alicia had rescued her from a peculiarly disagreeable position, and had assisted her to attain her great end, viz. that of becoming a pianiste. For these two ladies Mdlle. Arsenieff entertained that sort of attachment which a savage may be supposed to feel for a benefactor. By any means right or wrong, his benefactor is to be protected and benefited. Admitted as one of the intimates of the Ponsonby family, the Russian girl had discovered Alicia's attachment to Giuliani; and from the moment she had read in his eyes his admiration of Lill, she had taken for Miss Tufton an unreasoning aversion founded on her gratitude to Alicia. She hated Giuliani for being insensible to Alicia's superiority; in her heart she accused him of mean worship of wealth, and after all the Ponsonby's kindness to him! But Mdlle. Arsenieff possessed the powers of dissimulation, as well as the blind devotion, of a savage. She veiled her attacks under a show of frankness, which went well with her broad open face.

Lill, on the contrary, had taken a liking to Mdlle. Arsenieff, and whenever she heard of any one requiring music lessons, or some pianiste for the evening, she always recommended Lady Ponsonby's *protégée*. It was Lill who had proposed to Mrs. Townsend to invite the Russian. Nothing mollified by this good-nature, Mdlle. Arsenieff conducted a series of covert attacks against Lill, more especially when Giuliani was present, and always with rare precision hitting on incidents peculiarly distasteful to him. She described and exaggerated the expensive style of Miss Tufton's dress; spoke of her as being surrounded by a phalanx of admirers; one to hold her smelling bottle, others her fan, her bouquet; relating that she had entered a ball-room leaning on Mr. Tufton's arm, and that her manner was such to the young man, that every one said, if she were not his *fiancée*, she ught to be; that Madame Townsend was a woman to ruin a steadier girl than Madlle. Lill; and, in short, without bringing any real accusation against Lill, she managed to give Giuliani a lively image of pride, coquetry, and indiscretion.

There is a coarse, light way of relating, that throws listeners off their guard; besides, Giuliani had strong prejudices which allowed him to be led and misled when persons far his inferiors in intelligence escaped the trap.

One evening Valentine exclaimed after the departure of Mdlle. Arsenieff,—

"What motive can Mdlle. Arsenieff have for constantly speaking ill of Miss Tufton?"

This was after the pianiste had successfully mimicked Mons. Vertengris and Edward Tufton, and declared that there would be a duel between them to decide who should carry off the belle.

"No motive at all," said Lady Ponsonby, "but that she is amused by the vagaries of a set of persons hitherto undreamed of by her."

"Well, mother, I don't agree with you. She persists too much in one strain for it to be natural; it's very like a jealous woman."

As no one answered, he asked,—

"What has Miss Tufton done to you all, that you seem actually pleased with—"

"My dear Valentine!" interrupted the mother and daughter.

"Let me finish my sentence: yes, you are pleased, and do encourage Mdlle. Arsenieff's ill-nature by your laughter. Whatever Miss Tufton may do, I am sure she is never unladylike, and that is what you cannot say for your Russian favourite."

"Valentine, you mistake; no one here wishes ill to Miss Tufton," said Giuliani, gravely; "at the same time it is not easy to approve of her entire neglect of your mother With carriage and horses she might have made her way here once in the last three weeks; formerly she never allowed two days to pass without calling."

"There's something wrong, about which, I am not in the secret," said Valentine; "but I knew Miss Tufton before any of you: I have seen her surrounded by men and I swear she never flirted with one or a dozen, or gave her flowers or her handkerchief to any one to hold: she is as proud as a queen! But all women love to pull a pretty girl to pieces," and out of the room flung honest Valentine.

"Valentine is right," said Alicia; "we have all been encouraging Mdlle. Arsenieff. I shall speak seriously to her to-morrow; and as for Miss Tufton's visits here, probably she only states the fact when she says it is not her fault that she does not come."

This outburst of Valentine's had its effect on Giuliani; it determined him to accept of an invitation to dinner he shortly after received from Mrs. Caledon; the note said, to meet Mons. Villemasson, the great philosopher, and warm admirer of Italy, the Tuftons, and a few other friends. He would go and judge for himself.

The Tuftons were already in the Caledon's drawing-room when Giuliani was announced. Lill had heard he was expected, and hoped to be able to maintain a placid exterior when she should see him. But the sound of his voice—she could not look up—covered her face and throat with a scarlet blush. Edward Tufton was on one side of her and Mrs. Townsend on the other. Mrs. Caledon had hold of Giuliani's arm and was presenting him to Mons. Villemasson, her great lion, a most flourishing specimen of a philosopher; flowing grey hair combed back from a face with a complexion that looked like strawberries and cream, a figure portly as a bishop's, hands like those of a priest;—this nice old gentleman stood conversing with Giuliani for some time, and Lill hoped that every one would remark the extreme cordiality of the celebrity.

Mrs. Caledon was worse than the most terrible child for getting herself and her guests into scrapes; she presently brought Giuliani up to Lill, saying,—

"The master must take the pupil down to dinner; it will be a good opportunity for him to see whether she has forgotten her Italian."

And, having done this, she went away smiling.

Lill could not tell whether Sir Mark or Edward Tufton had heard or understood this speech, for almost immediately there was a move towards the dining-room and her arm lay on that of Giuliani. Neither had yet said a word to the other. If Lill had been aware in time that she was going to meet Giuliani in this way, she would not have had the courage to appear at Mrs. Caledon's. He took pity on her excessive embarrassment, and, meaning to broach some indifferent subject, asked, " if she had been riding that morning ?"

Lill fancied his question contained an allusion to the day when she had galloped away from his sight conscience-stricken; once again she flushed, saying,—

" I know you disapprove of ladies riding, but I cannot help it."

" My prejudices are not worth your remembering," he replied, with a forced smile. " Ah! what is that our neighbours are saying ?"

A very pleasant looking, handsome English woman, with that smooth, rosy *embonpoint* which denoted that she found this world the best of all possible worlds, was answering Mons. Villemasson, the amateur of Italy.

" My dear sir, I confess I have neither patience nor sympathy with twenty-six millions of people for ever gnashing their teeth, and crying out for some one to come and help them."

The benign philosopher, who, perhaps, found it easier to row with the current than against it, at all events at dinner-time, bethought him of a means of showing off his friendship for Italy and his Roman Italian at the same time; he burst forth :

" *Piangi chè ben' hai donde Italia mia,*" &c.

Kind Mrs. Caledon's eyes filled, and she glanced towards Giuliani, though the only words she had understood of the baron's quotation were, " Piangi" and " Italia ;" they were enough, however, to encourage her tears,

Lill had winced at the handsome lady's attack on Italians, and looked down on her plate ; but Mrs. Caledon, in her happy confusion of ideas, exclaimed, " Oh ! Mr. Giuliani, do say something for your own cause."

General attention being thus attracted to him, Giuliani exclaimed, with some warmth,—

" The question, I believe, is, why do the Italians not free themselves. Ask Enceladus why he does not shake off the mountain under which he is buried; or **Prometheus**, why he does not break his bonds and be free. There are attempts even beyond the strength of giants. Do you know, madame," more particularly addressing the handsome lady, "that Austria exercises an iron sway in Lombardy and Venetia; that she keeps, in spite of pope and cardinals, let alone the populations, garrisons at Ferrara, Comacchio, and Plaisance; that the rulers of Modena, Parma, and Tuscany, are offshoots of Austria; that all act, with the exception of Piedmont, as Austria bids? Are we then so wrong, after all, if we call upon Europe to undo the work of iniquity which in an evil hour she has done—if we protest against the breach of the most solemn promises? Yes, the promises made to Italians, to induce them to join the allies against the common enemy, have been forgotten, and Austria has been permitted to turn Italy into a prison. The Croat encamped within the very heart of our country, a hundred thousand foreign bayonets, was what peace blessed us with—a peace that was a bitter derision. Never was oppression, never was compression, for us, more pitiless."

"What a fool!" muttered Sir Mark to Mrs. Townsend.

"So he is," she answered, "to be talking sense here."

"Well," exclaimed Mrs. Caledon, "I always thought you such a moderate man."

"There are matters in which moderation is cowardice, Mrs. Caledon. And now," he added, smiling, "my violent fit is over, and I return to my natural disposition of a lamb." Then, addressing himself to Lill, he said, in a lower voice, "I am afraid I have disgraced myself irretrievably in the eyes of your fair *compatriote*. It is not like a gentleman to be warmly interested in anything, is it?"

"You speak English so well, Mr. Giuliani, why don't you say 'countrywoman' and not '*compatriote*,'" and Lill glanced at him with a pair of laughing eyes; she was so pleased with this return to his former friendly manner.

"Compatriot is English, I assure you," he said, with amusing gravity; "it is in Craig's dictionary."

"It is? then believe me, I am sure you have made a

warm friend of my fair *compatriote.* We English are given to enthusiams," and she blushed from sudden consciousness.

He changed the conversation by asking her if she still continued her lessons of Chopin.

" Given up," she said, " because I have no time, or rather because I can no longer command my time ; I wish you would believe me Mr. Giuliani."

" I do believe you," he answered ; " I regret to do so though, for, however amiable, it is a weakness to allow yourself to be so easily guided."

Before Lill could answer there was a general move into the drawing-room. As they passed thither, Giuliani's handsome adversary attacked him again with—

" I don't give up my point, Signor Giuliani. Let the Italians remember the proverb, ' Providence helps those who help themselves.' You see I am dreadfully combative : shall you be afraid to come and see me ?" and the lady handed him a card.

Seated by Lill's side at dinner, Giuliani had been unable to have a good view of her ; while he was listening to his new friend, his eyes wandered to the other end of the room. Beautiful always, but something had been stolen from her beauty ; something new given to it. There was less of brilliancy in her complexion ; her eyes seemed to have grown darker, their former proud bright look was softened, and there were traces of anxiety in the down drop of the mouth. She was leaning back in her chair, as if fatigued ; in short, Giuliani discovered alterations in her which went to his heart. He did not in the least suspect how much tenderness there had come into his own eyes while he thus contemplated Lill, nor how abstracted he had become ; he was passing sentence on himself as over severe.

The handsome lady, being a good-natured person, left him to his meditations, much amused, and not at all offended, to see how soon after he was by the side of the lovely Miss Tufton, who, according to the custom of young ladies, no sooner perceived him coming than she turned her head in the opposite direction.

" How is it Miss Crumpton is not here ?" began Giuliani.

"Because she has taken the most extraordinary dislike to Mrs. Townsend, and shuts herself up to avoid her."

"And you, do you sympathize with Miss Crumpton?"

"Not at all," answered Lill, warmly; then sobering her tone and looking almost deprecatingly at Giuliani, she added "I like her, and I cannot say why."

"The expression of your face reveals that you are expecting some reproof from me. Was I, then, so severe a master?"

The words! they were nothing, as words often are; but the voice, how eloquent it was! Lill did not speak, she was frightened at the tone; she looked round quickly to see who was near, she even made a movement as if she would have taken flight.

"Do you wish me to go away?" he asked.

"No, stay;" yet the transparent eyelids lay obstinately over the sweet eyes. At last, with a great effort compelling herself to speak, she said —

"Yes, you are inclined always to be severe."

"Do not call it severity," he said, then added, "But how can I expect you to understand what passes in a man's soul when he has *nothing* but the bread of the proscribed."

"*Prenez mon ours*," whispered a merry voice, and a slender figure insinuated itself betweeen Giuliani and Miss Tufton. "Mrs. Caledon will be with you immediately, you look so melancholy a couple; and, dear woman, wherever she has seen any one with a triste air, she has gone up to them with, '*Prenez mon ours.*' She had offered him twice to Sir Mark, and once to cousin Edward. Look how she makes him dance! how well he bows!"

Mrs. Caledon was, indeed, moving anxiously about with her arm within that of Mons. Villemasson, presenting him first to one person and then to another. Lill tried to laugh, and Giuliani smiled.

"If you will let me bring in my chair," continued Mrs. Townsend, "I'll tell you a story. There, now we are comfortable," she said, much as a child might have done. She began. "Once upon a time there was a famous pacha — I forget his name —"

"Schahabaham!" suggested Giuliani.

"How strange you should know anything of vaudevilles," observed Mrs. Townsend, staring at Giuliani. "Uncommonly sensible, though. Well, Mr. Schahabaham had a favourite, whom he prized far beyond his sultana, or his first minister, though that personage was half an idiot; and who do you think, or what do you think, this favourite of the pacha's might be? Do you give it up? why a great bear — *the* Great Bear probably — an excellent creature in its way, and which, under pretext of being a bear, never spoke. Poor beast! in spite of being adored by pacha, minister, and the whole nation, one day it died. It's dreadful in any country to the bearer of bad tidings; but in the kingdom of the Pacha Scha —" she looked at Giuliani.

"Schahabaham."

"Exactly; there it was dangerous to men's heads; so you may imagine the prime minister's joy when he heard of the arrival in the capital of the pacha's dominions of two European merchants. They would be a novelty which might divert the pacha's grief when he heard, as hear he must, of his irreparable loss. But to every proposition of the minister to present the strangers at court, they shook their heads saying '*Prenez mon ours.*'"

"Lill, my dear young friend," exclaimed Mrs. Caledon, "you are looking very serious to-night. Allow me to introduce Mons. Villemasson. Miss Tufton — Mons. Villemasson."

"I am afraid I am rather an unlikely person to drive away a young lady's melancholy," said the benign old man.

"You will find Miss Tufton incorrigible," said Mrs. Townsend, "because she knows a pensive attitude suits her so well. She has positively resisted my story of *L' Ours et le Pacha.*"

"Ha, ha! *prenez mon ours,*" said the Frenchman, promptly; "but one must see it acted to feel the drollery," and he laughed the good-natured laugh peculiar to very fat men.

By this time Mrs. Caledon had discovered some other Schahabaham in want of consolation, and carried off her precious guest. Mrs. Townsend, her bright eyes following the strangely assorted couple said to Giuliani, —

"Have you ever forgotten that men and women were men and women, and looked at them as you would do at the animals in the Jardin des Plantes. Really, when narrowly examined, humanity is not so very pretty, that any of us have a right to be proud of it. A crowded room always disgusts me with my fellow mortals. How clever of the Greeks and Romans to have draperies to hide the poorness of the human figure! I can bear the sight now and then of a man's head; don't you believe the soul to be in the brain?"

"We must call back Mons. Villemasson, he is just the man to answer your query," said Giuliani.

"To offer me one of his own peculiar hobbies, you mean; *prenez mon ours*, in fact."

"As for me," rejoined Giuliani, "I confess I have never tried to discover in what particular niche of our bodies the soul may be quartered; I know it is the principle of our life here and hereafter."

Mrs. Townsend buried her face in her bouquet, then said, —

"There! no more of such dreadful churchyard words; let us live the day and be satisfied. Lill, there's a pansy for you — it means sweet thoughts," and the little lady sauntered away.

"You must not judge of Mrs. Townsend by her manners in society," observed Lill. "She is very charitable, and always ready to oblige."

"She is interesting," he replied, "but like one whose mind is jangled and out of tune. I should say she possessed unusual penetration: her eyes actually seem to pierce into one's mind. I suspect she has a marvellous power of reading the thoughts of those about her, and—" he stopped.

"Well!" said Lill, a little anxiously.

"She will be no friend to me," he replied in a lower voice.

Lill did not make any attempt to continue the conversation and Giuliani, hurt at her silence, said no more, but he kept his place by her side. Once Edward Tufton came to Lill, under pretence of asking her if she would have an ice. Though she declined it, Edward remained standing before her, endeavoring to engross all her attention, pretending perfect unconsciousness of Giuliani's being there.

When the moment of departure came, the two men each offered her an arm. Lill felt bound to accept Giuliani's; not for the fear of twenty Sir Mark Tuftons, would she have mortified him by showing a prefence for Edward.

The Italian it was, also, who put her cloak round her. Mrs. Townsend was flirting with Sir Mark, who naturally had no eyes but for her, when she chose to be agreeable. Young Tufton looked on as sulky as a bear.

CHAPTER XXVII.

Seeing is believing.

EDWARD TUFTON's sulkiness having outlasted his slumbers, Lill resolved to get out of his way and go over to Mrs. Townsend.

As she was leaving the breakfast-room, Edward called out, " Where are you going so early ?"

" I beg your pardon, I did not distinctly hear your question ;" she opened her large eyes on him and spoke in a peculiarly quiet tone.   He was in his right place at once ; he muttered some words she did not care to hear, rang the bell furiously, and asked for *Galignani's Messenger.*

Lill found Mrs. Townsend in her own room, lying on a sofa in a *peignoir*, her long fair hair escaping from the comb with which it had been hastily caught up.   On a table before her was something like a toy, a piece of wood in the shape of a heart, mounted on three tiny wheels ; in her hands a book with a yellow paper cover. As Lill entered, she pushed the book under the sofa pillow, and said, "Sit down by me, Lill, 1 have something serious to say to you."

Lill remembered Giuliani's words, and was sure that she was going to be cross-examined.

" I have been consulting Planchette about you," went on Mrs. Townsend.

" Who is Planchette ?" asked Lill, doing all she could to seem at her ease under the scrutiny of the little lady.

" There she is," said Mrs. Townsend, pointing to the apparent toy, " Seeing is believing." So saying, she drew towards her a blank sheet of folio paper, and upon it placed what she called Planchette : in the broadest end of the heart was a hole, in which was already fixed a black-lead pencil, with the point downwards.   Mrs. Townsend put her hand on the wood, exactly as she would have done on the keys of a piano-forte.

" Now, Planchette," she exclaimed, " let us see what you can do."

In a second or two Planchette wildly scoured across the paper, first one way, then another; Mrs. Townsend's hands obeying every capricious turn of its wheels. At last they came to a standstill.

"Now then, Lill, see what she has written; there's no trick in it, I assure you."

"I can see nothing but a set of unmeaning strokes."

"Give it to me, child."

Lill handed the paper to her friend.

"What is the meaning of this, Planchette?" cried Mrs. Townsend. "Why do you persist in writing 'river;' every time I have tried her this morning," continued she, quite gravely, "she has written the same word 'river.' Don't smile; it means a warning to you, for I told Planchette that it was for you I consulted her. Come, Planchette, dear Planchette, do be a little more clear," and Mrs. Townsend with great seriousness, put another sheet of paper beneath the wood.

"You don't mean to say you are in earnest," said Lill.

"Of course you won't believe me," answered Mrs. Townsend. "A truth is always condemned at first: Galileo said the world moved, and it was called a heresy. Well, you may believe I move Planchette; I can only reply, '*e pure si muove.*'" A bright red spot of excitement was on each of the speaker's cheeks.

"It was one of your favourite Italians" (this was a side thrust at Lill) "who gave me Planchette, and if I had always attended to Planchette's counsel, I should be wiser and better than I am. Many a beautiful letter of advice she has written me, alluding to events no one knew but myself; and prayers, ah! Lill, I could show you such sublime prayers she has written."

"My dear Mrs. Townsend! dear Honora!" exclaimed Lill, quite shocked.

"I believed as little as you do once, but as I said before, seeing is believing; and one day I was dining out and people were talking of spirit-rapping and table-turning; I laughed and said I would believe if the dinner-table rose up and slapped my hand. I held my hand high above the table; you do not think I would tell you a fib, Lill. I give you my word of honour, suddenly everything in the room seemed to wave before my eyes, and

the table, a great heavy dining-table, jumped up and
slapped my hand. It was the same evening I first saw
Planchette and found out I was a medium. Oh! the
comfort I have had in Planchette; she has been a friend
to me in my loneliness."

Lill began now seriously to fear that Mrs. Townsend
was mad.

"No, my dear girl," said she; "I am as sane as you.
Poor Lill! I can read your face easier than this warn-
ing of Planchette's, 'River! river!'" she repeated.
"Come, you put your hands on it with mine."

It was quite droll to see the two ladies sitting silent
and expectant with their hands on the wooden heart,
which, however coaxed by her devotee, remained stub-
bornly immovable.

"Take your hands off; she knows you are an unbe-
liever;" away ran Planchette freed from Lill's pressure.
"Ah! she has written 'Lilian', and put a great cross
after it."

"Lilian is my christian name," said Lill.

"There now, do you believe? I swear to you I did
not know you were called Lilian, though I must say I
have often wondered what your real name was."

Lill did not choose to contradict her friend, or even
to say that the word she declared was Lilian might have
served as well as any other in the dictionary.

"Lilian, and a cross, and river; I can't make it out,"
and Mrs. Townsend pushed away Planchette, except
that she means you are likely to be crossed in love."

"She ought, then, to have written 'willow' instead of
'river.'" said Lill, with a faint attempt at a laugh; "or,
perhaps, I am to drown myself as poor Ophelia did."

"Who can tell?" said Mrs. Townsend. "Have you
seen Pedagogus to-day—that ugly man whose eyes were
like burning-glasses last night? Ah! Lill! Lill! stop
in time; it's such arrant folly."

"What can make you suppose —" Lill began.

"I don't suppose," interrupted Mrs. Townsend. "Do
you think Pedagogus is the first man in love I have
seen, and you the first girl, half fascinated, half frightened. Do you know what's the great cause of wickedness in the world, Lill? Poverty! Do you know why

I am trying to bring myself to marry Sir Mark? Because I am poor! O my dear girl! shun poverty more than death."

Here Mrs. Townsend rang a little hand bell; it was a summons for Madlle. Athenais.

"Give me my drops quick; you may give me a hundred. I married for love." continued she, after having swallowed her dose. "With *your* habits it would be the same with you as with me: borrowing, borrowing, Lill, first from one man, then another. Impossible, you say, you should do such things. You know nothing about it. Your husband's intimates see your distress, and one or other helps you, and then one gets accustomed. There's a whole set of men I hate to meet. If Sir Mark would pay them Mr. Townsend's debts I would marry the old gentleman to-morrow. Oh! dear, and then the end of love. What years I passed with a drunken, furious man, about as like the one I married as Satan to the angel Gabriel. Lill! Lill! what a life mine has been! I was meant for better things: nothing saved from the wreck; and time is going so fast, so fast, and I shall *never* have known what happiness is."

Lill kissed her, though unable to sympathize much. At Lill's age one feels so strong to overcome, so sure of winning where others have failed.

"You don't know Mr. Giuliani," she said with some spirit; "he is a gentleman by birth, education, and profession. He was a soldier when quite a boy."

"An amateur soldier," said Mrs. Townsend, with a sneer.

"He will be a count when his uncle dies; and it is only because he loves his principles better than his life, that he is poor."

"Ah! yes—his principles; I have an idea of the sort of man: he would sacrifice you too, my dear, for his principles! I hate Italians. My sister, my beautiful Caroline, would have her own way. She married one of these Hectors, and you should see the wreck. She is younger than me by years; she looks like my mother; grey-haired, haggard, neglected. What does her fine Marco care about her. He does not drink, to be sure, but he leaves her for the pleasure of conspiracy. While she sits at home trembling for his life and liberty, mending her children's clothes by the light of a miserable brass lamp, he is contributing his thousands of francs for some mad plot or other. I wish you could see her, or read her letters; you would then learn what comes of marrying a man with principles. Better far marry Edward Tufton, manage him and live respectably in your own country, than go roaming the world with a man whose greatest recommendation is his beard; he'd do famously for a Chasseur."

If Giuliani truly was deficient in the prestige of beauty, his physiognomy was one nevertheless full of serenity and nobleness, significant that the soul reigned supreme over the body.

"I cannot sit quietly by and hear you talk so of a person I respect; one, too, whom I have the greatest *reason* to respect," said Lill, her eyes full of angry tears.

"It is all for your good I speak," replied Mrs. Townsend' "He may be a good Italian, a white fly; but you don't love him I tell you, or you would behave very differently: you like his love, but not himself. Every girl almost has a scrape of this kind, out of which her friends extricate her, and she's all the better for it afterwards: it steadies her for life: I wish to God some one had helped me."

Mrs. Townsend was not to be recognized in this mood for the little coquetish sylph who seemed as if she had been fed on sugar plums all her life. She caught a view of herself in the mirror opposite, and was struck with her own appearance.

"I shan't say any more to you, Lill; see what a fright talking sense to you has made me. For the last time, take care what you are about. Sir Mark would be glad to see you starve, if you married that Italian. He had the face of a tiger all dinner-time yesterday; and Edward Tufton frizzled up his fancy little moustache just like an angry cat."

CHAPTER XXVIII.

The Little Man and his Little Speech.

A GREAT surprise awaited Lill on her return home. Edward Tufton asked her, with a very serious look on his baby face, to go with him into the boudoir: into that little room in which were the birds, and the flowers, and the memory of the Italian lessons.

"What can you want there? It's my sanctum, and not for visitors," said Lill, unwilling to leave Mr. Edward's company there.

"Isn't it, though?" burst out the angry youth. "Didn't you have that—that foreign fellow there, day after day?"

"Edward! Paris air does not agree with you, I advise you to go back to England."

"Paris air be —"

"I don't allow anybody but my grandfather to make use of ugly words in my presence;" and the young lady turned disdainfully from her cousin.

"Don't be angry with me, Lill," said Edward, coming up to her with a piteous face.

"I am not inclined to be angry with you, if you would only be good natured and merry as you used to be," answered Lill.

"But I can't; how *can* I be merry when I am misera·ble?"

"Miserable! then, you naughty boy, you have got into debt."

"I think I have a right to be considered something more than a boy at nearly twenty-two," returned Edward, in a highly offended tone.

"Naughty man, if that pleases you better. Tell me what makes you miserable."

"Can't you guess, Lill?" and he came close to where she was standing, in the embrasure of one of the windows.

"Not a bit: how do you think I can guess men's scrapes? Good heavens! perhaps you are in love, or secretly married."

"It's not right to laugh at a fellow, and trample on

his heart as you do. I mayn't be worth *much*, but I *do* care for you, Lill, more than for anything in the world."

Lill was grave enough now; she turned white and red, and red and white twenty times in as many seconds before she exclaimed, as she did very distinctly,—

"Oh, nonsense!"

"It's not nonsense at all," resumed Edward; "I know now that I have been in love with you all my life; but I never found it out till last night at Mrs. Caledon's. I felt ready to kill that Bombastes Furioso, when he was talking so close into your ear, and you taking everything he offered to you, and nothing from me; it's too bad of you, Lill: I see by your eyes you are laughing at me; but because I can't make rhymes and talk humbug poetry, it's no reason why I shouldn't be able to love you dearly all the days of my life."

"I am not laughing nor inclined to laugh; I am very, very sorry you do care so much about me," said Lill, in a little sad tone.

"Then you have made up your mind not to have me," exclaimed Edward, tears in his blue eyes; "you won't, won't you, Lill?"

"No;" and she said it decidedly.

"It's all those cursed lessons—"

Lill stopped him.

"Edward, don't trouble yourself to find out any cause for a woman's refusal; it is not manly. I very well see what has been the case: that you have been asking questions you had no business to ask of Miss Crumpton; which is about as honorable as listening at a door."

"Very well, go on hitting as hard as you please; but I'll tell you what: you shall *not* lower yourself, and if ever that foreign scoundrel dares to offer you his arm again, or to come near you, I'll knock him down."

"I leave Mr. Giuliani to take care of himself," said Lill, trying hard not to show her passion, but it got the better of her. "As for you, I thoroughly despise you," and with her head very erect she left the room.

She went in search of Miss Crumpton.

"Please to tell me exactly what questions Edward Tufton has had the audacity to put to you about me, and what you said to him?" began Lill, in a voice whose vibrations told Crummie that her unwise confidences had brought forth a crisis.

"My dear, it was something Mrs. Caledon said which put Mr. Edward on the track."

"Track! what a nice word! track of what? of Mr. Giuliani?"

Here the chaperone's love and fear made her brave the lightning of Lill's eyes, the angry quivering of the delicate nostrils. "Oh! Lill, my dear child, do be advised; don't go any more to Lady Ponsonby's."

"And so you have been giving him an account of her visitors. I am surrounded by spies!" and away rushed Lill to her own room, locking and double-locking her door.

What was she to do? How was she to act? Every one about her warning her against Mr. Giuliani. Even Mrs. Townsend, who, if any one could be so, must be unprejudiced. If she could only undo what she had done! That she might do so she knew, for she was sure that her folly (she called it folly unconsciously) was unknown to any one but their two selves. She was without fear of *his* claiming aught of her unforced promise to him—unforced, yes! but his face, his tone of voice, had overcome her. His face, the face with which he had told her he loved her; his air, the day her horse's hoofs had covered him with dust, rose before her. She clasped her hands before her eyes to shut out the apparition, but it pertinaciously thrust itself between her eyes and fingers. She could never—no, never—have the courage to play him false; to inflict misery on so good a man, so fond of her. He had always been so unhappy, so unfortunate; she must bear the consequences of her own act. Lill said so to herself, but her mind still worked to find some outlet of escape. No one prays audibly to the devil for help—but he is cognizant of the slightest conceived wish for his aid. The serpent reminded Lill instantly of Edward Tufton's menace against Mr. Giuliani: she told herself that she was afraid to brave that silly boy; impossible, therefore, that she could venture that Saturday evening to Lady Ponsonby's. She dared not risk a collision between the two men.

Edward must go away after what had just occurred,

and then she would be free to act as she pleased. Lill
gave a great sigh of relief; she had gained some breathing time. She had not courage to write another note of
apology, she had done so for three Saturdays running;
it would be almost insulting : she would let it appear a
chance. In the meanwhile she could consider whether
it would be better or not to avow her situation to Lady
Ponsonby. Lill did not sound the depths of her own
sincerity, or she would have owned that she feared too
much what Lady Ponsonby's advice might be, ever to
ask it. After having advanced rashly she had neither
the courage to draw back penitently nor to choose
the martyr's palm.

CHAPTER XXIX.

Champs Elysées.

Now let us look into the attic room of the Rue de Berlin. Giuliani in spite of himself had been beguiled at Mrs. Caledon's into renewed hope of Lill's affection, by the touch of sensibility in her manner towards him, and most of all by her courage in accepting his arm in presence of Sir Mark. Giuliani dreamed and hoped again. As for her little failings he loved her enough to bear patiently with them. What right had he to expect perfection? God knows he was far from it himself, and how could he be constantly weighing her faults and virtues in a balance when she gave up for him what was of such value in her estimation? He would make life smoother for her than she expected. Once his wife, she should be won, and not constrained, to think less of the world; at any rate, his gratitude should not take the shape of teasing her into the adoption of his opinions on that matter; she had seen the last of his severity. He winced as he recollected her deprecating, subdued look whenever she imagined what she was saying might be disagreeable to him.

" I have all along thought too much of myself," he went on—"too much of my own ideas—been more selfish, poor child, than she can ever be ; requiring self-sacrifice from her and giving no example of it myself. Always '*I* think so, *I* despise this or that, *therefore* it is right that *you* should so think, and so despise.' And so beautiful, so elegant, so accomplished, yet she bore with me. God bless her! whatever happens."

It was in this strain of feeling that Giuliani went on the Saturday to Lady Ponsonby. Lill would be there he was sure ; she had missed many evenings. but never without sending an apology, and this Saturday he knew from Alicia that no note had come from Miss Tufton. This evening he would tell her that he was sure of his professorship ; he had not done so before, because he had allowed himself to be angry with her neglect. She had owned that she let others guide her too easily ; this would not be a great fault when she was in the guidance of a loving friend. Never had Giuliani been so little like himself as since he had met Lill the evening before. The vexatious restraint of the past week, his doubts of her sincerity removed, his spirits bounded higher than they had ever done. Yes, he hoped, besides, that evening to explain his situation to his good friends, the Ponsonbys ; he longed for their sympathy.

"What good news have you to give us?" asked Madlle. Arsenief as he passed her.

"I have heard none," said he, unconscious of the expectant happiness radiating from his whole face.

It was nine o'clock and Miss Tufton was not come, half-past nine, then ten ; Alicia's eyes turned as anxiously as Giuliani's to the clock on the mantlepiece ; her face changed as his did. His old indignation was rising again : if Miss Tufton did not know her own mind, he knew his. He would not be played with. He left the *salon.* Alicia followed him into the ante-room and laid her hand on his arm.

"Are you ill ? What are you going to do ?" she asked, anxiously.

He stared at her for a minute. "Yes, my head aches ; I must have air."

"Shall we see you again this evening?" She wished to detain him to say something soothing, and she could only utter commonplaces.

"No, the noise and the lights ; I must be alone, if you please."

Alicia had grown timid and distant with Giuliani, how timid and distant she was not conscious of till now ; she felt the impatient movement of his arm under her detaining hand, and lifted it quickly.

"Good-night," and he almost sprang away. He hurried on, giving himself no explanation of what he was intending to do, hurried into the Champs Elysées without lessening his aimless speed, until he reached the house in which Sir Mark Tufton had apartments. A few carriages were stationed near the door ; loud strains of music filled the air—dance music, so inspiriting that some working girls passing by with their lover workmen,

were swinging round in the joyous polka; astonishing
how well and gracefully these common French people
moved. A little knot of elders, furnished by the different
porters' rooms, and by the *cafés*, were nodding their
heads approvingly in time to the measure. The branches
of the newly leafed trees, illumined by the lamps midway
between their trunks, had a pale splendour like what
we fancy in fairy grottoes. The dancers, their poor dress
coloured by the fantastic light, the gay sound, made a
good picture of Arcadia, for lookers-on with hearts at
rest enough to let their fancy play. To Giuliani's ear
the spirited music was like the braying of discordant
trumpets, the merriment was bitterness, his eyes were
fixed on the open windows of the first floor. The *salon*
was light as day; he drew back to the edge of the pave-
ment, so as to have a good view of the interior. Couples
were whirling there also; a figure in flowing white muslin was clasped close by another in black broad cloth,
long fair curls were wafted by the quick movement to
mingle with protuberant whiskers. "Love, exclusive,
deep-rooted love," muttered the unhappy gazer. "Amusement, *that's* the real business of life—perhaps she's
right."

CHAPTER XXX.

What Happened during Forty-eight Hours.

On the Sunday morning after the Saturday evening's dance improvised by Mrs. Townsend, which had sent Giuliani home frantic with angry disappointment, and almost resolved never again to seek Lill, the restless Honora made her appearance just as Miss Crumpton and Lill were sallying forth to the Chapel Marbœuf.

"You must both come with me to the Rue Taitbout. Mons. Monod is going to preach there, and every one is going."

Now the aristocracy of England and the Church of England were Miss Crumpton's strong points. Her faith in the infallibility and superiority of both was beyond danger. Nevertheless, she dreaded to enter even a French Protestant chapel as much as she despised continental nobility. Lill had once coaxed her into the Madeleine, but as soon as the little bell previous to the sacrifice of the mass was rung, she had bounced up from her seat, exclaiming, "They are going to do it now," and had, to the great scandal of the congregation, forced her way out, dragging Lill after her.

Miss Crumpton attempted no more interference with Mrs. Townsend than she would have done with Sir Mark himself; so she quietly, though with a sore conscience, left the field to the enemy, and went away by herself to the Chapel Marbœuf.

Lill took her seat by Mrs. Townsend in the hackney coach that lady had come in; Sir Mark's observance of the Sabbath consisting in forbidding his carriage and horses to be used for church-going.

"There's not much crowd," observed Mrs. Townsend, as they went up the stairs to the room where the service was to be performed. "More like a concert-room than a church," she whispered, as they took their chairs. "That bit of blue above the pulpit, I suppose, is for the preacher to address as heaven;" then looking round as members of the congregation came dropping in, "Religion is not a great beautifier; how ugly every one is ! what noses !"

"Hush, pray !" said Lill, who did not at all share in her friend's want of veneration.

"Oh ! here comes the avant-courier," again exclaimed Honora; "what a girlish face he has; doesn't he look like a greengrocer dressed up ? he would make a pretty woman though."

This was *à propos* of a very young man who had entered the pulpit.

"Good heavens ! he is not Mons. Monod, surely," cried Mrs. Townsend, as the youth gave out a psalm.

A very austere lady who was seated next to the English lady here handed her a psalm-book, saying,—

"*Non, ce n'est pas Mons. Monod ; c'est mon fils.*"

Mrs. Townsend, with a grimace, accepted the book ; but proposed to Lill that they should make their escape. Lill would not listen to her, nor even look at her.

Mrs. Townsend put on a resigned air, saying,—

"Fancy a brat like that setting up to teach."

When the sermon-book was produced, she arranged her bracelets, unbuttoned and rebuttoned her gloves, turned over the psalms, and did all she could to forget that preaching was going on. At last, however, from want of anything else to do, she looked at the young preacher. His blue eyes were sparkling; on the thin cheeks, pale as marble when he had begun, now burned the bright red of earnest enthusiasm. The tenderness of the woman was stirred by the terrible delicacy of his appearance. Poor fellow ! speaking must be death for him. His voice was singularly clear and piercing; he was saying, as his words caught her attention,—

"With the first fear of sin comes the first dawn of the joy of its pardon. Fear of God, my dear brethren, is not a terror of danger. There are two kinds of fear— fear of danger to ourselves personally, and fear of offending God, because of the offence to His love. Our fear of giving offence to one we love is not the fear of risk to ourselves, is it ? My brethren, I appeal to your hearts —to my own—and the answer is, no ! it is fear of the pain we necessarily inflict by our offence. Many a timid soul exclaims, 'There *is* pardon; but not for those in certain cases. I knew the right, I erred, then returned to the right, and again forsook it.'"

"'That's a hit at me," here muttered Mrs. Townsend.

" Dear brothers and sisters, take courage ; remember David,—is he not called the man after God's heart, though sinning, doubtless, more deeply than the timid soul I may now be addressing? With the first fear of his sin came to him the dawn of the joy of its pardon. I entreat you all hold this in mind. If God were extreme to mark the iniquities of the best of us, who do you imagine could stand before Him? When we look back at the way we have left behind, we see it crossed by our culpabilities, our repentances, our backslidings, each of them standing up clearly along the path we have trod ; we shrink—do we not?—from the road that still remains for us to tread, we fear for the future. Let us suppose that the most toilsome, suffering journey lay before us, at the end of which would be some once dear friend whom we had betrayed and alienated, and that we might make sure of receiving his forgiveness and love again, if we would venture on that terrible journey to obtain them. Which of us would hesitate to undertake so much for a dear earthly friend? Which of us, whose heart drops blood for the offences given to those who are gone before us to the silent land, would draw back from any sacrifice, any trial, any restraint, to have the sting of remorse drawn from his heart? Would we not rouse ourselves from all languor of hopelessness, and, faint, worn, and sobbing, set out bravely on our hard, forlorn way? Do I blame you because an earthly love would excite you thus? No; God himself has shown us that human affection teaches us heavenly affection. The Magdalene's human love for her Saviour and pardoner led her to heavenly love. Up, then, poor prostrate soul, prepare for the steep rough road; reconciliation, pardon, await you in God's bosom. Crossed, perplexed, disappointed soul, there you will read aright the enigma of your destiny here—of that anguish which has crucified your heart. Be sure, O my dear brethren ! be sure, as I am, that, once you have climbed that height, all the consolation, all the joy you have sought and missed so long, you will find there."

That afternoon Mrs. Townsend did not call to take Lill a drive in the Bois de Boulogne, as she had done every Sunday before; nor did Monday morning bring any note of a programme of busy idleness for the day.

" What's the matter with you and Mrs. Townsend ?" inquired Sir Mark of Lill, with grim suspicion.

" Nothing," said Lill.

" What a true woman's answer ! a world of subterfuge hid in a word !" he went on. " I tell you I will know. She was denied to me yesterday afternoon, and in the evening also."

" I am not Mrs. Townsend's keeper," said Lill; " probably she was at church."

Sir Mark gaped at his granddaughter : " What had she to do there ?"

" Pray," said Lill, "as it would be well for us all to do "

"A new freak," exclaimed he. " I like your fine lady's religion, dancing in Sunday morning, and then to church for absolution."

" They stopped dancing last night, Sir Mark," said Miss Crumpton, " before midnight struck, I assure you."

" I am delighted to hear it, madam," returned he, with a mocking bow. "And Edward Tufton ; what the deuce has come to him, that he says he must be off to England to-day ?"

Sir Mark stopped his walk up and down the room, and stared at Lill.

She said : " I suppose we are all going away soon ?"

Her heart beat fast while waiting for the answer.

" I thought you wanted to stay in Paris, Miss Tufton."

" *I* wanted !" repeated Lill, with some trepidation.

" *I* wanted," mimicked Sir Mark. " I wish to God the wind would shift as well as your mind !"

" Oh, dear me, Sir Mark, I hope you don't feel your neuralgia," put in Miss Crumpton.

" Yes, madam, I do feel my foot — I always do feel it in this sort of weather. I am not harder than wood, and I believe I am right in saying that it's the weather that made that table crack just now."

Lill rejoiced in this change of the conversation, though

she felt sure Edward had dropped some deleterious hints in Sir Mark's ear.

"Go and see after Mrs. Townsend, Miss Tufton," said Sir Mark with a grimace of pain. "Take the carriage, for I want Miss Crumpton to rub my foot, and mind you come back straight without going elsewhere."

Mrs. Townsend was not at home. Madlle. Athenais said madame had gone out, she thought by appointment. Lill was sorry. She had grown accustomed to Honora's companionship; it was a useful excuse, and helped to prevent her from thinking. Lill was far from imagining that the Saturday evening's polka and the Sunday morning's church were fixing her fate for her.

Sir Mark kept his whole household that day in a ferment. It was on these occasions that Miss Crumpton honourably emerged from obscurity, taking the foremost place of fatigue and danger, and astonishing the agitated French domestics, by her obstinate complacency under fire.

To be sure, while she only rubbed and moaned, he only snarled and growled; but when she ventured on any initiative, his roar was really terrific. It was droll to hear her answer his savage manifestations by, "Poor Sir Mark! is the pain so bad?"

In the evening Mrs. Townsend made her appearance. Sir Mark sent to beg her to come into his private room. He hid his wrapped-up foot under a fold of his dressing-gown, receiving her with a cheerfulness that made Miss Crumpton, with ineffable *naïveté*, exclaim,—

"Well, Sir Mark! you are a wonderful man for hiding pain! Mrs. Townsend, you have no idea how dreadful his poor foot has been."

Sir Mark's upper lip rose, showing his teeth; he was as like a vicious terrier as possible.

"What's come to you?" he said, when Mrs. Townsend sat down quietly, without the least approach to any joke "You have made yourself look like a Quakeress."

"Sir Mark, I have had other things to think of to-day than dress."

"The deuce you have! money to pay for it, perhaps?"

A faint pink coloured Mrs. Townsend's pale cheeks; she put a visible constraint on herself as she answered,—

"What would have been the consequence, Sir Mark, if I had married you three months ago when you were so urgent?"

"I should have been minus some 200*l.*,'" returned he, unconsciously unbuttoning his coat.

Mrs. Townsend's little puritanical air gave way under this provocation; she burst into one of her merriest laughs.

"Don't be afraid, I am not going to borrow even the fourth of the sum you would have had to pay for Lady Tufton; my question was meant as a consolation. You would rather part with me than your money, wouldn't you, Sir Mark?" she added in her coaxing way.

"By Jove!" he said, excitedly, "you are a perfect Cleopatra."

"I shan't add Antony to your name," quoth she, rising: "you wouldn't lose the world for a woman, I am sure."

"I don't know what you might not make me do, if you chose," said Sir Mark, holding out his hand towards her.

"You are very harsh to Lill," said Mrs. Townsend.

"She is so defiant, yet she is not aboveboard as you are; your truth is what I like in you."

"Thanks—I thought you liked everything about me."

"And so I do—I do," said the delighted old man, trying to take her hand.

"Promise that you'll grant my request, and I'll let you kiss my bluest vein. Cleopatra said that; you know my authority—Shakspeare."

"Well, what is it?" asked Sir Mark, rather peevishly.

"Afraid of his purse," pretended to whisper Mrs. Townsend to Miss Crumpton; then to Sir Mark: "Repeat after me these words: 'I promise faithfully upon my solemn word of honour to behave with decent temper to my pretty granddaughter in all cases, and *never* to turn her out of doors without a dowry, whether I, Sir Mark, marry without her consent, or she marries without mine, in faith of which I kiss the Bible and Mrs. Townsend's hands;' I will have it so," she continued, as she drew back from the small Bible she suddenly presented to him, adding,—

"Kiss both or none."

Sir Mark yielded, glueing his withered lips to the delicate hand.

"There, that will do," she said, drawing it back. "You are a witness, Miss Crumpton; now good-bye, and good luck to you all."

"What are you going away so soon for?" asked Sir Mark; "can't you stay? You magnetize my pain, you little enchantress."

"Sorry I can't oblige you," she said, nonchalantly; "duty calls me away."

"Nonsense! come, ask me for something more — something for yourself."

She shook her head.

"Pleasant dreams, old friend — dreams of the sums you have saved by not having me for a wife."

"You shall have the horses you set your heart upon," he began; he stopped, for she was gone.

Sir Mark mused a little, then he bid Miss Crumpton see if Mrs. Townsend was with Miss Tufton.

"Tell her I want to say only two words to her. I must see her again, do you hear?"

Mrs. Townsend had left the house.

"Send after her," said Sir Mark, angrily. "Go yourself, Miss Crumpton"

In a quarter of an hour, the chaperone returned. Mrs. Townsend was not at home. The annoyance helped to bring back a paroxysm of pain. Half a dozen times messages were sent to Rue de Cirque—always the same reply: Mrs. Townsend was not at home. Sir Mark would not allow Edward Tufton to leave for England. No one in Sir Mark's house had much rest that night.

CHAPTER XXXI.

Forever—Never.

BEFORE half-past nine o'clock the next morning Lill went with Ruth to the Rue de Cirque. No Mrs. Townsend; but a letter for Sir Mark, which Madlle. Athenais delivered with great volubility, praising herself for having followed Mrs. Townsend's instructions faithfully. "Madame had desired that no one should know of her departure till the next day, and Madlle. Athenais has been hard-hearted to every anxious inquiry. Madame had left plenty of money for her apartment and for Madlle. Athenais, who would seize the occasion to take a trip to see her parents at Orleans."

"Is Mrs. Townsend gone to England?" asked Lill, who had at first been struck dumb with astonishment.

"I could not say, mademoiselle; madame gave me no hint."

"Her luggage—surely you saw the directions?"

"Ha! that makes me think," said the *femme de chambre;* "madame has written mademoiselle's name on various small articles."

Madlle. Athenais *est de toute fidélité.*

Mademoiselle Tufton would be so good as to give her an acknowledgment that she had received these articles. The letter to Sir Mark would, without any doubt, explain Madame Townsend's movements; but if not, Madlle. Athenais would be tempted to think that Madame Townsend was still in Paris; she took away her trunks in *fiacre;* but Madlle. Athenais had only heard madame tell the *cocher* to drive to the Arc de l'Etoile; but that, as Madlle. Tufton could understand, was merely throwing dust into the listener's eyes.

At this stage of the conversation madame la propriétaire came down in her petticoat and camisole, her hair not yet dressed, looking ten years older in her morning than she did in her evening costume.

"Cette chère dame! ah! j'ai grande peur," and here came a significant tap on the propriétaire's forehead

"Quelque coup de tête, soyez sure, mademoiselle ; et la voiture et les jolis ponies.   Qu'est-ce qu'on en fera ?"

Miss Tufton supposed there were directions in the letter she held in her hand, addressed to Sir Mark ; "she would see madame la propriétaire again after having spoken to Sir Mark."

The letter consisted of half a dozen lines,—

"DEAR SIR MARK,

"It will be of no use your trying to find me, as I don't intend to marry you.   I make you a present of my carriage and ponies, and I give Lill Tufton all the baubles you lavished on me.   I am going where the adorning is not to be that of plaiting the hair and of wearing of gold. Let Lill have the trinkets in peace.   Don't forget your promise as to her.   Take example by me, and think of the next world before it is too late.

"HONORA TOWNSEND."

Sir Mark's face, as he read it, took the ashy hue it had had on his arrival from England with Mrs. Townsend.   Lill thought, but she might be mistaken, that there was a tear in each of Sir Mark's eyes as he threw down the letter on the table.

"May I read it, Sir Mark !" asked Lill.

"No ;" and he put it into his pocket.

He would wish Lill and every one around him to believe that there was still some link between him and Mrs. Townsend—that all was not broken off.

"We must start for England directly, Miss Tufton. Can you be ready this afternoon ?"

"Gracious me !" ejaculated Miss Crumpton ; "and your pain, Sir Mark."

"I am in no pain, Miss Crumpton."

"But Sir Mark, it's a physical impossibility to be ready to-day—not if I were to be on my knees before trunks from this time till sunset."

"No later than the midday train to-morrow," said Sir Mark, " if you have to leave all your frippery behind. Do you hear, Miss Tufton? to-morrow at midday—my business won't wait."

Sir Mark said his business wouldn't wait to every individual he came across.   His anxiety to hide the wound he had received gave him courage to control all outbreak of passion.

"I have some visits I ought to pay before going away," said Lill.

"Do what you like; but remember, ready or not, I go to-morrow."

Lill had heard and understood all her grandfather was saying, but her brain was busy with her own situation. She must see Giuliani; she must explain the present crisis to him. How was she to manage? No chance of finding him at his own lodgings in the forenoon, and even if he were at home, what would he think of her going to him alone? And dared she ask him to come and see her? Suppose Sir Mark should find him, or even Edward Tufton? well, then she would tell the truth and take the consequences. First of all, however, she would see Lady Ponsonby: she was determined now to ask that dear old lady to advise and guide her; how she wished she had done so sooner; but who could ever have dreamed of such a catastrophe. Where could Mrs. Townsend be? Was she in England? Did Sir Mark know? Lill doubted it, but she had no time for conjectures as to any one's affairs but her own.

She drove to Mrs. Caledon's and paid a hasty visit there, long enough, however, to hear that Giuliani had been named to a professorship somewhere in the south of France; Mrs. Caledon could not remember the town.

In a fever of excitement Lill then went to Lady Ponsonby's. The concierge told her that Miledi was out of Paris; she was gone to Marseilles to meet her son just returned from the Indies. Lill's heart sank—fate was against her. "Go to the Rue de Berlin," she said, brave from excess of fear.

"Mr. Giuliani was not at home." She wrote on one of her visiting cards that she begged him to call next morning on her as early as eight, before eight if he could, she was setting off for England the next day.

Sir Mark went through all the business preparations consequent on this rapid move with peculiar quiet. He did not swear once, that either Lill or Miss Crumpton heard. They saw little of him, however, Edward Tufton being there to execute his orders.

Lill sat in a sort of forlorn way, watching Ruth pack her trunks. She had not energy enough even to open the boxes brought to her by Madlle. Athenais.

When bedtime came, she called Miss Crumpton in her room.

Crummie, you must help me this once; I will never ask you again to do anything of the kind : this once you must; if you don't I am so thoroughly miserable I shall commit some folly; promise me, Crummie."

"Ah! well, my dear, if it must be so."

"I *must* see Mr. Giuliani before I go; I have asked him to come to-morrow morning at eight. I am sure he'll come. Crummie, you must stay in the drawing-room, while I speak to him in the little room. If you hear any one coming, call to us; will you, Crummie? I *must* and will see him, whether you agree or not. You may bring a downright misfortune on me if you won't help me."

Crummie, of course, promised.

Lill gave Ruth the strictest orders to call her at six; and left her blinds open that the light might rouse her. There seemed at first every chance of her being already awake at six o'clock, for she heard all the small hours of the night strike and was awake at five, but she fell into a heavy feverish slumber just before six. She started up, however, at Ruth's summons, her face like wax, except for the dark purple circle round her eyes.

"Ruth," she said, "I expect Mr. Giuliani to call this morning—my Italian master, you remember." Lill was trying to impose upon her maid. "Show him into the back drawing-room. I want you to watch for him, that there may be no mistake about his coming for Sir Mark or Mr. Tufton. I don't want to disturb Sir Mark."

Lill fetched Miss Crumpton downstairs; not a word passed between them. As eight o'clock struck, Lill heard the door of the apartment open quietly. Ruth understood her business. At that instant, Lill wished she had not asked Mr. Giuliani to come. What should she say to him? She ran into the little room with the feeling of one seeking escape from an avenger. She knew he was in the room with her, but she could not look up or speak.

He spoke to her in his usual voice; she did not hear

the words, but started, saying, "Hush! don't speak so loud."

"Why are you so agitated, Miss Tufton? Of what are you afraid?"

Then she raised her eyes to his face. He was perfectly composed; more, he had a sort of smile on his lips. Something in his look and bearing stung her to the quick.

"Won't you sit down?" she said mechanically.

"Thank you, no; you must have a great deal to arrange for your departure; very unexpected, I believe."

"Quite," she answered. "Sir Mark only said we were to go yesterday morning. I let you know as soon almost as I knew myself."

He did not reply.

"Mrs. Townsend is the cause of this move," she went on; "I did mean—I did not mean."

Why would he not speak? She was ruffled; it was not fair of him; he ought to make allowances for her, so she took the offensive.

"Mrs. Caledon told me yesterday you were going to leave Paris. Did you mean to go without telling me?"

"Probably."

"You are very unkind, Mr. Giuliani. I don't think I deserve that."

"Oh! Miss Tufton."

"Why do you call me Miss Tufton?" she flashed out.

"Do you wish me to call you *Perla?*" and he half smiled.

It was a curious battle, in which Lill would be sure to wound herself more deeply.

"You play with my feelings; you make me angry on purpose."

"God forbid! I wish, on the contrary, to make you understand yourself."

"My dear," here called in Miss Crumpton. Ruth had put her head anxiously into the drawing-room.

"Miss Crumpton warns you—us," said Giuliani, "that it is useless to prolong this scene. Miss Tufton, farewell! I will remember you in my prayers always, as Perla." He clasped her hand for an instant, and was hastening from the room, but she ran after him.

Mr. Giuliani, Mr. Giuliani, oh! don't go so; will you write to me?"

"I will answer any letter you address to me."

"You are not angry with me," and her pale lips worked with the effort not to cry.

"No, no, not angry," he said, much as he might have spoken to a child. "You could not help what you have done."

She clung to his arm. "I cannot bear to see you go away; oh! pray, if I only knew what was best."

He held her in his arms one instant, the next he placed her in those of Miss Crumptom, and Lill heard the door close.

"Don't let me scream, Crummie," she said—"don't," and she hid her face in her old friend's bosom.

CHAPTER XXXII.

The Sacred Hour of Four.

WHILE Lill, with a jarred heart and head, was with Sir Mark and his party on the road to Dover *viâ* Calais, Lady Ponsonby and Alicia were journeying from Marseilles to Paris, with their interesting invalid, Sir Frederick Ponsonby.

Sir Frederick is that eldest son of Lady Ponsonby already mentioned in the last chapter. He is come back to Europe on sick leave, and looks certainly a little languid, just sufficiently so to alarm his tender mother. But, in fact, the journey home has almost set to rights whatever had been the matter with his health.

Lady Ponsonby had not recognized in the tall, handsome, moustached man, the slender stripling of sixteen who had left her ten years ago. She was now obliged to look up to him, and she did so with a mother's pride in his strength and comeliness.

An intellectual face, or one expressive of frankness and benevolence, is all that a man need have of beauty, to insure him his portion of that peculiar affection which gives savour to life. Besides having this intelligent face, with the good expression, Sir Frederick Ponsonby had uncommonly regular features: fine dark gray eyes, a straight nose, a perfectly well shaped mouth, glossy chestnut hair; in a word, that sort of head which our neighbours over the water define as a *tête de Christ*.

Lady Ponsonby was full of admiration for this unknown son. She sat opposite to him in the railway carriage, and when he shortly fell asleep, as gentlemen occasionally do on railways, she watched him with exactly the same adoration in her eyes, as had been there when she kept vigil by his cradle some six-and-twenty years ago. She had had many fears for him during the last half-score of years — fears of battles and murder, of cholera and cobra capellos, of debts and duns, and the sundry other dangers, which, as every reflecting mother knows, exist for her son. But as she studies her Frederick's brow, almost as smooth as when he left her — when she traces no network of lines round his eyes, sees no dragging down of the corners of the mouth — she feels assured he has come out safely from the temptations of that wilderness called the world.

Lady Ponsonby arrives in Paris a happy woman and a proud mother. Her friends are enthusiastic about Sir Frederick; they are more attentive in calling than ever; even Madame de Rochepont de Rivière finds the young baronet endurable. "He was a man," she declared, "for whom a woman might be excusable in having a heartache. I maintain," she added, "that the English are the handsomest nation in the world," and her contemptuous glance at Giuliani gave point to the assertion.

Certainly Giuliani was not at that time a specimen of his country, that would do to set up as a rival to Sir Frederick. The Italian was thinner than ever, his face more rugged with deep lines, his magnificent eyes (they, at least could stand a comparison with the young Englishman's) were sunken and without lustre. His whole person revealed the indescribable marks made by the hand of sorrow. He appeared what he was, the incarnation of disappointment; Sir Frederick, that of success. The one man had been gathering thorns all his life; the other, figs. The one had seen his country in deadly throes of travail for liberty, when she had had no strength for the birth; the other had always known his motherland mistress of herself, triumphant in every quarter.

A blighted oak is a desirable object on canvass, or in a word-picture; a good subject to moralize or poetize on, but we all prefer to have fine flourishing trees in our avenues. Giuliani, was as much out of his place in Parisian society as a lightning-blasted oak in a parterre. He acknowledged this himself, by the disposition he showed to retreat from its musk-perfumed atmosphere, and when forced into it, felt no resentment towards those who made him the target of their *bonmots*.

He felt the discrepancy that existed between him and his admirable friend's beau-ideal of a son. They had met with the cordiality of old acquaintances; they never got beyond this outward show.

———

When Sir Frederick had been in Paris, let us say a month, his mother and sister remarked a certain method in his disposal of his day. Regularity had not been the distinguishing trait of his life on his first arriving in Paris. For the five years previous, a lucrative staff appointment had banished him to an outpost somewhere in the mountains of Scinde. Well, Paris was a great change; and Sir Frederick had not enough of eyes or ears for all he desired to see or hear.

At the end of four weeks, he subsided suddenly into a methodical person; his day was parcelled out minutely. He seemed to have put himself to school again; a professor of the French language attended to enable him to rub up his French, which had rusted considerably during the ten years in India. He had lessons of singing, attended some popular lectures, but invariably at the hour of four in the afternoon he went out, either on horseback or on foot, dressed in a manner that denoted a special wish to do his handsome person justice. On his return, there was always some costly flower in his button-hole which was afterwards transferred to a particularly elegant vase, on his writing-table; and which had not been placed there by either his mother or sister. Many other small articles of bijouterie, in exquisite taste, rather than costly, came to keep the pretty vase company.

Occasionally Lady Ponsonby met her son's valet with a letter in his hand, not for the post; and I am sorry to add, that her ladyship's *bonne* made an opportunity to inform madame, that a commissionnaire brought a *billet pour monsieur* every morning before monsieur was out of bed.

Lady Ponsonby saw, heard, and was silent. She had a great respect for every one's personality. She was rewarded by her son's never wishing to exchange her roof for a separate apartment of his own.

Sir Frederick was in love; nothing surprising in that at seven-and-twenty; but who with?

That at present was what he kept to himself.

At last, one day in July, Sir Frederick did not go out at four o'clock, but at that hitherto sacred hour walked into his mother's *salon*, languid and listless, like a fish

out of water, or rather, perhaps, like a man in the firs,
days after retiring from business. He had *Galignani's
Messenger* in his hand.

Giuliani was with the ladies, and Sir Frederick perceived at once that, whatever might have been the subject of their conversation, they changed it as soon as he
appeared. This of itself did not please him — it would
not have been easy to please him at that moment — so
he retired unsociably into the depths of an arm-chair,
and seemed engrossed by his newspaper. Lady Ponsonby made one or two efforts to draw him into conversation; she was very sensitive as to his showing any
slight to the Italian; but Frederick was determinedly
sulky. Suddenly, however, he asked, —

"Haven't I heard some of you mention Miss Tufton?
no, it was Valentine told me she and her grandfather
had been in Paris."

There was a little awkward silence in the room, such
as always occurs when some one mentions a subject in
ignorance of how interesting it is to one of those present.

Lady Ponsonby said,—

"What makes you think of the Tuftons at this moment?"

"Miss Tufton's name is here," he replied, tapping a
column of *Galignani*; "at the head of some preposterous description of the dress she went to court in; such
humbug, filling a newspaper with milliner's jargon. I
am thinking, mother, of running over to England to
take a look at the old Priory and Monk's Capel farm,
and as these Tuftons' will be my nearest neighbours, I
wanted to know how you liked them."

"Sir Mark is a character," said Lady Ponsonby.

"Which means he is disagreeable; and the young
lady?"

"A pretty creature."

Here Mr. Giuliani took his leave. Another pause.

"I suppose there are some habitable rooms in the
Priory?" went on Sir Frederick.

"Are you really off in such a hurry, Fred?" asked
Alicia.

"Oh, yes! Paris is insufferable in this weather.
Why shouldn't you both go over with me, eh, mother?'

"Not at this flash-of-lightning speed, my dear boy. You forget I am an old woman, accustomed to do as I like. Now, that is, perhaps, the only thing I shouldn't be able to do in England."

"My dear mother, what do you do here that you couldn't do in England?" Sir Frederick's voice showed disturbance.

"Fred, in our dear native land, all is convention, constraint, or fiction; everything done by rule; there's a particular way of eating, drinking, and speaking. Fancy your distress if I blundered in the way I held my knife, or ate my soup, or pronounced some word, or, worse still, made use of some word banished from genteel society. Alicia, too, would get into all sorts of scrapes, which you would have to take the responsibility of. There are a hundred other difficulties I could never conquer now; I am too old to learn. The servants!— no, my dear, I should be frightened to death at an English dinner-party; you know I have not been to one for twenty years, and your sister *never*."

"All which means, mother, that you have given up your own country."

"My good Fred, I am grown a citizen of the world. I do not believe any nation has a monopoly of goodness; there are probably as many righteous people on this side of the Channel as on the other. I stay here simply because fate transplanted me long ago, and I have taken root in the soil of France; old trees don't bear moving well, Fred. I would try it, however, for your sake, if I saw that you needed me; but you do not just now, when you have no house to put me in; and London I protest against. The Thames would kill me in a week."

"Oh, mother, mother! and you dare to say that with such nosegays of streets as you have here."

"Habit, my dear, has long since appeased my sensitiveness with regard to these; it is the being called on to accustom myself to a new atmosphere which I deprecate."

The day before Sir Frederick started for England Lady Ponsonby paid a visit to Mr. Giuliani in his attic.

"I have come to ask you," she said, "whether it might not be as well to take Sir Frederick into our confidence

—to explain to him how Miss Tufton is situated with regard to you."

Giuliani's olive complexion turned a shade darker as he listened to this speech. He took time before he gave his answer, and then it was given with deliberation and decision.

"No; certainly not. In fact, it is Miss Tufton's secret, not mine; besides, I am not the man to put forward claims, so as to isolate a girl, to hem her within a magic circle, out of which she cannot escape but into my arms, or by a painful exposure. My dear friend, let her alone, and look upon me as one recovering from a fit of insanity. I have swallowed one remedy to-day. I bought the *Galignani* which has her name in it. How reasonable it is to expect that the young lady figuring at the proudest court in Europe, on an equality with the proudest aristocracy in the world, could accept of this garret, or one similar to it, for her home! To suppose that Miss Tufton would consider the world well lost for love of me is simply absurd."

Lady Ponsonby sighed, but had no argument to oppose to what Giuliani said.

"I do not affirm, however," he added, "that were I still in the position in which I was born, that I would not have struggled against all rivals for her love. I do not affirm even now, that did my conscience allow me to pursue her, I might not make her love me. She is not entirely worldly, and all Englishwomen, to their praise be it said, believe in love, and desire to marry and *be* married for love; so that if she knew how I loved her.—Well, in all probability she will never be enlightened on that subject."

Lady Ponsonby sighed again, and said,—

"To be candid with you, Giuliani, I fear the impression she may make on my son, unless he is forewarned."

"He is forearmed against her, dear lady, and even were this not the case, I say again, let her alone—I must be all or nothing."

"Forearmed!" repeated Lady Ponsonby, in an eager voice.

She was not too perfect to feel very lively curiosity and particularly in this instance.

Giuliani bowed with a look that said plainly enough, " You will hear no more from me."

The intelligent, sympathizing friend left the attic, wondering at and admiring Giuliani's strength of character, while his heart, poor fellow, was scorching in the furnace of jealousy she had lighted; while he was ready to throw up his arms and cry out: " My trial is beyond my strength !" There was additional pain also, in the certainty that this faithful friend was unconscious of his great burden of sorrow. So it must always be. It is among the hard tasks life gives us to learn, that of the fruitlessness of the hunt we all undertake for the one who will sympathize with, and understand, and rightly judge us. It is not only death, which every one of us must meet alone, but every temptation, every agony, that assails us throughout our mortal career. If we require an example of the insufficiency of the best of earthly friends in our great needs, let us read the twenty-seventh chapter of St. Matthew. We shall find there, also, in what spirit we are to bear the loneliness, the desertion, the anguish, which perchance we reap unde-servedly.

17*

CHAPTER XXXIII

Country Neighbours.

The method of English life, laughingly caricatured by Lady Ponsonby was telling on Lill. After a month in London she was inclined to believe she had dropped down in Paris into a sphere immeasurably removed from that in which she lived in England: beginning to shrink from the recollection of many things she had done in Paris. Had she been in London, they could never have occurred; she had been moonstruck, possessed. She had ruined her life. There was an unfortunate similarity in this judgment on herself to that which Giuliani passed on himself; with this difference, that the result she feared as ruin would have been bliss to him, and *vice versâ.*

Lill certainly had never been so patriotic as since her return from the Continent. She allowed that she had not known before how beautiful her native land was. She could scarcely restrain a cry of delight when she first caught sight of Wavering, as they were driving from the station to the hall. The sun was setting, its long, slanting rays drawing a broad line of gold along the tops of the hedges; the summits of the wavy uplands beyond, sheets of brightness; the woods nestling within their folds of deep purple; the village houses clustered round the gray-walled church like a brood of chickens round a mother hen. Lill was completely captivated by the spell of familiar scenes.

"England seems to agree with you better than France, Miss Tufton," said Sir Mark, in the course of the evening. "You studied too hard, perhaps, in Paris."

Sly shots of this kind never failed to provoke Lill. To her, as to most impulsive people, suspense on any subject was intolerable. Better be killed at once than be always fearing death; so she replied,—

"It is very good of you, Sir Mark, to find so praiseworthy a motive for the dulness you seem to have remarked in me, but you are mistaken as to the cause.

I never was so idle in my life as during the last month of our stay in Paris."

"You had better not irritate me, Miss Tufton," was all he said.

"How much or how little do you think he knows?" asked Lill of Miss Crumpton, the first time they were alone.

The chaperone's answer was not consolatory.

"I never knew so cunning a man; he says things quite at hazard, just to throw people off their guard."

Lill thought the tone of voice in which this speech was made was very like that of one who had suffered from Sir Mark's shrewdness. She had her own ideas of the quarter from whence Sir Mark might have gleaned information, but she spared the old lady.

"I must write to Paris, Crummie," went on Lill; "I have not written a line since the note to say we had arrived." No answer from Miss Crumpton. "And then, Crummie, you will be so kind—will you not?—as to take my letter to the post-office at Wavering yourself. I cannot let the servants see the direction. Ruth would know the name, if none of the others did." Still ·a silence on Miss Crumpton's part. "Yes, Crummie; and please. *you* must write the address; if Mrs. Pybus remarks it, she will fancy you are writing to some one on business, and she might not think that, if she saw my hand. Dear Crummie, I am in the scrape, and you must help me."

"Oh, my dear girl, if you would be advised!"

Lill put her hands to her ears.

"Crummie, it's of no use," and she ran out of the room.

Certainly half-an-hour had not elapsed before the young lady reappeared with a letter in her hand.

"Done already!" exclaimed Miss Crumpton.

"Yes, and now, Crummie, direct it."

Miss Crumpton yielded—she always yielded—and wrote the address.

"Now, Crummie, you go at once, and I will come in the pony chaise, and meet you at the White Gate; and we'll go and call on the Pantons, to gratify you with a sight of your model of perfection. Miss Althemiah. Now go, dear Crummie, and don't let Sir Mark catch you."

"Poor Crummie!" went on Lill to herself, as she stood at the window watching Miss Crumpton stealing through the shrubbery, "you have cleverly adopted the stage walk of a traitor. Who that sees you could doubt you were bent on some unholy errand."

The Wavering post-office was at the village grocery. Every one knows what it is like: it stands high above the road, has a low white gate; then three steps of brick, and a yard of steep pathway between box borders; little plots, in which are heartsease, and a red geranium or two, some tall larkspurs, and a great red dahlia, dark red roses clustering up to the very roof, as they never will cluster on a gentleman's house; a latticed window on either side of the door, above which is a white board, with "Kezia Pybus licensed dealer in tea, tobacco, and coffee."

As Miss Crumpton came in sight of the little gate a tall gentleman was in the act of mounting a fine horse. Who could it be? Miss Crumpton has no idea. A stranger. She hurries a little, but before she is near enough to have a good view of his face, he throws a small silver coin to Kezia's youngest boy, who has been holding his horse, and rides away sitting in his saddle in that lounging way which makes uninitiated spectators wonder that the rider remains a rider two seconds. Miss Crumpton had intended to drop Lill's letter into the box, with a hope it might pass unheeded, but the sight of the careless horseman made her alter her mind. She opened Mrs. Pybus' door, which, as all similar doors do, rang out a loud peal.

"Your servant, Miss Crumpton," said Kezia. "How are you, miss, to-day?"

Wavering folks would have thought it bad manners to have said "ma'am" to a lady who was not married.

"Quite well, thank you, Mrs. Pybus," and as Miss Crumpton laid down her letter on the counter, she saw another lying there with "France" also on the counter. "And Miss Tufton, miss—is she pretty well? We haven't seen her since she came home; no, we haven't. Sure then, and yours is a furrin letter too. Strange times for us, miss. France seems a mighty deal nearer to us than it used to be in my young days. Yes, it do indeed."

"I did not make out who it was on horseback at your gate," said Miss Crumpton.

"Lawkus!" returned Kezia, "and don't you know, miss? That's Sir Frederick Ponsonby; he's been down at Monk's Capel Priory. Let me see, how long be Sir Frederick here, Charlotte?" turning to her sonsy daughter; "what with the letters, and the stamps, and the groceries, and Pybus' church duties, really my head ain't what it used to be—no, it ain't."

"Sir Frederick been well nigh on to a month here," put in Charlotte.

"Dear me!" ejaculated Miss Crumpton. "is he living at Monk's Capel, all alone in that mouldy barn of a place?"

"Yes, he be, Miss Crumpton: half of the windows be out; but he's a living in them two big rooms up-stairs, which Fordham done up last year in case he could let the shoot. I hear Sir Frederick a taken the shoot hisself, and bought Bill Fordham's black hunter; leastways, that's what I heard 'em say, Miss Crumpton."

Miss Crumpton, probably by accident, managed to see, without her spectacles, that the name in the direction of Sir Frederick's letter was not Ponsonby.

Lill drove—as she did everything else—impetuously; that pony-chaise, with the obstinate little Shetland pony, was among the trials of the chaperone's life. The news obtained from Mrs. Pybus was, therefore, related in a painfully disjointed manner; the rattle down the last hill fairly shook out of Miss Crumpton's head the best point of her story—the letter to some Madlle. Mathilde or Mélanie something.

"We shall have every particular here," said Lill, jumping out of the chaise to open a gate. "Now, Crummie, drive up in style."

Vale House was an unpretending, long, low building of red brick, bleached by years and storms to a charming warm gray. The drive to the door was not an atrocious circle round a centre plot of shrubs; no, it was broad and straight, between two sloping banks, covered with fuchsias and red geraniums, widening as it approached the porch. The drawing-room and dining-room windows looked out on a fine lawn, terminated by a grassy bank, on which at that moment a magnificent peacock was parading. As soon as the vain bird saw the ladies, he came strutting forward, his spread tail catching the wind; he almost tumbled under the nose of the mischievous pony.

The instant the hall door opened, you knew you were in a sailor's house. A couple of oil paintings decorated the walls. The first showed a blue sky overhead, and on the blue sea, under the soft azure, a schooner and a brig, the distance between them bridged over by gracefully curling smoke; this was a representation of the capture of the slave brig *Santa Maria* by H. M. schooner *Marmot* on the Great Bahama Bank in the year 18—. The second picture portrayed a night battle, a savage scene of the capture of the two-topsail slave schooner *Dulcinea*, by H. M. shooner *Scapegrace*, after a chase of twenty-four hours, and an action of one hour and twenty minutes within pistol-shot. The slaver's sails were riddled and falling down, and so was the mast, into an inky sea; so pitch black was the sky, that it was only by the grace of the moon peeping out of one corner, that you could see the *Scapegrace's* victory.

These two pictures proved the honourable way in which Admiral Panton, a man without a scrap of interest or a drop of blue blood in his veins, had come to be an admiral before he reached his sixtieth birthday; a fact that had occurred five years before Miss Tufton's pony chaise stopped at the porch of Vale House. They were actions fought at long odds, but no one will care to hear about it now, when such descriptions are in the papers as that of the battle of Volturno. Yet why not be interested about that old heart of oak, Admiral Panton? He and glorious Garibaldi are chips off very similar blocks: the old tar fought to free slaves also, did his duty: and what can a man do more? The opportunity is not given to every one to show himself a hero.

Above the one picture were a ship's cutlass and a sword; above the other a bit of manattee skin, made into a whip, and the backbone of a shark, at least Admiral Panton said it was a backbone.

"Tell me the shark has no backbone! why, sir, th .o

it is before your own eyes; you'll believe them, if you won't mine."

A loud hum of voices reached the hall, even through the closed door of the drawing-room.

"The colonel is here," whispered Lill to Miss Crumpton; "they are battling at the hop question."

Miss Tufton and her chaperone found the whole family assembled. Mrs. Panton, the two daughters Althemiah and Eliza, the admiral, his brother the colonel, and another to whom the colonel was holding forth in a loud voice. This stranger was introduced as Sir Frederick Ponsonby. Lill at once held out her hand, greeting him cordially, as she explained, for her dear Lady Ponsonby's sake. Let us look round the room while Sir Frederick is answering Miss Tufton's inquiries for his mother.

The admiral, a round-shouldered middle-sized man, will not take up many lines; his face is wonderfully variegated, all shades of red in it from scarlet down to dark purple, his eyes are weak with staring at the sun and heavenly bodies. He and his brother, the colonel, are two impatient men, always most peculiarly so to one another; they never wait to hear the answer to any question the one asks of the other.

Mrs. Panton has no great pretensions to individuality. She resembles hundreds and hundreds of other ladies of her age. She has thick bands of iron-grey hair, neat features, a faded complexion, rather bunchy in figure, though by no means stout. Her eldest daughter constantly invents new caps for her; but the admiral has never been brought to think any of them becoming.

"Why do you wear caps, my dear?" he invariably asks.

"My age, my own husband." Yes, that speech is Mrs. Panton's one peculiarity. The admiral is her "own husband."

Althemiah, named after a three-decker, is not pretty, but why she is not it would be difficult to tell; her eyes are good, and her nose, and her mouth, and her teeth, and her hair, yet she is not pretty; perhaps she is neither fair enough nor dark enough, or too short for the size of her head, or her shoulders too broad for her height; but pretty she is not. Mrs. Panton will assure you that Althemiah has not a fault—the most dutiful child parents ever had. Among Mrs. Panton's friends, however, her pet daughter was generally called "a nice unnoticeable little thing." Althemiah's every phrase begins with "Mamma thinks," or " Papa is of opinion." Mrs. Panton often thanked God fervently that Lill Tufton was not her daughter. Excellent woman! she had never felt any regrets that the poor girl had no mother to guide and protect her.

But Lizzie Panton, called Dolly after Dolly Vardon, aged sixteen, was pretty even by the side of Miss Tufton; such sweet hazel eyes, like a dove's, a *nez retroussé*, a clear nut-brown complexion. a short, round, active figure; met tripping along in the lanes or field. she was as pretty a model for a May queen as one could wish to see. The dear little thing has been sitting in a corner, silently nursing a lovely white kitten. with her soft eyes fixed on Sir Frederick—a bad habit she has acquired. She came out of her corner to greet her dear Lill.

And Sir Frederick—how did he appear to the visitor? She thought him handsome, but did not approve of his distrait air; he looked too much as if he were accustomed to break ladies' hearts. His dress also struck her as being finical. like one of the figures in a French fashion-book. Miss Tufton saw all this in the manner in which well-bred young ladies manage such examinations. Sir Frederick had no idea that he was being tried, and judged, and sentenced. by the pair of blue eyes. the curve of whose half-lowered eyelids he was admiring.

When Miss Tufton at last remembers that she must be civil to Mrs. Panton and Althemiah, the colonel pounces again on Sir Frederick.

" Now, if you will just listen to me. I will make it all clear as day to you. If the duty were taken off, then the Gaulshire hops would come into the market on a par with the Stonyshire. My brother and Fordham won't see this; but, sir, this county would be ruined—ruined—"

" Why the dickens," interrupted the admiral, who was humble under criticism as to nautical affairs, but ram

pant on the subject of farming; "Why the dickens, I
say, shouldn't brewers and consumers pay the duty, and
not the farmers? It's infamous, I say, that the produce
of one county should be taxed, and not that of another;
it's a crying injustice.!"

"My good gracious, sir—my good gracious—now just
stop a minute, and I will explain it all; put it all down
on paper."

Here ensued a confused duet of "Government," "By
George," "Profit," "Taxes," "Sixty pounds," "Shame-
ful." "Duty."

The admiral stuttered with impatience, the colonel
bearing down on him, and over him, with a rapidity of
utterance only to be paralleled by a first-rate comic
singer. Mrs. Panton throughout talked placidly, sometimes smiling when the uproar swelled.

Sir Frederick's eyes, full of good-natured mirth, went
in search of those of Lill. He seemed quite at home
with her already. A man and woman while listening to
very common-place remarks may receive very strong impression of each other. How otherwise account for the
attachments we see and hear of, and which we know positively have neither been sown nor nurtured by scientific,
philosophical nor sentimental discussions? Certainly
the epoch at which two persons meet who afterwards
love one another is seldom marked by clever conversation.

When Miss Tufton rose to take leave. Sir Frederick
also shook hands. The whole Panton family went with
them to the door, the admiral adjusting the apron of
chaise, and complimenting Miss Tufton on her pony and
her driving, and presenting her with a rose and a spray
of jessamine. They were a cordial and kind-hearted
family, these Pantons. See, there is Dolly fearlessly
shoving a lump of sugar into the mouth of Black Prince,
Sir Frederick's horse.

"Take care Dolly," says the colonel to his pet; "don't
put your silly face so near that fellow's lips. Come
away, I say."

Sir Frederick rode by the side of the pony chaise,
reining in Black Prince to keep step with Lill's shaggy-
maned Shetland; asking the usual questions young gen

tlemen ask of young ladies in the country. Was she fond of riding? Did she ride? Ever go to the meet, or to the balls at Z—? Sir Frederick had heard of a picnic to be given by the regiment there, to the ladies of the neighbourhood. Lill after an instant's skirmish with her conscience which reminded her of Giuliani's dislike for ladies riding, confessed she was very fond of riding; she did not expect to have an invitation to the picnic, as having been abroad, Sir Mark had had no opportunity of showing attention to the military now at Z—.

"The Pantons were going," Sir Frederick said; "he was sure as soon as Miss Tufton was known to be at Wavering she would be invited; in that case would she go?" and Sir Frederick's fine grey eyes pleaded most flatteringly for an affirmative. But Miss Tufton was a beautiful young lady of fashion, used to flattery; if the same look had been directed to Dolly Panton, she would have blushed and said, "Oh! yes," in a small, trembling voice.

Lill was sufficiently embarrassed, however, what to say as to Sir Mark's calling on the young baronet; she dared not answer that he would, though it seemed quite a matter of course that he should do so.

It was a glorious day, a little sharp breeze tempering the sun's rays, a little breeze just strong enough to make the aspens show the silver side of their leaves. Blossom and fruit were all around: the bronzing wheat-fields were pleasant to look upon, and the lazy cattle standing musing over their own reflections wherever they could find water; there was no song of birds, but the air was musical with insects' hum. Beautiful shadows coursed over the wavy uplands; as they rush over the hedge of the road, Black Prince lays back his quivering ears, and protests against them. Lill was pleased with the way Sir Frederick patted his horse's arched neck, in which every vein showed, and gently encouraged him by voice and hand to make acquaintance with the objects of his alarm; any show of gentleness in a great strong man, fascinates a woman's heart.

"My pony has tried your politeness long enough, Sir Frederick," says Lill at last; perfectly aware nevertheless, that her well-bred escort would not have remained such for five minutes had he not liked to do so.

Sir Frederick sees they are skirting the park paling, and understands he is dismissed; he raises his hat quite off his head, and bows low.

"A very good imitation of a Frenchman," observes Lill, saucily to Miss Crumpton as he rides away.

"Far better looking than his brother, Mr. Valentine,' answered the old lady.

"Better looking? Why, Crummie, Sir Frederick is handsome, and poor Valentine is only just tolerable."

"That's what I meant, Lill; I dare say Lady Ponsonby is not a little proud of this young gentleman."

"He gives me the impression of being too handsome for anything."

Lill mentioned to Sir Mark at dinner, the having met Sir Frederick Ponsonby at Admiral Panton's that afternoon.

"The son of the old woman in Paris? why hasn't he called here?"

"Because, I suppose, he is aware that in England, it is the custom for a stranger to be called on, by those who wish for his acquaintance."

"Is he going to build himself a house on his large property of six hundred acres?"

"He did not mention his plans to me, but as Lady Ponsonby was very kind to me when I was in Paris, I should be sorry we showed any slight to her son."

"Why didn't she come with her son?" asked Sir Mark, who had a pleasure in teasing Lill with questions; it amused him to see her colour rise and her eyes flash, and the effort it cost her to maintain her composure. The same sort of spirit which makes men and boys rouse dogs to snap, and bark, and fight.

Sir Mark, however, could be gentlemanly and courteous when it pleased him, and he had no sooner seen Sir Frederick than it pleased him to be both. The tall, handsome, elegant young man gratified Sir Mark's taste for the beautiful. As he looked at Sir Frederick, he wished Heaven had given him such a son. He fancied, as all do, that if this and that circumstance in his life had been otherwise ordered, he would have been a different and happier man. Why should that old-fashioned Lady Ponsonby have such a son to inherit those few acres of Monk's Capel, and the wide lands of Wavering go to a poor baby of a youth who could but just claim kith with him. "Ay, just the way all things go in the world, carefully arranged for man's disappointment," summed up Sir Mark.

Sir Mark promised the young baronet leave to shoot over his preserves ;—an unknown event in the recollection of the united parishes of Wavering and Bloomfield : moreover invited him to dinner, asking the choicest of the neighbourhood to meet him.

No wonder Sir Frederick mentioned Sir Mark in honourable terms in his letters to his mother Of Lill he observed,—

"She is an extremely pretty person, her manner rather too formed for her age. She reminds me, not her features, but the expression of her face, of Leonardo's Mona Lisa, her smile is not frank. Is she mocking at me and the world in general? Her voice is sweet, but has a tone of defiance in it. A shade more of gentleness and she would be charming

CHAPTER XXXIV.

Coming Events cast their Shadows before

A YOUNG man in the country, neither a clergyman, nor a farmer, without mother, sister, or wife, is expected to seek the society of the female relatives of his more fortunately endowed male acquaintances. Music and riding are more than excuses, they are excellent reasons for daily meetings with one's near neighbours. A canter on the short turf of a breezy common, is among the pleasantest and most innocent diversions of life. Sir Frederick was therefore often to be seen on Black Prince, by the side of Miss Tufton's horse, and the Miss Pantons' ponies. Duets and trios were practised in the morning, to be sung in the evening.

"It seems to me," said Lill, one day to Sir Frederick, "as if you and I had met before; your face and voice are so familiar to me."

"Probably some family likeness to my mother, or to Valentine or Alicia."

Lill smiled, but did not say, "No, indeed, your voice and your face have *that* in them of which none of the others of your family can boast."

Sir Frederick was indeed one of those men who are sure to bring a pleased smile on women's lips. He was clever, accomplished, handsome, never seeking to lead the conversation, but in following it, let such gems of information drop carelessly, that it gave the idea, that if he chose to take the trouble, he could be something superior to what he was. He laughed at sentiment in a manner, that inferred he had a great share of it. For instance, one evening the following skirmish took place between him and Lill.

"I saw by the way you arched your eyebrows, Miss Tufton, when I sat down to the piano, that you do not approve of men playing—you consider billiards and cigars more manly amusements."

"More common certainly; I hope you have a piano at the priory?"

"You think it must require a strong head to resist

the danger of long evenings, and nothing particular to
do."

"Indeed I was not reflecting on the perils of solitude
for you."

"You are not so charitable then, as some other of my
lady friends. I have been trying to ease the anxiety of
one, by promising to look out for an intellectual middle-
aged housekeeper."

"It puts me out of all patience," said Lill; "to think
of the vulgar, jocular advice which is always given to
every unmarried man. That is how the spirit of society
is spoiled."

"What? by the promotion of marriages?" he asked,
with laughing eyes.

"Yes, I think so," she said, pettishly.

Lill, it must be understood, had rushed to the conclusion from the beginning of their acquaintance, that Sir
Frederick being Lady Ponsonby's son, must know the
situation of Lady Ponsonby's friend, Giuliani, with regard to herself. Believing this, she talked to him with
the aplomb of a girl who considers herself out of danger
of being misunderstood.

"It is quite a relief," continued Sir Frederick, "to
meet with some one, whose opinions so entirely coincide
with my own. I see you are not the least romantic, Miss
Tufton."

"'A primrose by the river's brink, a primrose is to me,'
and nothing more, Sir Frederick."

"You prefer comfortable stone houses to the most
splendid of aërial castles,"

She answered: "The moment one awakens from a
dream, all pleasurable emotions are over, the comforts
of stone walls remain."

Miss Tufton spoke of Sir Frederick as very amusing,
with his nonsensical assumption of being matter-of-fact.

No diplomatist that ever was, or will be, can utter the
contrary of what he thinks and feels, with such a suc-
cessful air of truth as a young lady under twenty.

Never had Lill been possessed with such a spirit of
life and movement as now. She seemed to have forgotten what weariness was. Her heart had thrown off the
lethargy which had crept into it from the day she had
promised it to Giuliani. It beat quickly and happily;

far more rapidly than ever, and with a new delight. Her days were full and pleasant, too much so to leave any time for reflection.

This blessed truce with care lasted for Lill just as long as it ever lasts for any one.

Since her return to Wavering, it had been her habit to write once a fortnight to Mr. Giuliani, giving him a sort of diary of her life. She never omitted the name of Sir Frederick Ponsonby where it ought to occur. She meant to be in perfect good faith with the Italian. She abounded in expressions of interest for the Italian cause, dwelling long in touching words of womanly sympathy on the fate of the Bandiera brothers, a pamphlet about which she had lately been reading.

Giuliani used to dissect these letters word by word; every sentiment or expression should have satisfied him, and so they did, on the sixth perusal. It was the first impression that was painful and alarming. The heart has a terribly sure divination of its own. Jealousy never does exist without some cause; and as for letters, one may be certain that the real feeling of the dear one who writes, will filter through the most unconscious or the most elaborate effort at concealment.

Giuliani always sat down to answer Lill's letter with the intention of pouring out on paper some of the riches of his tenderness for her. But no sooner did he make the attempt, than his pen stopped as if by a spell. Some spirit or demon whispered to him, "She does not care for you, or your love. You will only frighten her." Thus his letters to her were essays on politics, literature, the fine arts; on any subject, but that of himself and his feelings. She might have read them aloud at any market cross, except that prudent people would have objected to her corresponding at all with one who had been her Italian master.

Lill, though she was too young, too inexperienced, and alas! too indifferent, to understand that this absence of all expression of his love, anxiety, and pain, was irrefragable proof of the existence of all three, or that, as from every other empty vessel, most noise is to be heard from an empty heart; still even she gathered from Giuliani's letters, what no one else would have perceived, viz.: that he was for some reason or other displeased with her

CHAPTER XXXV.

Merry England.

Such was the state of things when the great event of the year to the youthful agricultural population of that quiet nook of the world was to take place.

The Wavering and Bloomfield school feast shut out all incidents, however grand and important, which were at a distance, just as a gate or a sapling on the foreground will hide an alp on the horizon.

It was the day when John Larke the carpenter, famed for more than ten miles round, came out in great force as contriver and conductor of the revels.

At six o'clock on that morning, he might have been seen, his hand shading his eyes, examining the sky, east, west, north and south. However promising the appearance of the heavens, John with both a religious and scientific knowledge of the instability of all things shakes his head to his wife's cheerful anticipations, shakes it again when Mrs. Ashton, the rector's lady, comes to him at nine o'clock, and says in her spirited way, —

"Well, John, we may have the tables set in the field."

"Just as you please, ma'am."

"You don't pretend to fear rain to-day," exclaimed Mrs. Ashton, laughing.

"Why, you see, ma'am, it don't do no harm to expect."

"It does no harm to hope," interrupted the lady ; "I always hope the best, John, and the best always comes at last," she added to herself, as she tripped actively away.

Stretching across the glebe field, lying between the school-house and the church, were long deal tables, covered with white table cloths, looking from the turning of the road from which you first saw Bloomfield, like a sheet of water.

The feast would begin at two. At one, small parties of children debouched from all the lands and woods about; the Wavering children came also to Bloomfield school, each child carrying a basket containing a plate, sometimes two, a mug, and a knife and fork.

From the back of the rectory, servants issued with large dishes, on which reposed magnificent cold surloins, or a rockwork of buns and plumcake. Before two, the Panton family arrived; Dolly in a new muslin, rosebud pattern, cunningly procured by the colonel through Miss Tufton's help, being a facsimile of one of Lill's dresses which he had heard his pet admire. Dolly was famous for her achievements at school feasts—"a host in herself" agreed all the rectors of the surrounding parishes.

Lill and Miss Crampton soon appeared.

"Sir Mark is to follow us," said Lill to Mrs. Ashton. "Indeed he is coming," she added, seeing some incredulity on the face of the rector.

"It will be the first time he has honoured us," returned Mr. Ashton.

"How pale Dolly is!" remarked Lill to Althemiah. "Is she well?"

"Mamma does not think she is," replied Althemiah; "but Dolly would come."

The children were by this time clattering over the benches on either side of the tables, their glittering eyes riveted on the beef and buns, most of them with their knife and fork uplifted in readiness for the attack.

A smart lady's maid, in a fashionable bonnet and shawl down to her heels, is laughingly and daintily helping a footman to bring forward the large cans of tea. John Larke and his aid manage the beer. John is churchwarden, and will see to it, that there is no abuse of the malt. The schoolmistress calls out, "Now, children." The rector is at the head of one table, the admiral at the other. Dolly looks furtively round. It had been rumored that Sir Frederick, as Mr. Ashton's principal parishioner, would take the head of the third table; but she sees Mrs. Ashton whisper to the colonel, who, a moment after calls out to her:

"You come and help us, Dolly."

The young ladies begin to be very active; it seems impossible to satisfy the demands for beef and bread.

"Why are you not eating, little boy?" asked Lill.

"Mustard!" he utters gutturally.

"Mustard!" repeats the lady's maid, condescendingly; "poor fellow! I'll run for it directly, Miss Tufton."

"You stay where you are," says John Larke, church-wardenly; "one of the men'll go quicker than you with your mincing steps."

"Well, Mr. Larke, I am obliged to you for your good opinion."

Carriages are arriving, and more young ladies help. Mammas and married sisters are sitting on chairs and benches, or walking round the tables as spectators.

"I say, you Jim," cries out the rector's son, a fine boy of nine years old, "what's the matter with you?"

"I'm fasting, Master Harry."

Harry supplies him, whispering to Lill, —

"Goodness! and he has had two large helpings."

In Jim's defence, be it said, he never sees roast beef but at the school feast.

The lady spectators are interchanging news about their babies, or their boys and girls, or about their neighbours.

"Lill Tufton is prettier than ever."

"Do you think so? It strikes me her complexion was finer last year."

"She is paler; but Dolly Panton hast lost her colour altogether. Mrs. Panton ought to give those girls a chance of seeing more of the world; she never seems to think of the future."

"There is a fate in these things; Miss Tufton has been enough in the world, and pretty as she is, she is not settled."

"Probably her own fault. By-the-by, where's Sir Frederick? On dit, he's looking that way."

"Oh, those horrid children, what a noise they make!"

The beef had vanished, and so had the buns, and cakes, and bread, and the gallons of beer and tea.

"Now Miss Finch," says Mrs. Ashton, "set the girls off playing; Miss Eliza Panton will help you. Mr. Herbert Colfield and his brother are going to play cricket with the boys."

The boys' side of the field is very lively, actually some of them throw off their jackets, and appear in pink shirts. The girls as yet are too shy to play. Dolly leads languidly, and Tom Titler is very slow. A horseman waves his hat from the road in greeting to the assembly, and the boys give a small hurrah. Dolly's face grows bright, then clouds over. Only Sir Mark Tufton. Lill is leading a party, striving all she can to put some animation into them. "Come, then—"

> "Lady Queen Anne, she sits in the sun,
>   As fair as a lily, as brown as a bun," &c.

Another cheer, a very boisterous one. This time it is all right; Sir Frederick has come on foot, and there he is, bowing to the ladies; and now he is among the boys. The sports have received a new impetus. The true spirit of a leader has come back to Dolly; she makes the girls run. Who can catch her?

The sun is on a level with the church roof.

"It's time to leave off," whispers the rector's lady to the rector. "What are they doing?"

Who would have expected it from Sir Frederick? There he is running at the top of his speed; boys and girls in full chase. He runs famously: the moment he is in danger of being caught, he showers down gingerbread nuts, or those enticing red and yellow and white concoctions, which fill sundry huge glass bottles in Mrs. Pybus's left hand-window. She will need a new supply.

How odd! How kind! Approving looks, mocking smiles, follow the young baronet. Flushed, and the handsomer for it, Sir Frederick at last gives in, and falls, perhaps not undesignedly so, at Miss Tufton's feet; one of the smiles he thinks so mysterious is on her face, at that very instant. He looks away, meets Dolly's dear eyes, springs up as if stung, and hastens to Mrs. Ashton's side as though he had perceived that lady to be in need of his assistance.

A very substantial tea is provided on these occasions for the friends invited to the school feast. The tea is in point of fact a cold dinner. Ceremony belongs exclusively to hot dishes; certainly there was very little of it that evening in the rectory dining-room. The gentlemen who had a right to the highest seats were in the lowest. Sir Mark Tufton was beside Althemiah; Sir Frederick next to the rector's daughter, a young lady of eleven years old. Ralph Colfield had manœuvred himself into a seat by Dolly.

Every one and every thing in that handsome room denoted prosperity. All the guests round the rector's hospitable table were favoured children of the earth. Not one had ever known the heart-breaking, up-hill work of a struggle for mere material existence; none had an idea of the fruitless rolling of a wheel, or of pouring water into sieves. Yet smooth as those lives appeared, every one was troubled and vexed with a rumpled rose-leaf. Even that pretty sixteen year old Dolly would have said, had you asked her opinion of the world, "that it was all vanity and vexation of spirit."

The company parted early : while they were standing in a confused group, waiting for the carriages, Sir Frederick came to Miss Tufton with her burnous over his arm.

"This is yours, I am sure," he said.

" I am at a loss to guess how you made the discovery," returned Lill.

" Are you not partial to the perfume of violets?" asked he, laying his face on the soft cachmere.

" How dare you?" rose to Lill's lips. She only refrained on account of those about her; but she made an attempt to take the cloak from Sir Frederick; who misinterpreting her action, or pretending to do so, folded the warm soft wrap round her. That moment Lill's eyes met those of Dolly, who was standing where the light of the hall lamp fell on her; Lill shivered.

" You are catching cold;" said Sir Frederick in his rich voice ; such a dangerous voice sometimes.

" Good night, dear Dolly," said Lill.

What did Dolly do, but give the extended hand a sharp little flip, and run away with a laugh that had no mirth in it ?

Lill shivered again, and then Sir Frederick drew up the hood of her mantle, and led her to the carriage.

CHAPTER XXXVI.

False Appearances.

Could it be from cold that Lill shivered on that balmy July night? No, indeed: it was from a sudden revelation made to her by the earnestly interrogating eyes of her little friend. Lill knew now the reason of that species of surveillance with which Dolly had lately vexed her. She saw herself standing on the brink of a precipice. She had been gliding down a slope so smooth, that she had been unconscious of its descent. Only a violent backward movement could save her from going over.

Sir Mark was in high good-humour during the drive home, actually joking Miss Crumpton on Colonel Pauton's attentions. But Lill could hear nothing distinctly, for the piercing reiteration in her ear of one word. "disloyal." She threw back the hood, so carefully drawn round her head. undid the fastening of the burnous, sat forward with her head out of the window. panting for breath. Half a dozen subjects crowded her thoughts; she wonders the while at the green tinted flame of the glowworm, at the blackness of the trees against the sky; every leaf that stirs seems to her to have a threatening message. She once more cowers back into her corner.

"Are you asleep. Miss Tufton?" questioned Sir Mark.

"No, only too tired to talk."

"I have invited a dozen of the people we met to-day to dine with us the day after to-morrow."

Lill roused herself to say, "That is very short notice."

"So it is, Miss Tufton, but I wanted to have that capital fellow. Sir Frederick, before he goes to Paris. Metal more attractive there, than my partridges and pheasants."

"Thank God!" very nearly burst from Lill's lips.

"I beg your pardon," said Mark. politely.

"For what?"

"For not having heard what you said."

Lill at that instant would have been grateful for the prop of a friendly word; very good impulses were in her heart, but Sir Mark's ironical manner, as it always did, braced her spirit up to defiance.

"If you wish to know what I thought, but did not intend to express, it was that I was glad Sir Frederick was going to see his mother. After being away ten years, he might give some weeks to her."

"Upon my word, Miss Tufton, I am pleased at your austere ideas of duty to parents; surprised at your philosophic indifference to one of the handsomest and pleasantest young fellows I ever met."

"You ought to have said *rejoiced* instead of *surprized*, Sir Mark, considering, as you say, there is metal more attractive in Paris; but for my indifference, I should have had to wear a willow wreath at your dinner-party."

Sir Mark, at the mention of the willow wreath, abstained from a further attack.

Alone, with her bedroom door locked, Lill sat with her head within her hands. No need to reflect or examine herself. She knew what had happened, knew that her heart beat wildly for some one, and that one not Giuliani. He was for ever driven out of the sanctuary promised to him; her joys, her sorrows, her thoughts were grouped round Sir Frederick.

"What will become of me?" she muttered, and slow, scorching tears rolled over her hot cheeks. "I must try to do right. Oh! that I could go back to what I was only one year ago; how differently I would act! If any one were to ask me why I did not say no to Mr. Giuliani when he put it in my power, I could not give a reason. I had such a confusion of feelings at the time, a sort of stupid idea that I had encouraged him, and I did like him so much till directly afterwards."

Quite true, Lill; you had liked him until he added a new ingredient to your intercourse; this addition it was which had soured all the sweet that existed before.

"All wrong, always all wrong; so weak to be always wrong,—no, this time I will do right. Though I die for it, I will hold to my word."

She was pacing up and down the room, talking to herself. She would send a letter to Giuliani by Sir Frederick: if the young baronet was not aware of her

engagement, and now Lill doubted it, this act of hers
would make it clear to him. As for inflicting pain on
Sir Frederick in her present mood, she enjoyed the idea
of doing so—she felt revengeful towards him.

"No fear of this fine Leander dying for love of any
one."

It was a pleasure to her to mock at him. Then she
turned round on herself, "I am a detestable creature; I
declare to Heaven I despise myself, I know no good of
this man, but that he can sing like a nightingale and ride
like any trooper. I don't believe he cares a pin's head
for me, and yet I am ready to follow him to the end of
the world, and trample on a great and noble heart to do
so; no doubt of what I would do, had I the option.
Poor Giuliani! and you actually would give your life for
me, would make your body my shield any day. God help
me, God help me, and drive this evil spirit out of
me."

Love is as insatiable as death, and prayers such as
that put up by Lill never reached heaven. She had
other and worse trials before her, ere rest came.

The next morning Lill wrote her letter to Giuliani; a
very different one from any she had ever sent him. She
made use of words which, had they been the expression
of real sentiments, she could never have had the courage
to put down on paper for him to see. While she wrote
them she was thinking simply of the vexation they would
cause Sir Frederick could he read them. She sealed the
envelope, directed it, and added in one corner, "honoured
by Sir Frederick Ponsonby."

She was in the most overpowering spirits all day.
When Ruth came to dress her, unlike her usual habit of
reading while her hair was arranged, Lill rattled away
in an unconnected way to her maid.

"Try how I should look with that great rose in the
front of my hair, Ruth; I like it—fasten it somehow—
exactly in the parting."

Ruth objected, first the difficulty, and then the unbe-
coming oddness.

"I don't care, I will have it so," said Lill, with sudden
violence. "There, take some of the hair, and plait i
in." She tried to do it herself, but her fingers trembled

so, she was obliged to desist. The next moment she would not have any flowers in her hair at all.

When Ruth had finished her labours, and Lill was alone, she took the letter for Giuliani out of her desk, looked at the address, placed it within the folds of her handkerchief, and was about to go downstairs—yes, she was resolved—her hand was on the lock of the door, when the impulse born amidst a storm of emotion gave way. She grew faint-hearted, and the letter was destroyed, torn into the smallest atoms. She then went down with a feeling of relief.

The fever in Lill's veins flushed her cheeks and brightened her eyes. Even those most familiar with her beauty were struck by its radiance this evening.

"She is wonderfully lovely," thought Sir Frederick, and his eyes continually sought her.

"Where is Dolly?" Lill asked of Mrs. Panton.

"A bad headache—school feasts always knock her up; and indeed. I am afraid I am wrong to let her go to grown-up parties; Althemiah did not till she was eighteen."

"And the colonel, I suppose, has stayed at home with his pet?"

"Yes; we counted heads, for Sir Mark was so good as to tell Althemiah who were to be of the party, and we found we should be thirteen if the colonel came."

Sir Frederick was standing by Miss Tufton; she said, recklessly.—

"Once in Paris, at the Caledons'—do you know the Caledons, Sir Frederick?—I very nearly drove the lady of the house wild. Sir Mark wouldn't sit down thirteen to dinner, and I was late—that was where I first met Mr. Giuliani."

"Indeed! my mother's friend! I did not know you were acquainted."

"He is a particular friend of mine."

"Who is your particular friend, Miss Tufton?" asked Sir Mark.

"Mr. Giuliani," repeated Lill, in tones as clear as a trumpet.

"What! the Italian master?" said Sir Mark; the man

you got the opera box out of? Here's an opportunity for you—send him the money by Ponsonby."

"I told you once, Sir Mark—" but Sir Mark was at the other end of the room receiving Mr. Langden, the millionnaire, who now possessed the Ponsonby estate all of it. with the exception of Sir Frederick's farm of Menk's Capel and the Priory.

Mr. Langden was a middle-sized. heavy man, neither ugly nor handsome. neither young nor old. The only decided opinion that could be given about him was, that he was rich and unmarried.

Sir Frederick had expected to take Miss Tufton in to dinner. She did not see him, so occupied was she with Mr. Langden. The young baronet's lip curled, as she passed him leaning on Mr. Langden's arm.

During dinner, the lady at Sir Frederick's right made some remark to him which led to a discussion between them of the comparative merits of English and French women. Sir Frederick took care his opinion should be distinctly heard by Miss Tufton.

" Englishwomen are, I fancy, the handsomest and the best possible women in the universe, but in dress and in manner they do not shine. The best dressed Englishwoman always has something heavy and overdone about her ; while a Frenchwoman sets herself and her dress off, so that if there are imperfections, they do not strike the eye as they do in her English rival."

"And what do you say to their *hair?*" suddenly interposed Mr. Langden.

Sir Frederick was so surprised at the quarter whence the question issued, that he did not answer promptly enough to prevent Mr. Langden from proceeding.

" When I was in Paris, I never could bear to look at a Frenchwoman's head—it seemed as if they had torn the hair out by the roots. The parting was as wide as my finger." And he held up a particularly thick finger.

Sir Frederick's glance dwelt an instant on the finger, and then sought Miss Tufton's eyes with a look of congratulation.

" The fact is," went on Sir Frederick to his neighbour, as if Mr. Langden had not spoken, " A Frenchwoman knows how to be handsome without beauty; the why and the how remains a mystery to women of all other nations."

Lill laughed a mirthless laugh, and retorted,—

"And all the world knows that the English, particularly Englishmen, have a decided taste for the mysterious and supernatural."

"Indeed!" exclaimed Mr. Langden, "I thought that we were the most matter-of-fact people."

"Some of us are, most hopelessly so," said Lill, quietly, and dropped into silence.

Sir Mark in his loud, overbearing way, was saying,—

"Know Mrs. Venner! I think I do; she ought to be killed, strangled, choked; she made me drive once eleven miles to eat her haunch of venison, and it was cold, spoiled. I'll never forget it, never forgive her, never go into her house again."

Mrs. Panton's mild voice here intervened. Mrs. Panton was always graphic in description.

"A most respectable person, I assure you, Mr. Langden, only so deaf; comes of a good stock; his father was in the Church, and he had a cousin a lawyer; and that's the kind of person he is."

Lill listened, and it seemed to her that she had never heard such conversation before. Were all these people rational beings? Her head was aching sadly with the buzz and nonsense. She was thankful when Sir Mark frowned to her to take the ladies away.

CHAPTER XXXVII.

Cross Purposes.

WHEN the gentlemen came into the drawing-room, Sir Frederick sat down by Miss Tufton. She took no notice of him, so he began turning over the books on a table near him.

"Ah! I see you are of the same school, Miss Tufton, as my mother and sister," said Sir Frederick, showing her the pamphlet of the Bandiera.

"And you, of course, are of a different one?"

"Are your opinions of a delicate pink, or are they of the deepest sanguinary hue, Miss Tufton?"

"I should hope that respect for the rights of the people—respect and sympathy for men who prefer death to slavery—may be confessed without bringing down on me the charge of being a red republican."

Lill had an inner feeling of satisfaction in using against Sir Frederick some of what she recollected as Giuliani's sentiments.

"Ah! you have taken the infection strongly, I see; quite natural; you are at the age for enthusiasm without reflection."

"And you, I suppose, at the age which reflects that it is best to worship the powers that be," retorted Lill.

"All ladies have a tender weakness for conspiracy and conspirators—for what is beyond the law," said Sir Frederick.

"I suppose you will allow that people don't risk their lives merely for the pleasure of conspiring, and that it is not the rule to conspire against a good government."

Lill was growing very angry, the more so that she read something very like fun in Sir Frederick's eyes.

"Perhaps not a reasonable nation, such as our own, —but Italians! why, conspiracy is a part of their national character; they are a dramatic race, fond of pointed hats, and red cloaks, and of firing from behind rocks and walls on unarmed passengers."

Lill's eyes were two flashing fires now; why couldn't she find something sharply mortifying to say?

"My dear Miss Tufton, do not be angry, but do believe that when a nation is worthy of freedom they have it : no class, no nation, can be kept down, unless it has some inherent defect or vice which justifies the degradation."

"That is to say, weakness is a justification for injustice and oppression : a noble and generous doctrine summed up in three words,—might is right."

"You mistake me ; I do not consider might as right. I should be delighted to see that slyest and luckiest of conspirators, Louis Philippie, dethroned ; I hope to do so. I despise the stupidity of the French people who took the crown from a royal gentleman to give it to a huckster."

"You have been well received by the Faubourg St. Germain, I perceive," said Lill, coldly. "We are born to be enemies, Sir Frederick. I hate and detest the Bourbons—the root more than the branches."

"And, no doubt, for the capital reason ladies have for hating and loving,' retorted Sir Frederick.

Lill had hit him with the words Faubourg St. Germain. Lill said passionately,—

"Women sometimes can give reasons for doing both one and the other, Sir Frederick."

At that instant she believed she hated him. Lill, to avoid singing duets with Sir Frederick, proposed games. When he had rejoined the ladies in the drawing-room, he was quite willing to make peace with his pretty hostess ; but all through the evening, whenever the opportunity had occurred of giving him a sharp retort, she had seized on it. For instance, when they were playing at "Throwing a light upon it," twice running, sufficient light had been gained to see that the object to be discovered was a man ; Sir Frederick had asked the first time, "Is he good ?" When he put the same question again, Lill called out: "How very moral Sir Frederick Ponsonby is !"

Poor girl, she was dreadfully tired of the part she was acting, longing for every one to go and leave her to be miserable and silent.

Admiral Panton was the dread of all the musical young ladies of the neighbourhood. Never was there a man so devoid of tact, that fine extra sense which best enables its possessor to dispense with amiability or moral worth. The admiral would, with a smiling ruthlessness, interrupt the most interesting conversations with, — "Come, are we to have no music this evening?"

"Oh, yes, admiral," would his victim answer; "do make dear Althemiah play."

"No; no playing; who cares for Althemiah's playing? That's not what I want; it's a song from you, Miss Harriet, or Miss Rose," or whatever the name of the doomed might be.

This particular evening he pounced on Miss Tufton. He could not see the almost despair with which she said it was a pity to interrupt the game.

No, no, no: she must oblige him by singing "The Skipper and his Boy."

You might have heard a pin drop while Lill sang; her voice had in it that ring of intense feeling which, issuing from a soul in pain, cleaves its way to the hearts of the listeners. Even Sir Mark was quiet; he looked at his granddaughter as she left the instrument with curiosity. Admiral Pantou had achieved such a success by his first importunity, that he now attacked Sir Frederick. Sir Frederick would be delighted to sing a duet with Miss Tufton, but Miss Tufton said, dryly. "that she was hoarse; he might have heard she was."

Sir Frederick sat down to the piano; he was able to accompany himself in a simple song; on the present occasion he chose one of those foolish ditties in which every verse ends, "Forget thee, never!" Did he intend or not to throw any particular meaning into the words? That is among the facts of his history never to be known. It was out of his power to have calculated on the effect he produced. The third time he pronounced "Forget thee, never!" Lill rose from her seat with a sort of stiff, mechanical movement, stared wildly about her like one in need of help, then, with the same species of sleep-walking effort, sat down again. No one appeared to have observed her; Sir Frederick had. She was sitting sideways to the piano, and his head had been turned towards her. The mute appeal of agony had thrilled through him : he tried, but was unable to finish the fourth verse; he made a laughing apology for his want of memory.

"On! sing the third verse over again," implored one young lady.

Sir Frederick engaged his charming petitioner in a violent flirtation. during which he watched the expressive clenching of Lill's hands.

"Since he would not sing," said his fair admirer, "would he take a seat in our carriage? There was plenty of room, only papa and herself."

But Sir Frederick was determined on a moonlight ride home.

"Is there a moon?" said his frank companion.

"Always," replied Sir Frederick. rather saucily, and with a demonstration of changing his place, which sent the young lady to whisper to her father.

Lill heard Sir Frederick telling some one who was reproaching him for being no sportsman. that he might be back for the hunting season. Everybody was shaking hands with her at once. Would they never go?

"Farewell, Miss Tufton," said Frederick's rich musical voice.

"Good-bye," she answered, and looked straight at him. "Remember me, if you please, to Lady Ponsonby, and to your brother and sister."

They shook hands, and left the room with some of the other guests. Lill remained standing in the same place. She fancied she was watching Sir Mark's very tender parting with Althemiah. As the door closed on the Pantons. Sir Mark came towards Lill.

"Why, how tired you look!" he exclaimed.

"I *am* tired; I can scarcely stand."

"Why don't you sit down, then?" and Sir Mark actually wheeled forward an arm-chair for her.

"I'll go to bed." she said, turning sharply away, that he might not see the tears that rose to her eyes. The trifling sympathy shown by Sir Mark made her quite hysterical.

Sir Frederick went home that night an instance of the possibility of what some affirm often happens; that of a man being in love with two women at once.

There exists a great dissolving power in absence, and

a very creative one in presence. One does not forget,
but the clear outlines of the past get blurred and faint.
Constancy requires to be cultivated and exercised, just
as our other virtues do, by self-denial and self-control.

Sir Frederick Ponsonby only paid a flying visit to
Paris; just the number of hours requisite to refresh his
wardrobe and make him presentable at the Bains d'
Amélie.

> "Pour qui veut du repos, du soleil, un air pur,
>   Le séjour d'Amélie est le port le plus sûr."

Whether repose, sun and pure air, were the peculiar
objects of Sir Frederick's journey to the Canigou à Mon-
tagne des Airs, must be left to the reader's penetration.
Lady Ponsonby and Alicia kindly took it for granted,
that after having been subjected to the damp English
climate, Sir Frederick felt the necessity of a course of
drying, at the foot of the Roche d'Annibal.

The evening before Sir Frederick was to start for the
Pyrenees, Lady Ponsonby, believing that she was showing a real turn for diplomacy, began a sort of cross-examination of her son about his fair neighbours at Monk's
Capel.

"Well, Fred, I have been half expecting some confidences from you."

He asked of what kind.

"The only one usually vouchsafed by men to their
mothers,—an intimation that at some period or other
they may marry."

"Does it disappoint you, mother, that I have no such
confession to make?"

"I wonder a little, considering the descriptions you
have sent me of the girls you have seen so much of."

"My dear mother, I dreamed the night before I left
England, that I was going to be married, and I awoke
and found my pillow wet with my tears."

"That is a put-off, and not an answer to my question."

"You shall have the frankest of negatives then, No—
I have not the slightest idea of placing my heart under
the despotism of Miss Tufton; nor have I the presump-
tion to believe it would be accepted "

"I see, then, that Miss Tufton was the only one who excited your attention."

"Quite true: Miss Althemiah—"

"What a name!" ejaculated Alicia.

"Miss Althemiah was excellent, but monotonous. Her dear little sister still played with the kitten. The member's daughter's eyes treated me with the most haughty indifference."

"That will do," said Lady Ponsonby. laughing; "I am satisfied you have returned heart-whole."

Sir Frederick for all answer, shrugged his shoulders: he was most hermetically discreet.

Lady Ponsonby retailed the above conversation with zest to Mr. Giuliani. Her anxiety about her son while he was in Sir Mark Tufton's neighborhood had been revealed to the Italian by the excess of her precautions to hide it. He could hardly suppress a smile at the naïveté with which his good friend believed that the only danger to Lill's constancy lay in Sir Frederick's presence.

CHAPTER XXXVIII.

Lill Breaks.

THE next week was endless to Miss Tufton. She would go out with the intention of taking a long walk or ride, and return tired within the hour. Everything wearied her, everything annoyed her; the least noise or movement in the room where she was, made her nervous. Everybody was disagreeable or to blame, and she felt a profound disgust for life, indeed, for humanity in general.

Miss Crumpton at last began to be aware that something was amiss with Lill. She had known her impatient and passionate, but never languid and listless; had never seen her occupied for hours with one single page of a book—for the leaf was never turned, that the chaperone could vouch for—still less had Lill ever remained half a morning with her hands in her lap, apparently watching the raindrops on the window running into one another. Nor was it only when Miss Crumpton and the young lady were *tête à tête* that Lill fell into these fits of absence. In the evenings, when Sir Mark was present, she would sit motionless, staring at the lamp or the fire.

Intense thought produced this longing for physical repose. From a child to a woman she had had a craving for information of all kinds, but Lill had never shown any reflective faculty; she acquired—she did not originate. The present call upon her head to direct her heart, singularly distressed her. She was confused by a mingling of sentiment and sensation. But for her entanglement with Mr. Giuliani, she would not have been called on to struggle against a preference for Sir Frederick Ponsonby. It was the necessity for the struggle, the difficulty to be overcome, which fixed his image indelibly on her soul. Difficulty acts on some natures as a magnet. Otherwise, the probabilities are, that Lill, with her sharp perception of weaknesses, her high standard of worth, would have sifted Sir Frederick, and decided that the grain of his character was not equal to his external merits. As it was, her whole being, heart, soul, mind, were engrossed by him. She must suffer—might die (she was one of the girls who might die for love), but it was one of those terrible passions which never leave their victims so long as they live.

One morning Lill was roused from her apathy by Miss Crumpton laying a letter silently before her. The colour and shape of the envelope told her at once from whom it came. The sight instantly summoned up the recollection of a lively debate she had had with Giuliani. She averring that she never thought or spoke of people, but they were sure to appear in person, or else to write; and Giuliani asking her, if she had ever noted how often such a concurrence had failed.

"It had not failed now," thought Lill, as she opened his letter; no, nor it could not have failed for many a day past; never had Giuliani been so present to her spirit, as during these last weeks.

Giuliani had written less than usual, only two sides of his paper were covered. There were neither apologies nor excuses for not having written sooner. Why should any one condemn himself as inattentive or idle? or resort to so stupid a manœuvre to escape the effort necessary to find something worth saying. To give a reason for unusual silence is another thing, and always as acceptable as excuses are unpalatable.

Giuliani began his letter much in the same way he would have done had he come to speak to Lill by word of mouth, instead of with his pen.

"You will smile," he wrote, "to hear that my letter is prompted by a dream. We moderns scout at most things that were reverenced by the ancients, just as youths quiz the counsels of gray-beards. You remember that we have high authority for believing that warnings are sometimes sent in dreams.

"Last night I dreamed that I saw you in a church, assuredly a church in Italy, for the women with which it was crowded had on either the pezzotto or the mezzaro. Among them I was startled by seeing you, kneeling on a chair as Italian women do. You also wore the Genoese scarf over your head. Astonishing the distinctness with which I heard the music, it was that of a military mass

As I gazed at you, you turned and saw me. The first expression of your face was that of terror, the next moment you stretched your hands towards me with a cry for help. In the struggle to reach you, I awoke.

"I am not prone to superstition, not afraid to commence a journey on a Friday, or on the thirteenth of a month, not unwilling to sit down thirteen to table. Still this dream has been the deciding cause of this letter. Are you in any difficulty, any peril? you told me once, you did not want a friendship that should show itself but once in a life, like coronation trappings. To some, nevertheless, is given the chance of proving their devotion but once, some never have even that one chance. Do not grudge me the opportunity if it occurs; remember that you have one true friend willing to help you. Be your trouble what it may, give me at least my share of it.

"Your faithful

"G. G."

Lill read this letter, revealing a constant thought of her, revealing love with all love's tender superstitions, another sort of superstition from the one disclaimed, and saw in it, what? only the chance of an escape. Strong passion seldom sees anything beyond or above its own aims. Lill, so generous when heart-whole, so sensitive to inflicting mortification, now believed this letter to be nothing less than an interposition of Providence in her behalf.

Unconsciously cruel as a woman always is, when she does not love the man who loves her, she wrote on the spur of the moment:—

"Yes, indeed, Mr. Giuliani; I do believe you are my sincere friend, the truest I shall ever have. I have been very foolish, very erring; I must try not to do worse yet, and I should do worse if I deceived you. I cannot expect you or any one to believe me, to believe that I meant well. I have endeavoured, indeed I have, to keep faith with you, but I know I have broken it; not willingly, not gaily and carelessly, oh, no! indeed,—pray believe *that* at least. I have cried out for help, and your letter has come like a good angel to guide me; I feel as if it were a voice from heaven. You would have led me right long ago, but I *did* wish to make you happy

I see I was very stupid, but not wicked, not intentionally
so ; will you ever forgive me ? I am sure I shall never
be happy, because all my life long I shall remember my
fault to you. I will always pray that you may forget me
and be happy.   "Your poor pupil,
                                       "LILL TUFTON."

She hastily gathered together every scrap she had of
his writing, putting them into the same envelope with
her letter. In the centre, carefully wrapped in silver
paper, was the ring Giuliani had given her. He had
chosen it to suit her fortunes, not his. and the price had
entailed on him manifold privations. "I don't want to
part with you, poor little ring, but I must, though it will
hurt him to see you again," and a great tear fell and
dimmed the diamonds. She heard again the fond, foolish
words which had accompanied the gift. "Why *cannot*
I love him !" she exclaimed with a great gasp.

She ran upstairs for her bonnet ; this time she never
thought of Miss Crumpton as a messenger. When she
was within sight of Wavering, she stopped ; two minutes
more and the letter would be beyond recall ; her heart
beat fearfully.

At this crisis, she was startled by John Larke's voice.

"Good-day, Miss."

"Good-morning, John," and she walked on.

"When I seed you a-coming along so fast. Miss, says
I to myself, now Miss Tufton be a-going to the post, sure
as anything. Every one do have a way of hurrying when
they be bound for the post."

"Because they be generally too late, John," said Lill,
trying to speak calmly.

"I expects it's just that, Miss. Hurry is bad. and delay is bad ; it's a precious hard job, so it is, to find out
when it's the right time for one or t' other. Them
Lon'on architects now, I ain't for finding fault with 'em,
nor with Mr. Langden for employing of 'em, he hadn't
no time to lose to get his work done afore winter set in ;
but bless you. Miss Tufton there ain't nothing now in
that house that don't want setting to rights."

"I suppose you are to do that," said Lill ; guessing
the old man's wish, that she should understand he had
been working at Longlands.

"Why, yes, Miss   Mr. Langden and me's been agree-ing about a heap of things. Says I, Mr. Langden, sir, I ain't by no means a quick man in getting through jobs, —Mr. Ashton 'll tell you that. I likes to do the thing as it shan't want doing again. Shall I put the letter in the box for you, Miss ?"

Lill hurriedly gave him her packet ; so John Larke completed a job that day, which certainly would not re-quire doing again.

After dinner, when they were alone, Lill said to Miss Crumpton,

"You have your wish Crummie. I have broken with Mr. Giuliani."

Miss Crumpton laid down her work.

"Don't say a word of thankfulness," went on Lill, "or I shall hate you as much as I do myself."

She got up and walked to and fro in the room several times, then stopped, and confronting the astonished chaperone, said,—

"Christians do not exult in the pain of their enemies, do they? Mr. Giuliani was my enemy : if it had not been for him, I should not have had a dark speck as big as a pin on my life : but still I don't enjoy paining him. Why didn't you do your duty, Crummie, and tell Sir Mark—"

"My dear, you begged me not."

"Would you stand by and see me stab myself if I begged you? let me throw myself over a precipice, if I begged you ? When one is mad our friends are bound to take care of us, to use force to prevent our doing our-selves harm."

"O Lill ! I am not,—I never was,—able to guide you. I was wrong to keep a situation for which I knew my-self unfit. I was not clever enough for you ;" and Miss Crumpton began to cry.

The secret of Lill's power of inspiring affection, in spite of a temper variable and impetuous as the wind, was, that she redeemed her outbreaks by such warm tenderness, such abundant repentance.

"Dear Crummie !" she now exclaimed, throwing her arms around her old friend, "forgive me, I am naughty, because I am unhappy. Don't look so pitiful, Crummie, —you break my heart."

Miss Crumpton stroked the fair head so coaxingly laid on her knee.

"Ah! poor thing, if ever any one was born to break their own heart, it is you; always such a tempest of a child."

"Pity me," said Lill; "for this day, I have cured a wrong action, by one worse."

This state of mind lasted till the fifth day, when she received a packet from Paris. She found in it only her own letters—they were all there, even to the note asking for lessons: yes, even the very note of invitation she had written by Valentine's desire. No one need envy Lill's sensations when she took up these bits of paper, so carefully preserved. In the faded writing, as in a magic mirror, she saw herself the saucy beauty, the eager pupil; saw the kind master, the anxious friend—the devoted lover. His voice was in her ears: "Pray God take that sound away." She did not faint, but she could not see—the room had grown dark, and always that voice close to her ear.

Miss Crumpton, who had herself received the packet from the postman, though full of curiosity to know the contents, had discreetly left Lill alone for half an hour.

Having heard that the best way of recovering persons from a stupor of grief was to scold them heartily, Miss Crumpton no sooner saw Lill's state than she began,—

"Come, my dear, get up from off the floor; come, Lill, it's not nice to give way so, particularly about—hem! hem!—particularly in this case."

Lill looked at her with burning eyes, tried to speak, but her throat was too dry, and her poor lips too parched. Miss Crumpton raised her up.

"You had better go and lie down, my dear: let me help you."

Lill dragged herself wearily along by Miss Crumpton's arm, went up stairs slowly, and lay down on her bed, without a word.

"Drink some water, Lill."

Miss Crumpton drew down the blinds, and then bustled away, recollecting the letters left open on the table in the morning room. As she gathered them together she muttered, "Fretting about a man she doesn't care a pin for: who can manage girls?"

CHAPTER XXXIX.

Adieu.

AFTER Giuliani had read Lill's letter, he came to a rapid decision. Paris and his pupils were alike hateful to him.—he would leave both, and at once. He had only two duties to perform before he began his journey. The first to send back Miss Tufton's letters, the second to bid farewell to that true friend, Valentine's mother.

His interview with Lady Ponsonby had much in it of the solemnity of a death-bed parting; neither of the two ever expected to meet again. There was a sincere friendship between them, though the one was an old woman, and the other a young man. Giuliani had always enjoyed Lady Ponsonby's cheerfullness, as much as her good sense. In her house alone and in her society, had he felt that serenity which a man instinctively seeks and needs, to restore the equilibrium of his faculties after the day's struggle. She, on her side, was proud of, even grateful for his respectful attachment.

He gave her now his full confidence, ending thus: "I am wearied of this aimless agitation; wearied of forced tranquillity: my soul is like an empty boat on a rough sea: I must have action, I cannot remain longer, where everything tends to enfeeble my dearest convictions. The atmosphere of Paris stifles me."

"Where do you go?" asked Lady Ponsonby.

"The world is all before me where to choose," he replied. "The pope's amnesty would allow of my returning to Bologna, but I cannot bend my will to the condition of signing the exacted declaration. No; I will go to Piedmont; there it is where our national resurrection will begin; already the dead there are lifting their gravestones. I must conquer this unfortunate passion, or it will conquer me. I have done with books and dreams. I am going to live. *A Dio, cara amica.*"

"*A Dio,* Giuliani."

"I should wish to shake Miss Ponsonby by the hand before I go"

Lady Ponsonby said she would find her daughter. A great fear made her anxious to break the news of Giuliani's immediate departure to Alicia without witnesses.

For all answer to her mother's sudden information Alicia joined her hands together, like a child praying. Lady Ponsonby could see how tremulous the fingers were—could see every nerve of the usually calm features working. But Alicia had been brave too long—had too long governed her emotions to fail now.

"One moment, mother," she said.

When she believed herself mistress of her voice and of her face, Miss Ponsonby went forward to meet the great anguish of her innocent life.

Giuliani hastened towards her; the touch of her clammy cold hand, that invincible sign of inward disturbance, and the vibrating motion of her head, were not in accordance with the firmly spoken,—

"*C'est donc vrai, qu'il faut dire adieu?*"

He raised the hand he had taken to his lips; perhaps his own wretchedness gave him an insight into hers; for as he looked at her, his eyes filled with tears: perhaps he understood at last that happiness had been so close to him, that he had overlooked it.

Farewell was finally said, and he was at the door when he suddenly turned back, and again taking a hand of both mother and daughter, said in low husky tones,—

"I have a legacy, a last wish, to leave with you, dear friends. Do not desert *her*, poor young thing; life is always difficult, the world hard, for such impetuous, uncalculating natures." The knot in his throat made his last words scarcely audible. "Be kind to her for my sake."

"I will," was solemnly pronounced by Lady Ponsonby and Alicia.

"Adieu, adieu, adieu."

CHAPTER XL.

A Question of Buying and Selling.

SUMMER, with its deep greens and luminous skies, autumn, with its purple and gold, have vanished; winter is at hand, with its short gray days and its long nights; no more walks in the early morning to watch the transparent mists lifted from the face of the hills; silent now are the tender harmonies, absent the aromatic scents, choice gifts of the dying year.

Upwards of two months have elapsed since Lill received back her letters from Mr. Giuliani. She knows nothing further of him, nor of Sir Frederick Ponsonby; she has not had the courage to write to Lady Ponsonby; nor has the young baronet's name dropped from the lips of any of the Pantons, who might have been expected to have had news of him, as the admiral and colonel constantly saw Sir Frederick's tenant, Fordham.

Sir Frederick seemed forgotten, for neither did Sir Mark nor Miss Crumpton ever allude to him. Lill resented this general forgetfulness of one who had been so flatteringly sought, and without whose company none of the neighbours had appeared to consider the assembling themselves together worth while. She learned the disagreeable lesson then, of how very little any one person is missed, of how very soon a vacant place is filled.

Lill's thoughts did not dwell constantly and with coherence on Sir Frederick; they fluttered about the recollection of him with a distressing confusion. Occupation, which required any exercise of intelligence, was intolerable to her. Music sickened her; she was in that sad condition when an inward depression shows itself in outward displeasure against every one and everything. Everybody was wrong or disagreeable, because *her* soul was dull and heavy.

This was the moment that poor Miss Crumpton chose to enlighten Lill as to Sir Mark's attentions to Miss Althemiah Panton.

" It will be all the same a hundred years hence, Crummie. Whatever is to be, will be; so don't puzzle your poor head as to what may or may not happen. Hav'n't you heard that men are the sport of circumstance ? Fate will overtake us, make what haste we will."

It was just before Christmas that Sir Mark did what he had never done before in his life, invited Lill into his private room. Nor was the irony with which he had always seasoned his intercourse with her, and which had not been diminished by Mrs. Townsend's flight, to be traced either in the voice or words, in which he began the interview. On the contrary, there was even a touch of deference in his manner.

"Surely some one has left me a fortune," was Lill's conjecture as she took a seat.

"I wish, Miss Tufton, to obtain from you a frank opinion of some of our neighbours. My reasons for this shall be made obvious to you by and by. Let us begin, for instance, with Mr. Geoffrey Colfield. What do you think of him, seriously speaking."

"A good enough person, I believe, but a most grotesque fop."

"Short and graphic. Well ! and Mr. Swainton ?"

"Very amusing, but ill-natured, and without self-respect, or delicacy of feeling."

"Capital ! and Sir Frederick Ponsonby ?"

"Vain of his good looks. Thinks himself irresistible, I should say."

Sir Mark rubbed his hands.

"Now, what of Mr. Langden ?"

"Oh ! he is utterly insignificant."

"Upon my word, young lady, you strike hard. I wonder what you think of yourself."

"Not so badly as I deserve. Sir Mark. Nature grants to every one a self-love and esteem of themselves in inverse proportion to their merits."

"I am to infer, then, that with or without reason, Miss Tufton thinks herself the superior of these gentlemen."

"Comparisons are odious and unfair, Sir Mark."

The old gentleman seemed at a loss how to proceed. When he spoke again, Lill started, as if she had forgotten his being there.

"Miss Tufton, perhaps you may change your opinion of Mr. Langden, when I tell you he has done you the honour of offering you his hand and a share of his enormous fortune."

"I grant the half of his prayer, and blow the rest away. I will accept the share of his fortune, but not so much as the little finger of his hand."

"You are pretty and young; use your time for being impertinent,—I don't prevent you; but Miss Tufton, remember, before it is too late, that you are portionless."

"Am I?" said Lill, calmly.

"You are poor; Mr. Langden can make you rich better listen to reason. Every year takes away from your value. You won't be half as good-looking next year as you are now. I don't suspect you of much romance. You like the good things of this world, and quite right too. Langden offers princely settlements. He is not a learned man, nor a man of birth, but what of that? Riches will get an entrée everywhere."

"I think not, Sir Mark." He stared at her; and she added, gravely, "not into heaven."

"Difficult, Miss Tufton, if you please, not impossible; and with your sharpness you will be able to turn Langden round your finger, make a saint of him;—he'll be a puppet in your hands."

"Thank you; but I have observed, that though silly women can make clever men do what they like, clever women never can manage foolish, stupid men. I will not marry Mr. Langden, Sir Mark. Do believe that girls are not so generally to be bought, as it suits satirists to say."

"That's the fruit of *your* experience, eh!"

Lill had unconsciously thrown a sop to Cerberus; he was thinking of Althemiah Panton.

"Well, your own folly be on your head; but, stop a minute,—suppose I were about to marry, Miss Tufton, would that change your decision?"

"Not at all; I do not like Mr. Langden; I cannot bear him. If you were to turn me out of doors, that would not induce me to walk into his house. I will have none of his heart, hands, purse or lands," and with a little half curtsey she left the room.

Miss Crumpton plied Lill so well with questions that she was soon in possession of the fact of the proposal and the refusal.

"Do you know, Crummie," said Lill, " Sir Mark wanted to frighten me into accepting Mr. Langden by a threat of marrying himself?"

" My dear, I did my best to make you observe Sir Mark's attentions to Althemiah Panton."

Lill shrugged her shoulders.

" My dear, I heard him telling her the other evening when he was praising her for counting so well at picquet, that she was the first woman he had ever met who understood that two and two only did make four. I am sure he might have found out that I knew as much long ago, if he had asked me to play with him. Miss Panton *does* so smile at him, Lill."

" She smiles at everybody," said Lill. " Oh, Crummie, what does it matter to anybody but the people themselves who marries who?" And that was all the interest Miss Crumpton could get Lill to take in her grandfather's supposed marriage.

CHAPTER XLI.

Fencing.

ONE forenoon of the new year 1848, when the drawing-room at the Hall was full of morning visitors, Lill suddenly stopped short in what she was saying, and bent down her head in the attitude of one striving to catch some distant sound. The next instant she rose, walked some steps towards the door, then turning away again, took a chair, and made some indistinct remark to the person nearest to her.

The moment after the door opened, and Sir Frederick Ponsonby was announced.

Lill received him as if she had seen him the day before. He did not perceive—what man ever does?—that her fingers trembled, so that she could not hold up the screen she had seized, under pretence that the fire scorched her face.

While Sir Frederick was speaking to the rest of the party, all of them his acquaintances, Lill looked at him, and saw that he was pale and thin, like one recovering from illness. She gathered from his answers to various inquiries, that he had been some days already at the Priory; she heard him talk of hunting, as if that had been the reason of his return. The more she looked at him, the more certain she was that foxhounds had had nothing to do with his coming to England, and she felt angry that he should try to make any one believe it had. Then her grandfather came in, and asked him to stay dinner; and Sir Frederick agreed, without any pressing, that Black Prince should be sent to the stables.

To give herself an air of indifference, Lill drew out of a basket some long neglected piece of worsted work; a fashionable amusement at that period. Sir Frederick settled himself comfortably near her, and began forthwith playing with the contents of her workbox.

"You did not show any surprise at seeing me, Miss Tufton."

"I was not more surprised at your coming back to England, than at your going to Paris. I have remarked before now, that whenever people are not compelled by some necessity to remain in one place, they always are restless. I should myself be extremely pleased if Sir Mark would take a fancy to go to Brighton to-morrow."

Sir Frederick accepted this speech in silence; he did not doubt she intended to be unkind. The next moment Lill was consulting him about the particular shade of red to be used for the innermost petal of a damask-rose.

"How are Lady Ponsonby and Miss Ponsonby?"

"Quite well, thank you."

"I suppose Paris is very gay. Were you often at the opera? How could you come away in the middle of the Carnival?"

"I have not been in Paris. I merely slept one night there in passing through."

"Oh!"

"You were not aware, then, that I went to the Pyrenees?"

"No, indeed; but I was struck by how well you were looking; the air of the Pyrenees has agreed with you,—it does with everybody, I am told,"

Miss Crumpton raised her head.

"What nonsense was Lill talking! Any one with half an eye might see that Sir Frederick was altered for the worse."

Lill took good care to meet no inquiring glances; she went on:—

"You were at Biarritz, of course? Did you make excursions into Spain? How did you like riding in the Bayonne *cacolets?*"

"My dear girl," here interposed Miss Crumpton, with her usual tact "you don't give Sir Frederick time to answer."

"I beg Sir Frederick's pardon," said Lill, gravely. "One moment more, till I find my black skein, and then I shall be able to give him all my attention."

"I have not been to Biarritz, Miss Tufton. I went to the Bains d'Amélie, in the Eastern Pyrenees."

"May I ask what they are famous for, Sir Frederick?"

"For tranquillity, old ladies, and sulphur, I believe, Miss Tufton."

"Dear me! I never before guessed your tastes, Sir Frederick."

He smiled, and went on to describe the picturesque scenery of the banks of the Mondoni, and of the valley of Montalba, the grandeur of Canigou and the Roche d' Annibal. No winter there, always summer.

"Charming! what a fascination hunting must have, to bring you to this Siberia! I am sure you must wish yourself back again."

He said, in a low voice,—

"You are doing your best to make me understand you wish I were there, or at Jericho—anywhere but where I am."

"You are quite wrong, Sir Frederick. I am as glad as any other of your acquaintances to see you again. The sight of an unaccustomed face is reviving in this dull place."

Lill, for many more days, made fruitless struggles to impose on Sir Frederick the belief of her indifference towards him. She deceived herself into a persuasion that she would willingly accomplish any penance which could cure her of her love for him. She could give no clear reason for the secret spite she nourished against him. She was not frank with herself, would not examine into a certain mental reservation which embittered all her feelings towards him, and made her almost savage to him, if he uttered a word expressive of interest in her. Had she forced herself to confess, she would have understood that it was not remorse for her conduct to Giuliani which influenced her, but that she was suspicious Sir Frederick had discovered her affection for him, even while he loved some one else. Loved some other! What else could be the meaning of that sudden journey to the Pyrenees, his haggard appearance, and those letters to France, of which she had never thought till lately? Could she have more circumstantial evidence against him? No, poor Lill! rather against yourself. Yet whenever she had succeeded in mortifying or wounding Sir Frederick by some careless or cruel word or act, she

would heap the most violent reproaches on herself, con-
demn herself as mean and ungenerous, and exalt him as
high as she lowered herself.

After one of these occasions, Sir Frederick remained
away from the hall much longer than he had ever done
before. "So much the better for me," thought Lill.
Every night her pillow could have told how bitterly she
wept her supposed success.

CHAPTER XLII.

Airy, Fairy Lilian.

THERE was an artificial lake in Wavering Park, with a drive round it. The older folks in the village remembered the "grand madam," as Sir Mark's predecessor's wife had been always called, driving her phaeton with the cream-coloured ponies there, when she happened to be at the hall; and gay parties rowing or sailing on the lake. Road, and boats, and lake, were now solitary and neglected. In summer, rustling green flags stretched into the water, and broad leaves with golden balls hid its surface. No noises there now, but the plash of leaping fish, the dabbling of the coot's bill, and now and then the hurried note of the sedge warbler.

An old deep-bayed quarry was at the north end of the lake, famous in the season among the school-children for the blackberries which grew at its base.

On one of the last days of February in 1848 Lill took shelter in one of the nooks of this quarry from a sudden heavy shower of mingled sleet and rain.

The news of the revolution in Paris had reached her. She had hoped Sir Frederick would have forgiven her last unkind rebuff, and come over to give her news of his family. She tried to induce Sir Mark to ride over to the Priory, but, seeing how much she wished it, he took an obstinate fit and rode the contrary way. When the 28th of the month came, and no Sir Frederick, Lill made certain that, uneasy about his mother, he must have himself gone to Paris; she might never see him again; she wished she had sent him a note; there could have been no harm in showing anxiety for Lady Ponsonby; he could not have misconstrued anything so natural. On second thoughts she would go to Vale House; she could not fail to hear there, if he had left the Priory.

Indifferent to menacing clouds, Lill set off, going by the lake: that way being half a mile shorter than by the road. She had walked on notwithstanding a drizzle,

and only stopped when the rain began to fall in heavy
earnest. She had not long taken shelter when she
heard the trot of a horse. She thought she recognized
the particular sound of those hoofs; she turned white
and red with fear and hope. Sir Frederick had almost
passed when some involuntary movement of hers made
him glance to the side.

"Miss Tufton!" he exclaimed. She was frightened
at the joy the sight of him gave her. "Can I not help
you?" he asked, dismounting and hanging his bridle on
the branch of a birch. "You are getting quite wet,"
and, drawing off his waterproof cloak, he wrapped it
round her in spite of her refusal. "I can't help you out
of the scrape, but I can share it with you; in ten
minutes the worst will be over; it is clearing to wind-
ward."

He placed himself so as to protect her from the wind,
saying, as his eyes rested on her delicate face and figure,
"What brought you out in such weather? it is surely
imprudent."

"I am a country girl; I don't mind a wetting," she
replied, hastily. "Have you heard from Lady Ponsonby?"

"I was on my way to the hall to tell you that I had
received excellent news from herself. I ran up to London with the intention of going across, but the business
was all over, and my presence, considering my horrible
political tendencies," he looked into her eyes, "would
have thrown a drop of gall into my dear mother's cup
of joy. Poor mother! she believes in republicans, and
writes as though she were in the seventh heaven."

Lill had spirit enough left to say,—

"You can afford to be generous. You have had your
wish granted. Louis Philippe has lost his crown."

"You don't forget easily," he said.

Then they were both silent; the wind playing sad
tricks with Lill's hair, blinding Sir Frederick's eyes
with it, and sending it across his mouth, and she could
do nothing to prevent it, for he had imprisoned her,
arms and all, within his cloak, which he held closed
round her with one hand. Once he raised the hand that
he had at liberty, not to put away the long flowing

curls; on the contrary, it was to hold them against his lips. Lill bent down her face, to hide from him the deep flush of consciousness which covered it.

"Miss Tufton, I have something to tell you," he said. Her heart flew into her throat, and she made a sudden movement of flight. "No, you cannot go yet; it still rains heavily. Do you know, I have just discovered that this is the very scene of an adventure that happened to me some years ago? I don't believe my life would be safe with Sir Mark, did he find it out. I scarcely know if I should disclose it even to you."

Relieved, yet disappointed, Lill answered:

"You have said so much, you must say more."

"Do you know that we are very old acquaintances?" he said. "Once, you were very much kinder to me than you are now. Look back in your memory, or rather I will tell you a tale that will make you remember. Once upon a time, there was a cruel rich man, and he lived in an island whose inhabitants hate oppression and cruelty in every shape. But, nevertheless—in the island I mean —every man may have a slave—a woman—who is called the slave of the ring, because the condition on which he may have her is, that he gives her a gold ring. The man I am telling you of bought such a slave. One day, the tyrant and his slave came to just such a place as this, accompanied by a lovely little fairy some good Genie had sent to comfort the slave of the ring. It was a fine autumn day, when ripe blackberries covered the bramble-bushes; and the slave was tempted, and stayed behind her master to pick some. The master turned round and struck her with his walking-stick. Poor little fairy did what she could to help, screamed with all her might, and her cries brought to the spot a great rough boy."

"Oh! was it you—was it you?" cried Lill, her heart in her eyes. "Oh! now I know why I loved Lady Ponsonby from the first moment I saw her. Poor grandmamma! she gave me *The Seven Champions* and we called the boy St. George."

What a rapturous gratitude there was in the beautiful eyes fixed on him! He seized her hand, and said, impetuously,—

"But my story is not done. The fairy kissed my hand, and promised to love me all her life. Lill, will you keep that promise?"

No answer; he laid the hand he held upon his open palm, and asked in a whisper—his face on a level with hers, his breath among her curls,—

"A gift, a frank gift?"

The small fingers pressed themselves closer to his.

"Look at me, Lill." She shook her head.

He gently lifted the drooping face, and saw a tear on either cheek.

"The last I will ever make you shed, Lill; my pearl of beauty. Your eyes—let me see your eyes."

She looked up at last. When she turned her glance from him, what a heavenly world she saw before her! The rain had ceased, the sun had pierced the clouds, and the bow of promise spanned the space between heaven and earth.

"A good omen," said Sir Frederick. He lifted her into his saddle and walked by her side, Black Prince behaving with most perfect decorum.

When Sir Frederick rose that February morning, he had had no formed intention of making a proposal of marriage to Miss Tufton. He had been led on partly by previous circumstances, partly by the feeling of the moment. As Lill had said to Miss Crumpton. "Fate will overtake us." Are not two-thirds, at least, of our actions the result of circumstances? Is it not even generous measure to allot one-third as the fruit of previous firm resolve? Never, however, had a man more assurances of having done exactly what he ought to have done than Sir Frederick. To say nothing of Sir Mark's gracious consent, the whole neighbourhood was unanimous in approbation. Not that an overpowering majority in our favour is always a proof of our being in the right, any more than success is always a measure of merit. Many reasons produced this touching unanimity. Sir Frederick's birth and Miss Tufton's were on an equality; that was doing their duty in the class in which it had pleased Providence to place them: though the beauty of the county made no misalliance, she yet had not achieved any mortifying triumph. Sir Frederick though handsome and accomplished as a Crichton, was not a man of fortune, and his bride, a treasure in herself, had no other treasure to bestow; so that, altogether, it was a most suitable match, and created no envy; on the contrary, there was plenty of room to wonder how two such elegant persons meant—unless Sir Frederick went back to India, and got a staff appointment—to exist on an income under a thousand a year. Everybody was pleased.

Congratulations arrived in person, and by post, and presents were not slow in appearing. Lill received a kind letter from Lady Ponsonby; much kinder than she had dared to hope for. Sir Frederick was not so well satisfied with the one addressed to himself. He wanted every one to assure him he was the happiest man in the world; and his mother's letter, though full of kind wishes, was sparing in congratulations. Of course Sir Frederick imagined that Lady Ponsonby was not free from that jealousy, which all mothers are accused of feeling, with respect to the marriage of their sons.

"I wonder if it is all real happiness, or if it is only a dream?" said Lill to Miss Crumpton, one night when she was going to bed. "I shouldn't be a bit surprised, if something dreadful were to happen, to put an end to it all. A murder, or a fire, or Sir Frederick turn out to be married, like Mr. Rochester. Now, Crummie, don't look as if you didn't know who Mr. Rochester is."

"I don't, indeed, Lill."

"Jane Eyre's Mr. Rochester. If I had been Jane Eyre, I would have killed him."

"My dear girl, what's the use of agitating yourself?" for Lill's face was as white as paper.

"I would forgive anything but being deceived," went on Lill. "No, I never could nor would forgive that."

"There's no deceit about Sir Frederick," said Miss Crumpton. "His eyes are as clear as day."

"So they are, dear old woman," exclaimed Lill, kissing Miss Crumpton. "I don't deserve to be so happy,—do I, Crummie? I don't deserve him. I have told him the whole story about Mr. Giuliani; he was so good about it; I could not be easy till he knew it. We are never, never to have a secret from one another."

CHAPTER XLIII.

The End of the Beginning.

One unclouded day of bliss followed another, until at last Sir Frederick pressed Lill to fix her wedding day.

"Why did he want a change? Were they not perfectly happy? Why could he not let well alone?" this was the first answer he received.

"Lill, my darling. your promise was to marry me, not to remain my betrothed."

"Ah, yes; but you were not thinking yesterday of our being married; I am certain you were not."

"I have thought of nothing else for the last month."

"You said it would take more than six months to make the Priory habitable."

"So it will. The repairs can go on while we are in Switzerland. I have never seen the Alps, and my desire is to see them for the first time in your company. Fortunately there is no displacing of the monarch of mountains contemplated."

"It is very early to go to Switzerland. June is soon enough."

"Let us divide the difference, and say May."

"May! not for the treasures of the world. Are you not aware that May is the unfortunate marriage month? Mary Stuart married Bothwell in May."

After a long debate Sir Frederick carried his point, and the twenty-third of April was fixed for the marriage. During the week previous Lill would have tried the patience of an angel, and yet Sir Frederick never lost his; but his spirits were evidently depressed.

Althemiah Panton was to be the principal bridesmaid, and little Rosy Ashton the second. By the way, Dolly Panton had been sent away to school, by her own desire, immediately after the beginning of the year. She had taken leave of Lill Tufton without kissing her, and on the night before she went away burned her diary.

Althemiah, who was staying at the hall to perform some of the onerous duties of a bridesmaid, ventured to

take the initiative for the first time since she could
speak, and remonstrated with Lill on her behaviour to
Sir Frederick; it was not respectful, etc.

"Suppose I don't respect him—don't care for him?"
said Lill.

"The day before you are to marry him is too late to
find that out," replied Althemiah.

"Too late?—not at all. I hear his step on the stairs;
I'll tell him so before you."

Althemiah fled.

Sir Frederick had come prepared to find Lill agitated;
tender thoughts were in his heart, tender words on his
lips: he was quite bewildered by the mocking gaiety of
the pair of eyes she fixed on him. He was puzzled
what to do or say: that which he had come to speak
would never suit her present mood. He watched her
uneasily; her gaiety, fictitious he was sure, affected him
more painfully than the deepest melancholy would have
done.

"You have no fears, no anxiety for the future, Lill—
have you?" he asked, taking both her hands in his.

"Afraid of the future? How can I be afraid of what
does not exist?"

"You quaint poetical child."

"But it is not original, you know." she said, with a
defiant smile—one of those he called mysterious. "I
borrowed it for the occasion."

"Will you come out and take a walk with me? Come
out. poor pet, it is a day that makes mere existence a
happiness."

"I don't wish to be happy to-day. You do not understand me at all, if you do not feel that I must be sorry—
sorry is not the word—wretched, to break away as I am
doing from everybody and thing I have known from my
birth, for the sake of a stranger."

"You do not love me, Lill," he said, sorrowfully.

"No, I think I hate you."

He turned pale. She looked long at him. and gradually
the proud mocking spirit that had been peering through
her eyes vanished. She went up to him with quivering
lips.

"Frederick, I don't know what is the matter with me. I cannot help being unkind to you; but I—I couldn't bear you to be away from me."

Sir Frederick led her to the chimney-piece, and holding both her hands, so as to prevent her escape, he rang the bell.

When the servant came, he desired that Miss Tufton's maid should bring her mistress's walking dress. He took the mantle from Ruth, and himself placed in on Lill's shoulders.

"I am not your property yet," she said, drawing back.

"Now for the hat," he went on; "and the goloshes," and kneeling down he drew them, as he spoke, over her shoes; then putting her arm within his, opened the glass door, and led her, reluctant but submissive, down the steps into the garden.

"Now then," he said, "we will go to the lake; there was the beginning of the happiest time of my life, and it shall end there also if it be true that you hate me."

He led her along as tenderly as though she had been a little child, careful that her foot should touch no stone, nor rough place. The air was piercing, but a sun of gold gilded the lake—the banks were covered with primroses. He drew a long breath of enjoyment, and pressed the hand lying on his arm closer to his side.

"Talk of an end!" he said. "No, no sweet one, I have you, and I shall not let you escape me. I will make you believe in love." He stooped to obtain a sight of her face. "Good heavens! how beautiful you are," he added, passionately.

"Is that why you care for me?" she asked.

"She calls it caring for her, and I have given her my life."

It was not the words, but the inflections of his voice, the expression of his eyes, that made her heart beat to suffocation. At that moment she believed fully and confidently that he loved her. Alarmed at her own emotion, she tried to answer him playfully,—

"When I am old and wrinkled—will you love me then?"

"I shall see no change, you will be Lill, my own Lill, for me."

"And do you really love me well enough, never to ask me to smile when I want to cry, or to sing and dance, when I am sad?"

"O one of little faith! but question for question; Lill, do you love me, or hate me?"

Up from her heart came the answer, "I love you:" it trembled on her lip, but to say it was impossible.

"Can you not say 'I love you?' I have never heard you pronounce those three blessed syllables."

"Time will show," she whispered, slipping her hand into his, and not denying him the sight of her loving eyes. It was one of those moments for both neither man nor woman ever forgets, let life be ever so long, or so smooth, or so troubled.

They were opposite the quarry—he loosened his hold of her hand to take her in his arms, but she sprang away from him, up the steep grassy path at the side. She was out of sight in an instant.

"Good-bye. good-bye." came floating through the air

"Till to-morrow," he called to her. "Strange, fantas tic girl!" he muttered; "but *she* is no coquette."

Excepting Sir Mark's private rooms, there was not one in the Hall which Lill did not visit that afternoon. She spent some time in what had been her schoolroom, taking down from the dusty shelves one book after another. In most of them was scrawled in pencil or ink, "Lilian, surnamed Espiègle." amid devices of fabulous animals, such as flying serpents or owls' heads on men's bodies astride a winged globe. Plenty of caricatures, too, on the fly-leaves; sufficient signs everywhere to prove that the name of Espiègle had been thoroughly deserved. No one in the house or out of the house had been spared, but Lady Tufton. Under several of the figures meant for the tall governess, was written "Juno"

"I am sure she wouldn't call me Espiègle if she saw me now," thought Lill. "I feel as tame as a barn-door fowl. How I used to tease and terrify her with my ambitions! I fancy, I hear her sonorous voice repeating over and over again, 'You have no judgment to guide your talents or your good impulses. Patience is genius.' Poor Juno! I wonder where you are. I should be glad to send you cake and wedding cards, and receive a letter of advice from you, full of concealed pity for Sir Frederick."

Other chambers also were visited by Lill, fraught with too sacred remembrances to be mentioned here; out of those rooms she came with reddened eyes.

When Lill went into the drawing-room before dinner, she found there, besides Sir Mark, Miss Crumpton and Althemiah, Mrs. Tufton, her son Edward, and Sir Mark's man of business from London, with the settlements.

Mrs. Tufton was a little, lively, elderly lady, who never failed to let strangers know she had been very pretty in her youth. She did so very ingeniously, by repeating that she had been told she was like some picture by Sir Joshua; or had been mistaken for Miss O'Neil, or some other celebrity. Her present claim to notice was her knowledge of the genealogy, and the past and present intermarriages of the landed gentry of England. She did not meddle with Scotland.

She was already at work informing the solicitor who Sir Frederick Ponsonby's grandfather and grandmother were on the maternal side, and whom his paternal great aunts and their sons and daughters had married. She was saying as Lill entered, "Curious thing! but the baronetcy has never descended from father to son, but to some collateral relation." Mrs. Tufton liked to talk legally, as she termed it.

Edward Tufton had been ordained since he and Lill had parted, and on the following morning was to appear in his beautiful new surplice, as Mr. Ashton's assistant in marrying Miss Tufton to Sir Frederick Ponsonby. Edward was dignified and reserved in manner; his waistcoat peculiarly shaped, and the collars of his shirt almost nothing.

He informed Lill that Valentine Ponsonby had travelled down from London, in the same carriage with himself and Mrs. Tufton.

"He is to be Sir Frederick's best man, he told me. Do you take the same interest in revolutions and republicans as you did? There seems to be plenty of that sort of thing going on in Paris just now?"

The Rev. Edward believed he had hit the cousin who had been so blind to his merits, a very hard blow.

Dinner was about as dull as dinners are, when most of the company are preoccupied by some serious interest, of which they do not consider it polite to talk.

Sir Mark made quite a solemn ceremony of the signing of the settlements. The parchments were spread out ostentatiously on a round table, on which were wax candles in two enormous silver candlesticks, and Sir Mark asked Mr. Baldwin questions in a loud voice, and did all that man could do to force Lill to understand what was settled on her. But her signature was all that could be obtained from the young lady; who immediately afterwards, to Sir Mark's astonishment, left the room, followed by Miss Althemiah, and thus caused Sir Mark to lose his game of picquet with the only woman who understood that two and two made four.

As soon as Lill could rid herself of Althemiah's well-meant attentions, and was alone with Miss Crumpton, she flung herself on her knees before the chaperone, begging to be forgiven for all her many naughtinesses.

"Crummie, you know that it is not my heart that is wicked. Crummie, dear, you will come and live with me—you must go to India with me, and ride on an elephant"—here Lill tried to laugh, but cried instead. "Tell me, you love me, Crummie; tell me that I have not made you unhappy all these many past years. I have never yet been good for anything; but I *can* and *do* love. I think I shall be a better woman now; you have hopes of me, Crummie."

Miss Crumpton, sobbing for company, said,—

"I'll tell you what's best for you, my dear, though I am an old maid : you must go to bed at once, and have a good tumbler full of hot port wine negus. God bless you, my dear. O Lill, what will become of me, without your dear face to look at?" and then the two women fell into each other's arms, and wept.

Lill's marriage was very quiet,—it was so at her own request,—but it was a very pretty wedding. She was popular in Wavering; and the girls of the village assembled, of their own accord, to strew flowers before her as she walked up the path through the churchyard.

Every woman in the two parishes was in the church; and they all considered it their duty to weep copiously.

John Larke, who from his office as parish clerk, had excellent opportunities of observing the bridal party, described the bride as more like waxwork than live flesh and blood.

"She behaved grandly; though I could see her shaking like an aspen, not a tear did she let drop."

"I wish she hadn't a tore her beautiful dress on that ere nail of Sir Mark's pew," said Mrs. Pybus. "It ain't lucky, no, it ain't."

Miss Crumpton had conducted herself with her usual propriety during the ceremony, but after the breakfast she became unruly, running up and down stairs with flushed cheeks, and giving wild directions about Lady Ponsonby's cloaks and bags.

"Something is the matter with the old lady," whispered Mrs. Tufton to Althemiah. "I am sure she has had too much champagne."

Poor Crummie! when the bride gave her the last kiss, she exclaimed in a high key,—

"The happiest day of my life, my dear Lady Ponsonby."

She went to the windows with the rest to see the carriage drive off.

"Have you got an old shoe?" she asked of the person next her, who chanced to be Sir Mark. "I have, rose-coloured, too; what a little foot she has, poor dear," with a sob, bringing an old dancing shoe of Lill's out of her pocket. "There!" she flung it with all her strength on the roof of the carriage, and then fainted away for the first time in her life.

CHAPTER XLIV.

The Beginning of the End.

On the 25th of June. Sir Frederick and Lady Ponsonby drove up the long avenue of poplars, in the little town of Aix les Bains. Never had two handsomer or happier faces appeared at the Hôtel de la Poste.

There was a special reason for the visit of the young couple to this noisy, gay place, hid away in a fold of the Alps. They had come thither to meet Mrs. Townsend by appointment.

One of the first letters which had been forwarded by Miss Crumpton to Lill, was from that flighty and long-missing lady. It was dated Paris, from the Rue des Trois Sabres :—

"Dearest Lill,

"I am so glad to see by *Galignani's Messenger* (I have not been able to renounce that particular snare of the soul). that you have been a sensible girl. and married a civilized and reasonable being, a countryman and friend : for though there are other honourable men belonging to other nations, I suppose, **gray eyes, brown hair,** and a fair complexion are three more trustworthy signs, believe me,—hem! than their opposites. Of course you fancy yourself in Elysium at this present moment, so I implore of you, do not write to me. By the by, you must wonder where I am, my dear; I am in a semi-demi religious community. No vows or shaving required. I may go away when I like, so I like to stay. I wear a black gown and plain white cap, which the evil spirit, still rampant in me, makes dangerous to my spiritual pastors and masters. They found out I had no vocation for preaching to stray sheep. Their sad stories make me so horribly indignant, that I rant forth philippics instead of pointing out errors ; so I am set to mend bodies instead of souls, and when there is no hospital duty for me, I teach little children. Their great round eyes. so stupidly ignorant of evil, are amusing to look at. When I am flat, I ask for a spell of the schoolroom : children are nice inventions.

"The youth who preached that day in the chapel Taitbout, has gone away on the long journey, from which no one comes back. I can't write to you about it; some day, perhaps, I may show you his letters to me. His mother—you remember her—so like some wooden effigy of the dark ages, poor soul—well, can you believe it, she says,—foolish body—that I have been a comfort to her?

"After all, yes, I should like to hear everything about you and your husband: he is the son, of course, of the charming lady you ran after in Paris. Good-bye, my pretty Lill. Don't forget,

"Your loving friend,
"Honora Townsend.

"P.S.—What of Sir Mark and the dear chaperone? Why shouldn't they be joined together in holy matrimony? Don't mention the proposal as coming from me."

"Not a bit changed," said Lill, after giving Sir Frederick a short account of Mrs. Townsend.

"People don't change," replied he.

"Yes, they do," affirmed his wife. "I am perfectly unlike an espiègle; or even the Lill Tufton you met at Wavering."

"Modified, not changed, Lill."

"Changed outright, I am grown too lazy to be impulsive," she answered. "Looking back, I am full of wonder and fear at the way I used to rush into difficulties. It was my way, Fred, to leap first and look afterwards."

"And I am to believe you are quite incapable of such enormities now?"

"Oh, yes, I am as slavish as your spaniel, who always consults your eyes before he even wags his tail. It's very nice to have some one to take all the trouble of thinking what's best to be done off one's hands. Yes, yes; I have quite, quite done with rash decisions."

At Geneva, another letter letter from Mrs. Townsend reached Lill. After thanking her for having written so immediately, Mrs. Townsend explained that she had been induced to leave Paris and join her sister (the one she had once spoken of to Lill), the wife of the Major Marco Alberti. The Signora Alberti was in a frantic state; her husband had been wounded in the face and the arm

He was ordered to Aix les Bains, the waters there being considered good for sword wounds. "As you mean to go to Geneva," the letter went on to say, " out of charity extend your travels to Aix les Bains, and give me the comfort of some rational conversation. My dear Lill, you cannot be too thankful for your escape from these crazy, crusading Italians. Why couldn't the Piedmontese be satisfied with setting a good example? I shall hate the words, freedom and liberty, for the rest of my life. I am dying to see Sir Frederick. I really shall be grateful if you will agree to my request."

When people are very happy, they are generally very good-natured, and therefore Mrs. Townsend's petition was granted. There was a note waiting for Lady Ponsonby at the Hôtel de la Poste, when she arrived. Mrs. Townsend wrote that she would be at Aix with the Albertis on the day but one after, adding, "Marco is suffering horribly."

"Then to-morrow we can devote to Haute Combe," said Lill.

The husband and wife passed that evening by the side of the water; they saw the sun set behind the steep naked summits of the Mont du Chat, which stretches for two leagues along the southern side of the Lac de Bourget. They remained out even when twilight had darkened into night. Overleaping the present, they made plans for the future, their intimate talk often dying into those silences which are no interruption to the communication of two loving hearts.

The next day was as fine as could be desired, and immediately after breakfast Sir Frederick and Lill set off in a sailing boat for the Abbey of Haute Combe, the burial-place, as most people know, of the royal house of Savoy. After having been for two months in the midst of all the grand picturesqueness of the Alps, rocks, valleys, pine forests, lakes, and glaciers of Switzerland, neither of the travellers were prepared to be fascinated by the scenery of a defile in Savoy. But the immense mass of the Mont du Chat has a sombre, savage splendour of its own, and the Lac de Bourget, from the left shore of which the mountain rises sheer, has its own peculiar loveliness. Within its transparent, narrow bounds meet and mingle mountain, sunny vineyards, church and church-yards, with the blue firmament. No separation there between hard earth and soft heaven.

"You will not persuade me to move from here for at least a week," said Lill to her husband; "this place bewitches me. Listen to the water. Fred—it *is* musical, I always thought that a poetical license—listen—and what a sky!"

"Not so blue and pure as your own eyes, Lill."

"Sacrilege," she said, quickly; then throwing herself back on the seat half in a reclining attitude, she added, "I am too happy to talk," and remained silent. An **ex**-pression of ecstasy spreading itself over her face.

The two boatmen looked at her, and then at each other; one uttered a significant "*J'espère!*" a very comprehensive contraction, meaning, "Well! I hope she's handsome enough." They then suddenly began to sing one of their native love songs, a mixture of strident, with monotonous complaining notes. The crew of another boat, not far off, took up the melody. Tears filled Lill's eyes as she listened, and she slipped her hand into that of her husband.

After the romance of the morning, came the comedy of the evening. They went to the Casino. Lill's appearance was greeted with that murmur, which is so flattering to a woman, "Beautiful as a dream," observed more than one young man.

Lill had never been vain, but she was delighted with this homage—it was something more to lay on the altar she had built in her heart to her husband.

They had made the circuit of the rooms, stopping to look on at the *rouge et noir* tables. One of the gamblers, a lovely woman, who might once have disputed the palm of beauty with the young English wife, particularly attracted Lill's notice. A heap of gold lay by the elbow of this person: every time she staked she won. Presently she moved as if to go away.

"Madame, don't forget your money," said one of her neighbours.

"I play for excitement, not gold," she said aloud, and left it.

"Poor thing! how I pity her," said Lill: 'let us go away."

As Lill entered the ball-room leaning on her husband's arm, another couple advanced from the opposite end of the salon. The lady was not young, about thirty, and of a doubtful beauty, at least as far as features went; "striking," was the word to use in describing her. She took your attention by storm. Her almond-shaped eyes were of a light, undecided colour, but the thick long lashes in which they were set made them seem black as night. Heavy bands of black hair surrounded her face, the complexion of which was clear and pale as alabaster. She was tall—taller than Lill, slight, upright, and magnificently curved.

Lill felt Sir Frederick start: he made a swerve to the side, indicative of a wish to avoid the dazzling stranger, but he recovered himself, and as they passed he bowed low, the lady slightly moving her head in return.

Lill had scarcely time to feel fluttered and annoyed, when she heard a well-known, bold voice, and Mdlle. Arsenieff was addressing her. With the Russian's usual freedom she was already catechizing Lady Ponsonby on how she came to be at Aix, volunteering the information that she had come thither herself under the patronage of Madame la Comtesse Mathilde de Ravignau.

"My concert is to-morrow. I shall expect you to take a dozen tickets for friendship's sake. *Et ce pauvre Giuliani ?*"

At this moment the gentleman, on whose arm the Comtesse Mathilde had been leaning, spoke to Sir Frederick.

"Will you sit down a moment, love," he said. "I must go and speak to an old acquaintance."

He led Lill to a chair. Mdlle. Arsenieff followed Lady Ponsonby, and sitting down by her pursued her course of cross-examination. Lill answered her politely and calmly, though she felt a terrible tightness in her chest, her lips quivered, but too slightly to attract the attention of her companion.

Lill fancied Sir Frederick avoided looking towards where she was; and that he moved his shoulders with a gesture she knew denoted impatience when she turned her eyes in his direction.

At last he came back to her; she whispered:

You have been a long time away."

" You must not expect that we can remain always to-gether," he said, shortly.

These were the first rough words she had ever heard from him.

She was in society, so she smiled.

Mdme. la Comtesse and Lady Ponsonby exchanged a look as they again repassed each other in the salon. A painful shudder ran through Lill's frame, and she told Sir Frederick she had had enough of the Casino.

When they reached their own apartments in the hotel, Lill perceived an air of defiance on Sir Frederick's face. In that little wilful head of hers one maxim had fixed itself, and that was to avoid the first quarrel. Be-sides, she loved him, and love had taught her humility and fear. She was not quite confident of her power over him: a woman's instinct is fine enough always to tell her if she *may* be the tyrant, or *must* be the slave.

CHAPTER XLV.

A Peep into Bluebeard's Closet.

THE next morning Lill rose with the idea that she had been very foolish the evening before. It had been preposterous of her to reproach her husband for conversing for half-an-hour with a former acquaintance. She to do so, who had so often ridiculed the silly exactingness of young wives! She accused herself in order to have an excuse for Sir Frederick's roughness.

Night had brought good inspirations to him also; he regretted having spoken harshly to Lill, but she must understand that and not require any acknowledgment of his fault.

Thus inclined for amity, their breakfast was as cheerful as usual, though each was sensible of making an effort. This was the first time that they had experienced that sensation in each other's company since their marriage. Lill, always as impulsive as ever, in spite of her belief to the contrary, wanted some extra demonstration of affection from Sir Frederick to set her heart at ease, and to obtain this she began to flatter him with the cunning of love.

"Not one quarrel, and we have been married nearly nine weeks?" she said; "no thanks to me, for I have tried to do so a dozen times," and she linked her arm in his. "Dear Fred, will you always be so kind and forbearing with such a wilful wife?"

"Will my dear little wife," he playfully tapped her fair cheek, "continue to look at me through the rose-coloured spectacles she has been wearing for the last two months? I don't think even your eyes, Lill, would be beautiful behind green glasses."

Lill winced, and let go her hold of him. She felt rising of her old impatience.

"Are you still angry with me?" she said.

"Angry! when was I angry? Come, Lill, let us go out into the air, and have a gallop on something; if we cannot find horses, there are capital donkeys here."

"I should like it, but I must stay at home to receive

Mrs. Townsend: she did not mention at what hour she would arrive." Lill was vexed that Sir Frederick did not understand how she was trying to conquer herself, and her voice had, unintentionally so, a little grieved tone, which is in general peculiarly irritating to husbands.

"That's a bore!" he exclaimed. "I'll go and take a ook round, ask for letters, and bring you the news."

Even while he spoke he had the door open in his hand. He was gone without the usual caress, without even a glance.

Lill feels aggrieved; ah! he is returning repentant? no; it is only Ruth with a small packet.

"Your master is just gone to the post," and Lill leaned out of the window in hopes of seeing Sir Frederick.

"This did not come by post, my lady," explained Ruth; "one of the waiters gave it to me."

The envelope was addressed in that fine small writing known all over the civilized world as "*Pattes de mouches*." Yes, it certainly was for Lady Ponsonby, though she wondered who her correspondent could be. Now she guesses; no doubt Mdlle. Arsenieff has sent her, as she threatened, the dozen tickets for the concert. Lill opened the packet: it was full of letters, written on thin foreign paper. She at once recognized her husband's hand; she had presence of mind enough to say: "You need not wait, Ruth."

There they are on her lap, the direction tells her to whom written: "Mdme. la Comtesse de Ravignan." She shuffled them like a pack of cards, recalling poor Crummie's first confidence about Sir Frederick. Some were to Paris, some to the Bains d'Amélie, one or two had Brétagne on them. What business has she with any correspondence of Sir Frederick Ponsonby's before her marriage? Is she going to be a spy? She threw the letters on the table, and in so doing a small note fell out. It ran thus:—

"MADAME,

"Ayez l'extrême gracieuseté de rendre à Sir Frederick Ponsonby les lettres ci-incluses. Je vous demande ce petit service, croyez-le, Madame, pour vous éviter un moment d'inquiétude, ce qui pourrait bien arriver si vous voyiez une lettre dans l'écriture d'une femme à l'adresse de votre mari. Sir Frederick m'ayant déjà remis mes pauvres lettres à moi, je me suis appelée à en faire autant des siennes. Depuis que je vous aie vu, Madame, je puis comprendre et même pardonner l'inconstance de quelque homme que ce soit.

"Agréez mes sentimens de respect,

"MATHILDE, Comtesse de Ravignan

"(Née de Loisic)."

Was it possible to stab any one with more politeness? Lill determined to play her part equally well; she would present the letters to her husband without a question, without even a look that he could misconstrue into vexation. Droll indeed if she, the winner of the victory, were going to be jealous of the past—of an elderly coquettish Frenchwoman? She ought rather to joke him about his taste for antiques. She wished with all her heart he would come in and relieve her of the charge of his property—his sole property; she had no claim on anything that was his before they were married.

Again and again she stretched her slender neck out of the window, to see if he were returning. Every time she glanced towards the table on which lay the letters, she lessened the distance between them and her. They had the same fascination for her that a serpent is said to have for a bird. Her eyes seemed to penetrate the paper, to read words that would render her the most miserable of creatures for the rest of her life. Two cries of impatient pain issued from her lips. She put her hands behind her to keep them out of temptation, still her neck was extended, revealing a most torturing excitation. The voice of Sir Frederick resounded beneath the window. She did not catch what he was saying, but suddenly, actuated by one of those impulses so beyond our own consciousness that they seem to come from a power above and beyond us, she seized the whole of the letters, to thrust them out of sight into her carriage bag open on a sofa. As she did so, one dropped at her feet; in picking it up she saw the postmark of " Wavering," and " 23rd April," the date of her wedding-day.

"Mine, mine," she muttered, and she put it into her bosom, only the next instant to draw it out; the touch had stung her.

"I will know all soon, though it kill me." Yes, that is the desire which swallows up in such moments all others. To know the whole of one's misery, to do that, the jealous become endowed with the dissimulation, the patience, the stoical endurance of the Indian. Her husband came back.

"No letters," said he, sitting down by her, and throwing his arm round her waist.

The blessed influences of a serene sky and beautiful nature had banished his irritation; he had been his own confessor by the side of the blue waters of the lake. Yes, the sight of the Comtesse Mathilde had made him unjust, rude to his fair, trusting, loving bride.

"What has been, cannot be sponged out," he said to himself. "The love I had for Mathilde was different from what I feel for my poor Lill; but I am honestly glad that Lill, not Mathilde, is my wife."

The more he analyzed the sensations the more satisfied he felt with his lot. Mathilde's image faded in the presence of that of his charming, pure young wife. In this happy state of mind he returned to the hotel.

"By-the-by, Frederick, you have never told me anything about the lady you met last night: not even her name," began Lill.

"Madame la Comtesse de Ravignan."

"Ought I to call on her, or she on me? It seems to me that you having known her so well, she and I ought to be civil to one another."

"What put it into your head that we were intimate?"

"One can't always demonstrate mathematically how impressions are received," she answered carelessly. "Is she the lady of the Faubourg St. Germain, who made you a legitimist?"

"She, and some others."

"Well, shall I send her a card or call? I suppose she is in this hotel."

"You would not like her; she would not suit you at all."

"I could avoid politics with her, you know. I am

rather curious to be acquainted with a *grande dame* of the old aristocracy. I never had that pleasure, for Sir Mark would not visit French families."

Sir Frederick by this time felt a storm in the air. He was in reality too honest, too inexperienced in deceiving, to know how to manage. The notion never entered his head that a frank avowal of his former love for Madame de Ravignan would cut the knot that already existed, he went on tying another.

"Well, if you wish it, I will see her and tell her you are coming."

"Does she need to be prepared for the sight of me?"

"If you had expressed the same wish when we met her at the Casino, an introduction would have taken place naturally; now, it might seem like a caprice."

"You kept away so determinately last evening, I had no opportunity of proposing anything," said Lill.

"You looked so forbidding and angry, I was afraid of some *éclat*."

The conversation was going all wrong. Sir Frederick took away his arm, then changed his seat.

Lill hesitated; should she insist on the veil being raised? Was she quite prepared for what might be the consequences!

Had Sir Frederick looked at her, he might have seen a sort of ripple passing over her skin and spoiling its evenness. He was, however, sitting half turned away, with the paper of the day before in his hand.

"Fred, do you remember the walk we had together the day before we were married?"

"Of course I do: there's been scarcely time for forgetting."

He rose and took his hat.

"Going out again?"

"Yes: you don't make it so agreeable that I should remain in this stupid little room."

"Stay a minute, Frederick;" she ran between him and the door; "I have something to say."

She was tingling from head to foot; her eyes grew glassy, and her face green with the agony of her suppressed feelings.

"I have had a letter from Madame de Ravignan."

Quite involuntarily he sat down again.

"Read it." She spread it out before him.

"Where are the letters?" he asked, after running his eye over the note.

"In my bag—all but one."

"And you have read them?"

He was very fierce.

She answered him by a look of indignation only. He understood her.

"I beg your pardon, Lill."

"I have not yet read a syllable. There is your correspondence intact, up to my wedding-day. Possibly Madame de Ravignan judged me as you did. This one I withhold. the one written on the day you married me."

He interrupted her.

"Not written."

"Sent away, then. on the day you married me. I mean to read it in your presence."

"You will do a very foolish act, Lill. Can you not understand, there may be times when a man, who is a man, feels bound to use soft language to a woman, to cover hard truth?"

"Perfectly," she said, and she opened the letter. "I will read it aloud."

"I beg of you, Lill, as a favour. to give me that foolish scrawl. I forget what is in it; but I swear to you that I loved you. and you only, the day we were married. Give it to me."

She sprang past him through the door connecting the *salon* and bedroom; before he could prevent it, he heard the key turned in that door, and also in the one on the stairs.

She opened the letter and hesitated as a gambler does, who is about to stake all he possesses on one throw. But she could not withstand that ravenous appetite for certainty which is one of the invariable symptoms of jealousy: she sought it, and found it.

The letter, dated the 22nd of April; began with,—

"Too late, too late; your relenting is like a reprieve to a dead man." Here was confirmation of those suspicions allayed, not uprooted, which had tortured her at Wavering. She writhed now under the knowledge that she was not the one he would have chosen. She pursued her reading. "You should have my life willingly; but not my honour. My word is given to Miss Tufton, and not even to call you my own, would I now draw back. You alone know whether your heart is racked by the anguish you so well describe; or whether your pen was guided by the infernal desire to stir into life the embers of a passion you provoked, and then disdained. That mad, soul-absorbing passion which I have felt for you, I shall never feel again. You have had the first bloom of my heart, but it will flower again, tended and sheltered by my sweet girl-bride. I can confidently trust my happiness in her hands. She loves me simply, affectionately. Her love was a spontaneous gift; I accepted it gratefully, as a shipwrecked wretch does a saving plank. In return I give her firm faith and deep devotion. I look back on the year gone by as on an epoch of folly and delusion. It belongs to the shadowy past. My heart will be re-baptized to happiness through the innocent love of the beautiful, noble creature who will be my wife within less than twenty-four hours."

The signature, and that was all.

As she read, Lill felt with horrible distinctness every single hair of her head moving. She could not keep her teeth from chattering. She had seen what was in Blue Beard's closet. Rub, rub, as she may, she will never rub out from her heart the testimony of her unwise visit.

23*

CHAPTER XLVI.

Love in Hate.

THOUGHTS are too rapid in the terrible crises of life, to be caught hold of and described. Lill's soul was like a ship between Scylla and Charybdis. It was tossing on hissing, bubbling waves, without compass and without steersman. Only two months! and already at the end of her happiness. It would be of no avail to follow the impulse, sprung from the cowardice rather than from the courage of her love, which was urging her to throw herself on her husband's neck, counselling her to seek no further enlightenment as to how much or how little she had of his heart, but rather to undertake the conquest of the whole.

" I should fail," she said to herself, " for I could never forget. My faith in him is lost. Where, then, would be my standing point? The words, addressed to that woman on the very eve of our marriage day, would for ever come between my heart and his."

She overheard Sir Frederick push back his chair. She heard his step: that well-known sound, which had always been a signal of joy to her : it brought tears into her eyes, scorched by the reading of the letter. Sir Frederick knocked at the inner door. His sensations about Madame de Ravignan's spiteful conduct were a curious compound of anger and mortification ; but knowing that whatever had been the doubtful state of his affections when he proposed to Lill, that now she was undisputed sovereign of his heart, when he cooled, he was ready to smile at the tragic manner in which his wife had rushed out of the room, clutching his last unlucky effusion to Madame de Ravignan. Sir Frederick was handsome as an archangel, amiable, affectionate, and generous-hearted, but by no means the hero of romance Lill had erected him into. Moreover, though he had made a great show of vehemence towards Madame de Ravignan, he had no great capability of passion ; the gentle tenderness he felt for Lill was what was most in accordance with his character.

"Lill, come back to me," he called, through the closed door.

The voice had its effect—she opened the door; he seized her in his arms, and kissed her violently—with a violence, indeed, that was new to her.

There is no calculating with sensitive natures. Lill drew back offended. She felt the caress almost an insult.

"I am not Madame de Ravignan, the object of a 'mad, soul-absorbing passion,' but your wife," and she walked to the sofa.

"My dear Lill!" exclaimed Sir Frederick. "I would as soon have met a tigress in my path as that lady."

"You forget that the window is open. Sir Frederick; *that* lady may hear you. You need not use such strong language to reassure me; I am not going to play the jealous wife."

"You have no cause for doing so. My dear love, how ill you look!"

"No wonder!"

Sir Frederick's ease of manner, which she was too agitated to perceive was assumed, threw her into one of those terrible excesses of passion in which a woman is capable of killing the man she adores.

"I marvel you have survived your trials. There's your letter," she said, and threw it on the ground, giving him a look of scorn that was equivalent to a blow on the face.

He coloured, and stooped to pick up the letter. He was in the act of tearing it, when she darted forward and tried to snatch it from him.

"No you shall not destroy it; I have changed my mind,—I shall keep it."

He stopped what further she would have said, by placing his hand on her mouth, exclaiming,—

"Listen!"

A man in the street was shouting, "Révolution à Paris! Massacres. Battaille sanglante à Montmartre; l'Archevêque assassiné."

Sir Frederick ran out, leaving Lill undisputed possession of the letter.

"How much he loves me!" she thought, bitterly. "My anguish is nothing to him; he does not even see it. Oh! what a fool I have been!"

Sir Frederick was away nearly half an hour; he came back very pale.

"The French mail has come in, and I have a letter from Alicia. Valentine has been severely wounded in the streets of Paris; the doctors give little hope. My poor mother! a shaft from her own bow has done it. I must be off for Geneva this afternoon, Lill. Do what I will, I cannot be in Paris before the day after to-morrow, probably too late."

Lill made no remark, though she had a momentary sympathy in his distress.

"Your friend will be here to-day or to-morrow," he continued; "and, with Ruth and Jacques, you will not be afraid to remain here without me."

"I shall do very well," said Lill.

She did not ask to see Alicia's letter, nor for any explanation as to how Valentine came to be wounded, nor yet interest herself in Sir Frederick's preparation for his journey.

She sat like one overcome by invincible sleep. He was going away, then, without their having come to any understanding about those letters; he seemed to have forgotten that she was offended, and had good right to be offended. Her heart was wounded, and her pride irritated. She was very unhappy.

More than once Sir Frederick in his hurried entries and exits, looked at her; he knew she was not deficient in feeling. He looked, but Lill was cold as ice, unyielding as iron.

"I shall go to the *salle à manger*, and have a *potage* and a *chop*," he said. "I have not more than three quarters of an hour to spare."

"Yes; I suppose you will not stop before you reach Geneva."

He had expected something more. He went out of the room; the sharp closing of the door made Lill spring from her seat. She sat miserable and undecided while he was away; her good and bad angel at either ear—the one repeating, "Self-sacrifice is heavenly; the greater the sacrifice the diviner;" the other dinning in her ears, "Not married for love." The room seemed papered with "spontaneous gift." She could never forgive his writing chat; besides, she had seen a man in love: memory too faithfully helped her with her comparison. All the out-pourings of Sir Frederick fell short of the mark Giuliani's restraint had reached.

She did not move when Sir Frederick came back, already with his hat on.

"Lill!" he raised her up in his arms, "are we friends?"

She turned aside. He stooped to kiss her. She moved so rapidly, that the kiss fell on her head.

"You are very unkind, Lill."

"Unkind! how dare you accuse me when *you* have made *me* miserable?"

"It's too bad!" he said, and letting go his hold, he walked slowly to the door. He lingered; not a syllable, not a breath even, met his ear; he was outside the door —no relenting; downstairs—in the street. When Lill heard the clacking of the postilion's whip, her heart had such a pang she thought it must have broken; she felt like one annihilated. How long she remained in that stony sorrow, she never knew—perhaps a minute, perhaps an hour. Nothing that had been, ever would be the same again; never, never more. Her eyes had been opened; distrust had entered her soul, with grief.

The next morning Lill was tormented by a visit from Mdlle. Arsenieff. The Russian had begun by being jealous of Lill for her friend Alicia's sake; but as nothing is at a standstill in this world of ours, but is either diminishing or increasing, so did this dislike of Mdlle. Arsenieff augment into unreasoning hatred of young Lady Ponsonby.

"I am come now to place myself under your patron-age, Lady Ponsonby," said Mdlle. Arsenieff. "Madame de Ravignan set out for Paris last evening; so did Sir Frederick, I hear; perhaps, they may make the journey together."

"I think that is not probable. Sir Frederick will hurry on without a moment's delay; it is with him a matter of life and death."

"They were old friends, you know. People say—"

Lill interrupted her: "People say that Sir Frederick proposed to her. Oh, yes; he told me that story

Young men's first loves, he said, are apt to be rather elderly. They are maternal, and not exacting."

Another letter came from Mrs. Townsend.

Marco Alberti was too ill to be moved from Turin. Could not the Ponsonbys come on there? At that season of the year the journey was nothing from Chambéry.

"I will go to her," said Lill; "he has set me an example of devotion to friends."

She thoroughly believed what Mdlle. Arsenieff meant her to believe. And in following out her own quickly conceived plan, she was not likely to be soon undeceived. What she felt was love in hate. She adored him, yet she wished with all her heart to pain him; she did not care at what cost to herself: vengeance on him, vengeance on herself. She told Ruth to pack her trunks, and to desire Jacques to get Sir Frederick's luggage ready. She sent him off in charge of it to Paris the same day that she herself started for Italy.

From Turin, Lill wrote to Sir Frederick. She told him in a very few lines that she had deliberately left Aix, and that, after the discovery she had made, she felt the necessity of their not meeting again at the present moment. She begged, therefore, he would agree to her request to be allowed twelve months for reflection. He was, she believed too delicate-minded to refuse her. For the present it was settled she would remain with Mrs. Townsend and Madame Alberti. It was the maddest act of poor Lill's life.

Had Sir Frederick had some more experience, he would have treated her malady more leniently. Unfortunately, also, when this crazy document reached him, he had not the heart to lay an additional burden on Lady Ponsonby. Valentine breathed, and that was all. Ever by the bedside of the gentle, kindly-natured young man, the mother's heart ached with self-reproach that this child had hitherto been the one of her children about whom she had thought least. Alicia, therefore, was Sir Frederick's confident, and shared in his indignation. She was, as most single women usually are, unmercifully severe as to the duties of a wife; without any knowledge of the vagaries of an impetuous human being like Lill, with her terrible susceptibility to a sense of wrong,

Alicia advised her brother to agree to his wife's demand.
Lady Ponsonby, on the contrary, would have prevailed
on her son to go at once to Lill. She knew that the
sight of the beloved one would act on Lill's heart like
the sun on frost. However, this was not to be. Sir
Frederick wrote in the first heat of his anger:

"You have been absurd—take care you stop short at
merely making yourself and me ridiculous. You have
revengefully calculated how to mortify and wound me.
You have, therefore, for ever lowered yourself in my estimation. I comply with the request you have made;
but do not be astonished if, at the end of the period you
have named, I may in my turn have terms to impose
upon you."

He enclosed at the same time a cheque for a consider
able amount of money. Lill, at the first reading felt
flushed with victory.

CHAPTER XLVII.

La Superba.

FLOODS of bright warm light bathed the expanse of sky, sea, and earth, that lay stretched out before the open windows of the old palace of Doria. The sunbeams danced upon the blue waters of the wide harbour, embraced, as it were, between the loving arms of the old and new mole. The sea arched itself beyond to meet the firmament in a far horizon, and showed on its broad breast of varied blue and green many a white sail.

A vessel coming majestically into port under a cloud of canvas, and a steamer shooting outwards, crossed on the threshold of the marine gateway. On the left, far within the immense basin, tapered the masts of a throng of merchant ships, lying at anchor, under the shelter of the town and quays. Behind and around the shipping, up an amphitheatre of hills, extend the many-coloured palaces at Genoa, well named the "Superba." On the most eastern eminence is the dome of the noble Carignano church, flanked on either side by a tower.

Beyond the city rise the peaks of the lofty Apennines, each crested by its fort; from the highest point, the summits fall in a graceful gradation, like waves suddenly crystallized by some wizard power. At the extreme verge of the view to the left juts forth the bold, picturesque headland of Porto Fino, blue in the softening distance as lapis-lazuli. Opposite to the town rises against the western sky the tall, slender column of the Lanterna, or lighthouse. After ranging over this extensive, brilliant prospect, the eye returns with pleasure to rest upon the grove of dark ilex-trees, shading part of the terrace of the palace. This terrace, based upon a rock, projects in front of the building into the sea. It is the spot where the Doge Andrea Doria spread the princely repast he offered to the Emperor Charles the Fifth.

On a sunny day of March, 1849, three ladies were walking under the shade of the ilex-trees. They were Lill, Signora Marco Alberti, and Mrs. Townsend. Sorrow and years had faded the faces of the sisters, but

Lill, who had not yet attained her majority, actually looked aged. Absence from those they love ages women quickly, and such had been the revolution in Lill's being during the last nine months, that they might well count as a lifetime. She had the haggard eyes which one fixed thought gives.

' What three specimens of matrimony we are ! Scare crows !" exclaimed Mrs. Townsend.

"But I am innocent," said Signora Alberti, with frightful egotism. "I have done nothing to deserve *my* troubles; and Marco would, I verily believe, see me die of grief before his eyes, rather than remain behind his regiment, though the general himself told him he was not fit for active service."

"And you complain of that ?" asked Lill. "You have chosen an odd subject for lamentation—your husband's heroism."

"That sort of thing is charming to read of," retorted the Signora Alberti; "but when a wife sees her husband insisting on joining a forlorn hope—going to certain defeat, if not to certain death—ah ! but a very few years ago we were so comfortable, no one thinking about these detestable ideas **of liberty**."

'Only heroes lead forlorn hopes," answered Lill.

"Mamma ! mamma !" shouted two children; and a couple of pretty little boys came bounding forward. They threw themselves on the ground at the Signora Alberti's feet, speaking as much with their hands as their lips, telling her that "papa had said they might go to the cathedral to attend the first service of the Triduum to be celebrated in behalf of the Army, if she, or their aunt, or Scià Lilla" (the name by which Lill went in the Alberti family) "would take them."

The armistice called Salasco had been denounced in the first week of March, and the Piedmontese and Austrian armies were already assembling on the frontiers of Lombardy and Piedmont. It is only justice to Genoa to say that no city in the north of Italy made more costly or willing sacrifices than she did towards the end of ridding the country of foreign dominion. The Genoese are a proud, stiff-necked, distrustful, rebellious people there is, indeed, a great similarity in their history to that of the chosen people of God, as described in the Old Testament; and, like the Jews, the Genoese are undaunted lovers of their own superb city. When they claim for it now also the title of *Italianissima*, they do so with a good right.

The Signora Alberti, like all persons who insist on nursing their grievances, never accepted any means of diverting her thoughts from dwelling solely on self. So now, as usual, she left the chance of her children's going to the cathedral to the good-nature of her sister and Lady Ponsonby.

San Lorenzo is a considerable distance from the Palazzo Doria, so that, in spite of the precaution of setting out early, the regiments to be present at the mass were turning into the Piazza Nuova as Mrs. Townsend, Lill, and the boys were entering the cathedral doors. A great crowd was already within, principally composed of country people—probably the families of the soldiers.

It was with some difficulty that the ladies obtained chairs; the little Albertis had to stand. A moment after there was a clank and ring of swords and spurs, and that peculiar muffled sound which is produced by the regular tread of a great body of men. The general, his aides-de-camp, and the field officers, accompanied by the well-known deputy Buffa, with the intendente of the city and other officials, filled the chancel. The subaltern officers and the soldiers were in double lines down the nave and aisles.

A military mass is always an imposing ceremony; in this instance it was both exciting and heart-rending. Who could help feeling, that for many among that host of vigorous men, animated by the one sentiment which makes war a virtue, this was a funeral service?

The women shed their tears quietly; once only during the *prône* or sermon, a sob interrupted the preacher and made him pause. His words hitherto had been commonplace, a mere string of popular phrases; now he turned his face in the direction from whence had arisen that solitary outcry of woe: it had come from the peasant woman by Lill's side. He began a sentence, meant to convey comfort to the desolate, broke down, and was only able to exclaim over and over again, "Italia! O Italia nostra!"

A great murmur, like that of a wave breaking on the sea shore, filled the cathedral: it was the offering up of one prayer, the registering of one vow, to break the chains of Italy. Mrs. Townsend with surprise saw Lill suddenly rise from her chair and look about her, as if meditating an escape from the group which encircled her.

" Are you ill ?" whispered Honora.

Lill sat down again without speaking, glanced towards the chancel, then covered her face with her hands.

When they were again in the street, Lill said, abruptly.—

" Honora, Mr. Giuliani was in the chancel; he was next to Major Alberti."

" Who ?   O heavens ! pedagogus ?"

" Don't call him names : he saw me too, but I am sure he did not recognize me at first.   Am I so changed, Honora ?"   As she asked this she turned her face to her friend.

Mrs. Townsend began to say something jokingly about none so blind as those that won't see ; she ended by an earnest " Yes, you are killing yourself by your obstinacy," so suddenly struck was she by the change in Lill's appearance.

It does often happen that to judge of what is daily before us, we require to look at it through unaccustomed eyes.   Mrs. Townsend now perceived for the first time the sad alteration that had prevented Giuliani's immediate recognition.   A pang of fear shot through her. Remorse makes no account of time or place ; it gives its stab anywhere.   In the twinkling of an eye Mrs. Townsend was thus wounded.   She felt that she had not been a wise friend to Lill in the late crisis.

" I hear his voice now," exclaimed Lill, touching Mrs. Townsend's arm.

Giuliani, with some other officers, was coming up quickly behind the two English ladies.   As the gentlemen passed they all lifted their hats.   Mrs. Townsend fancied Giuliani had hesitated, as though he had thought of speaking to her and Lady Ponsonby, but he went on with the others.

"Mr. Giuliani wrote to me once that he shouldn't die even if I refused him," observed Lill. "Did you hear how strong and cheerful his voice was? He is not changed. Men don't break their hearts for love."

"The tolerably wise among them don't exhibit the cracks in a public street," said Mrs. Townsend; "that's probably why Mr. Giuliani did not stop to speak to you."

"I behaved ill to him—very; but somehow I had a faith that he would be my friend in any case—he was so unlike other men; I always acknowledged that."

Mrs. Townsend made no reply; her excitable imagination had composed a whole poem while Lill was speaking. What a grand, heroic, chivalrous act it would be in Mr. Giuliani, the rejected lover, to plead the cause of the beloved rival! The Italian had always had an extraordinary influence over Lill; indeed, how could the most obstinate woman resist such noble self-devotion? "She stands on her dignity with me, poor darling! Stupid me! not to have guessed she was pining to death to be forced to make friends with that young goose of a husband of hers."

Mrs. Townsend lost no time in thinking over her scheme; she wrote at once to Mr. Giuliani, in most lucid phrases explaining what she hoped and expected from him. She begged also that his visit might appear un-prompted, made by his own wish.

Giuliani had heard Lill's unhappy story from Alicia, who, during Valentine's long and nearly hopeless illness, had supplied her mother's place as his correspondent. He knew that she had received in obstinate silence Lady Ponsonby's maternal entreaties. He did not con-demn the young wife so severely as did his other friends; he understood the almost supernatural trial it must have been to her, in all the pride of her youth, beauty, and love, to imagine herself accepted as a sick nurse for her husband's wounded heart. Love, he knew, would not be satisfied with less than love in return. By the light of his own burning passion he had seen deeper into himself and his fellow-beings, and had learned what to hope and what to despair of in himself and others. He had not recovered happiness, but he felt a greater fortitude to bear his own suffering, and a new power of sympathy with which to help others.

In this belief it was that he would dare to obey Mrs Townsend's invitation, which had reached him the same afternoon by the hands of Major Marco Alberti.

Before Mr. Giuliani pays his visit to the Palace Doria, it will be well to understand Lill's frame of mind at this critical juncture.

During these many months of self-imposed exile from Sir Frederick, Lill had endured silently an ever-renewed, horrible internal combat; from which she always came forth exhausted, and ever undecided as to her husband's feelings with regard to her. Her rejoicing at having left him had become very bitter rejoicing. So young as she was, was she to live to the end of her life with this bleeding heart? She opened its wounds constantly and with predetermination; she could not let them heal.

Hours and hours of every day, hours and hours of every night, she gave to recalling Sir Frederick's words, his silences; to picturing to herself his looks, his actions, every scene in which they had been together from the day of their first meeting to that of their parting. Often she would seize on some particular expression or sentence as on a prey, rending it to pieces, and always finding in it the poison she sought for with such curious avidity. Or she would recollect the omission of some trifling attention; perhaps something of no more consequence than a yawn in a *tête-à-tête* with her, and, with wilful, dexterous sophistry, persuade herself to accept the error of omission or commission as a proof of indifference.

There were other even more painful phases, when she had an agony of longing to see him again; many and many a time had she exclaimed aloud in the solitude of her own room, "I am forgetting his face; I don't remember him." Then she would have intervals of doubt whether she had judged him rightly; doubts that racked her more cruelly than even her distrust of his love. Oh! that she might have another opportunity of testing him.

As the period of separation she had demanded was approaching its termination, a new fear gnawed at her heart. What would he do? What might be the terms which he had hinted the probability of his imposing in his turn? Anything, anything, but not to breathe the same air, not to dwell under the same roof with him ; and yet, while feeling this, she could not keep her thoughts from glancing continually at the chance of a denial. Her woman's pride could not brook the possibility of that shame, and so she hardened herself to await her sentence in unbroken silence.

What wonder that this miserable state of excitement and restlessness undermined Lill's health and consumed her beauty!

CHAPTER XLVIII.

Master and Pupil.

The suite of apartments in the Palazzo Doria occupied by the Albertis was to the left of the great entrance; the numerous windows of their spacious dwelling-rooms all had a view of the bay. When Lill, according to custom, went to the *salon* after dinner, the sisters did not accompany her, for Mrs. Townsend had determined that the meeting she had arranged between master and pupil should take place without witnesses. It had been a day of hurry, confusion, and lamentation, for Marco Alberti was to start that same night, *en route* for Novara; therefore, Lill was not surprised at being allowed to leave the dining-room alone.

As she entered the *salon*, a gentleman came from the embrasure of a window to meet her. For an instant Lill stood motionless; then said, in the unmodulated voice that had become usual to her,—

"Mr. Giuliani! this is being kinder than I expected. I am glad to see you."

He said, with a visible effort,—

"You have been ill."

"Do you know nothing else about me——, but pray sit down," and she repeated again, "I am glad to see you."

"Are you?" he asked, mechanically, not with any notion of questioning the reality of what she said, but because he was bewildered by being near her again.

"Yes; the first unpainful feeling I have had for three quarters of a year, was when I caught sight of you in San Lorenzo. Even if you are pleased to know that I am unhappy, I am still glad to see you Mr. Giuliani."

One must have heard the sweet voice that has been heavenly music to one's ears, changed to a hard, cracked, toneless sound, to understand the heartache with which Giuliani listened to Lill. Hitherto, she had avoided looking at him; now her eyes slowly wandered over his face as he sat silent, striving to collect his thoughts, so as to find the right words to speak to her; she continued,—

"What an odd, unlikely coincidence, our meeting in the cathedral, with the dream you wrote me of. Do you remember?"

He nodded, unable to talk on that subject with calmness.

"You are altered; I did not think so at first: but I have changed most. You did not recognize me at first."

Giuliani had sought Lill's presence, believing his heart wounds healed over; painful throbs told him now the contrary. His tongue was at fault; he had avowedly come there to advise, and influence her to be reconciled to her husband; but he felt that if he opened his lips just then, it would be to speak words he was as bound not to utter, as she not to hear. Meagre, worn, sad, she had as great an attraction for him as in all the brightness of her beauty. Envied, triumphant, surrounded by homage, or neglected, alone, and faded, she was equally dear to him; not more so in other days—not less so now. He sat on wordless, feeling that his soul was like a ship between Scylla and Charybdis.

Lill could not bear the silence.

"How are your Paris friends, Mr. Giuliani? Is Valentine better? Of course I ought to know, but I do not."

"He is lamed for life," said Giuliani.

"Poor Valentine! only think of his turning out a hero; and Mrs. Caledon, is she as lively and clever as ever?"

How the assumption of that gay manner jarred with the dejection stamped on Lill's countenance and figure. She was no longer poised, erect, giving the idea of a bird ready to take wing; on the contrary, her head was bent forward like one accustomed to carry a heavy burden.

Giuliani roused himself from his first stupefaction of pain: he said,—"It is of what concerns yourself I wish to hear."

"Of me! oh! dear, I don't think there is much to tell—nothing extraordinary: disappointment is very common. However, I don't wish you to have a worse opinion of me than I deserve. I did not marry for money, I assure you; it was 'all for love and the world well lost;'" she gave a little dry laugh as she added, "at least on my side."

"I never doubted your disinterestedness," he said,

with infinite pity; "and you believe, I am sure, that even in my most selfish moments I thought of your happiness and that now to know you were happy would give me joy."

For an instant the muscles round her mouth quivered, then they resumed their rigidity, and she said, quietly, " I cannot believe in anything, Mr. Giuliani."

"So you refuse even my friendship!" He tried to speak cheerfully, but his real sadness showed through the attempted disguise.

"How good you are to me!" she exclaimed, and laid a hand over her eyes.

He saw first one tear, then another, and another, fall on her black silk dress. His heart quaked; he rose and hurried to the window. The sun was already low in the cloudless west; a long tremulous line of fiery gold lay on the small dancing waves. Oh! blessed nature, that never refuses encouragement, if men would only open their eyes to see, their ears to hear.

He had touched the fountain of her tears, and softened the hardness of her heart. She followed him to the window, saying,—

" I do believe in you; it was not true what I said. I am so unhappy; I cannot help trying to hurt others." Her glistening eyes were raised to his, and she held out her hand to him.

He made as though he had not seen the offered pledge of amity, but, drawing a chair forward, said,—"Come, let us reason a little together:" then pointing to the luminous line on the sea, he added, " Can you not fancy *that* to be a golden path leading from this world to one brighter?"

" You are very good, indulgent, forbearing," she said, answering the train of her own thoughts, not his words.

" You will not bribe me not to speak truths to you," he said, pretty firmly.

" I see you *have* heard about me," returned Lill, "probably from no friendly source: hear now my side of the story."

He guessed the comfort it would be to her to have a new auditor for her sorrows; he guessed that she might have found, after the first burst of sympathy from the kind but unstable Mrs. Townsend, little of the patience

of a listener. He was aware also of the egotistical de
mands of a heart new to suffering.

Lill, now that the element which had disturbed her
liking for the Italian was absent, once more drew near
to him with faith and confidence. She told him her tale
with entire trust, but with cruel *naiveté*. She did not
remark his frightful pallor, as her words, revealing such
treasures of tenderness for another man met his ear.
His feelings were stirred almost beyond his control. He
suffered at one and the same moment for her and by her.
Rage seized his heart, and held him by the throat, keeping him dumb.

Lill ended: "There are some illusions which when wo
once lose, the light of life goes out. Is it a part of the
primeval curse, Mr. Giuliani, that affection should never
be mutual?" She looked at him as she finished speaking. The expression of his face puzzled her, and made
her add,—"You, too, are angry with me."

He struggled to recover possession of himself, and
said, in a voice rough with emotion,—

"Angry? no, but I know not how to comfort you. I
can only urge you to obey duty."

"You are no better than one of Job's friends," she
said, disappointed, then added, with a miserable attempt
at sarcasm.—"Why don't you go on and tell me that my
suffering is deserved; that it is a fair retribution; that
I deceived you, who trusted in me, and now it is my turn
to be deceived and betrayed; that I should bear my
punishment patiently; that it is weak to complain? All
undeniably true. I have said it for you. Now let us talk
of something else." The last words came forth in little
hard sobs.

Giuliani turned away his head, that she might not see
how unmanned he was. Presently he said,—

"You have reminded me of Job's denunciation against
a false friend. 'He that speaketh flattery to his friends,
even the eyes of his children shall fail.' I must fulfil
my duty as a friend, though truth is always hard to
bear. God knows how willingly I would spare you even
the passing pain I know I shall now give you. You are
but twenty, I believe; supposing that, by persistence in
your present resolution not to seek to be reconciled to

your husband, this separation should become a lasting one, how do you mean to pass the next ten years of your youth? You have not probably taken that into consideration yet, Lady Ponsonby. The heart does not die at your age, and, however monstrous and impossible the supposition appears to you now, I warn you, that you will inevitably seek compensation for your sorrow."

"Stop, sir," she exclaimed, vehemently.

"One moment bear with me," he said. "We cannot concentrate the consequences of our actions in one point; we cannot say, thus far shall they go and no farther. You are so young; have pity on yourself." There were tears in his eyes. "It is not God who will have made this fate for you; you will have made it for yourself, because you have not known how to discipline your own passions."

"I am not a mere vulgar, jealous wife, Mr. Giuliani. I *can* forgive; I *do* forgive: but I know that the evil under which I bend is without remedy for me; the past cannot be undone: if I could only forget! But wherever I turn I see every syllable of that horrible letter; deceived! deceived in the moment of greatest trust! Mr. Giuliani, you don't know the words he spoke to me the very day, almost within the very, hour that he wrote to her—how could he have the heart? Oh! never, never to believe in him again; it is *too* hard, too hard."

The scientific physician, the keen-witted barrister lie in wait for accidents to guide them in delicate, intricate cases. What science, what practised penetration does for the man of medicine or of law, love did for Giuliani. Forgetful of self, he thought only of how to reach and counteract the poison corroding Lill's heart. He said,—

"Look at me, Lady Ponsonby."

She turned to him in surprise.

"Well, you recognize in me—do you not?—the same signs of repressed agitation—you detect in me the same quivering of the muscles, the weakness of the flesh when under the hot ploughshare of agony—that were visible in Sir Frederick Ponsonby when he found himself so unexpectedly in Madame de Ravignan's presence?"

"No," she faltered, joining her hands in dawning hopeful prayer, or in intercession to be spared his reproaches, or a mingling of one feeling and the other.

"You perceive a difference; now, then, you can understand that selfishness, pride, revenge, all man's base passions, would naturally urge me to influence you against Sir Frederick Ponsonby; you can understand how much power you have given me, by complaining of him; now, then, will you refuse to credit me, when I protest to you, what indeed any commonly experienced man would laughingly tell you was as evident as the light of day, that your husband once had a caprice, a fancy, for this French widow, and that he extricated himself from this awkward predicament in the most gentlemanly manner he could; that is, by giving her the honours of war? Deep wounds have visible scars, believe me, Lady Ponsonby." As he thus tore open his own heart to comfort her, he saw a gleam of joy light up her eyes. She had no thought for his pain, unless as an acceptable witness in her husband's favour.

"But he said he would give her his life, but not his honour," she objected.

"Ay! men not only say so, but they do give their lives, when the loss of honour implies anything *but* the giving up a woman they love for one they do not. Constancy, in this last case, is a very rare example to find among men."

"You would not deceive me," she said, almost coaxingly.

He had no strength left for further argument, but yet enough to trample out the last spark of feeling for himself; he answered,—

"Write to him, recall him, say come."

"But will he? Will he really forgive me?" she asked, in a tremulous, eager voice.

She would not then spare him one pang; he said, hastily,—

"And when he comes, fall on his neck—" utterance failed him.

There was a long pause. When Lill looked again at Giuliani, he was gazing intently at the western horizon

"Oh! you are good!" once more said Lill.

He smiled on her, and, pointing to the radiance above

the sea line, quoted to her these words: "'Man, of what dost thou complain? Of struggle? It is the condition of victory. Of injustice? What is that to an immortal being? Of death? It is freedom.' And now, Lady Ponsonby, farewell!"

"When shall I see you again, Mr. Giuliani?"

"I leave to-night for Novara."

"I forgot—oh! I am so ungrateful—I have not asked about yourself."

"Thank you, there is little to say on that subject. I am in the Piedmontese service. We have been unfortunate, but the good seed is sown; it will yet bear a rich harvest; I am content in that belief, though perhaps I may not see the reaping."

He was gone, and she had not even shaken hands with him.

He left her, knowing that she had scarcely a glimmering consciousness of the hard victory he had won over self for her sake.

Before he quitted Genoa, Giuliani wrote to the dowager Lady Ponsonby; he said that he considered there was no time to be lost, if Lill's life was to be saved. He explained that her emaciation was extreme, while her eyes were unspeakably lustrous, and on her cheeks were carmine spots, fatal indications of internal devouring fever. Happiness and tranquillity must undo the work of grief and agitation.

Lill obeyed Giuliani's advice with the submission of a child. She wrote to her husband, "Come and forgive me."

These two letters went by the next day's mail; but it was not in 1849 as it is now: there were then no railways completed between Italy and Paris. Moreover Sir Frederick was in England.

CHAPTER XLIX.

Pazienza!

AFTER the departure of the troops in Genoa to Novara, there was a pause of all external demonstration in the city; it seemed to settle into calm, but it was like that hot, seething calm which precedes a physical or moral tempest.

The same unnatural tranquillity was visible in Lill. She had calculated that her letter, leaving Genoa on the 19th of March, would reach Sir Frederick on the 25th or 26th. She allowed him a day to reply to it; she might hear from him, therefore, as soon as the 2nd of April—might, perhaps, see him. "Pazienza!" she said, using the word as the Italians did with respect to Austrian rule; that is, to indicate a never-dying impatience.

On the 24th of March this strange quiet in the town disappeared. No one knew whence the rumours of disaster to the Piedmontese army, but the very air seemed alive with them. Treachery, defeat, victory, alternated on pale, quivering lips; and yet the fact was patent, that all the couriers from Turin to head-quarters at Novara had been intercepted, and obliged to return, so that all communication between Charles Albert and his capital was cut off.

The following day's alarm and perturbation were still more general. At noon on the 27th, the news of the battle and defeat of Novara, and of the King's abdication, came like a thunderclap. The Genoese would not swallow this bitter cup, without giving signs of life; the words said to have been uttered by Charles Albert, "All is lost; even honour!" maddened the Ligurians.

"Not so," said they. "If all is lost, we will save our honour; for that people which can survive infamy is no longer a people, but a flock of slaves, bearing on their brows the mark of God's Curse."

That very evening there were tumults in the streets, and the rappel was beaten.

It was not till the 31st of March that matters assumed

an uncomfortable aspect. The presence, however, of H.M.S. *Vengeance* in the bay kept the minds of the few English families in Genoa at rest.

Madame Alberti, who had heard of her husband's safety, began preparations for leaving; but Lill declared she would not stir for all the cannon in the world till she had received her letter. Of Giuliani there had been no news.

On the 1st April, a Sunday, Lill and Mrs. Townsend, after church, took a walk on the bastions of Santa Chiara, and so into the heart of the town. The walk was long and the sun hot. Feeling tired, they went into the little church of the Madonna delle Grazie to rest. They had remarked the entire absence of all soldiers or sentinels on the ramparts, and that the cannon were left to their own care. Lill had just said, " How quiet everything is!" when suddenly there was a sound of drums and shouts.

The two ladies, though accustomed to street demonstrations during the last week, thought it nevertheless wise to hasten homewards. They met a few men vociferating loudly, "All' armi, all' armi!" and frightened women's faces looked out of the windows, but as yet, though they saw plenty of cause for hurry, they saw none for alarm. They had to pass the Ducal Palace; as they neared it the scene changed. There was an uproar and a crowd. Masses of men were dragging cannon, then there was a rushing sound, and Lill felt herself caught hold of and pushed back into a little wooden shed. She tried to see what was going on, but a strong hand turned her forcibly away from the street. One of those horrible popular retributions was being enacted. A spy, one of those whose trade is to sell blood, had been found, and was sacrificed in a moment of mob fury.

" This is no time for women to be abroad," said an English voice. "Ladies, allow me to take you home."

The person speaking was in the British naval uniform, a middle-aged man. Lill glanced at him, and then accepted his offered arm, Mrs. Townsend taking the other. His uniform was of the shabbiest; but they both instinctively recognized in him a man of their own rank.

" What is going to happen?" asked Mrs. Townsend.

"Nothing less than treason and rebellion, though I believe the perpetrators in good faith will consider themselves the new King's best subjects."

"You think there will be real, downright fighting?" said Honora.

"Perhaps, but there's the big ship for you. I dare say, there are some young men on board who will willingly give you up their quarters."

"I am not afraid," said Lill.

The officer made a half-comic grimace. "Not the first time you have been in action, I suppose. You don't even start when the great guns bellow; so much the better. You know the Consul, of course. Now, my advice to you is, if he abandons the town, you do the same. When the sight of his gray hat no longer makes these *Zeneixi* fly right and left, you come away."

He left them at the door of the palazzo with a good-natured "Don't forget my advice; above all, take your measures to be well informed about the gray hat, and keep out of the streets."

"I wonder who he is himself," said Honora, "that he makes so free with the hats of dignitaries. How I wish English people would not go about in such shabby clothes when they are on the Continent!"

In those times Genoa had no letter carriers. On the next afternoon, the 2nd of April, Lill, in spite of the warning advice of the day before, unknown to Mrs. Townsend, went by herself to the post-office. If disappointment awaited her, she could bear it best by herself. "No letter," was the answer she received, but would not believe; she thrust forward her passport a second and even a third time. It was a moment when incivility might have been excused, but the Italians are fundamentally good-natured, and even the third negative was pronounced without acerbity.

As she was returning to the palace, she met in the Strada Nuova an officer of the Piedmontese line, blindfolded and with a white flag on his musket. That same afternoon De Asarta surrendered; the soldiers were all to leave Genoa within twenty-four hours. De Asarta's family were to remain as hostages until the troops were beyond the Apennines.

The reader will be so good as to bear in mind that the
Genoese were not in rebellion to their king, but believed
themselves, as the English captain had said, to be acting
for Victor Emmanuel against a *party* who were selling
the country to the Austrians. Among the articles of
capitulation, signed between De Asarta, the commandant
of the Sardinian troops, on the one side, and Avezzana,
the general-in-chief of the National Guard, on the other,
was this one : " Genoa will remain *unalterably* united to
Piedmont."

The siege of Genoa belongs to history. It is only
mentioned here because some of the events had to do
with Lill Tufton's story. She refused attention to all reports or prophecies of danger; and when the sound of
the cannon and musketry was not to be denied, she said
" that she was as safe in the Palazzo Doria as at S. Pier
d'Arena or along the coast; where, according to all ac-
counts, there was not only a mad populace, but a mad
army." She would not go to the big ship; she hated
ships. Her remaining, however, was no rule for others.

"At present I feel as if I bore a charmed life; I have
something to do. I can't die yet; besides, you know,
Honora, Planchette bid me beware of water, not bullets."

Mrs. Townsend was quite heroic in her proofs of
friendship to Lill at this period. " I am glad to have
the opportunity of proving to myself that I have not
wholly relapsed into my old selfish ways," she said once
to a burst of Lill's gratitude. " I am not quite cured
though; so, as soon as Alberti can stay at home, I shall
be off to the Rue des Trois Sabres, for another dose of
goodness."

Madame Alberti, who was dubious as to what she
would do, stayed also, because Lill refused to move, and
Mrs. Townsend refused to leave Lill. Madame Alberti
took great credit to herself afterwards for this, when she
heard that the English who had gone on board the man-
of-war had been obliged to quit when the ship cleared
for action, and that they were now dispersed in the small
towns of Cornegliano and Sestri di Ponente.

It had been believed that La Marmora would attack
the Porta Pila, at the opposite extremity of the town;
on the contrary, he appeared before the gate of S. Pier

d'Arena, so that what fighting there was took place in extremely disagreeable proximity to the Doria Palace. La Marmora's orders, and without doubt his own feelings also, led him rather to menace than to act against the deluded city; and this naturally protracted the siege for days.

Lill would have gone again to the post office had she not been assured by some Genoese friends of Madame Alberti that no mails had arrived. One whole day the party in the palace passed in the cellars, another crouching in a space between the roof and the ceiling of the upper suite of apartments. At last came the news of an armistice for forty-eight hours. La Marmora was master of some of the forts, the Begatto and the Specola, and a deputation of citizens had gone off to Turin. Poor people! what they wanted was to be allowed to go on fighting the Austrians; one of the terms of capitulation offered was the immediate recommencement of the war. No sooner did Lill hear of the truce than she sprang out like a greyhound freed from a leash; the only precaution she took was to wear the Genoese *mezzaro*. Foreigners are never safe in moments of popular tumult, and of course there was no end of heaven-crying injustice in the papers against English interference. Lill stepped over or through the barricades with great intrepidy, or rather indifference; at last she came to one guarded by a woman with a musket on her shoulder.

"Determined to see what is going on," said the same strong English voice Lill had heard before. It was the naval captain.

"I *must* go to the post office," she returned, rather sharply.

"Luckily our road lies the same way; otherwise, as you are unarmed, the pretty sentinel here wouldn't let you pass."

In fact, the girl he alluded to (she was quite a girl) was presenting her musket in a very ferocious manner at the English gentleman and lady.

The captain said, "*scià scusi*" (allow me), put by the musket, sprang over the barricade in a moment, kissed the astonished sentinel, and saying, "Pretty little girls

were never meant for such sort of fighting," helped Lili
to pass.

By this time he had come to see that his companion
was in no state of mind to enjoy joking; so he walked
soberly enough by her side.

"Shall I inquire for your letters?" he asked, when
they reached the post office.

She gave him the paper on which her name was written; he remarked how her hand trembled.

"Good luck," he said, with a sort of paternal kindness, "here are two letters for you."

When she saw the letter addressed to her in her
husband's writing, Lill's knees became as weak as water.

"Take my arm, and lean well on me," said the captain.
"Read your letter; I am as blind as a bat."

"No; take me home quickly," and so he did, and not
another word passed between them

CHAPTER L.

Who Breaks—Pays.

LOCKED into her own room, Lill opened her husband's letter. "Oh! I cannot see, I cannot see," she cried in agony, but the blindness passed away, and she read,—

"Monk's Capel Priory, March 27, 1849.

"I SHALL be with you almost as soon as my letter, I go by Paris to Marseilles, and from thence by steamer to Genoa. I shall thus escape all risk of being detained by either snow on Mont Cenis, or by the fighting of which we hear rumours. There is no fear of a French steamer being interfered with, and I know through my mother that the Doria Palace can be reached by water. O Lill! how foolish we have both been. Is life so long that one can afford to squander in unhappiness so many months? Look out for me, my love; let me see you as I pass, waving me a welcome. No more partings on this side of the grave, Lill; hand in hand for the rest of our lives, my only darling.

"Believe me now and always your own
"FREDERICK."

Down on her knees. Thank God! thank God! Then she rushed into the *salon*, crying out "Honora! Honora! Ruth! Where is Ruth?"

Mrs. Townsend came running to the call.

"He *is* coming, Honora; he may be in sight now. Where is Ruth?"

Mrs. Townsend asked no questions. "Dear Lill!" she said, and would have embraced her, but Lill kept crying out for Ruth.

"Honora! you help me off with this black gown; he would not like to see me in black to welcome him. Ruth, find my blue muslin, the one your master was so fond of."

While Ruth was seeking for the blue dress, Mrs Townsend took up the second letter, lying still unopened. It was from Miss Crumpton, and Mrs. Townsend fancied

it might tend to tranquillize Lill if her thoughts could be
diverted, even for a few minutes, from dwelling on Sir
Frederick's arrival. She therefore said, " Perhaps there
is some news here, Lill."

" Open it, and tell me what there is in it. Honora
dear, I have such a strange sensation. My knees are as
weak as water."

" Do sit down like a darling, till Ruth is ready for you.
Listen to your dear Crummie."

" Wavering Hall,
March 29, 1849.

" DEAREST LILL,

" WE are wearying for news of you. The notion that
you may be still in Genoa among those bloodthirsty
Italians is dreadful. Surely Mrs. Townsend ought to
have sense enough to perceive that Italy is not a place
for English women at this time. I never did approve
of your intimacy with that lady; she always led you
wrong."

" Much obliged to you, dear Miss Crumpton," here
ejaculated Mrs. Townsend. "Are you listening, Lill?"

" Yes! oh, yes!"

Mrs. Townsend went on reading—"Sir Mark is growing old; dear Lill, what do you think he asked me the
other day? Why, there was no picture of you at the
Hall, and he said it was my fault for not reminding him
to have a likeness taken of you. The spring is cold and
backward, not at all like what I remember. Everything
seems changing for the worse. Some one — Colonel
Panton I think — was saying the other day. that it was
because of some derangement of the earth's orbit; it
may be that, or just as likely something else,—I am sure
I can't pretend to say. You scold me for not giving you
any news, but there is none to give.

" Lill, my dear girl, do not be angry if I tell you one
thing; I have kept it on my mind till my conscience
won't bear it any longer: Sir Frederick is not living as
he ought to do; he sent away all the workpeople from
the Priory when he came back, and there he is with
scarcely any sashes in the windows : the wind may blow
in just as it likes; and he has only old Betty Pagan to

wait on him, and a man for his horse. I hear he sits in his wet clothes when he comes in from hunting, and never knows whether there will be a dinner for him or not. O my dear child! think before it's too late, and pray forgive me for telling you what is disagreeable.

"Sir Mark does not say anything, but somehow he is not so tantalizing as he was; he asks often if there's been any letter from Genoa. That little dowdy, Althemiah, is going to be married to Lord Durrington's eldest son. What he sees in her, *I* don't know.

' With my warm love and blessing,

"Your faithful friend,

"M. Crumpton."

"Don't cry, Lill," said Mrs. Townsend; "happy days are in sight for you."

"He *did* love me," whispered Lill; "I will be so good, Honora. I will never doubt, I will try never to pain any one again. How many friends I have, and I have never deserved one!"

"All right now, dear girl, so dry your eyes and smile."

Ruth here brought in the blue muslin dress. Lill's fingers trembled so, that she could not fasten the buttons. "It hangs like a bag on me," she exclaimed.

"Never mind," said Mrs. Townsend; "It looks charming, and you are like a violet wet with dew."

"What a comfort this armistice is!" observed Lill; for now I can go and find out when the French steamer is expected."

"Stefano the cook had suddenly reappeared," said Mrs. Townsend; "we can send him to Banchi. You must not leave the house; there is no saying who might arrive in the meantime."

"The steamer from Marseilles was due that day, but might not arrive before night," was the information brought back by Stefano. Lill, as may be supposed, was pitiably restless. It was so evidently painful to her to be forced to speak, that at last Mrs. Townsend gave up her well-meant efforts to distract her attention from the one subject, and left her free to wander from window to window. Looking at the port through a small telescope, and examining her watch, were the alternations in which Lill passed hours. She could not be induced to sit down to dinner; she was sure the steamer would pass exactly then, and she should never forgive herself if she were out of the way. They must send her a crust of bread and a glass of wine.

Half an hour after, when Signora Alberti and Mrs. Townsend returned to the *salon*, Lill was not there; tho sisters took it for granted that she had gone to her own room.

Just afterwards there was a tap at the door, and with a " *Con licenza,*" Mr. Giuliani came in.

"You know," said Mrs. Townsend. hurrying to him, "that Sir Frederick Ponsonby is expected to-day by the French steamer."

"I came with the news in case it might not have reached you" he replied.. "I had a letter from his mother two days ago." Giuliani sat down like one thoroughly wearied with long watching. "I am just from Turin," he added.

"Sad times," said Mrs. Townsend, struck by his worn appearance His lips moved, but she distinguished no words.

The sharp report of a rifle, sounding quite close to the windows, made the two ladies start, the Signora Alberti exclaiming, "Oh dear, those weary guns. I don't think these Genoese understand the meaning of the word truce."

"Men discharging their muskets probably," said Giuliani, Here little Lorenzo Alberti came into the room; he sidled up to his mother, looking frightened.

"Mamma, mamma, come to Scià Lilla; come, she won't speak."

"Good-heavens!" cried the mother, "what is the matter? You have hurt yourself, Renzo. Look at the child's frock."

"It's blood, it's blood," shrieked the boy, in horror of the red spots he now saw. "Scià Lilla! Scià Lilla!"

"Where is Scià Lilla?" asked Mrs. Townsend, hurriedly.

"On the terrace ;—oh, my frock!"
There was something infectious in the little fellow's distress and terror. Giuliani, closely followed by Mrs.

Townsend, ran out into the court, beyond which is the ilex-shaded terrace jutting into the sea. There they saw Lill lying, face downwards, on the ground, her head in the direction of the entrance of the port.

"She has fainted!" exclaimed Mrs. Townsend.

Giuliani knelt down; he touched Lill's hand, gently raised her head; he looked up at Mrs. Townsend.

"Well?" she cried sharply.

"She is dead," he said.

"Impossible! nonsense!" burst out Mrs. Townsend. "She was well half an hour ago. She has fainted."

Giuliani pointed to a small red circle on the bosom of the blue dress. "She has been shot; God help her!" He tried to lift up the prostrate body; that slim form weighed like a heavy load of lead. "I cannot do it," he muttered, and the sweat-drops fell from his forehead.

Plenty of help—half a dozen surgeons were soon on the spot. They were useless—Lill Tuftou's spirit had fled from this world.

————

Some hours after—it was dark by that time—Mrs. Townsend, a candle in her hand, came into the *salon* where Giuliani was waiting for her. She found him in the recess of the same window where he and Lill had sat together during their last interview. He had not missed the light from the sky, so full of expectation was he; all was not at an end yet for him. Mrs. Townsend beckoned to him; he rose and went to her.

"You can go in now," she said, pointing to a door.

"Alone, if you please."

She bowed and left him.

He went calmly enough up to the side of the bed, on which lay the remains of the woman he had so truly loved.

Could anything so lovely be death?

A smile of hope was on the sweet white face.

Every trace of the care and grief that had so changed her when he last saw her, had vanished. She looked younger than he had ever known her. He stooped down to press a kiss on those exquisite lips.

"Lill!" he ejaculated; it was the first time he had

thus named her—"Lill! you would say No, if you could speak; I will not rob you now."

He drew forward a chair and sat down by the body. Those who have kept a similar vigil know how faithfully memory paints in such moments. Every scene in which he and Lill had met, every word, every look of hers, came livingly back to Giuliani. There she was again before him in all the grace of her piquant beauty playfully defying Sir Mark. That picture dissolved into another, in which she appeared first as the pretty petulant pupil, soon subdued to gentleness by his repellent coldness—a coldness only skin deep, God knows. If any had been by to mark him, they would have seen him sometimes smile, so lifelike were the visions passing before him. Once, he fancied she called him "Mr. Giuliani."

He started to his feet; it surely was not possible that he had only recollected the sound of her voice speaking his name.

He had not yet drained the bitter cup to the lees. He had done for the best; but why had he, a man marked down by calamity, tried twice to influence the fate of that bright creature? If—

What worlds of agony that little word can hold—ah! it was a pitiful case.

*   *   *   *   *   *   *   *   *   *

At midnight there **was a great** stir in the Palazzo Doria; Sir Frederick Ponsonby had arrived.

" Who was to tell him what had happened ?"

"Not I, not I," cried Mrs. Townsend, wringing her hands.

Mercifully. Sir Frederick knew his misfortune. He had heard of it before leaving the steamer from some custom-house officers, who, in ignorance of his interest in the tragical occurrence—already become town talk—had related every detail in his presence.

Once again Mrs. Townsend was a guide to the Chamber of Death.

Giuliani was still seated by the bed, his look riveted to Lill's face. He was violently moved when Sir Frederick went in; Mrs. Townsend saw his eyes lighten with passion; then he turned to take one more glance of those beloved features; subdued, he bowed to Sir Frederick, quietly left the room, and immediately after the house. Of him none of his former friends know aught, save that he went to Rome, one of Manara's deathless band.

Lill lies buried in the Protestant Cemetery of San Benigno.

It was never ascertained with any certainty how she met her death; it was supposed she had slipped out to watch for the French steamer, and been hit by mere accident. In all probability, the sharp report which by its proximity had so startled the Signora Alberti, had sounded poor Lill's knell. The surgeons one and all agreed that her death had been too instantaneous for pain of body or mind.

"She was so happy, so very happy, the whole of that day," was all the comfort Mrs. Townsend could think of for the wretched husband;—"she will never know grief again; she is safe in the Land of Promise."

THE END.